The yellowbacks... classics of popular fiction

The yellowjackets or yellowbacks were a great series of bestselling adventure and crime thrillers that had its origins in the mid to late 19th century following on from the 'penny dreadfuls'. They virtually began the mass market revolution of the early 20th century with a clear standard format and imprint/series livery (what would today be called branding). Hodder & Stoughton published the yellowjackets in two main series with series run dates of: 1923-1939 and later 1949-1957.

As the tagline ('where thrillers really began') on the back cover implies, the imprint and series focused on thrillers that were the bestsellers of their time. This current reissue or retro revival if you will, brings back many of these masterpieces, now classics in their own way and extends it further by including key titles from that period that were either great crime or thriller or even general commercial fiction (including sub-genres of noir, horror, gothic, romance, westerns, etc.) influences of their time. There are some perennial favourites and many rarities either lost or not easily available being revived in the current series. Writers and characters ranged from adventure heroes like Bulldog Drummond, Allan Quatermain, Richard Hannay or the Saint through thriller grandmasters Edgar Wallace and E. Phillips Oppenheim, crime and mystery maestros like Patricia Wentworth, GK Chesterton, Agatha Christie and the Detection club, to western and swashbucklers like Zane Grey, Max Brand, Captain Blood and even romance or general fiction classics like Hermina Black, Denise Robins, Marie Corelli or Stella Morton. These were books that had storytelling at their heart and always entertained.

The yellowbacks had both hardback (with varying design elements) and paperback (which built the series look) versions with the latter still carrying the imprint 'yellowjacket'. The current reissues pay tribute to both and use an amalgam of elements from both editions while retaining the complete yellow (or 'mustard-plaster') livery with the author's name in blue beveled type with a 'simulated emboss' effect and a white outer 'outline', and the book title in black. These reissues retain the distinctive size of the original mass market paperback and follow the three main category variations—the thrillers (crime, westerns, mystery, adventure) had blue lettering for the author's name, while Romance and softer general fiction had red; and other categories like humour had green.

For more detail and a full list of titles visit https://www.hachetteindia.com/home/yellowbacks

INTRODUCING CLUBFOOT

INTRODUCING CLUBFOOT

George **Valentine Williams** (1883–1946) was the son of G. Edward Williams, Chief Editor of the Reuters News Agency. After being privately educated in Germany, he joined Reuters as a sub editor in 1902. In 1909, Williams became a reporter for the *Daily Mail* (then the most popular British newspaper and the first to achieve a daily circulation of one million copies). In this capacity, he reported on international events such as the Portuguese Revolution of 1910 and the Balkan Wars of 1912–1913. During the early stages of the First World War, reporters were not permitted direct access to the Western Front. Williams therefore obtained a commission with the Irish Guards in December 1915. He saw action during the Battle of the Somme, where he was seriously wounded in 1916, and was awarded the Military Cross. Williams then joined the small group of accredited war correspondents based at British General Headquarters and continued to serve as the accredited correspondent for the *Daily Mail* until the end of the War. After the War, Valentine Williams was in charge of reporting the Versailles Peace Conference in 1919 for the *Daily Mail*. In addition to journalism, Williams also became a popular writer of mystery fiction, publishing a series of 28 books from 1918 until his death in 1946.

INTRODUCING
CLUBFOOT

Valentine Williams

The Man with the Clubfoot
The Return of Clubfoot

Introducing Clubfoot by Valentine Williams
The Man with the Clubfoot first published in 1918 by Herbert Jenkins and then as a yellowback by Hodder & Stoughton in 1936. *The Return of Clubfoot* first published by Herbert Jenkins in 1923 and then as a yellowback by Hodder & Stoughton in 1936.

This Hodder Yellowback edition © Hachette India 2023
(Registered Name: Hachette Book Publishing India Pvt. Ltd.)
An Hachette UK Company www.hachetteindia.com

1

All rights reserved. No part of the publication may be reproduced, stored in a retrieval system (including but not limited to computers, disks, external drives, electronic or digital devices, e-readers, websites), or transmitted in any form or by any means (including but not limited to cyclostyling, photocopying, docutech or other reprographic reproductions, mechanical, recording, electronic, digital versions) without the prior written permission of the publisher, nor be otherwise circulated in any form of binding or cover other than that in which it is published and without a similar condition being imposed on the subsequent purchaser.

The texts in these editions in most cases have been reprinted as is, with minimal editorial changes and by and large no bowdlerizing for political correctness; though in some editions, a few words and phrases considered archaic, or those considered offensive now, along with archaic punctuation may have been modified in places to make the text more accessible to today's readers. The narratives, language, beliefs, social mores and/or cultural depictions, in these volumes are a reflection of their times and must be viewed as such. They may also contain certain cultural, racial and gender prejudices and stereotypes that may be outdated or clearly wrong then and wrong today; but their removal would be tantamount to claiming these prejudices never existed. The Publisher does not endorse or support those depictions or stereotypes; and these books have been made available for a discerning audience that will read it for entertainment value and a chronicle/record of popular fiction of past times.

Cover design by Priya Singh adapted from the original classic yellowjacket by Hodder & Stoughton.

Cover illustration: Hodder original.

Series note: Some of the books in the series (unless otherwise credited) may have cover or inside illustrations from the original yellowbacks or early editions, and while full restoration has been attempted, some images may be grainy or faded due to the condition of the original material. The end notes or bonus material or blurb details may have been sourced from the public domain or free use publications such as Wikipedia and attribution is hereby made also allowing similar free use reproduction from here. Sources requiring further specific attribution may write in and further detailing and/or corrections shall be made in subsequent printings/editions.

Reprint specifications may be subject to change including but not limited to finishes, paper, colour sections.

ISBN: 978-93-5731-218-9

Hachette Book Publishing India Pvt. Ltd.
4th & 5th Floors, Corporate Centre,
Plot No. 94, Sector 44, Gurugram - 122 003, India

Typeset in Electra LT STD 10/12.5 pt by Manipal Technologies Limited, Manipal

Printed and bound in India by Manipal Technologies Limited, Manipal

CONTENTS

THE MAN WITH THE CLUBFOOT

1.	I Seek a Bed in Rotterdam	3
2.	The Cipher with the Invoice	8
3.	A Visitor in the Night	15
4.	Destiny Knocks at the Door	22
5.	The Lady of the Vos In't Tuintje	34
6.	I Board the Berlin Train and Leave a Lame Gentleman on the Platform	45
7.	In Which a Silver Star Acts as a Charm	59
8.	I Hear of Clubfoot and Meet his Employer	69
9.	I Encounter an Old Acquaintance Who Leads Me to a Delightful Surprise	82
10.	A Glass of Wine with Clubfoot	95
11.	Miss Mary Prendergast Risks her Reputation	107
12.	His Excellency the General is Worried	119
13.	I find Achilles in his Tent	132
14.	Clubfoot Comes to Haase's	142
15.	The Waiter at the Café Regina	153
16.	A Hand-Clasp by the Rhine	161
17.	Francis Takes up the Narrative	173
18.	I Go on With the Story	181
19.	We Have a Reckoning with Clubfoot	191
20.	Charlemagne's Ride	199
21.	Red Tabs Explains	212

THE RETURN OF CLUBFOOT

22.	Doña Luisa	223
23.	In Which a Gentleman Pays his Debt	230
24.	The Message	243
25.	A Footstep in the Lane	255
26.	The Girl in the Smoke-room	262
27.	I Receive an Invitation	274
28.	The Vice-Consul's Warning	281
29.	Dr Custrin	288
30.	Concerning a Long Drink	295
31.	The Grave in the Clearing	305
32.	A Voice in the Forest	317
33.	I Meet an Old Acquaintance	325
34.	El Cojo	332
35.	"Die Fünf-Und-Achtziger"	340
36.	Marjorie's Adventure	349
37.	Black Pablo Makes his Preparations	356
38.	The Escape	363
39.	A Face Among the Ferns	369
40.	Which Proves that Two Heads are Better than One	374
41.	The Burial Chamber	382
42.	A Light in the Darkness and What Came of it	395
43.	I Interrupt a Tête-à-Tête	403
44.	Capitulation	409
45.	Ulrich Von Hagel's Treasure	414
46.	The End of a Dream	423
47.	In which a Black Box Plays a Decisive Part	430

The Man with the Clubfoot

1

I SEEK A BED IN ROTTERDAM

The reception clerk looked up from the hotel register and shook his head firmly.

"Very sorry, saire," he said, "not a bed in ze house." And he closed the book with a snap.

Outside the rain came down heavens hard. Everyone who came into the brightly lit hotel vestibule entered with a gush of water. I felt I would rather die than face the wind-swept streets of Rotterdam again.

I turned once more to the clerk who was now busy at the key-rack.

"Haven't you really a corner? I wouldn't mind where it was, as it is only for the night. Come now..."

"Very sorry, saire. We have two gentlemen sleeping in ze bathrooms already. If you had reserved..." And he shrugged his shoulders and bent towards a visitor who was demanding his key.

I turned away with rage in my heart. What a cursed fool I had been not to wire from Groningen! I had fully intended to, but the extraordinary conversation I had had with Dicky Allerton had put everything else out of my head. At every hotel I had tried it had been the same story—Cooman's, the

Maas, the Grand, all were full even to the bathrooms. If I had only wired...

As I passed out into the porch I bethought myself of the porter. A hotel porter had helped me out of a similar plight in Breslau once years ago. This porter, with his red, drink-sodden face and tarnished gold braid, did not promise well, so far as a recommendation for a lodging for the night was concerned. Still...

I suppose it was my mind dwelling on my experience at Breslau that made me address the man in German. When one has been familiar with a foreign tongue from one's boyhood, it requires but a very slight mental impulse to drop into it. From such slight beginnings do great enterprises spring. If I had known the immense ramifications of adventure that was to spread its roots from that simple question, I verily believe my heart would have failed me and I would have run forth into the night and the rain and roamed the streets till morning.

Well, I found myself asking the man in German if he knew where I could get a room for the night.

He shot a quick glance at me from under his reddened eyelids.

"The gentleman would doubtless like a German house?" he queried.

You may hardly credit it, but my interview with Dicky Allerton that afternoon had simply driven the war out of my mind. When one has lived much among foreign peoples, one's mentality slips automatically into their skin. I was now thinking in German—at least so it seems to me when I look back upon that night—and I answered without reflecting:

"I don't care where it is as long as I can get somewhere to sleep out of this infernal rain!"

"The gentleman can have a good, clean bed at the Hotel Sixt in the little street they call the Vos in't Tuintje, on the canal behind the Bourse. The proprietress is a good German, jawohl... Frau Anna Schraff her name is. The gentleman need only say he comes from Franz at the Bopparder Hof."

I gave the man a gulden and bade him get me a cab.

It was still pouring. As we rattled away over the glistening cobble-stones, my mind travelled back over the startling events of the day. My talk with old Dicky had given me such a mental jar that I found it at first wellnigh impossible to concentrate my thoughts. That's the worst of shell-shock. You think you are cured, you feel fit and well, and then suddenly the machinery of your mind checks and halts and creaks. Ever since I had left hospital convalescent after being wounded on the Somme ("gunshot wound in head and cerebral concussion" the doctors called it) I had trained myself, whenever my brain was *en panne*, to go back to the beginning of things and work slowly up to the present by methodical stages.

Let's see then... I was "boarded" at Millbank and got three months' leave: then I did a month in the Littlejohns' bungalow in Cornwall: there I got the letter from Dicky Allerton, who, before the war, had been in partnership with my brother Francis in the motor business at Coventry. Dicky had been with the Naval Division at Antwerp and was interned with the rest of the crowd when they crossed the Dutch frontier in those disastrous days of October, 1914.

Dicky wrote from Groningen, just a line. Now that I was on leave, if I were fit to travel, would I come to Groningen and see him? "I have had a curious communication which seems to have to do with poor Francis," he added. That was all.

My brain was still halting, so I turned to Francis. Here again I had to go back. Francis, rejected on all sides for active service owing to what he scornfully used to call "the shirkers' ailment, varicose veins," had flatly declined to carry on with his motor business after Dicky had joined up, although their firm was doing government work. Finally, he had vanished into the maw of the War Office and all I knew was that he was "something on the Intelligence." More than this not even *he* would tell me, and when he finally disappeared from London, just about the time that I was popping the parapet with my battalion at Neuve Chapelle, he left me his London chambers as his only address for letters.

Ah! Now it was all coming back... Francis' infrequent letters to me about nothing at all, then his will, forwarded to me for safe keeping when I was home on leave last Christmas, and after that, silence. Not another letter, not a word about him, not a shred of information. He had utterly vanished.

I remembered my frantic inquiries, my vain visits to the War Office, my perplexity at the imperturbable silence of the various officials I importuned for news of my poor brother. Then there was that lunch at the Bath Club with Sonny Martin of the Heavies and a friend of his, some kind of staff captain in red tabs. I don't think I heard his name, but I know he was at the War Office, and presently over our cigars and coffee I laid before him the mysterious facts about my brother's case.

"Perhaps you knew Francis?" I said in conclusion. "Yes," he replied, "I know him well."

"*Know* him," I repeated, "*know* him... then... then you think... you have reason to believe he is still alive...?"

Red Tabs cocked his eye at the gilded cornice of the ceiling and blew a ring from his cigar. But he said nothing.

I persisted with my questions but it was of no avail. Red Tabs only laughed and said: "I know nothing at all except that your brother is a most delightful fellow with all your own love of getting his own way."

Then Sonny Martin, who is the perfection of tact and diplomacy—probably on that account he failed for the Diplomatic—chipped in with an anecdote about a man who was rating the waiter at an adjoining table, and I held my peace. But as Red Tabs rose to go, a little later, he held my hand for a minute in his and with that curious look of his, said slowly and with meaning:

"When a nation is at war, officers on *active service* must occasionally disappear, sometimes in their country's interest, sometimes in their own."

He emphasised the words "on active service."

In a flash my eyes were opened. How blind I had been! Francis was in Germany.

2

THE CIPHER WITH THE INVOICE

Red Tabs' sphinx-like declaration was no riddle to me. I knew at once that Francis must be on secret service in the enemy's country and that country Germany. My brother's extraordinary knowledge of the Germans, their customs, life and dialects, rendered him ideally suitable for any such perilous mission. Francis always had an extraordinary talent for languages: he seemed to acquire them all without any mental effort, but in German he was supreme. During the year that he and I spent at Consistorial-Rat von Mayburg's house at Bonn, he rapidly outdistanced me, and though, at the end of our time, I could speak German like a German, Francis was able, in addition, to speak Bonn and Cologne *patois* like a native of those ancient cities—ay, and he could drill a squad of recruits in their own language like the smartest *Leutnant* ever fledged from Gross-Lichterfelde.

He never had any difficulty in passing himself off as a German. Well I remember his delight when he was claimed as a fellow Rheinlander by a German officer we met, one summer before the war, combining golf with a little useful espionage at Cromer.

I don't think Francis had any ulterior motive in his study of German. He simply found he had this imitative faculty:

philology had always interested him: so, even after he had gone into the motor trade, he used to amuse himself on business trips to Germany by acquiring new dialects.

His German imitations were extraordinarily funny. One of his "star turns" was a noisy sitting of the Reichstag with speeches by Prince Bulow and August Bebel and "interruptions"; another, a patriotic oration by an old Prussian General at a Kaiser's Birthday dinner. Francis had a marvellous faculty not only of *seeming* German, but even of almost looking like a German, so absolutely was he able to slip into the skin of the part.

Yet never in my wildest moments had I dreamt that he would try and get into Germany in war-time, into that land where every citizen is catalogued and pigeon-holed from the cradle. But Red Tabs' oracular utterance had made everything clear to me. Why, a mission to Germany would be the very thing that Francis would give his eyes to be allowed to attempt! Francis with his utter disregard of danger, his love of taking risks, his impish delight in taking a rise out of the stodgy Hun... why, if there were Englishmen brave enough to take chances of that kind, Francis would be the first to volunteer.

Yes, if Francis were on a mission anywhere it would be to Germany. But what prospect had he of ever returning—with the frontiers closed and ingress and egress practically barred even to pro-German neutrals? Many a night in the trenches I had a mental vision of Francis, so debonair and so fearless, facing a firing-squad of Prussian privates.

From the day of the luncheon at the Bath Club to this very afternoon I had had no further inkling of my brother's whereabouts or fate. The authorities at home professed ignorance, as I knew, in duty bound, they would, and I had nothing to hang any theory on to until Dicky Allerton's letter came. Ashcroft at the F.O. fixed up my passports for me and I lost no time in exchanging the white gulls and red cliffs of Cornwall for the windmills and trim canals of Holland.

And now in my breast pocket lay, written on a small piece of cheap foreign note-paper, the tidings I had come to Groningen to seek. Yet so trivial, so nonsensical, so baffling was the message that I already felt my trip to Holland to have been a fruitless errand.

I found Dicky fat and bursting with health in his quarters at the internment camp. He only knew that Francis had disappeared. When I told him of my meeting with Red Tabs at the Bath Club, of the latter's words to me at parting and of my own conviction in the matter he whistled, then looked grave.

He went straight to the point in his bluff direct way.

"I am going to tell you a story first, Desmond," he said to me, "then I'll show you a piece of paper. Whether the two together fit in with your theory as to poor Francis' disappearance will be for you to judge. Until now—I must confess—I had felt inclined to dismiss the only reference this document appears to make to your brother as a mere coincidence in names, but what you have told me makes things interesting—by Jove, it does, though. Well, here's the yarn first of all!

"Your brother and I have had dealings in the past with a Dutchman in the motor business at Nymwegen, name of van Urutius. He has often been over to see us at Coventry in the old days and Francis has stayed with him at Nymwegen once or twice on his way back from Germany—Nymwegen, you know, is close to the German frontier. Old Urutius has been very decent to me since I have been in gaol here and has been over several times, generally with a box or two of those nice Dutch cigars."

"Dicky," I broke in on him, "get on with the story. What the devil's all this got to do with Francis? The document..."

"Steady, my boy!" was the imperturbable reply, "Let me spin my yarn in my own way. I'm coming to the piece of paper...

"Well, then, old Urutius came to see me ten days ago. All I knew about Francis I had told him, namely, that Francis had entered the army and was missing. It was no business of the old Mynheer if Francis was in the Intelligence, so I didn't tell him that. Van U. is a staunch friend of the English, but you know the saying that if a man doesn't know he can't split.

"My old Dutch pal, then, turned up here ten days ago. He was bubbling over with excitement. 'Mr Allerton,' he says, 'I haf had a writing, a most mysterious writing—a writing, I t'ink, from Francis Okewood.'

"I sat tight. If there were any revelations coming they were going to be Dutch, not British. On that I was resolved.

"'I haf received,' the old Dutchman went on, 'from Gairemany a parcel of metal shields, plates—what you call 'em—of tin, *hein*? What I haf to advertise my business. They arrife las' week—I open the parcel myself and on the top is the envelope with the invoice.'

"Mynheer paused: he has a good sense of the dramatic.

"'Well,' I said, 'did it bite you or say "Gott strafe England," or what?'

"Van Urutius ignored my flippancy and resumed. 'I open the envelope and there in the invoice I find this writing—here!'

"And here," said Dicky, diving into his pocket, "is 'the writing'!"

And he thrust into my eagerly outstretched hand a very thin half-sheet of foreign note-paper, of that kind of cheap glazed note-paper you get in Cafés on the Continent when you ask for writing materials.

Five lines of German, written in fluent German characters in purple ink beneath the name and address of Mynheer van Urutius... that was all.

My heart sank with disappointment and wretchedness as I read the inscription.

Here is the document:

> Herrn Willem van Urutius,
> Automobilgeschaft,
> Nymwegen.
> *Alexander-Straat* 81 *bis*.
>
> Berlin, 1ten Juli, 16.
>
> O Eichenholz! O Eichenholz,
> Wie leer sind deine Blatter.
> Wie Achiles in dem Zelte.
> Wo zweie sich zanken
> Erfreut sich der Dritte.

(Translation.)

> Mr Willem van Urutius,
> Automobile Agent,
> Nymwegen.
> 81 bis *Alexander-Straat*.
>
> Berlin, 1st July, 16.
> O Oak-tree! O Oak-tree,
> How empty are thy leaves.
>
> Like Achiles in the tent.
>
> When two people fall out
> The third party rejoices.

I stared at this nonsensical document in silence. My thoughts were almost too bitter for words.

At last I spoke.

"What's all this rigmarole got to do with Francis, Dicky?" I asked, vainly trying to suppress the bitterness in my voice. "This looks like a list of copybook maxims for your Dutch friend's advertisement cards..."

But I returned to the study of the piece of paper.

"Not so fast, old bird," Dicky replied coolly, "let me finish my story. Old Stick-in-the-mud is a lot shrewder than we think.

"'When I read the writing,' he told me, 'I think he is all robbish, but then I ask myself, Who shall put robbish in my invoices? And then I read the writing again and once again, and then I see he is a message.'

"Stop, Dicky!" I cried, "Of course, what an ass I am! Why *Eichenholz*..."

"Exactly," retorted Dicky, "as the old Mynheer was the first to see, *Eichenholz* translated into English is 'Oak-tree' or 'Oak-wood'—in other words, Francis."

"Then, Dicky..." I interrupted.

"Just a minute," said Dicky, putting up his hand. "I confess I thought, on first seeing this message or whatever it is, that there must be simply a coincidence of name and that somebody's idle scribbling had found its way into old van U.'s invoice. But now that you have told me that Francis may have actually got into Germany, then, I must say, it looks as if this might be an attempt of his to communicate with home."

"Where did the Dutchman's packet of stuff come from?" I asked.

"From the Berlin Metal Works in Steglitz, a suburb of Berlin: he has dealt with them for years."

"But then what does all the rest of it mean... all this about Achilles and the rest?"

"Ah, Desmond!" was Dicky's reply, "that's where you've got not only me, but also Mynheer van Urutius."

"'O oak-wood! O oak-wood, how empty are thy leaves!'... That sounds like a taunt, don't you think, Dicky?" said I.

"*Or* a confession of failure from Francis... to let us know that he has done nothing, adding that he is accordingly sulking 'like Achilles in his tent'."

"But, see here, Richard Allerton," I said, "Francis would never spell 'Achilles' with one 'l'... now, would he?"

"By Jove!" said Dicky, looking at the paper again, "nobody would but a very uneducated person. I know nothing about German, but tell me, is that the hand of an educated German? Is it Francis' handwriting?"

"Certainly, it is an educated hand," I replied, "but I'm dashed if I can say whether it is Francis' German handwriting: it can scarcely be because, as I have already remarked, he spells 'Achilles' with one 'l'."

Then the fog came down over us again. We sat helplessly and gazed at the fateful paper.

"There's only one thing for it, Dicky," I said finally, "I'll take the blooming thing back to London with me and hand it over to the Intelligence. After all, Francis may have a code with them. Possibly they will see light where we grope in darkness."

"Desmond," said Dicky, giving me his hand, "that's the most sensible suggestion you've made yet. Go home and good luck to you. But promise me you'll come back here and tell me if that piece of paper brings the news that dear old Francis is alive."

So I left Dicky but I did not go home. I was not destined to see my home for many a weary week.

3

A VISITOR IN THE NIGHT

A volley of invective from the box of the cab—bad language in Dutch is fearfully effective—aroused me from my musings. The cab, a small, uncomfortable box with a musty smell, stopped with a jerk that flung me forward. From the outer darkness furious altercation resounded above the plashing of the rain. I peered through the streaming glass of the windows but could distinguish nothing save the yellow blur of a lamp. Then a vehicle of some kind seemed to move away in front of us, for I heard the grating of wheels against the kerb, and my cab drew up to the pavement.

On alighting, I found myself in a narrow, dark street with high houses on either side. A grimy lamp with the word "Hôtel" in half-obliterated characters painted on it hung above my head, announcing that I had arrived at my destination. As I paid off the cabman another cab passed. It was apparently the one with which my Jehu had had words, for he turned round and shouted abuse into the night.

My cabman departed, leaving me with my bag on the pavement at my feet gazing at a narrow dirty door, the upper half of which was filled in with frosted glass. I was at last awake to the fact that I, an Englishman, was going to spend the night in a German hotel to which I had been specially recommended by a German porter on the understanding that I was a German. I knew that, according to the Dutch neutrality regulations, my passport would have to be handed in for inspection by the police and that therefore I could not pass myself off as a German.

"Bah!" I said to give myself courage, "This is a free country, a neutral country. They may be offensive, they may overcharge you, in a Hun hotel, but they can't eat you. Besides, any bed in a night like this!" and I pushed open the door.

Within, the hotel proved to be rather better than its uninviting exterior promised. There was a small vestibule with a little glass cage of an office on one side and beyond it an old-fashioned flight of stairs, with a glass knob on the post at the foot, winding to the upper stories.

At the sound of my footsteps on the mosaic flooring, a waiter emerged from a little cubby-hole under the stairs. He had a blue apron girt about his waist, but otherwise he wore the short coat and the dicky and white tie of the Continental hotel waiter. His hands were grimy with black marks and so was his apron. He had apparently been cleaning boots.

He was a big, fat, blonde man with narrow, cruel little eyes. His hair was cut so short that his head appeared to be shaven. He advanced quickly towards me and asked me in German in a truculent voice what I wanted.

I replied in the same language, I wanted a room.

He shot a glance at me through his little slits of eyes on hearing my good Bonn accent, but his manner did not change.

"The hotel is full. The gentleman cannot have a bed here. The proprietress is out at present. I regret..." He spat this all out in the offhand insolent manner of the Prussian official.

"It was Franz, of the Bopparder Hof, who recommended me to come here," I said. I was not going out again into the rain for a whole army of Prussian waiters.

"He told me that Frau Schratt would make me very comfortable," I added.

The waiter's manner changed at once.

"So, so," he said—quite genially this time—"it was Franz who sent the gentleman to us. He is a good friend of the house, is Franz. Ja, Frau Schratt is unfortunately out just now, but as soon as the lady returns I will inform her you are here. In the meantime, I will give the gentleman a room."

He handed me a candlestick and a key.

"So," he grunted, "No. 31, the third floor."

A clock rang out the hour somewhere in the distance.

"Ten o'clock already," he said. "The gentleman's papers can wait till tomorrow, it is so late. Or perhaps the gentleman will give them to the proprietress. She must come any moment."

As I mounted the winding staircase I heard him murmur again:

"So, so, Franz sent him here! Ach, der Franz!"

As soon as I had passed out of sight of the lighted hall I found myself in complete darkness. On each landing a jet of gas, turned down low, flung a dim and flickering light a few yards around. On the third floor I was able to distinguish by the gas rays a small plaque fastened to the wall inscribed with an arrow pointing to the right above the figures: 46-30.

I stopped to strike a match to light my candle. The whole hotel seemed wrapped in silence, the only sound the rushing of water in the gutters without. Then from the darkness of the narrow corridor that stretched out in front of me, I heard the rattle of key in a lock.

I advanced down the corridor, the pale glimmer of my candle showing me as I passed a succession of yellow doors, each bearing a white porcelain plate inscribed with a number in black. No. 46 was the first room on the right counting from the landing: the even numbers were on the right, the odd on the left: therefore I reckoned on finding my room the last on the left at the end of the corridor.

The corridor presently took a sharp turn. As I came round the bend I heard again the sound of a key and then the rattling of a door knob, but the corridor bending again, I could not see the author of the noise until I had turned the corner.

I ran right into a man fumbling at a door on the left-hand side of the passage, the last door but one. A mirror at the end of the corridor caught and threw back the reflection of my candle.

The man looked up as I approached. He was wearing a soft black felt hat and a black overcoat and on his arm hung an umbrella streaming with rain. His candlestick stood on the floor at his feet. It had apparently just been extinguished, for my nostrils sniffed the odour of burning tallow.

"You have a light?" the stranger said in German in a curiously breathless voice. "I have just come upstairs and the wind blew out my candle and I could not get the door open. Perhaps you could..." He broke off gasping and put his hand to his heart.

"Allow me," I said. The lock of the door was inverted and to open the door you had to insert the key upside-down. I did so and the door opened easily. As it swung back I noticed the number of the room was 33, next door to mine.

"Can I be of any assistance to you? Are you unwell?" I said, at the same time lifting my candle and scanning the stranger's features.

He was a young man with close-cropped black hair, fine dark eyes and an aquiline nose with a deep furrow between the eyebrows. The crispness of his hair and the high cheekbones gave a suggestion of Jewish blood. His face was very pale and his lips were blueish. I saw the perspiration glistening on his forehead.

"Thank you, it is nothing," the man replied in the same breathless voice. "I am only a little out of breath with carrying my bag upstairs. That's all."

"You must have arrived just before I did," I said remembering the cab that had driven away from the hotel as I drove up.

"That is so," he answered, pushing open his door as he spoke. He disappeared into the darkness of the room and suddenly the door shut with a slam that re-echoed through the house.

As I had calculated, my room was next door to his, the end room of the corridor. It smelt horribly close and musty and the first thing I did was to stride across to the windows and fling them back wide.

I found myself looking across a dark and narrow canal, on whose stagnant water loomed large the black shapes of great barges, into the windows of gaunt and weather-stained houses over the way. Not a light shone in any window. Away in the distance the same clock as I had heard before struck the quarter—a single, clear chime.

It was the regular bedroom of the *maison meublée*—worn carpet, discoloured and dingy wall-paper, faded rep curtains and mahogany bedstead with a vast *édredon*, like a giant pin-cushion. My candle, guttering wildly in the unaccustomed breeze blowing dankly through the chamber, was the sole illuminant. There was neither gas nor electric light laid on.

The house had relapsed into quiet. The bedroom had an evil look and this, combined with the dank air from the canal, gave my thoughts a sombre tinge.

"Well," I said to myself, "you're a nice kind of ass! Here you are, a British officer, posing as a brother Hun in a cut-throat Hun hotel, with a waiter who looks like the official Prussian executioner. What's going to happen to you, young feller my lad, when Madame comes along and finds you have a British passport? A very pretty kettle of fish, I must say!

"And suppose Madame takes it into her head to toddle along up here tonight and calls your bluff and summons the gentle Hans or Fritz or whatever that ruffianly waiter's name is to come upstairs and settle your hash! What sort of a fight are you going to put up in that narrow corridor out there with a Hun next door and probably on every side of you, and no exit this end? You don't know a living soul in Rotterdam and no one will be a penny the wiser if you vanish off the face of the earth... at any rate no one on this side of the water."

Starting to undress, I noticed a little door on the left-hand side of the bed. I found it opened into a small *cabinet de toilette*, a narrow slip of a room with a wash-hand stand and a very dirty window covered with yellow paper. I pulled open this window with great difficulty—it cannot have been opened for years—and found it gave on to a very small and deep interior court, just an air shaft round which the house was built. At the bottom was a tiny paved court not more than five foot square, entirely isolated save on one side where there was a basement window with a flight of steps leading down from the court through an iron grating. From this window a faint yellow streak of light was visible. The air was damp and chill and horrid odours of a dirty kitchen were wafted up the shaft. So I closed the window and set about turning in.

I took off my coat and waistcoat, then bethought me of the mysterious document I had received from Dicky. Once more I looked at those enigmatical words:

> O Oakwood! O Oakwood (for that much was clear),
> How empty are thy leaves.
> Like Achiles (with one "l") *in the tent.*
> *When two people fall out*
> *The third party rejoices.*

What did it all mean? Had Francis fallen out with some confederate who, having had his revenge by denouncing my brother, now took this extraordinary step to announce his victim's fate to the latter's friends? "Like Achilles in the tent!" Why not "in *his* tent"? Surely...

A curious choking noise, the sound of a strangled cough, suddenly broke the profound silence of the house. My heart seemed to stop for a moment. I hardly dared raise my eyes from the paper which I was conning, leaning over the table in my shirt and trousers.

The noise continued, a hideous, deep-throated gurgling. Then I heard a faint foot-fall in the corridor without.

I raised my eyes to the door.

Someone or something was scratching the panels, furiously, frantically.

The door-knob was rattled loudly. The noise broke in raucously upon that horrid gurgling sound without. It snapped the spell that bound me.

I moved resolutely towards the door. Even as I stepped forward the gurgling resolved itself into a strangled cry.

"Ach! ich sterbe," were the words I heard.

Then the door burst open with a crash, there was a swooping rush of wind and rain through the room, the curtains flapped madly from the windows.

The candle flared up wildly.

Then it went out.

Something fell heavily into the room.

4

DESTINY KNOCKS AT THE DOOR

There are two things at least that modern warfare teaches you, one is to keep cool in an emergency, the other is not to be afraid of a corpse. Therefore I was scarcely surprised to find myself standing there in the dark calmly reviewing the extraordinary situation in which I now found myself. That's the curious thing about shell-shock: after it a motor back-firing or a tyre bursting will reduce a man to tears, but in face of danger he will probably find himself in full possession of his wits as long as there is no sudden and violent noise connected with it.

Brief as the sounds without had been, I was able on reflection to identify that gasping gurgle, that rapid patter of the hands. Anyone who has seen a man die quickly knows them. Accordingly I surmised that somebody had come to my door at the point of death, probably to seek assistance.

Then I thought of the man next door, his painful breathlessness, his blueish lips, when I found him wrestling with his key, and I guessed who was my nocturnal visitor lying prone in the dark at my feet.

Shielding the candle with my hand I rekindled it. Then I grappled with the flapping curtains and got the windows shut. Then only did I raise my candle until its beams shone down upon the silent figure lying across the threshold of the room.

It was the man from No. 33. He was quite dead. His face was livid and distorted, his eyes glassy between the half-closed lids, while his fingers, still stiffly clutching, showed paint and varnish and dust beneath the nails where he had pawed door and carpet in his death agony.

One did not need to be a doctor to see that a heart attack had swiftly and suddenly struck him down.

Now that I knew the worst I acted with decision. I dragged the body by the shoulders into the room until it lay in the centre of the carpet. Then I locked the door.

The foreboding of evil that had cast its black shadow over my thoughts from the moment I crossed the threshold of this sinister hotel came over me strongly again. Indeed, my position was, to say the least, scarcely enviable. Here was I, a British officer with British papers of identity, about to be discovered in a German hotel, into which I had introduced myself under false pretences, at dead of night alone with the corpse of a German or Austrian (for such the dead man apparently was)!

It was undoubtedly a most awkward fix.

I listened.

Everything in the hotel was silent as the grave.

I turned from my gloomy forebodings to look again at the stranger. In his crisp black hair and slightly protuberant cheek-bones I traced again the hint of Jewish ancestry I had remarked before. Now that the man's eyes—his big, thoughtful eyes that had stared at me out of the darkness of the corridor—were closed, he looked far less foreign than before: in fact he might almost have passed as an Englishman.

He was a young man—about my own age, I judged—(I shall be twenty-eight next birthday) and about my own height, which is five feet ten. There was something about his appearance and build that struck a chord very faintly in my memory.

Had I seen the fellow before?

I remembered now that I had noticed something oddly familiar about him when I first saw him for that brief moment in the corridor.

I looked down at him again as he lay on his back on the faded carpet. I brought the candle down closer and scanned his features.

He certainly looked less foreign than he did before. He might not be a German after all: more likely a Hungarian or a Pole, perhaps even a Dutchman. His German had been too flawless for a Frenchman—for a Hungarian, either, for that matter.

I leant back on my knees to ease my cramped position. As I did so I caught a glimpse of the stranger's three-quarters face.

Why! He reminded me of Francis a little!

There certainly was a suggestion of my brother in the man's appearance. Was it the thick black hair, the small dark moustache? Was it the well-chiselled mouth? It was rather a hint of Francis than a resemblance to him.

The stranger was fully dressed. The jacket of his blue serge suit had fallen open and I saw a portfolio in the inner breast pocket. Here, I thought, might be a clue to the dead man's identity. I fished out the portfolio, then rapidly ran my fingers over the stranger's other pockets.

I left the portfolio to the last.

The jacket pockets contained nothing else except a white silk handkerchief unmarked. In the righthand top-pocket of the waistcoat was a neat silver cigarette case, perfectly plain, containing half a dozen cigarettes. I took one out and looked at it. It was a Melania, a cigarette I happen to know for they stock them at one of my clubs, the Dionysus, and it chances to be the only place in London where you can get the brand.

It looked as if my unknown friend had come from London.

There was also a plain silver watch of Swiss make.

In the trousers pocket was some change, a little English silver and coppers, some Dutch silver and paper money. In the right-hand trouser pocket was a bunch of keys.

That was all.

I put the different articles on the floor beside me. Then I got up, put the candle on the table, drew the chair up to it and opened the portfolio.

In a little pocket of the inner flap were visiting cards. Some were simply engraved with the name in small letters:

> Dr Semlin

Others were more detailed:

> Dr Semlin
> Brooklyn, N.Y.
>
> The Halewright Mfg. Coy., Ltd.

There were also half a dozen private cards:

> Dr Semlin,
> 333 E. 73rd St.,
> New York.
> Rivington Park House.

In the packet of cards was a solitary one, larger than the rest, an expensive affair on thick, highly glazed millboard, bearing in Gothic characters the name:

Otto von Steinhardt.

On this card was written in pencil, above the name:

"Hotel Sixt, Vos in't Tuintje," and in brackets, thus:
"(Mme. Anna Schratt.)"

In another pocket of the portfolio was an American passport surmounted by a flaming eagle and sealed with a vast red seal, sending greetings to all and sundry on behalf of Henry Semlin, a United States citizen, travelling to Europe. Details in the body of the document set forth that Henry Semlin was born at Brooklyn on 31st March, 1886, that his hair was Black, nose Aquiline, chin Firm, and that of special marks he had None. The description was good enough to show me that it was undoubtedly the body of Henry Semlin that lay at my feet.

The passport had been issued at Washington three months earlier. The only *visa* it bore was that of the American Embassy in London, dated two days previously. With it was a British permit, issued to Henry Semlin, Manufacturer, granting him authority to leave the United Kingdom for the purpose of travelling to Rotterdam; further, a bill for luncheon served on board the Dutch Royal mail steamer *Koningin Regentes* on yesterday's date.

In the long and anguishing weeks that followed on that anxious night in the Hotel of the Vos in't Tuintje, I have often wondered to what malicious promptings, to what insane impulse, I owed the idea that suddenly germinated in my brain as I sat fingering the dead man's letter-case in that squalid room. The impulse sprang into my brain like a flash and like a flash I acted on it, though I can hardly believe I meant to pursue it to its logical conclusion until I stood once more outside the door of my room.

The examination of the dead man's papers had shown me that he was an American businessman, who had just come from London, having but recently proceeded to England from the United States.

What puzzled me was why an American manufacturer, seemingly of some substance and decently dressed, should go to a German hotel on the recommendation of a German, from his name, and the style of his visiting card, a man of good family.

Semlin might, of course, have been, like myself, a traveller benighted in Rotterdam, owing his recommendation to the hotel to a German acquaintance in the city. Still, Americans are cautious folk and I found it rather improbable that this American businessman should adventure himself into this evil-looking house with a large sum of money on his person — he had several hundred pounds of money in Dutch currency notes in a thick wad in his portfolio.

I knew that the British authorities discouraged, as far as they could, neutrals travelling to and fro between England and Germany in war-time. Possibly Semlin wanted to do business in Germany on his European trip as well as in England. Knowing the attitude of the British authorities, he may well have made his arrangements in Holland for getting into Germany lest the British police should get wind of his purpose and stop him crossing to Rotterdam.

But his German was so flawless, with no trace of Americanism in voice or accent. And I knew what good use the German Intelligence had made of neutral passports in the past. Therefore I determined to go next door and have a look at Dr Semlin's luggage. In the back of my mind was ever that harebrain resolve, half-formed as yet but none the less firmly rooted in my head.

Taking up my candle again, I stole out of the room. As I stood in the corridor and turned to lock the bedroom door behind me, the mirror at the end of the passage caught the reflection of my candle.

I looked and saw myself in the glass, a white, staring face.

I looked again. Then I fathomed the riddle that had puzzled me in the dead face of the stranger in my room.

It was not the face of Francis that his features suggested.

It was mine!

* * *

The next moment I found myself in No. 33. I could see no sign of the key of the room; Semlin must have dropped it in his fall, so it behoved me to make haste for fear of any untoward interruption. I had not yet heard eleven strike on the clock.

The stranger's hat and overcoat lay on a chair. The hat was from Scott's: there was nothing except a pair of leather gloves in the overcoat pockets.

A bag, in size something between a small kit-bag and a large handbag, stood open on the table. It contained a few toilet necessaries, a pair of pyjamas, a clean shirt, a pair of slippers... nothing of importance and not a scrap of paper of any kind.

I went through everything again, looked in the sponge bag, opened the safety razor case, shook out the shirt, and finally took everything out of the bag and stacked the things on the table.

At the bottom of the bag I made a strange discovery. The interior of the bag was fitted with that thin yellow canvas-like material with which nearly all cheap bags, like this one was, are lined. At the bottom of the bag an oblong piece of the lining had apparently been torn clean out. The leather of the bag showed through the slit. Yet the lining round the edges of the gap showed no fraying, no trace of rough usage. On the contrary, the edges were pasted neatly down on the leather.

I lifted the bag and examined it. As I did so I saw lying on the table beside it an oblong of yellow canvas. I picked it up and found the under side stained with paste and the brown of the leather.

It was the missing piece of lining and it was stiff with something that crackled inside it.

I slit the piece of canvas up one side with my penknife. It contained three long fragments of paper, a thick, expensive, highly glazed paper. Top, bottom and left-hand side of each was trim and glossy: the fourth side showed a broken edge as though it had been roughly cut with a knife. The three slips of

THE MAN WITH THE CLUBFOOT

paper were the halves of three quarto sheets of writing, torn in two, lengthways from top to bottom.

At the top of each slip was part of some kind of crest in gold, what, it was not possible to determine, for the crest had been in the centre of the sheet and the cut had gone right through it.

The letter was written in English but the name of the recipient as also the date was on the missing half.

Somewhere in the silence of the night I heard a door bang. I thrust the slips of paper in their canvas covering into my trousers pocket. I must not be found in that room. With trembling hands I started to put the things back in the bag. Those slips of paper, I reflected as I worked, at least rent the veil of mystery enveloping the corpse that lay stiffening in the next room. This, at any rate, was certain: German or American or hyphenate, Henry Semlin, manufacturer and spy, had voyaged from America to England not for the purposes of trade but to get hold of that mutilated document now reposing in my pocket. Why he had only got half the letter and what had happened to the other half was more than I could say... it sufficed for me to know that its importance to somebody was sufficient to warrant a journey on its behalf from one side to the other of the Atlantic.

As I opened the bag my fingers encountered a hard substance, as of metal, embedded in the slack of the lining in the joints of the mouth. At first I thought it was a coin, then I felt some kind of clasp or fastening behind it and it seemed to be a brooch. Out came my pocket knife again and there lay a small silver star, about as big as a regimental cap badge, embedded in the thin canvas. It bore an inscription. In stencilled letters I read:

Here was Dr Semlin's real visiting-card.

I held in my hand a badge of the German secret police.

You cannot penetrate far behind the scenes in Germany without coming across the traces of Section Seven of the Berlin Police Presidency, the section that is known euphemistically as that of the Political Police. Ostensibly it attends to the safety of the monarch, and of distinguished personages generally, and the numerous suite that used to accompany the Kaiser on his visits to England invariably included two or three top-hatted representatives of the section.

The ramifications of *Abteilung Sieben* are, in reality, much wider. It does such work in connection with the newspapers as is even too dirty for the German Foreign Office to touch, comprising everything from the launching of personal attacks in obscure blackmailing; sheets against inconvenient politicians to the escorting of unpleasantly truthful foreign correspondents to the frontier. It is the obedient handmaiden of the Intelligence Department of both War Office and Admiralty in Germany, and renders faithful service to the espionage which is constantly maintained on officials, politicians, the clergy and the general public in that land of careful organisation.

Section Seven is a vast subterranean department. Always working in the dark, its political complexion is a handy cloak for blacker and more sinister activities. It is frequently entrusted with commissions of which it would be inexpedient for official Germany to have cognizance and of which, accordingly, official Germany can always safely repudiate when occasion demands.

I thrust the pin of the badge into my braces and fastened it there, crammed the rest of the dead man's effects into his bag, stuck his hat upon my head and threw his overcoat on my arm, picked up his bag and crept away. In another minute I was back in my room, my brain aflame with the fire of a great enterprise.

Here, to my hand, lay the key of that locked land which held the secret of my lost brother. The question I had been asking myself, ever since I had first discovered the dead man's American papers of identity, was this. Had I the nerve to avail myself of Semlin's American passport to get into Germany? The answer to that question lay in the little silver badge. I knew that no German official, whatever his standing, whatever his orders, would refuse passage to the silver star of Section Seven. It need only be used, too, as a last resource, for I had my papers as a neutral. Could I but once set foot in Germany, I was quite ready to depend on my wits to see me through. One advantage, I knew, I must forgo. That was the half-letter in its canvas case.

If that document was of importance to Section Seven of the German Police, then it was of equal, nay, of greater importance to my country. If I went, that should remain behind in safe keeping. On that I was determined.

"Never before, since the war began," I told myself, "can any Englishman have had such an opportunity vouchsafed to him for getting easily and safely into that jealously guarded land as you have now! You have plenty of money, what with your own and this..." and I fingered Semlin's wad of notes, "and provided you can keep your head sufficiently to remember always that you are a German, once over the frontier you should be able to give the Huns the slip and try and follow up the trail of poor Francis.

"And maybe," I argued further (so easily is one's better judgment defeated when one is young and set on a thing), "maybe in German surroundings, you may get some sense into that mysterious jingle you got from Dicky Allerton as the sole existing clue to the disappearance of Francis."

Nevertheless, I wavered. The risks were awful. I had to get out of that evil hotel in the guise of Dr Semlin, with, as the sole safeguard against exposure, should I fall in with the dead man's employers or friends, that slight and possibly imaginative resemblance between him and me: I had to take such measures as would prevent the fraud from being detected when the body was discovered in the hotel: above all, I had to ascertain, before I could definitely resolve to push on into Germany, whether Semlin was already known to the people at the hotel or whether—as I surmised to be the case—this was also his first visit to the house in the Vos in't Tuintje.

In any case, I was quite determined in my own mind that the only way to get out of the place with Semlin's document without considerable unpleasantness, if not grave danger, would be to transfer his identity and effects to myself and vice versa. When I saw the way a little clearer I could decide whether to take the supreme risk and adventure myself into the enemy's country.

Whatever I was going to do, there were not many hours of the night left in which to act, and I was determined to be out of that house of ill omen before day dawned. If I could get clear of the hotel and at the same time ascertain that Semlin was as much a stranger there as myself, I could decide on my further course of action in the greater freedom of the streets of Rotterdam. One thing was certain: the waiter had let the question of Semlin's papers stand over until the morning, as he had done in my case, for Semlin still had his passport in his possession.

After all, if Semlin was unknown at the hotel, the waiter had only seen him for the same brief moment as he had seen me.

Thus I reasoned and argued with myself, but in the meantime I acted. I had nothing compromising in my suit-case, so that caused no difficulty. My British passport and permit and anything bearing any relation to my personality, such as my watch and cigarette case, both of which were engraved with my initials, I transferred to the dead man's pockets. As I bent over the stiff, cold figure with its livid face and clutching fingers, I felt a difficulty which I had hitherto resolutely shirked forcing itself squarely into the forefront of my mind.

What was I going to do about the body?

At that moment came a low knocking.

With a sudden sinking at the heart I remembered I had forgotten to lock the door.

5

THE LADY OF THE VOS IN'T TUINTJE

Here was Destiny knocking at the door. In that instant my mind was made up. For the moment, at any rate, I had every card in my hands. I would bluff these stodgy Huns: I would brazen it out: I would be Semlin and go through with it to the bitter end, aye, and if it took me to the very gates of Hell.

The knocking was repeated.

"May one come in?" said a woman's voice in German.

I stepped across the corpse and opened the door a foot or so.

There stood a woman with a lamp. She was a middle-aged woman with an egg-shaped face, fat and white and puffy, and pale, crafty eyes. She was in her outdoor clothes, with an enormous vulgar-looking hat and an old-fashioned sealskin cape with a high collar. The cape which was glistening with rain was half open, and displayed a vast bosom tightly compressed into a white silk blouse. In one hand she carried an oil lamp.

"Frau Schratt," she said by way of introduction, and raised the lamp to look more closely at me.

Then I saw her face change. She was looking past me into the room, and I knew that the lamplight was falling full upon the ghastly thing that lay upon the floor.

I realized the woman was about to scream, so I seized her by the wrist. She had disgusting hands, fat and podgy and covered with rings.

"Quiet!" I whispered fiercely in her ear, never relaxing my grip on her wrist. "You will be quiet and come in here, do you understand?"

She sought to shrink from me, but I held her fast and drew her into the room.

She stood motionless with her lamp, at the head of the corpse. She seemed to have regained her self-possession. The woman was no longer frightened. I felt instinctively that her fears had been all for herself, not for that livid horror sprawling on the floor. When she spoke her manner was almost business-like.

"I was told nothing of this," she said. "Who is it? What do you want me to do?"

Of all the sensations of that night, none has left a more unpleasant odour in my memory than the manner of that woman in the chamber of death. Her voice was incredibly hard. Her dull, basilisk eyes, seeking in mine the answers to her questions, gave me an eerie sensation that makes my blood run cold whenever I think of her.

Then suddenly her manner, arrogant, insolent, cruel, changed. She became polite. She was obsequious. Of the two, the first manner became her vastly better. She looked at me with a curious air, almost with reverence, as it seemed to me. She said, in a purring voice:

"Ach, so! I did not understand. The gentleman must excuse me."

And she purred again:

"So!"

It was then I noticed that her eyes were fastened upon my chest. I followed their direction.

They rested on the silver badge I had stuck in my braces.

I understood and held my peace. Silence was my only trump until I knew how the land lay. If I left this woman alone, she would tell me all I wanted to know.

In fact, she began to speak again.

"I expected *you*," she said, "but not... *this*. Who is it this time? A Frenchman, eh?"

I shook my head.

"An Englishman," I said curtly.

Her eyes opened in wonder.

"Ach, nein!" she cried—and you would have said her voice vibrated with pleasure—"An Englishman! Ei, ei!"

If ever a human being licked its chops, that woman did.

She wagged her head and repeated to herself:

"Ei, ei!" adding, as if to explain her surprise, "He is the first we have had."

"You brought him here, eh! But why up here? Or did der Stelze send him?"

She fired this string of questions at me without pausing for a reply. She continued:

"I was out, but Karl told me. There was another came, too: Franz sent him."

"This is he," I said. "I caught him prying in my room and he died."

"Ach!" she ejaculated... and in her voice was all the world of admiration that a German woman feels for brute man... "The Herr Englander came into your room and he died. So, so! But one must speak to Franz. The man drinks too much. He is always drunk. He makes mistakes. It will not do. I will..."

"I wish you to do nothing against Franz," I said. "This Englishman spoke German well: Karl will tell you."

"As the gentleman wishes," was the woman's reply in a voice so silky and so servile that I felt my gorge rise.

"She looks like a slug!" I said to myself, as she stood there, fat and sleek and horrible.

"Here are his passport and other papers," I said, bending down and taking them from the dead man's pocket. "He was an English officer, you see?" And I unfolded the little black book stamped with the Royal Arms.

She leant forward and I was all but stifled with the stale odour of the patchouli with which her faded body was drenched.

Then, making a sheaf of passport and permit, I held them in the flame of the candle.

"But we always keep them!" expostulated the hotel-keeper.

"This passport must die with the man," I replied firmly. "He must not be traced. I want no awkward enquiries made, you understand. Therefore..." and I flung the burning mass of papers into the grate.

"Good, good!" said the German and put her lamp down on the table. "There was a telephone message for you," she added, "to say that der Stelze will come at eight in the morning to receive what you have brought."

The deuce! This was getting awkward. Who the devil was Stelze?

"Coming at eight is he?" I said, simply for the sake of saying something.

"Jawohl!" replied Frau Schratt. "He was here already this morning. He was nervous, oh! very, and expected you to be here. Already two days he is waiting here to go on."

"So," I said, "he is going to take... it on with him, is he?" (I knew where he was "going on" to, well enough: he was going to see that document safe into Germany.)

There was a malicious ring in the woman's voice when she spoke of Stelze. I thought I might profit by this. So I drew her out.

"So Stelze called today and gave you his orders, did he?" I said, "and... and took charge of things generally, eh?"

Her little eyes snapped viciously.

"Ach!" she said, "der Stelze is der Stelze. He has power; he has authority; he can make and unmake men. But I... I in my time have broken a dozen better men than he and yet he dares to tell Anna Schratt that... that..."

She raised her voice hysterically, but broke off before she could finish the sentence. I saw she thought she had said too much.

"He won't play that game with me," I said. Strength is the quality that every German, man, woman and child, respects, and strength alone. My safety depended on my showing this ignoble creature that I received orders from no one. "You know what he is. One runs the risk, one takes trouble, one is successful. Then he steps in and gathers the laurels. No, I am not going to wait for him."

The hotel-keeper sprang to her feet, her faded face all ravaged by the shadow of a great fear.

"You wouldn't dare!" she said.

"I would," I retorted. "I've done my work and I'll report to headquarters and to no one else!"

My eyes fell upon the body.

"Now, what are we going to do with this?" I said. "You must help me, Frau Schratt. This is serious. This must not be found here."

She looked at me in surprise.

"That?" she said, and she kicked the body with her foot. "Oh, that will be all right with die Schratt! 'It must not be found here'" (she mimicked my grave tone). "It will *not* be found here, young man!"

And she chuckled with all the full-bodied good humour of a fat person.

"You mean?"

"I mean what I mean, young man, and what you mean," she replied. "When they are in a difficulty, when there are complications, when there is any unpleasantness... like *this*... they remember die Schratt, 'die fesche Anna,' as they called me once, and it is 'gnadige Frau' here and 'gnadige Frau' there and a diamond bracelet or a pearl ring, if only I will do the little conjuring trick that will smooth everything over. But when all goes well, then I am 'old Schratt,' 'old hag,' 'old woman,' and I must take my orders and beg nicely and... bah!"

Her words ended in a gulp, which in any other woman would have been a sob.

Then she added in her hard harlot's voice:

"You needn't worry your head about *him*, there! Leave him to me! It's my trade!"

At those words, which covered God only knows what horrors of midnight disappearances, of ghoulish rites with packing-case and sack, in the dark cellars of that evil house, I felt that, could I but draw back from the enterprise to which I had so rashly committed myself, I would do so gladly. Only then did I begin to realize something of the utter ruthlessness, the cold, calculating ferocity, of the most bitter and most powerful enemy which the British Empire has ever had.

But it was too late to withdraw now. The die was cast. Destiny, knocking at my door, had found me ready to follow, and I was committed to whatever might befall me in my new personality.

The German woman turned to go.

"Der Stelze will be here at eight, then," she said. "I suppose the gentleman will take his early morning coffee before."

"I shan't be here," I said. "You can tell your friend I've gone."

She turned on me like a flash.

She was hard as flint again.

"Nein!" she cried. "You stay here!"

"No," I answered with equal force, "not I..."

"...Orders are orders and you and I must obey!"

"But who is Stelze that he should give orders to me?" I cried.

"Who is...?" She spoke aghast.

"... And you yourself," I continued, "were saying..."

"When an order has been given, what you or I think or say is of no account," the woman said. "It is an order: you and I know *whose* order. Let that suffice. You stay here! Good night!"

With that she was gone. She closed the door behind her; the key rattled in the lock and I realized that I was a prisoner. I heard the woman's footfalls die away down the corridor.

That distant clock cleaved the silence of the night with twelve ponderous strokes. Then the chimes played a pretty jingling little tune that rang out clearly in the still, rain-washed air.

I stood petrified and reflected on my next move.

Twelve o'clock! I had eight hours' grace before Stelze, the man of mystery and might, arrived to unmask me and hand me over to the tender mercies of Madame and of Karl. Before eight o'clock arrived I must—so I summed up my position—be clear of the hotel and in the train for the German frontier—if I could get a train—else I must be out of Rotterdam, by that hour.

But I must *act* and act without delay. There was no knowing when that dead man lying on the floor might procure me another visit from Madame and her myrmidons. The sooner I was out of that house of death the better.

The door was solid; the lock was strong. That I discovered without any trouble. In any case, I reflected, the front-door of the hotel would be barred and bolted at this hour of the night, and I could scarcely dare hope to escape by the front without detection, even if Karl were not actually in the entrance hall. There must be a back entrance to the hotel, I thought, for I had seen that the windows of my room opened on to the narrow street lining the canal which ran at the back of the house.

Escape by the windows was impossible. The front of the house dropped sheer down and there was nothing to give one a foothold. But I remembered the window in the *cabinet de toilette* giving on to the little air-shaft. That seemed to offer a slender chance of escape.

For the second time that night I opened the casement and inhaled the fetid odours arising from the narrow court. All the windows looking, like mine, upon the air-shaft were shrouded in darkness: only a light still burned in the window beneath the grating with the iron stair to the little yard. What was at the foot of the stair I could not descry, but I thought I could recognize the outline of a door.

From the window of the *cabinet de toilette* to the yard the sides of the house, cased in stained and dirty stucco, fell sheer away. Measured with the eye the drop from window to the pavement was about fifty feet. With a rope and something to break one's fall it might, I fancied, be managed...

From that on, things moved swiftly. First with my penknife I ripped the tailor's tab with my name from the inside pocket of my coat and burnt it in the candle: nothing else I had on was marked, for I had had to buy a lot of new garments when I came out of hospital. I took Semlin's overcoat, hat and bag into the *cabinet de toilette* and stood them in readiness by the window. As a precaution against surprise I pushed the massive mahogany bedstead right across the doorway and thus barricaded the entrance to the room.

From either side of the fireplace hung two bell-ropes, twisted silk cords of faded crimson with dusty tassels. Mounting on the mantel-piece I cut the bell-ropes off short where they joined the wire. Testing them I found them apparently solid—at any rate they must serve. I knotted them together.

Back to the *cabinet de toilette* I went to find a suitable object to which to fasten my rope. There was nothing in the little room save the washstand, and that was fragile and quite unsuited for the purpose. I noticed that the window was fitted with shutters on the outside fastened back against the wall. They had not been touched for years, I should say, for the iron peg holding them back was heavy with rust and the shutters were covered with dust. I closed the left-hand shutter and found that it fastened solidly to the window-frame by means of massive iron bolts, top and bottom.

Here was the required support for my rope. The poker thrust through the wooden slips of the shutter held the rope quite solidly. I attached my rope to the poker with an expert knot that I had picked up at a course in tying knots during a preposterously dull week I had spent at the base in France. Then I dragged from the bed the gigantic eiderdown pincushion and the two massive pillows, stripping off the pillow-slips lest their whiteness might attract attention whilst they were fulfilling the unusual mission for which I destined them.

At the window of the *cabinet de toilette* I listened a moment. All was silent as the grave. Resolutely I pitched out the eiderdown into the dark and dirty air shaft. It sailed gracefully earthwards and settled with a gentle plop on the stones of the tiny yard. The pillows followed. The heavier thud they would have made was deadened by the billowy mass of the *édredon*. Semlin's bag went next, and made no sound to speak of; then his overcoat and hat followed suit.

I noticed, with a grateful heart, that the eiderdown and pillows covered practically the whole of the flags of the yard.

I went back once more to the room and blew out the candle. Then, taking a short hold on my silken rope, I clambered out over the window ledge and started to let myself down, hand over hand, into the depths.

My two bell-ropes, knotted together, were about twenty feet long, so I had to reckon on a clear drop of something over thirty feet. The poker and shutter held splendidly firm, and I found little difficulty in lowering myself, though I barked my knuckles most unpleasantly on the rough stucco of the wall. As I reached the extremity of my rope I glanced downward. The red splash of the eiderdown, just visible in the light from the adjoining window, seemed to be a horrible distance below me. My spirit failed me. My determination began to ebb. I could never risk it.

The rope settled the question for me. It snapped without warning—how it had supported my weight up to then I don't know—and I fell in a heap (and, as it seemed to me at the time, with a most reverberating crash) on to the soft divan I had prepared for my reception.

I came down hard, very hard, but old Madame's plump eiderdown and pillows certainly helped to break my fall. I dropped square on top of the eiderdown with one knee on a pillow and, though shaken and jarred, I found I had broken no bones.

Nor did my sense leave me. In a minute I was up on my feet again. I listened. All was still silent. I cast a glance upwards. The window from which I had descended was still dark. I could see the broken bell-ropes dangling from the shutter, and I noted, with a glow of professional pride, that my expert join between the two ropes had not given. The lower rope had parted in the middle...

I crammed Semlin's hat on my head, retrieved his bag and overcoat from the corner of the court where they had fallen and the next moment was tiptoeing down the ladder.

The iron stair ran down beside the window in which I had seen the light burning. The lower part of the window was screened off by a dirty muslin curtain. Through the upper part I caught a glimpse of a sort of scullery with a paraffin lamp standing on a wooden table. The room was empty. From top to bottom the window was protected by heavy iron bars.

At the foot of the iron stair stood, as I had anticipated, a door. It was my last chance of escape. It stood a dozen yards from the bottom of the ladder across a dank, little paved area where tins of refuse were standing—a small door with a brass handle.

I ducked low as I clambered down the iron ladder so as not to be seen from the window should anyone enter the scullery as I passed. Treading very softly I crept across the little area and, as quietly as I could, turned the handle of the door.

It turned round easily in my hand, but nothing happened.

The door was locked.

6

I BOARD THE BERLIN TRAIN AND LEAVE A LAME GENTLEMAN ON THE PLATFORM

I was caught like a rat in a trap. I could not return by the way I had come and the only egress was closed to me. The area door and window were the only means of escape from the little court. The one was locked, the other barred. I was fairly trapped. All I had to do now was to wait until my absence was discovered and the broken rope found to show them where I was. Then they would come down to the area, I should be confronted with the man, Stelze, and my goose would be fairly cooked.

As quietly as I could I made a complete, thorough, rapid examination of the area. It was a dank, dark place, only lit where the yellow light streamed forth from the scullery. It had a couple of low bays hollowed out of the masonry under the little courtyard, and one filled with wood blocks, the other with broken packing-cases, old bottles and like rubbish. I explored these until my hands came in contact with the damp bricks at the back, but in vain. Door and window remained the only means of escape.

Four tall tin refuse bins stood in line in front of these two bays, a fifth was stowed away under the iron stair. They were all nearly full of refuse, so were useless as hiding-places. In any case it accorded neither with the part I was playing nor with my sense of the ludicrous to be discovered by the hotel domestics hiding in a refuse bin.

I was at my wits' end to know what to do. I had dared so much, all had gone so surprisingly well, that it was heartbreaking to be foiled with liberty almost within my grasp. A great wave of disappointment swept over me until I felt my very heart sicken. Then I heard footsteps and hope revived within me.

I shrunk back into the darkness of the area behind the refuse bins standing in front of the bay nearest the door.

Within the house footsteps were approaching the scullery. I heard a door open, then a man's voice singing. He was warbling in a fine mellow baritone that popular German ballad:

> "Das haben die Madchen so gerne
> Die im Stübchen und die im *Salong*."

The voice hung lovingly and wavered and trilled on that word "*Salong*": the effect was so much to the singer's liking that he sang the stave over again. A bumping and a rattle as of loose objects in an empty box formed the accompaniment to his song.

"A cheery fellow!" I said to myself. If only I could see who it was! But I dare not move into that patch of yellow light from which the only view into the scullery was afforded.

The singing stopped. Again I heard a door open. Was he going away?

Then I saw a thin shaft of light under the area door.

The next moment it was flung back and the waiter, Karl, appeared, still in his blue apron, a bucket in either hand.

He was coming to the refuse bins.

Pudd'n Head Wilson's advice came into my mind: "When angry count up to four: when very angry, swear." I was not angry but scared, terribly scared, scared so that I could hear my heart pulsating in great thuds in my ears. Nevertheless, I followed the advice of the sage of Dawson's Landing and counted to myself: one, two, three, four, one, two, three, four; while my heart hammered out: Keep-cool, keep-cool, keep-cool! And all the time I remained crouching behind the first two refuse bins nearest the door.

The waiter hummed to himself the melody of his little ditty in a deep bourdon as he paused a moment at the door. Then he advanced slowly across the area.

Would he stop at the refuse bins behind which I cowered?

No, he passed them.

The third? The fourth?

No!

He walked straight across the area and went to the bin beneath the stairs.

I muttered a blessing inwardly on the careful habits of the German who organizes even his refuse into separate tubs.

The man had his back to the door.

Now or never was my chance.

I crawled round my friendly garbage bins, reached the area door on tip-toe and stepped softly into the house. As I did so I heard the clank of tin as Karl replaced the lid of the tub.

A dark passage stretched out in front of me. Immediately to my right was the scullery door wide open. I must avoid the scullery at all costs. The man might remain there and I could not risk him driving me before him back to the entrance hall of the hotel.

I crept down the dark passage with hands outstretched. Presently they fell upon the latch of a door. I pressed it, the door opened inwards into the darkness and I passed through. As I softly closed the door behind me I heard Karl's heavy step and the grinding of the key as he locked the area door.

I stood in a kind of cupboard in pitch darkness, hardly daring to breathe.

Once more I heard the man singing his idiotic song. I did not dare look out from my hiding-place, for his voice sounded so near that I feared he might be still in the passage.

So I stood and waited.

* * *

I must have stayed there for an hour in the dark. I heard the waiter coming and going in the scullery, listened to his heavy tramp, to his everlasting snatch of song, to the rattle of utensils, as he went about his work. Every minute of the time I was tortured by the apprehension that he would come to the cupboard in the passage.

It was cold in that damp subterranean place. The cupboard was roomy enough, so I thought I would put on the overcoat I was carrying. As I stretched out my arm, my hand struck hard against some kind of projecting hook in the wall behind me.

"Damn!" I swore savagely under my breath, but I put out my hand again to find out what had hurt me. My fingers encountered the cold iron of a latch. I pressed it and it gave.

A door swung open and I found myself in another little area with a flight of stone steps leading to the street.

* * *

I was in a narrow lane driven between the tall sides of the houses. It was a cul-de-sac. At the open end I could see the glimmer of street lamps. It had stopped raining and the air was fresh and pleasant. Carrying my bag I walked briskly down the lane and presently emerged in a quiet thoroughfare traversed by a canal—probably the street, I thought, that I had seen from the windows of my bedroom. The Hotel Sixt lay to the right of the lane: I struck out to the left and in a few minutes found myself in an open square behind the Bourse.

There I found a cab-rank with three or four cabs drawn up in a line, the horses somnolent, the drivers snoring inside their vehicles. I stirred up the first and bade the driver take me to the Café Tarnowski.

Everyone who has been to Holland knows the Café Tarnowski at Rotterdam. It is an immense place with hundreds of marble-topped tables tucked away among palms under a vast glazed roof. Day or night it never closes: the waiters succeed each other in shifts: day and night the great hall resounds to the cry of orders, the patter of the waiters' feet, the click of dominoes on the marble tables.

Delicious Dutch *café au lait*, a beefsteak and fried potatoes, most succulent of all Dutch dishes, crisp white bread, hot from the midnight baking, and appetizing Dutch butter, largely compensated for the thrills of the night. Then I sent for some more coffee, black this time, and a railway guide, and lighting a cigarette began to frame my plan of campaign.

The train for Berlin left Rotterdam at seven in the morning. It was now ten minutes past two, so I had plenty of time. From that night onward, I told myself, I was a German, and from that moment I set myself assiduously to *feel* myself a German as well as enact the part.

"It's no use dressing a part," Francis used to say to me: "you must *feel* it as well. If I were going to disguise myself as a Berliner, I should not be content to shave my head and wear a bowler hat with a morning coat and get my nails manicured pink. I should begin by persuading myself that I was the Lord of creation, that bad manners is a sign of manly strength and that dishonesty is the highest form of diplomacy. Then only should I set about getting the costume!"

Poor old Francis! How shrewd he was and how well he knew his Berliners!

There is nothing like newspapers for giving one an idea of national sentiment. I had not spoken to a German, save to a few terrified German rats, prisoners of war in France, since the beginning of the war and I knew that my knowledge of German thought must be rusty. So I sent the willing waiter for all the German papers and periodicals he could lay his hands on. He returned with stacks of them. *Berliner Tageblatt, Kölnische Zeitung, Vorwärts*; the alleged comic papers, *Kladderadatsch, Lustige Blätter* and *Simplicissimus*; the illustrated press, *Leifziger Illus-trirte Zeitung, Der Weltkrieg im Bild*, and the rest: that remarkable café even took in such less popular publications as Harden's *Zukunft* and semi-blackmailing rags like *Der Roland von Berlin*.

For two hours I saturated myself with German contemporary thought as expressed in the German press. I deliberately laid my mind open to conviction; I repeated to myself over and over again: "We Germans are fighting a defensive war: the scoundrelly Grey made the world-war: Gott strafe England!" Absurd as this proceeding seems to me when I look back upon it, I would not laugh at myself at the time. I must be German, I must feel German, I must think German: on that would my safety in the immediate future depend.

I laid aside my reading in the end with a feeling of utter amazement. In every one of these publications, in peace-time so widely dissimilar in conviction and trend, I found the same mentality, the same outlook, the same parrot-like cries. What the *Cologne Gazette* shrieked from its editorial columns, the comic (God save the mark) press echoed in foul and hideous caricature. Here was organization with a vengeance, the mobilization of national thought, a series of gramophone records fed into a thousand different machines so that each might play the selfsame tune.

"You needn't worry about your German mentality," I told myself, "you've got it all here! You've only got to be a parrot like the rest and you'll be as good a Hun as Hindenburg!"

A Continental waiter, they say, can get one anything one chooses to ask for at any hour of the day or night. I was about to put this theory to the test.

"Waiter," I said (of course, in German), "I want a bag, a handbag. Do you think you could get me one?"

"Does the gentleman want it now?" the man replied.

"This very minute," I answered.

"About that size?"—indicating Semlin's.

"Yes, or smaller if you like: I am not particular."

"I will see what can be done."

In ten minutes the man was back with a brown leather bag about a size smaller than Semlin's. It was not new and he charged me thirty gulden (which is about fifty shillings) for it. I paid with a willing heart and tipped him generously to boot, for I wanted a bag and could not wait till the shops opened without missing the train for Germany.

I paid my bill and drove off to the Central Station through the dark streets with my two bags. The clocks were striking six as I entered under the great glass dome of the station hall.

I went straight to the booking-office, and bought a first-class ticket, single, to Berlin. One never knows what may happen and I had several things to do before the train went.

The bookstall was just opening. I purchased a sovereign's worth of books and magazines, English, French and German, and crammed them into the bag I had procured at the café. Thus laden I adjourned to the station buffet.

There I set about executing a scheme I had evolved for leaving the document which Semlin had brought from England in a place of safety, whence it could be recovered without difficulty, should anything happen to me. I knew no one in Holland save Dicky, and I could not send him the document, for I did not trust the post. For the same reason I would not post the document home to my bank in England: besides, I knew one could not register letters until eight o'clock, by which hour I hoped to be well on my way into Germany.

No, my bag, conveniently weighted with books and deposited at the station cloakroom, should be my safe. The comparative security of station cloak-rooms as safe deposits has long been recognized by jewel thieves and the like, and this means of leaving my document behind in safety seemed to me to be better than any other I could think of.

So I dived into my bag and from the piles of literature it contained picked up a book at random. It was a German brochure: *Gott strafe England!* by Prof. Dr Hugo Bischoff, of the University of Göttingen. The irony of the thing appealed to my sense of humour. "So be it!" I said. "The worthy Professor's fulminations against my country shall have the honour of harbouring the document which is, apparently, of such value to *his* country!" And I tucked the little canvas case away inside the pages of the pamphlet, stuck the pamphlet deep down among the books and shut the bag.

Seeing its harmless appearance the cloak-room receipt—I calculated—would, unlike Semlin's document, attract no attention if, by any mischance, it fell into wrong hands *en route*. I therefore did not scruple to commit it to the post. Before taking my bag of books to the cloak-room I wrote two letters Both were to Ashcroft—Ashcroft of the Foreign Office, who got my passport and permit to come to Rotterdam. Herbert Ashcroft and I were old friends. I addressed the envelopes to his private house in London. The Postal Censoi, I knew, keen though he always is after letters from neutral countries, would leave old Herbert's correspondence alone.

The first letter was brief. "Dear Herbert," I wrote, "would you mind looking after the enclosed until you hear from me again? Filthy weather here. Yours, D.O." This letter was destined to contain the cloak-room receipt. To conceal the importance of an enclosure, it is always a good dodge to send the covering letter under a separate cover.

"Dear Herbert," I said in my second letter, "If you don't hear from me within two months of this date regarding the enclosure you will have already received, please send someone, or, preferably, go yourself and collect my luggage at the cloak-room of the Rotterdam Central Station. I know how busy you always are. Therefore you will understand my reasons for making this inordinate claim upon your time. Yours, D.O." And, by way of a clue, I added, inconsequently enough: "Gott strafe England!"

I chuckled inwardly at the thought of Herbert's face on receiving this preposterous demand that he should abandon his dusty desk in Downing Street and betake himself across the North Sea to fetch my luggage. But he'd go all right. I knew my Herbert, dull and dry and conventional, but a most faithful friend.

I called a porter at the entrance of the buffet and handing him Semlin's bag and overcoat, bade him find me a first-class carriage in the Berlin train when it arrived. I would meet him on the platform. Then, at the cloak-room opposite, I gave in my bag of books, put the receipt in the first letter and posted it in the letter-box within the station. I went out into the streets with the second letter and posted it in a letterbox let into the wall of a tobacconist's shop in a quiet street a few turnings away. By this arrangement I reckoned Herbert would get the letter with the receipt before the covering letter arrived.

Returning to the railway station I noticed a kind of slop shop which despite the early hour was already open. A fat Jew in his shirt-sleeves, his thumbs in his waistcoat pockets, stood at the entrance framed in hanging overcoats and hats and boots. I had no umbrella and it struck me that a waterproof of some kind might not be a bad addition to my extremely scanty wardrobe. Moreover, I reflected that with the rubber shortage rain-coats must be at a premium in Germany.

So I followed the bowing son of Shem into his dark and dirty shop and emerged presently wearing an appallingly ugly green mackintosh reeking hideously of rubber. It was a shocking garment but I reflected that I was a German and must choose my garb accordingly.

Outside the shop I nearly ran into a little man who was loafing in the doorway. He was a wizened, scrubby old fellow wearing a dirty peaked cap with a band of tarnished gold. I knew him at once for one of those guides, half tout, half bully, that infest the railway termini of all great Continental cities.

"Want a guide, sir?" the man said in German.

I shook my head and hurried on. The man trotted beside me. "Want a good, cheap hotel, sir? Good, respectable house... Want a..."

"Ach! gehen Sie zum Teufel!" I cried angrily. But the man persisted, running along beside me and reeling off his tout's patter in a wheezing, asthmatic voice. I struck off blindly down the first turning we came to, hoping to be rid of the fellow, but in vain. Finally, I stopped and held out a gulden.

"Take this and go away!" I said.

The old fellow waved the coin aside.

"Danke, danke," he said nonchalantly, looking at the same time to right and left.

Then he said in a calm English voice, utterly different from his whining accents of a moment before:

"You must be a dam' cool hand!"

But he didn't bluff me, staggered though I was. I said quickly in German:

"What do you want with me? I don't understand you. If you annoy me any more I shall call the police!"

Again he spoke in English and it was the voice of a well-bred Englishman that spoke:

"You're either a past master at the game or raving mad. Why! The whole station is humming after you! Yet you walked out of the buffet and through the whole lot of them without turning a hair. No wonder they never spotted you!"

Again I answered in German:

"Ich verstehe nicht!"

But he went on in English, without seeming to notice my observation:

"Hang it all, man, you can't go into Germany wearing a regimental tie!"

My hand flew to my collar and the blood to my head. What a cursed amateur I was, after all I had entirely forgotten that I was wearing my regimental colours. I was crimson with vexation but also with a sense of relief. I felt I might trust this man. It would be a sharp German agent who would notice a small detail like that.

Still I resolved to stick to German: I would trust nobody.

But the guide had started his patter again. I saw two workmen approaching. When they had passed, he said, this time in English:

"You're quite right to be cautious with a stranger like me, but I want to warn you. Why, I've been following you round all the morning. Lucky for you it was me and not one of the others..."

Still I was silent. The little man went on:

"For the past half-hour they have been combing that station for you. How you managed to escape them I don't know except that none of them seems to have a very clear idea of your appearance. You don't look very British, I grant you; but I spotted your tie and then I recognized the British officer all right.

"No, don't worry to tell me anything about yourself—it is none of my business to know, any more than you will find out anything about me. *I* know where you are going, for I heard you take your ticket; but you may as well understand that you have as much chance of getting into your train if you walk into the railway hall and up the stairs in the ordinary way as you have of flying across the frontier."

"But they can't stop me!" I said. "This isn't Germany..."

"Bah!" said the guide. "You will be jostled, there will be an altercation, a false charge, and you will miss your train! *They* will attend to the rest!

"Damn it, man," he went on, "I know what I'm talking about. Here, come with me and I'll show you. You have twenty minutes before the train goes. Now start the German again!"

We went down the street together for all the world like a "mug" in tow of one of those blackguard guides. As we approached the station the guide said in his whining German:

"Pay attention to me now. I shall leave you here. Go to the suburban booking-office—the entrance is in the street to the left of the station hall. Go into the first-class waiting-room and look out of the window that gives on to the station hall. There, you will see some of the forces mobilized against you. There is a regular cordon of guides—like me—drawn across the entrances to the main-line platforms—unostentatiously, of course. If you look you will see plenty of plainclothes Huns, too..."

"Guides?" I said.

He nodded cheerfully.

"Looks bad for me, doesn't it? But one gets better results by being one of them. Oh! it's all right. In any case you've got to trust me now.

"See here! When you have satisfied yourself that I'm correct in what I say, take a platform ticket and walk upstairs to platform No. 5. On that platform you will find a train. Go to the end where the metals run out of the station, where the engine would be coupled on, and get into the last first-class carriage. On no account move from there until you see me. Now then, I'll have that gulden!"

I gave him the coin. The old fellow looked at it and wagged his head, so I gave him another, whereupon he took off his cap, bowed low and hurried off.

In the suburban side waiting-room I peered out of the window on to the station hall. True enough, I saw one, two, four, six guides loafing about the barriers leading to the main-line platforms. There seemed to be a lot of people in the hall and certainly a number of the men possessed that singular taste in dress, those rotundities of contour, by which one may distinguish the German in a crowd.

I now had no hesitation in following the guide's instructions to the letter. Platform No. 5 was completely deserted as I emerged breathless from the long staircase and I had no difficulty in getting into the last first-class carriage unobserved. I sat down by the window on the far side of the carriage.

Alongside it ran the brown panels and gold lettering of a German restaurant car.

I looked at my watch. It was ten minutes to seven. There was no sign of my mysterious friend. I wondered vaguely, too, what had become of my porter. True, there was nothing of importance in Semlin's bag, but a traveller with luggage always commands more confidence than one without.

Five minutes to seven! Still no word from the guide. The minutes ticked away. By Jove! I was going to miss the train. But I sat resolutely in my corner. I had put my trust in this man. I would trust him to the last.

Suddenly his face appeared in the window at my elbow. The door was flung open.

"Quick!" he whispered in my ear, "Follow me."

"My things..." I gasped with one foot on the foot-board of the other train. At the same moment the train began to move.

The guide pointed to the carriage into which I had clambered.

"The porter..." I cried from the open door, thinking he had not understood me.

The guide pointed towards the carriage again, then tapped himself on the chest with a significant smile.

The next moment he had disappeared and I had not even thanked him.

The Berlin train bumped ponderously out of the station. Peering cautiously out of the carriage, I caught a glimpse of the waiter, Karl, hurrying down the platform. With him was a swarthy, massively built man who leaned heavily on a stick and limped painfully as he ran. One of his feet, I could see, was misshapen and the sweat was pouring down his face.

I would have liked to wave my hand to the pair, but I prudently drew back out of sight of the platform.

Caution, caution, caution, must henceforward be my watchword.

7

IN WHICH A SILVER STAR ACTS AS A CHARM

I have often remarked in life that there are days when some benevolent deity seems to be guiding one's every action. On such days, do what you will, you cannot go wrong. As the Berlin train bumped thunderously over the culverts spanning the canals between the tall, grey houses of Rotterdam and rushed out imperiously into the plain of windmills and pollards beyond, I reflected that this must be my good day, so kindly had some fairy godmother shepherded my footsteps since I had left the café.

So engrossed had I been, indeed, in the great enterprise on which I was embarked, that my actions throughout the morning had been mainly automatic. Yet how uniformly had they tended to protect me! I had bought my ticket in advance; I had given my overcoat and bag to a porter that I now knew to have been my saviour in disguise; I had sallied forth from the station and thus given him an opportunity for safe converse with me. The omens were good: I could trust my luck today, I felt, and, greatly comforted, I began to look about me.

I found myself, the only occupant, in a first-class carriage. On the window was plastered a notice, in Dutch and German, to the effect that the carriage was reserved. Suddenly I thought of my bag and overcoat. They were nowhere to be seen. After a little search I found them beneath the seat. In the overcoat pocket was a black tie.

I lost no time in taking the hint. If any of you who read this tale should one day notice a ganger on the railway between Rotterdam and Dordrecht wearing the famous colours of a famous regiment round his neck you will understand how they got there. Then, wearied out with the fatigues of my sleepless night, I fell into a deep slumber, my verdant waterproof swathed round me, Semlin's overcoat about my knees.

* * *

I was dreaming fitfully of a mad escape from hordes of wildly clutching guides, led by Karl the waiter, when the screaming of brakes brought me to my senses. The train was sensibly slackening speed. Outside the autumn sun was shining over pleasant brown stretches of moorland bright with heather. The next moment and before I was fully awake we had glided to a standstill at a very spick and span station and the familiar cry of "Alles aussteigen!" rang in my ears.

We were in Germany.

The realization fell upon me like a thunderclap. I was in the enemy's country, sailing under false colours, with only the most meagre information about the man whose place I had taken and no plausible tale, such as I had fully intended to have ready, to carry me through the rigorous scrutiny of the frontier police.

What was my firm? The Halewright Manufacturing Company. What did we manufacture? I had not the faintest idea. Why was I coming to Germany at all? Again I was at a loss.

The clink of iron-shod heels in the corridor and an officer, followed closely by two privates, the white cross of the Landwehr in their helmets, stood at the door.

"Your papers, please," he said curtly but politely.

I handed over my American passport.

"This has not been viséd," said the officer.

With a pang I realized that again I was at fault. Of course, the passport should have been stamped at the German Consulate at Rotterdam.

"I had no time," I said boldly. "I am travelling on most important business to Berlin... I only reached Rotterdam last night, after the Consulate was closed."

The lieutenant turned to one of his guards.

"Take the gentleman to the Customs Hall," he said and went on to the next carriage.

The soldier appropriated my overcoat and bag and beckoned me to follow him. Outside the platform was railed off. Everyone, I noticed, was shepherded into a long narrow pen made with iron hurdles leading to a locked door over which was written: Zoll-Revision. I was going to take my place in the queue when the soldier prodded me with his elbow. He led me to a side door which opened in the gaunt, bare Customs Hall with its long row of trestles for the examination of the passengers' luggage. In a corner behind a desk was a large group of officers and subordinate officials, all in the grey-green uniform I knew so well from the life in the trenches. The principal seemed to be an immense man, inordinately gross and fat, with a bloated face and great gold spectacles. He was roaring in a loud angry voice:

"He's not come! There you are! Again we shall have all the trouble for nothing!"

I thought he looked an extraordinarily bad-tempered individual and I fervently prayed that I should not be brought before him.

The doors were flung open. With a rush the hall was invaded with a heterogeneous mob of people huddled pellmell together and driven along before a line of soldiers. For an hour or more babel reigned. Officials bawled at the public: the place rang with the sounds of angry altercation. After a furious dispute one man, wildly gesticulating, was dragged away by two soldiers.

I never saw such a thorough examination in my life. People's bags were literally turned upside down and every single object pried into and besnuffled. After the Customs' examination passengers were passed on to the searching rooms, the men to one side, the women to the other. I caught sight of a female searcher lolling at a door... a monstrous and grim female who reminded me of those dreadful bathing women at the seaside in our early youth.

The fat official had vanished into an office leading off the Customs Hall. He was, I surmised, the last instance, for several passengers, including a very respectably dressed old lady, were driven into the side office and were seen no more.

During all this scene of confusion no one had taken any notice of me. My guard looked straight in front of him and said never a word. When the hall was all but cleared, a man came to the office door and made a sign to my sentinel.

At a table in the office which, despite the sunshine outside, was heated like a greenhouse, I found the fat official. Something had evidently upset him, for his brows were clouded with anger and his mastiff-like cheeks were trembling with irritation. He thrust a hand out as I entered.

"Your papers!" he grunted.

I handed over my passport.

Directly he had examined it, a red flush spread over his cheeks and forehead and he brought his hand down on the table with a crash. The sentry beside me winced perceptibly.

"It's not viséd," the fat official screamed in a voice shrill with anger. "It's worthless... what good do you think is this to me?"

"Excuse me..." I said in German.

"I won't excuse you," he roared. "Who are you? What do you want in Germany? You've been to London, I see by this passport."

"I had no time to get my passport stamped at the Consulate at Rotterdam," I said. "I arrived there too late in the evening. I could not wait. I am going to Berlin on most important business."

"That's nothing to do with it," the man shouted. He was working himself up into a fine frenzy. "Your passport is not in order. You're not a German. You're an American. We Germans know what to think of our American friends, especially those who come from London."

A voice outside shouted: "Nach Berlin alles einsteigen." I said as politely as I could, despite my growing annoyance:

"I don't wish to miss my train. My journey to Berlin is of the utmost importance. I trust the train can be held back until I have satisfied you of my good faith. I have here a card from Herr von Steinhardt."

I paused to let the name sink in. I was convinced he must be a big bug of some kind in the German service.

"I don't care a rap for Herr von Steinhardt or Herr von anybody else," the German cried. Then he said curtly to a cringing secretary beside him:

"Has he been searched?"

The secretary cast a frightened look at the sentry.

"No, Herr Major," said the secretary.

"Well, take him away and strip him and bring me anything you find!"

The sentry spun on his heel like an automaton.

The moment had come to play my last card, I felt: I could not risk being delayed on the frontier lest Stelze and his friends should catch up with me. I was surprised to find that apparently they had not telegraphed to have me stopped.

"One moment, Herr Major," I said.

"Take him away!" The fat man waved me aside.

"I warn you," I continued, "that I am on important business. I can convince you of that, too. Only..." and I looked round the office. "All these must go."

To my amazement the fat man's anger vanished utterly. He stared hard at me, then took off his spectacles and polished them with his handkerchief. After this he said nonchalantly: "Everybody get outside except this gentleman!" The sentry, who had spun round on his heel again, seemed about to speak: his voice expired before it came out of his mouth: he saluted, spun round again and followed the rest out of the room.

When the place was cleared I pulled my left brace out of the armhole of my waistcoat and displayed the silver star.

The fat man sprang up.

"The Herr Doktor must excuse me: I am overwhelmed: I had no idea that the Herr Doktor was not one of these tiresome American spies that are overrunning our country. The Herr Doktor will understand... If the Herr Doktor had but said..."

"Herr Major," I said, endeavouring to put as much insolence as I could into my voice (that is what a German understands), "I am not in the habit of bleating my business to every fool I meet. Now I must go back to the train."

"The Berlin train has gone, Herr Doktor, but..."

"The Berlin train gone?" I said. "But my business brooks no delay. I tell you I must be in Berlin tonight!"

"There is no question of your taking the ordinary train, Herr Doktor," the fat man replied smoothly, "but unfortunately the special which I had ready for you has been countermanded. I thought you were not coming again."

A special? By Jove! I was evidently a personage of note. But a special would never do! Where the deuce was it going to take me?

"The Berlin train was to have been held back until your special was clear," the Major went on, "but we must stop her at Wesel until you have passed. I will attend to that at once!"

He gave some order down the telephone and after a brisk conversation turned to me with a beaming face:

"They will stop her at Wesel and the special will be ready in twenty-five minutes. But there is no hurry. You have an hour or more to spare. Might I offer the Herr Doktor a glass of beer and a sandwich at our officers' casino here?"

Well, I was in for it this time. A special bearing me Heaven knows whither on unknown business...! Perhaps I might be able to extract a little information out of my fat friend if I went with him, so I accepted his invitation with suitable condescension.

The Major excused himself for an instant and returned with my overcoat and bag.

"So!" he cried, "we can leave these here until we come back!" Behind him through the open door I saw a group of officials peering curiously into the room. As we walked through their midst, they fell back with precipitation. There was a positive reverence about their manner which I found extremely puzzling.

A waggonette, driven by an orderly, stood in the station yard, one of the Customs officials, hat in hand, at the door. We drove rapidly through very spick-and-span streets to a little square where the sentry at an iron gate denoted the Officers' Club. In the anteroom four or five officers in field-grey uniform were lounging. As we entered they sprang to their feet and remained stiffly standing while the Major presented them, Hauptmann Pfahl, Oberleutnant Meyer... a string of names. One of the officers had lost an arm, another was very lame, the remainder were obvious dug-outs.

"An American gentleman, a good friend of ours," was the form in which the Major introduced me to the company. Again I found myself mystified by the extraordinary demonstrations of respect with which I was received. Germans don't like Americans, especially since they took to selling shells to the Allies, and I began to think that all these officers must know more about me and my mission than I did myself. A stolid orderly, wearing white gloves, brought beer and some extraordinarily nasty-looking sardine sandwiches which, on sampling, I realized to be made of "war bread."

While the beer was being poured out I glanced round the room, bare and very simply furnished. Terrible chromolithographs of the Kaiser and the Crown Prince hung on the walls above a glass filled with war trophies. With a horrible sickness at heart I recognized amongst other emblems a glengarry with a silver badge and a British steel helmet with a gaping hole through the crown. Then I remembered I was in the region of the VIIth Corps, which supplies some of our toughest opponents on the Western front.

Conversation was polite and perfunctory.

"It is on occasions such as these," said the lame officer, "that one recognizes how our brothers overseas are helping the German cause."

"Your work must be extraordinarily interesting," observed one of the dug-outs.

"All your difficulties are now over," said the Major, much in the manner of the chorus of a Greek play. "You will be in Berlin tonight, where your labours will be doubtless rewarded. American friends of Germany are not popular in London, I should imagine!"

I murmured: "Hardly."

"You must possess infinite tact to have aroused no suspicion," said the Major.

"That depends," I said.

"Pardon me," replied the Major, in whom I began to recognize all the signs of an unmitigated gossip, "I know something of the importance of your mission. I speak amongst ourselves, is it not so, gentlemen? There were special orders about you from the Corps Command at Münster. Your special has been waiting for you here for four days. The gentleman who came to meet you has been in a fever of expectation. He had already left the station this morning when... when I met you. I sent word for him to pick you up here."

The plot was thickening. I most certainly was a personage of note.

THE MAN WITH THE CLUBFOOT   67

"What part of America do you come from, Mr Semlin?" said a voice in perfect English from the corner. The one-armed officer was speaking.

"From Brooklyn," I said stoutly, though my heart seemed turned to ice with the shock of hearing my own tongue.

"You have no accent," the other replied suavely.

"Some Americans," I retorted sententiously, "would regard that as a compliment. Not all Americans talk through their noses any more than we all chew or spit in public."

"I know," said the young man. "I was brought up there!"

We were surrounded by smiling faces. This officer who could speak English was evidently regarded as a bit of a wag by his comrades. I seized the opportunity to give them in German a humorous description of my simplicity in explaining to a man brought up in the United States that all Americans were not the caricatures depicted in the European comic press.

There was a roar of laughter from the room.

"Ach, dieser Schmalz!" guffawed the Major, beating his thigh in ecstasy. "Kolossal!" echoed one of the dug-outs. The lame man smiled wanly and said it was "incredible how humorous Schmalz could be."

I had hoped that the conversation might now be carried on again in German. Nothing of the kind. The room leant back in its chairs, as if expecting the fun to go on.

It did.

"You get your clothes in London," the young officer said.

He was a trimly built young man, very pale from recent illness, with flaxen hair and a bright, bold blue eye—the eye of a fighter. His left sleeve was empty and was fastened across his tunic, in a buttonhole of which was twisted the black and white ribbon of the Iron Cross.

"Generally," I answered shortly, "when I go to England. Clothes are cheaper in London."

"You must have a good ear for languages," Schmalz continued; "you speak German like a German and English..." he paused appreciably, "... like an Englishman."

I felt horribly nervous. This young man never took his eyes off me: he had been staring at me ever since I had entered the room. His manner was perfectly calm and suave.

Still I kept up my end very creditably, I think.

"And not a bad accomplishment, either," I said, smiling brightly, "if one has to visit London in war-time."

Schmalz smiled back with perfect courtesy. But he continued to stare relentlessly at me. I felt scared.

"What is Schmalz jabbering about now?" said one of the dug-outs. I translated for the benefit of the company. My resume gave the dug-out who had spoken the opportunity for launching out on an interminable anecdote about an ulster he had bought on a holiday at Brighton. The story lasted until the white gloved orderly came and announced that "a gentleman" was there, asking for the Herr Major.

"That'll be your man," exclaimed the Major, starting up— I noticed he made no attempt to bring the stranger in. "Come, let us go to him!"

I stood up and took my leave. Schmalz came to the door of the anteroom with us.

"You are going to Berlin?" he asked.

"Yes," I replied.

"Where shall you be staying?" he asked again.

"Oh, probably at the Adlon!"

"I myself shall be in Berlin next week for my medical examination, and perhaps we may meet again. I should much like to talk more with you about America... and London. We must have mutual acquaintances."

I murmured something about being only too glad, at the same time making a mental note to get out of Berlin as soon as I conveniently could.

8

I HEAR OF CLUBFOOT AND MEET HIS EMPLOYER

As we went down the staircase, the Major whispered to me:

"I don't think your man wished me to know his name, for he did not introduce himself when he arrived and he does not come to our Casino. But I know him for all that: it is the young Count von Boden, of the Uhlans of the Guard: his father, the General, is one of the Emperor's aides-de-camp: he was, for a time, tutor to the Crown Prince."

A motor-car stood at the door, in it a young man in a grey-blue military great-coat and a flat cap with a pink band round it. He sprang out as we appeared. His manner was most *empressé*. He completely ignored my companion.

"I am extremely glad to see you, Herr Doktor," he said. "You are most anxiously expected. I must present my apologies for not being at the station to welcome you, but, apparently, there was some misunderstanding. The arrangements at the station for your reception seem to have broken down completely..." and he stared through his monocle at the old Major, who flushed with vexation.

"If you will step into my car," the young man added, "I will drive you to the station. We need not detain this gentleman any longer."

I felt sorry for the old Major, who had remained silent under the withering insolence of this young lieutenant, so I shook hands with him cordially and thanked him for his hospitality. He was a jovial old fellow after all.

The young Count drove himself and chatted amiably as we whirled through the streets. "I must introduce myself," he said: "Lieutenant Count von Boden of the 2nd Uhlans of the Guard. I did not wish to say anything before that old chatterbox. I trust you have had a pleasant journey. Von Steinhardt, of our Legation at the Hague, was instructed to make all arrangements for your comfort on this side. But I was forgetting, you and he must be old acquaintances, Herr Doktor!"

I said something appropriate about von Steinhardt's invariable kindness. Inwardly, I noted the explanation of the visiting card in the portfolio in my pocket.

At the station we found two orderlies, one with my things, the other with von Boden's luggage and fur *pélisse*. The platforms were now deserted save for sentries: all life at this dreary frontier station seemed to die with the passing of the mail train.

I could not help noticing, after we had left the car and were strolling up and down the platform waiting for the special, that my companion kept casting furtive glances at my feet, I looked down at my boots: they wanted brushing, certainly, but otherwise I could see nothing wrong with them. They were brown, it is true, and I reflected that the German man about town has a way of regulating his tastes in footgear by the calendar, and that brown boots are seldom worn in Germany after September Ist.

Our special came in... an engine and tender, a brakesman's van, a single carriage and a guard's van. The stationmaster bid us a most ceremonious adieu, and the guard, cap in hand, helped me into the train.

It was a Pullman car in which I found myself, with comfortable arm-chairs and small tables. One of the orderlies was laying the table for luncheon, and here, presently, the young Count and I ate a meal, which, save for the inevitable "*Kriegsbrod*," showed few signs of the stringency of the British blockade. But by this time I had fully realized that, for some unknown reason, no pains were spared to do me honour, so probably the fare was something out of the common.

My companion was a bright, amusing fellow and delightfully typical of his class. He had seen a year's service with the cavalry on the Eastern front, had been seriously wounded and was now attached to the General Staff in Berlin in what I judged to be a decorative rather than a useful capacity, for, apart from what he had learnt in his own campaigning he seemed singularly ignorant of the development of the military situation. Particularly, his ignorance of conditions on the Western front was supreme. He was full to the brim with the most extraordinary fables about the British. He solemnly assured me, for example—on the faith of a friend of his who had seen them—that Japanese were fighting with the English in France, dressed as Highlanders—his friend had heard these Asiatic Scotsmen talking Japanese, he declared. I thought of the Gaelic-speaking battalions of the Camerons and could hardly suppress a smile.

Young von Boden was superbly contemptuous of the officers of the obscure and much reduced infantry battalion doing garrison duty at Goch, the frontier station he had just left, where—as he was careful to explain to me—he had spent four days of unrelieved boredom, waiting for me.

"Of course, in war time we are a united army and all that," he observed unsophistically, "but none of these fellows at Goch was a fit companion for a dashing cavalry officer. They were a dull lot. I wouldn't go near the Casino. I met some of them at the hotel one evening. That was enough for me. Why, only one of them knew anything at all about Berlin, and that was the lame fellow. Now, there is one thing we learn in the cavalry..."

But I had ceased to listen. In his irresponsible chatter the boy used a word that struck a harsh note which went jarring through my brain. He had mentioned "the lame fellow," using a German word "der Stelze." In a flash I saw before me again that scene in the squalid bedroom in the Vos in't Tuintje—the candle guttering in the draught, the livid corpse on the floor and that sinister woman crying out: "Der Stelze has power, he has authority, he can make and unmake men!"

The mind has unaccountable lapses. The phrase had slipped out of my German vocabulary. I had not even recognized it until the boy had rapped it out in a context with which I was familiar and then it had come back. With it, it brought that tableau in the dimly lit room, but also another—a picture of a vast and massive man, swarthy and sinister, with a clubfoot, limping heavily after Karl, the waiter, on the platform at Rotterdam.

That, then, was why the young lieutenant had glanced down at my feet at the station at Goch. The messenger he had come to meet, the bearer of the document, the man of power and authority, was clubfooted, and I was he!

But seeing I was free of any physical deformity, to say nothing of the fact that I in no way resembled the clubfooted man I had seen on the platform at Rotterdam, why had the young lieutenant accepted me so readily? I hazarded the reason to be that he had orders to meet a person who had not been further designated to him except that he would arrive by a certain train. The Major at the station would be responsible for establishing my *bona fides*. Once that officer had turned me over to the emissary, the latter's sole responsibility consisted in conducting me to the unknown goal to which the special train was rapidly bearing us. Such are the marvels of discipline!

My companion was, indeed, the model of discretion in everything touching myself and my business. Curiosity about your neighbour's affairs is a cardinal German failing, yet the

Count manifested not the slightest desire to learn anything about me or my mission to Berlin. You may be sure that I, for my part, did nothing to enlighten him. It was not, indeed, in my power to do so. Yet the young man's reserve was so marked that I was convinced he had his orders to avoid the topic.

As the train rushed through Westphalia, through busy stations with glimpses of sidings full of trucks loaded to the brim, past towns whose very outlines were blurred by the mirk of smoke from a hundred factory chimneys, my thoughts were busy with that swarthy cripple. I had broken away from him with one portion of a highly prized document, yet he had made no attempt to have me arrested at the frontier. Clearly, then, he must still look upon me as an ally and must therefore be yet in ignorance of the identity of the dead man lying in my chamber at the Hotel Sixt. The friendly guide had told me that the party "combing out" the station at Rotterdam for me did not appear to know what I looked like.

Was it possible, then, that Clubfoot did not know Semlin by sight?

The fact that Semlin had only recently crossed the Atlantic seemed to confirm this supposition.

Then the document. Semlin had half. Who had the other half? Surely Clubfoot... Clubfoot who was to have called at the hotel that morning to receive what I had brought from England. Perhaps, after all, my random declaration to the hotel-keeper had not been so far wrong; Clubfoot wanted to take the whole document to Berlin and reap all the laurels at the cost of half the danger and labour. That would explain his present silence. He suspected Semlin of treachery, not to the common cause, but to him!

It looked as if I might have a free run until Clubfoot could reach Berlin. That, unless he also took a special, could not be until the next evening at earliest. But, more redoubtable than a meeting with the man of power and authority, hung over me, an ever-present nightmare, the interview which I felt awaited me at the end of my present journey... the interview at which I must render an account of my mission.

Evening was falling as we ran through the inhospitable region of sand and water and pine that engirdles Berlin. We glided at diminished speed through the trim suburbs, skirted the city, on whose tall buildings the electric sky-signs were already beginning to twinkle, crashed heavily over a vast network of metals at some great terminus, then tore off again into the gathering darkness. In a little, we slowed down again. We were running through wooded country. From the darkness ahead a lantern waved at us and the train stopped with a jerk at a little wayside station, a tiny box of an affair. A tall, solid figure, wearing a spiked helmet and grey military great-coat, stood in solitary grandeur in the centre of the little platform, the wavering rays of a flickering gas lamp reflected in his brilliantly polished topboots.

"Here we are at last!" said my companion.

I stepped out to meet my fate.

* * *

The young lieutenant was rigid at the salute before the figure on the platform.

I heard the end of a sentence as I alighted "... the gentleman I was to meet, Excellency!"

The other looked at me. He was a big man with a crimson face. He made no attempt at greeting, but said in a hoarse voice: "Have the goodness to come with me. The orderlies will attend to your things." And, with clinking spurs, he strode out through some big kind of anteroom, swathed in wrappings, into a yard beyond, where a big limousine was throbbing gently.

He stood aside to let me get in, then mounted himself, followed, rather to my surprise, by the young Count, whose responsibility for myself had ended, I imagined, on "delivering the goods." My surprise was of short duration, for once in the car the young Uhlan dropped all the formality he had displayed on the platform and addressed the elder officer as "papa." This, then, was old General von Boden, of whom the Major had spoken, Aide-de-Camp to the Kaiser and formerly tutor to the Crown Prince.

Father and son chatted in a desultory fashion across the car, and I took the opportunity of studying the old gentleman. His face was of the most prodigious purple hue, and so highly polished that it continually caught the reflection of the small electric lamp in the roof. Huge gold spectacles with glasses so thick that they distorted his eyes, straddled a great beak-like nose. He had doffed his helmet and was mopping his brow, and I saw a high, perfectly bald, dome-like head, brilliantly polished and almost as red as his face. He was clean shaven and by no means young, for the flesh hung in bags about his face. Long years of the habit of command had left their mark in an imperiousness of manner which might easily yield to ruthlessness I judged.

"I thought I should have had orders before I left the Villa," the General said to his son, "then you could have gone straight there. I suppose he means to see him here: that is why he wanted him brought to the Villa. But he's always the same: he never can make up his mind." And he grunted.

"Perhaps there will be something waiting at home," he added in his hoarse barrack-yard voice.

We drove through a white gate into a little drive which brought us up in front of a long, low villa. Neither father nor son had opened their lips to me during the drive from the station and I had not ventured to put a question to either of them, but I knew we were in Potsdam. The little station in the woods was Wild-Park, I suspected, the private station used by the Emperor on his frequent journeys and situated in the grounds of the New Palace. All the officials of the Prussian Court have villas at Potsdam, though why I had been brought there in connection with an affair that must surely rather interest the Wilhelm-Strasse or the Police Presidency was more than I could fathom.

There was a frightful scene in the hall. Without any warning the General turned on the orderly who had opened the door and screamed abuse at him. "Camel! Ox! Sheep's-head!" he roared, his face and shining pate deepening their vermilion hue. "Do I give orders that they shall be forgotten? What do you mean? You ass... He put his white-gloved hands on the man's shoulders and shook him until the fellow's teeth must have rattled in his head. The orderly, white to the lips, hung limp in the old man's grasp, muttering apologies: "Ach! Exzellenz! Exzellenz will excuse me..."

It was a revolting spectacle, but it did not make the least impression on the son, who, putting down his cap and great-coat and unhooking his sword, led me into a kind of study. "These orderlies are such thickheads!" he said.

"Rudi! Rudi!" a hoarse, strident voice screamed from the hall. The lieutenant ran out.

"You've got to take the fellow to Berlin tonight. The message was here all the time—that numskull Heinrich forgot it. And we've got to keep the fellow here till then! An outrage, having the house used as a barrack for a rascally detective!" Thus much I heard, as the door had been left open. Then it closed and I heard no more.

As I had heard this much, there was a certain irony in the invitation to dinner subsequently conveyed to me by the young Uhlan. There was nothing for it but to accept. I knew I was caught deep in the meshes of Prussian discipline, every one had his orders and blindly carried them out, from the garrulous Major on the frontier to this preposterous *Exzellenz*, this Imperial aide-de-camp of Potsdam. I was already a tiny cog in a great machine. I should have to revolve or be crushed.

His Excellency left me in no doubt on this point: When I was ushered into his study, after a much-needed wash and a shave, he received me standing and said point-blank: "Your orders are to stay here until ten o'clock tonight, when you will be taken to Berlin by Lieutenant Count von Boden. I don't know you, I don't know your business, but I have received certain orders concerning you which I intend to carry out. For that reason you will dine with us here. After you have seen the person to whom you are to be taken tonight, Lieutenant Count von Boden will accompany you to the railway station at Spandau, where a special train will be in readiness in which he will conduct you back to the frontier. I wish you clearly to understand that the Lieutenant is responsible for seeing these orders carried out and will use all means to that end. Have I made myself clear?"

The old man's manner was indescribably threatening. "This is the machine we are out to smash," I had said to myself when I saw him savaging his servant in the hall and I repeated the phrase to myself now. But to the General I said: "Perfectly, your Excellency!"

"Then let us go to dinner," said the General. It was a nightmare meal. A faded and shrunken female, to whom I was not introduced—some kind of relative who kept house for the General, I supposed—I was the only other person present. She never opened her lips save, with eyes glazed with terror, to give some whispered instruction to the orderly anent the General's food or wine. We dined in a depressing room with dark brown wallpaper decorated with dusty stags' antlers, an enormous green-tiled stove dominating everything. The General and his son ate solidly through the courses while the lady pecked furtively at her plate. As for myself I could not eat for sheer fright. Every nerve in my body was vibrating at the thought of the evening before me. If I could not avoid the interview, I was resolutely determined to give Master von Boden the slip rather than return to the frontier empty-handed. I had not braved all these perils to be packed off home without, at least, making an attempt to find Francis. Besides, I meant if I could to get the other half of that document.

There was some quite excellent Rhine wine, and I drank plenty of it. So did the General, with the result that, when the veins starting purple from his temples proclaimed that he had eaten to repletion, his temper seemed to have improved. He unbent sufficiently to present me with quite the worst cigar I have ever smoked.

I smoked it in silence whilst father and son talked shop. The female had faded away. Both men, I found to my surprise, were furious and bitter opponents of Hindenburg, as I have since learnt most of the old school of the Prussian Army are. They spoke little of England: their thoughts seemed to be centred on Russia as the arch-enemy. They pinned their faith on Falkenhayn and Mackensen. They had no words strong enough in their denunciation of Hindenburg, whom they always referred to as "the Drunkard"... "der Saufer." Nor were they sparing of criticism of what they called the Kaiser's "weakness" in letting him rise to power.

The humming of a car outside broke up our gathering. Remembering that I was but a humble servant before this great military luminary, I thanked the General with due servility for his hospitality. Then the Count and I went out to the car and presently drove forth into the night.

We entered Berlin from the west, as it seemed to me, but then struck off in a southerly direction and were soon in the commercial quarter of the city, all but deserted at that hour, save for the trams. Then I caught a glimpse of lamps reflected in water, and the next moment the car had stopped on a bridge over a canal or river. My companion sprang out and hurried me to a small gate in an iron railing enclosing a vast edifice looming black in the night, while the car moved off into the darkness.

The gate was open. Half a dozen yards from it was a small, slender tower with a pointed roof jutting out from the corner of the building. In the tower was a door which yielded easily to my companion's vigorous push as a clock somewhere within the building beat a double stroke—half-past ten.

The door led into a little vestibule brilliantly lit with electric light. There a man was waiting, a fine, upstanding bearded fellow in a kind of green hunting costume.

"So, Payer I," said the young Uhlan. "Here is the gentleman. I shall be at the west entrance afterwards. You will bring him down yourself to the car."

"Jawohl, Herr Graf!" answered the man in green, and the lieutenant vanished through the door into the night.

A terrifying, an incredible suspicion that had overwhelmed me directly I stepped out of the car now came surging through my brain. That vast, black edifice, that slender tower at the corner—did I not know them?

Mechanically, I followed the man in green. My suspicions deepened with every step. In a little, they became certainty. Up a shallow and winding stair, along a long and broad corridor, hung with rich tapestries, the polished parquet glistening faintly in the dim light, through splendid suites of gilded apartments with old pictures and splendid furniture... here a lackey with powdered hair yawning on a landing, there a sentry in field-grey, immobile before a door... I was in the Berlin Schloss.

The Castle seemed to sleep. A hushed silence lay over all. Everywhere lights were dim, staircases wound down into emptiness, corridors stretched away into dusky solitude. Now and then an attendant in evening dress tiptoed past us or an officer vanished round a corner, noiselessly save for a faint clink of spurs.

Thus we traversed, as it seemed to me, miles of silence and of twilight, and all the time my blood hammered at my temples and my throat grew dry as I thought of the ordeal that stood before me. To whom was I thus bidden, secretly, in the night?

We were in a broad and pleasant passage now, panelled in cheerful light brown oak with red hangings. After the desolation of the State apartments, this comfortable corridor had at least the appearance of leading to the habitation of man. A giant trooper in field-grey with a curious silver gorget suspended round his neck by a chain paced up and down the passage, his jackboots making no sound upon the soft, thick carpet with which the floor was covered.

The man in green stopped at the door. Holding up a warning hand to me, he bent his head and listened. There was a moment of absolute silence. Not a sound was to be heard throughout the whole Castle. Then the man in green knocked softly and was admitted, leaving me outside.

A moment later, the door swung open again. A tall, elegant man with grey hair and that indefinite air of good breeding that you find in every man who has spent a life at court, came out hurriedly. He looked pale and harassed.

On seeing me, he stopped short.

"Dr Grundt? Where is Dr Grundt?" he asked and his eyes dropped to my feet. He started and raised them to my face.

The trooper had drifted out of earshot. I could see him, immobile as a statue, standing at the end of the corridor. Except for him and us, the passage was deserted.

Again the elderly man spoke and his voice betrayed his anxiety.

"Who are you?" he asked almost in a whisper. "What have you done with Grundt? Why has he not come?"

Boldly I took the plunge.

"I am Semlin," I said.

"Semlin," echoed the other, "—ah yes! The Embassy in Washington wrote about you—but Grundt was to have come..."

"Listen," I said, "Grundt could not come. We had to separate and he sent me on ahead..."

"But... but..."—the man was stammering now in his anxiety—"... you succeeded?"

I nodded.

He heaved a sigh of relief.

"It will be awkward, very awkward, this change in the arrangements," he said. "You will have to explain everything to him, everything. Wait there an instant."

He darted back into the room.

Once more I stood and waited in that silent place, so restful and so still that one felt onself in a world far removed from the angry strife of nations. And I wondered if my interview—the meeting I had so much dreaded—was at an end.

"Pst, pst!" The elderly man stood at the open door.

He led me through a room, a cosy place, smelling pleasantly of leather furniture, to a door. He opened it, revealing across a narrow threshold another door. On this he knocked.

"Herein!" cried a voice—a harsh, metallic voice.

My companion turned the handle and, opening the door, thrust me into the room. The door closed behind me.

I found myself facing the Emperor.

9

I ENCOUNTER AN OLD ACQUAINTANCE WHO LEADS ME TO A DELIGHTFUL SURPRISE

He stood in the centre of the room, facing the door, his legs, straddled apart, planted firmly on the ground, one hand behind his back, the other, withered and useless like the rest of the arm, thrust into the side pocket of his tunic. He wore a perfectly plain undress uniform of field-grey, and the unusual simplicity of his dress, coupled with the fact that he was bareheaded, rendered him so unlike his conventional portraits in the full panoply of war that I doubted if I should have recognized him—paradoxical as it may seem—but for the havoc depicted in every lineament of those once so familiar features.

Only one man in the world today could look like that. Only one man in the world today could show, by the ravage in his face, the appalling weight of responsibility slowly crushing one of the most vigorous and resilient personalities in Europe. His figure, erstwhile erect and well-knit, seemed to have shrunk, and his withered arm, unnaturally looped away into his pocket, assumed a prominence that lent something sinister to that forbidding grey and harassed face.

His head was sunk forward on his breast. His face, always intensely sallow, almost Italian in its olive tint, was livid. All its alertness was gone; the features seemed to have collapsed, and the flesh hung flabbily, bulging in deep pouches under the eyes and in loose folds at the corners of the mouth. His head was grizzled an iron-grey but the hair at the temples was white as driven snow. Only his eyes were unchanged. They were the same grey, steely eyes, restless, shifting, unreliable, mirrors of the man's impulsive, wayward and fickle mind.

He lowered at me. His brow was furrowed and his eyes flashed malice. In the brief instant in which I gazed at him I thought of a phrase a friend had used after seeing the Kaiser in one of his angry moods—"His icy, black look."

I was so taken aback at finding myself in the Emperor's presence that I forgot my part and remained staring in stupefaction at the apparition. The other was seemingly too busy with his thoughts to notice my forgetfulness, for he spoke at once, imperiously, in the harsh staccato of a command.

"What is this I hear?" he said. "Why has not Grundt come? What are you doing here?"

By this time I had elaborated the fable I had begun to tell in the corridor without. I had it ready now: it was thin, but it must suffice.

"If your Majesty will allow me, I will explain," I said. The Emperor was rocking himself to and fro, in nervous irritability, on his feet. His eyes were never steady for an instant. Now they searched my face, now they fell to the floor, now they scanned the ceiling.

"Dr Grundt and I succeeded in our quest, dangerous though it was. As your Majesty is aware, the... the... the object had been divided..."

"Yes, yes, I know! Go on!" the other said, pausing for a moment in his rocking.

"I was to have left England first with my portion. I could not get away. Everyone is searched for letters and papers at Tilbury. I devised a scheme and we tested it, but it failed."

"How? It failed?" the other cried.

"With no detriment to the success of our mission, Your Majesty."

"Explain! What was your stratagem?"

"I cut a piece of the lining from a hand-bag and in this I wrapped a perfectly harmless letter addressed to an English shipping agent in Rotterdam. I then pasted the fragment of the lining back in its place in the bottom of the bag. Grundt gave the bag to one of our number as an experiment to see if it would elude the vigilance of the English police."

A light of interest was growing in the Emperor's manner, banishing his ill-temper. Anything novel always appealed to him.

"Well?" he said.

"The ruse was detected, the letter was found and our man was fined twenty pounds at the police court. It was then that Dr Grundt decided to send me..."

"You've got it with you?" the other exclaimed eagerly.

"No, your Majesty," I said. "I had no means of bringing it away. Dr Grundt, on the other hand..." And I doubled up my leg and touched my foot.

The Emperor stared at me and the furrow reappeared between his eyes. Then a smile broke out on his face, a warm, attractive smile, like sunshine after rain, and he burst into a regular guffaw. I knew His Majesty's weakness for jokes at the expense of the physical deformities of others, but I had scarcely dared to hope that my subtle reference to Grundt's clubfoot as a hiding-place for compromising papers would have had such a success. For the Kaiser fairly revelled in the idea and laughed loud and long, his sides fairly shaking.

"Ach, der Stelze! Excellent! Excellent!" he cried. "Plessen, come and hear how we've diddled the Engländer again!"

We were in a long room, lofty, with a great window at the far end, where the room seemed to run to the right and left in the shape of a T. From the big writing-desk with its litter of photographs in heavy silver frames, the little bronze busts of the Empress, the water-colour sea-scapes and other little touches, I judged this to be the Emperor's study.

At the monarch's call, a white-haired officer emerged from the further end of the room, that part which was hidden from my view.

The Kaiser put his hand on his shoulder.

"A great joke, Plessen!" he said, chuckling. Then, to me: "Tell it again!"

I had warmed to my work now. I gave as drily humorous an account as I could of Dr Grundt, fat and massive and podgy, hobbling on board the steamer at Tilbury, under the noses of the British police, with the document stowed away in his boot.

The Kaiser punctuated my story with gusty guffaws, and emphasized the fun of the *dénouement* by poking the General in the ribs.

Plessen laughed very heartily, as indeed he was expected to. Then he said suavely:

"But has the stratagem succeeded, Your Majesty?"

The monarch knit his brow and looked at me.

"Well, young man, did it work?"

"...Because," Plessen went on, "if so, Grundt must be in Holland. In that case, why is he not here?"

My heart sank within me. Above all things, I knew I must keep my countenance. The least sign of embarrassment and I was lost. Yet I felt the blood fleeing from my face and I was glad I stood in the shadow.

A knock came to the door. The elderly chamberlain who had met me outside appeared.

"Your Majesty will excuse me... General Baron von Fischer is there to report..."

"Presently, presently," was the answer in an irritable tone. "I am engaged just now..."

The old courtier paused irresolutely for a moment.

"Well, what is it; what is it?"

"Despatches from General Headquarters, your Majesty! The General asked me to say the matter was urgent!"

The Kaiser wakened in an instant.

"Bring him in!" Then, to Plessen, he added in a voice from which all mirth had vanished, in accents of gloom:

"At this hour, Plessen? If things have again gone wrong in the Somme!"

An officer came in quickly, rigid with a frozen face, helmet on head, portfolio under his arm. The Kaiser walked the length of the room to his desk and sat down. Plessen and the other followed him. I remained where I was. They seemed to have forgotten all about me.

A murmur rose from the desk. The officer was delivering his report. Then the Kaiser seemed to question him, for I heard his hard metallic voice:

"Contalmaison... Trones Wood... heavy losses... forced back... terrific artillery fire..." were words that reached me. The Kaiser's voice rose on a high note of irritability. Suddenly he dashed the papers on the desk from him and exclaimed:

"It is outrageous! I'll break him! Not another man shall he have if I must go myself and teach his men their duty!"

Plessen hurriedly left the desk and came to me. His old face was white and his hands were shaking.

"Get out of here!" he said to me in a fierce undertone. "Wait outside and I will see you later!" Still, from the desk, resounded that harsh, strident voice, running on in an ascending scale, pouring forth a foaming torrent of menace.

I had often heard of the sudden paroxysms of fury from which the Kaiser was said to suffer of recent years, but never in my wildest day-dreams did I ever imagine I should assist at one.

Gladly enough did I exchange the highly charged electrical atmosphere of the Imperial study for the repose of the quiet corridor. Its perfect tranquillity was as balm to my quivering nerves. Of the man in green nothing was to be seen. Only the trooper continued his silent vigil.

Again I acted on impulse. I was wearing my grassgreen raincoat, my hat I carried in my hand. I might therefore easily pass for one just leaving the Castle. Without hesitation, I turned to the left, the way I had come, and plunged once more into the labyrinth of galleries and corridors and landings by which the man in green had led me. I very soon lost myself, so I decided to descend the next staircase I should come to. I followed this plan and went down a broad flight of stairs, at the foot of which I found a night porter, clad in a vast overcoat bedizened with eagles and seated on a stool, reading a newspaper.

He stopped me and asked me my business. I told him I was coming from the Emperor's private apartments, whereupon he demanded my pass. I showed him my badge which entirely satisfied him, though he muttered something about "new faces" and not having seen me before. I asked him for the way out. He said that at the end of the gallery I should come to the west entrance. I felt I had had a narrow squeak of running into my mentor outside. I told the man I wanted the other entrance... I had my car there.

"You mean the south entrance?" he asked, and proceeded to give me directions which brought me, without further difficulty, out upon the open space in front of the great equestrian statue of the Emperor William I.

It was a clear, starry night and I heaved a sigh of relief as I saw the Schloss-Platz glittering in the cold light of the arc lamps. So pressing had been the danger threatening me that the atmosphere of the Castle seemed stifling in comparison with the keen night air. A new confidence filled my veins as I strode along, though the perils to which I was advancing were not a whit less than those I had just escaped. For I had burnt my boats. My disappearance from the Castle must surely arouse suspicion and it was only a matter of hours for the hue and cry to be raised after me. At best it might be delayed until Clubfoot presented himself at the Castle.

I could not remain in Berlin, that was clear. My American passport was not in order, and if I were to fall back upon my silver badge, I should instantly come into contact with the police with all kinds of unwelcome consequences. No, I must get out of Berlin at all costs. Well away from the capital, I might possibly utilize my silver badge or by its help procure identity papers that would give me a status of some kind.

But Francis? Baffled as I was by that obscure jingle of German, something seemed to tell me that it *was* a message from my brother. It was dated from Berlin, and I felt that the solution of the riddle, if riddle it were, must be found here.

I had reached Unter den Linden. I entered a cafe and ordered a glass of beer. The place was a blaze of light and dense with a blue cloud of tobacco smoke. A noisy band was crashing out popular tunes and there was a loud buzz of conversation rising from every table. It was all very cheerful and the noise and the bustle did me good after the strain of the night.

I drew from my pocket the slip of paper I had had from Dicky and fell to scanning it again. I had not been twelve hours in Germany, but already I was conscious that, for anyone acting a part, let anything go wrong with his identity papers and he could never leave the country. If he were lucky, he might lie doggo; but there was no other course.

Supposing, then, that this had happened to Francis (as, indeed, Red Tabs had hinted to me was the case) what course would he adopt? He would try and smuggle out a message announcing his plight. Yes, I think that is what I myself would do in similar circumstances.

Well, I would accept this as a message from Francis. Now to study it once more.

> *O Eichenholz! O Eichenholz!*
> *Wie leer sind deine Blätter.*
> *Wie Achiles in dem Zelte.*
> *Wo zweie sich zanken*
> *Erfreut sich der Dritte.*

The message fell into three parts, each consisting of a phrase. The first phrase might certainly be a warning that Francis had failed in his mission.

"*O Okewood! How empty are thy leaves!*"

What, then, of the other two phrases?

They were short and simple. Whatever message they conveyed, it could not be a lengthy one. Nor was it likely that they contained a report of Francis' mission to Germany, whatever it had been. Indeed, it was not conceivable that my brother would send any such report to a Dutchman like van Urutius, a friendly enough fellow, yet a mere acquaintance and an alien at that.

The message carried in those two phrases must be, I felt sure, a personal one, relating to my brother's welfare. What would he desire to say? That he was arrested, that he was going to be shot? Possibly, but more probably his idea in sending out word was to explain his silence and also to obtain assistance.

My eye recurred continually to the final phrase: "When *two* people fall out, the *third* party rejoices."

Might not these numerals refer to the number of a street? Might not in these two phrases be hidden an address at which one might find Francis, or at the worst, hear news of him?

I sent for the Berlin Directory. I turned up the streets section and eagerly ran my eye down the columns of the "A's." I did not find what I was looking for, and that was an "Achilles-Strasse," either with two "Is" or with one.

Then I tried "Eichenholz." There was an "Eichen-baum-Allee" in the Berlin suburb called West-End, but that was all. I tried for a "Blatter" or a "Blatt-Strasse" with an equally negative result.

It was discouraging work, but I went back to the paper again. The only other word likely to serve as a street remaining in the puzzle was "Zelt."

"*Wie Achiles in dem Zelte.*"

Wearily I opened the directory at the "Z's."

There, staring me in the face, I found the street called "*In den Zelten.*"

I had struck the trail at last.

In den Zelten, I had discovered, on referring to the directory again, derived its name "In the Tents," from the fact that in earlier days a number of open-air beer-gardens and booths had occupied the site which faces the northern site of the Tiergarten. It was not a long street. The directory showed but fifty-six houses, several of which, I noticed, were still beer-gardens. It appeared to be a fashionable thoroughfare, for most of the occupants were titled people. No. 3, I was interested to see, was still noted as the Berlin office of *The Times*.

The last phrase in the message decidedly gave the number. *Two* must refer to the number of the house: *third* to the number of the floor, since practically all dwelling-houses in Berlin are divided off into flats.

As for the "Achiles," I gave it up.

I looked at my watch. It was twenty past eleven: too late to begin my search that night. Then I suddenly realized how utterly exhausted I was. I had been two nights out of bed without sleep, for I had sat up on deck crossing over to Holland, and the succession of adventures that had befallen me since I left London had driven all thought of weariness from my mind. But now came the reaction and I found myself yearning for a hot bath and a nice comfortable bed. To go to an hotel at that hour of night, without luggage and with an American passport not in order, would be to court disaster. It looked as though I should have to hang about the cafes and night restaurants until morning, investigate the clue of the street called In den Zelten, and then get away from Berlin as fast as ever I could.

But my head was nodding with drowsiness. I must pull myself together. I decided I would have some black coffee, and I raised my eyes to find the waiter. They fell upon the pale face and elegant figure of the one-armed officer I had met at the Casino at Goch... the young lieutenant they had called Schmalz.

He had just entered the cafe and was standing at the door, looking about him. I felt a sudden pang of uneasiness at the sight of him, for I remembered his cross-examination of me at Goch. But I could not escape without paying my bill; besides, he blocked the way.

He settled my doubts and fears by walking straight over to my table.

"Good evening, Herr Doktor," he said in German, with his pleasant smile. "This indeed is an unexpected pleasure! So you are seeing how we poor Germans are amusing ourselves in wartime. You must admit that we do not take our pleasures sadly. You permit me?"

Without waiting for my reply, he sat down at my table and ordered a glass of beer.

"I wish you had appeared sooner," I exclaimed in as friendly a tone as I could muster, "for I am just going. I have had a long and tiring journey and am anxious to go to an hotel."

Directly I had spoken I realized my blunder.

"You have not got an hotel yet?" said Schmalz. "Why, how curious! Nor have I? As you are a stranger in Berlin, you must allow me to appoint myself your guide. Let us go to an hotel together, shall we?"

I wanted to demur, difficult as it was to find any acceptable excuse, but his manner was so friendly, his offer seemed so sincere, that I felt my resolution wavering. He had a winning personality, this frank, handsome boy. And I was so dog-tired!

He perceived my reluctance but also my indecision.

"We'll go to any hotel you like," he said brightly. "But you Americans are spoilt in the matter of luxurious hotels, I know. Still, I tell you we have not much to learn in that line in Berlin. Suppose we go to the Esplanade. It's a fine hotel... the Hamburg American line run it, you know. I am very well known there, quite the *Hauskind*... my uncle was a captain of one of their liners. They will make us very comfortable: they always give me a little suite, bedroom, sitting-room and bath, very reasonably: I'll make them do the same for you."

If I had been less weary—I have often thought since—I would have got up and fled from the cafe rather than have countenanced any such mad proposal. But I was drunk with sleep heaviness and I snatched at this chance of getting a good night's rest, for I felt that, under the aegis of this young officer, I could count on any passport difficulties at the hotel being postponed until morning. By that time, I meant to be out of the hotel and away on my investigations.

So I accepted Schmalz's suggestion.

"By the way," I said, "I have no luggage. My bag got mislaid somehow at the station and I don't really feel up to going after it tonight."

"I will fix you up," the other replied promptly, "and with pyjamas in the American fashion. By the by," he added, lowering his voice, "I thought it better to speak German. English is not heard gladly in Berlin just now."

"I quite understand," I said. Then, to change the subject, which I did not like particularly, I added:

"Surely, you have been very quick in coming down from the frontier. Did you come by train?"

"Oh, no!" he answered. "I found that the car in which you drove to the station... it belonged to the gentleman who came to meet you, you know... was being sent back to Berlin by road, so I got the driver to give me a lift."

He said this quite airily, with his usual tone of candour. But for a moment I regretted my decision to go to the Esplanade with him. What if he knew than he seemed to know?

I dismissed the suspicion from my mind.

"Bah!" I said to myself, "You are getting jumpy. Besides, it is too late to turn back now!"

We had a friendly wrangle as to who should pay for the drinks, and it ended in my paying. Then, after a long wait, we managed to get a cab, an antique-looking "growler" driven by an octogenarian in a coat of many capes, and drove to the Esplanade.

It was a regular palace of a place, with a splendid vestibule with walls and pavement of different-hued marbles, with palm trees overshadowing a little fountain tinkling in a jade basin, with servants in gaudy liveries. The reception clerk overwhelmed me with the cordiality of his welcome to my companion and "the American gentleman," and after a certain amount of coquettish protestations about the difficulty of providing accommodation, allotted us a double suite on the entresol, consisting of two bedrooms with a common sitting-room and bathroom.

In his immaculate evening dress, he was a Beau Brummell among hotel clerks, that man. The luggage of the American gentleman should be fetched in the morning. The gentleman's papers? There was no hurry: the Herr Leutnant would explain to his friend the forms that had to be filled in: they could be given to the waiter in the morning. Would the gentlemen take anything before retiring? A whisky-soda—ah! Whisky was getting scarce. No? Nothing? He had the honour to wish the gentlemen pleasant repose.

We went to the lift in procession, Beau Brummell in front, then a waiter, then ourselves and the gold-braided hall porter bringing up the rear. One or two people were sitting in the lounge, attended by a platoon of waiters. The whole place gave an impression of wealth and luxury altogether out of keeping with British ideas of the stringency of life in Germany under the British blockade. I could not help reflecting to myself mournfully that Germany did not seem to feel the pinch very much.

At the lift the procession bowed itself away and we went up in charge of the liftman, a gorgeous individual who looked like one of the Pope's Swiss Guards. We reached the entresol in an instant. The Lieutenant led the way along the dimly lighted corridor.

"Here is the sitting-room," he said, opening a door. "This is my room, this the bathroom, and this," he flung open the fourth door, "is your room!"

He stood aside to let me pass. The lights in the room were full on. In an armchair a big man in an overcoat was sitting.

He had a heavy square face and a clubfoot.

10

A GLASS OF WINE WITH CLUBFOOT

I walked boldly into the room. All sense of fear had vanished in a wave of anger that swept over me, anger with myself for letting myself be trapped, anger with my companion for his treachery.

Schmalz stood at my elbow with a smile full of malice on his face.

"There now!" he cried, "you see, you are among friends! Am I not thoughtful to have prepared this little surprise for you? See, I have brought you to the one man you have crossed so many hundreds of miles of ocean to see! Herr Doktor! This is Dr Semlin. Dr Semlin: Dr Grundt."

The other had by now heaved his unwieldy frame from the chair.

"Dr Semlin?" he said, in a perfectly emotionless voice, *une voix blanche*, as the French say, "this is an unexpected pleasure. I never thought we should meet in Berlin. I had believed our rendezvous to have been fixed for Rotterdam. Still, better late than never!" And he extended to me a white, fat hand.

"Our friend, the Herr Leutnant," I answered carelessly, "omitted to inform me that he was acquainted with you, as, indeed, he failed to warn me that I should have the pleasure of seeing you here tonight."

"We owe that pleasure," Clubfoot replied with a smile that displayed a glitter of gold in his teeth, "to a purely fortuitous encounter at the Casino at Goch, as, indeed, it would appear, I am similarly indebted to chance for the unlooked-for boon of making your personal acquaintance here this evening."

He bowed to Schmalz as he said this.

"But come," he went on, "if I may make bold to offer you the hospitality of your own room, sit down and try a glass of this excellent Brauneberger. Rhine wine must be scarce where you come from. We have much to tell one another, you and I."

Again he bared his golden teeth in a smile.

"By all means," I said. "But I fear we keep our young friend from his bed. Doubtless, you have no secrets from him, but you will agree, Herr Doktor, that our conversation should best be *tête-à-tête*."

"Schmalz, dear friend," Clubfoot exclaimed with a sigh of regret, "much as I should like... I am indeed truly sorry that we should be deprived of your company, but I cannot contest the profound accuracy of our friend's remark. If you could go to the sittingroom for a few minutes..."

The young lieutenant flushed angrily.

"If you prefer my room to my company... by all means," he retorted gruffly, "but I think, in the circumstances, that I shall go to bed."

And he turned on his heel and walked out of the room, shutting the door with rather more force than was necessary, I thought.

Clubfoot sighed.

"Ach! youth I youth!" he cried, "The same impetuous youth is at this very moment hacking out for Germany a world empire amidst the nations in arms. A wonderful race, a race of giants, our German youth, Herr Doktor... the mainspring of our great German machine—as they find who resist it. A glass of wine!"

The man's speech and manner boded ill for me, I felt. I would have infinitely preferred violent language and open threats to the subtle menace that lay concealed beneath all this suavity.

"You smoke?" queried Clubfoot. "No!"—he held up his hand to stop me as I was reaching for my cigarette case, "You shall have a cigar—not one of our poor German Hamburgers, but a fine Havana cigar given me by a member of the English Privy Council. You stare! Aha! I repeat, by a member of the English Privy Council, to me, the Boche, the barbarian, the Hun! No hole-and-corner work for the old doctor. *Der Stelze* may be lame, Clubfoot may be past his work, but when he travels *en mission*, he travels *en prince*, the man of wealth and substance. There is none too high to do him honour, to listen to his views on poor, misguided Germany, the land of thinkers sold into bondage to the militarists! Bah! The fools!"

He snarled venomously. This man was beginning to interest me. His rapid change of moods was fascinating, now the kindly philosopher, now the Teuton braggart, now the Hun incorporate. As he limped across the room to fetch his cigar-case from the mantelpiece I studied him.

He was a vast man, not so much by reason of his height, which was below the medium, but his bulk, which was enormous. The span of his shoulders was immense, and, though a heavy paunch and a white flabbiness of face spoke of a gross, sedentary life, he was obviously a man of quite unusual strength. His arms particularly were out of all proportion to his stature, being so long that his hands hung down on either side of him when he stood erect, like the paws of some giant ape. Altogether, there was something decidedly simian about his appearance... his squat nose with hairy, open nostrils, and the general hirsuteness of the man, his bushy eyebrows, the tufts of black hair on his cheekbones and on the backs of his big spade-like hands. And there was that in his eyes, dark and courageous beneath the shaggy brows, that hinted at accesses of ape-like fury, uncontrollable and ferocious.

He gave me his cigar which, as he had said, was a good one, and, after a preliminary sip of his wine, began to speak.

"I am a plain man, Herr Doktor," he said, "and I like plain speaking. That is why I am going to speak quite plainly to you. When it became apparent that the person whom it is not necessary to name further greatly desired a certain letter to be recovered, I naturally expected that I, who am a past master in affairs of this order, notably, on behalf of the person concerned, would have been entrusted with the mission. It was I who discovered the author of the theft in an English internment camp; it was I who prevailed upon him to acquiesce in our terms; it was I who finally located the hiding-place of the document... all this, mark you, without setting foot in England."

My thoughts flew back again to the three slips of paper in their canvas cover, the divided crest, the big sprawling, upright handwriting. I should have known that hand. I had seen it often enough on certain photographs which were accorded the place of honour in the drawing-room at Consistorial-Rat von Mayburg's at Bonn.

"I therefore had the prior claim," Clubfoot continued, "to be entrusted with the important task of fetching the document and handing it back to the writer. But the gentleman was in a hurry; the gentleman always is; he could not wait for that old slowcoach of a Clubfoot to mature his plans for getting into England, securing the document, and getting out again.

"So Bernstorff is called into consultation, the head of an embassy that has made the German secret service the laughing-stock of the world, an ambassador that has his private papers filched by a common sneakthief in the underground railway and is fool enough to send home the most valuable documents by a jackass of a military attaché who lets the whole lot be taken from him by a dunderheaded British customs officer at Falmouth! *This* was the man who was to replace *me!*

"Bernstorff is accordingly bidden to despatch one of his trusty servants to England, with all suitable precautions, to do *my* work. You are chosen, and I will pay you the compliment of saying that you fulfilled your mission in a manner that is singularly out of keeping with the usual method of procedure of that gentleman's emissaries.

"But, my dear Doktor... pray fill your glass. That cigar is good, is it not? I thought you would appreciate a good cigar... As I was saying, you were handicapped from the first. When you reach the place indicated to you in your instructions, you find only half the document. The wily thief has sliced it in two so as to make sure of his money before parting with the goods. They didn't know, of course, that Clubfoot, the old slowcoach, who is past his work, was aware of this already, and had made his plans accordingly. But, in the end, they had to send for me. 'The good Clubfoot,' 'old chap,' 'sly old fox,' and all the rest of it—would run across to England and secure the other half, while Count Bernstorff's smart young man from America would wait in Rotterdam until Herr Dr Grundt arrived and handed him the other portion.

"But Count Bernstorff's young man does nothing of the kind. He is one too many for the old fox. He does not wait for him. He runs away, after displaying unusual determination in dealing with a prying Englander—whose fate should be a lesson to all who interfere in other people's business—and goes to Germany, leaving poor old Clubfoot in the lurch. You must admit, Herr Doktor, that I have been hardly used—by yourself as well as by another person?"

My throat was dry with anxiety. What did the man mean by his veiled allusions to "all who interfere in other people's business?"

I cleared my throat to speak.

Clubfoot raised a great hand in deprecation.

"No explanation, Herr Doktor, I beg" (his tone was perfectly unconcerned and friendly), "let me have my say. When I had found out that you had left Rotterdam—by the way, you must let me congratulate you on the remarkable fertility of resource you displayed in quitting Frau Schratt's hospitable house—when I found you were gone, I sat down and thought things out.

"I reflected that an astute American like yourself (believe me, you are very astute) would probably be accustomed to look at everything from the business standpoint. 'I will also consider the matter from the business standpoint,' I said to myself, and I decided that, in your place, I too would not be content to accept, as sole payment for the danger of my mission, the scarcely generous compensation that Count Bernstorff allots to his collaborators. No, I should wish to secure a little renown for myself, or, were that not possible, then some monetary gain proportionate with the risks I had run. You see, I have been at pains to put myself wholly in your place. I hope I have not said anything tactless. If so, I can at least acquit myself of any desire to offend."

"On the contrary, Herr Doktor," I replied, "you are the model of tact and diplomacy."

His eyes narrowed a little at this. I thought he wouldn't like that word "diplomacy."

"Another glass of wine? You may safely venture; there is not a headache in a bottle of it. Well, Herr Doktor, since you have followed me so patiently thus far, I will go further. I told you, when I first saw you this evening, that I was delighted at our meeting. That was no mere banality, but the sober truth. For, you see, I am the very person with whom, in the circumstances, you would wish to get in touch. Deprived of the honour, rightly belonging to me, of undertaking this mission single-handed and fulfilling it alone, I find that you can enable me to carry out the mission to a successful conclusion, whilst I, for my part, am able and willing to recompense your services as they deserve and not according to Bernstorff's starvation scale.

"To make a long story short, Herr Doktor... How much?"

He brought his remarks to this abrupt anti-climax so suddenly that I was taken aback. The man was watching me intently for all his apparent nonchalance, and I felt more than ever the necessity for being on my guard. If I could only fathom how much he knew. Of two things I felt sure: the fellow believed me to be Semlin and was under the impression that I still retained my portion of the document. I should have to gain time. The bargain he proposed over my half of the letter might give me an opportunity of doing that. Moreover, I must find out whether he really had the other half of the document, and in that case, where he kept it.

He broke the silence.

"Well, Herr Doktor," he said, "do you want me to start the bidding? You needn't be afraid. I am generous."

I leant forward earnestly in my chair.

"You have spoken with admirable frankness, Herr Doktor," I said, "and I will be equally plain, but I will be brief. In the first place, I wish to know that you are the man you profess to be: so far, you must remember, I have only the assurance of our excitable young friend."

"Your caution is most praiseworthy," said the other, "but I should imagine I carry my name written on my boot." And he lifted his hideous and deformed foot.

"That is scarcely sufficient guarantee," I answered, "in a matter of this importance. A detail like that could easily be counterfeited, or otherwise provided for."

"My badge," and the man produced from his waistcoat pocket a silver star identical with the one I carried on my braces, but bearing only the letter "G" above the inscription "Abt. VII."

"That, even," I retorted, "is not conclusive."

Clubfoot's mind was extraordinarily alert, however gross and heavy his body might be.

He paused for a moment in reflection, his hands crossed upon his great paunch.

"Why not?" he said suddenly, reached out for his cigar-case, beside him on the table, and produced three slips of paper highly glazed and covered with that unforgettable, sprawling hand, a portion of a gilded crest at the top—in short, the missing half of the document I had found in Semlin's bag. Clubfoot held them out fanwise for me to see, but well out of my reach, and he kept a great, spatulate thumb over the top of the first sheet where the name of the addressee should have been.

"I trust you are now convinced, Herr Doktor," he said, with a smile that bared his teeth, and, putting the pieces together, he folded them across, tucked the away in his cigar-case again, and thrust it into his pocket.

I must test the ground further.

"Has it occurred to you, Herr Doktor," I asked, "that we have very little time at our disposal? The person whom we serve must be anxiously waiting..."

Clubfoot laughed and shook his head.

"I want that half-letter badly," he said, "but there's no violent hurry. So I fear you must leave that argument out of your presentation of the case, for it has no commercial value. The person you speak of is not in Berlin."

I had heard something of the Kaiser's sudden appearances and disappearances during the war, but I had not thought they could be so well managed as to be kept from the knowledge of one of his own trusted servants, for such I judged Clubfoot to be. Evidently, he knew nothing of my visit to the Castle that evening, and I was for a moment unpatriotic enough to wish I had kept my half of the letter that I might give it to Clubfoot now to save the coming exposure.

"A thousand dollars!" Clubfoot said.

I remained silent.

"Two? Three? Four thousand? Man, you are greedy. Well, I will make it five thousand—twenty thousand marks..."

"Herr Doktor," I said, "I don't want your money. I want to be fair with you. When the... the person we know of sends for you, we will go together. You shall tell the large part you have played in this affair. I only want credit for what I have done, nothing more..."

A knock came at the door. The porter entered.

"A telegram for the Herr Doktor," he said, presenting a salver.

Somewhere near a band was playing dance music... one of those rousing, splendidly accented Viennese waltzes. There seemed to be a ball on, for, through the open door of the room, I heard, mingled with the strains of the music, the sound of feet and the hum of voices. Then the door closed, shutting out the outer world again.

"You permit me," said Grundt curtly, as he broke the seal of the telegram. So as not to seem to observe him, I got up and walked across to the window, and leaned against the warm radiator.

"Well?" said a voice from the arm-chair.

"Well?" I echoed.

"I have made you my proposal, Herr Doktor: you have made yours. Yours is quite unacceptable. I have told you with great frankness why it is necessary that I should have your portion of the document and the sum I am prepared to pay for it. I set its value at five thousand dollars. I will pay you the money over in cash, here and now, in good German bank-notes, in exchange for those slips of paper."

The man's suavity had all but vanished: his voice was harsh and stern. His eyes glittered under his shaggy brows as he looked at me. Had I been less agitated, I should have noted this, as a portent of the coming storm, also his great ape's hands picking nervously at the telegram in his lap.

"I have already told you," I said firmly, "that I don't want your money. You know my terms!"

He rose up from his seat and his figure seemed to tower. "Terms?" he cried in a voice that quivered with suppressed passion, "Terms? Understand that I give orders. I accept terms from no man. We waste time here talking. Come, take the money and give me the paper."

I shook my head. My brain was clear, but I felt the crisis was coming. I took a good grip with my hands of the marble slab covering the radiator behind me to give me confidence. The slab yielded: mechanically I noted that it was loose.

The man in front of me was shaking with rage.

"Listen!" he said. "I'll give you one more chance. But mark my words well. Do you know what happened to the man that stole that document? The English took him out and shot him on account of what was found in his house when they raided it. Do you know what happened to the interpreter at the internment camp, who was our go-between, who played us false by cutting the document in half? The English shot *him* too, on account of what was found in letters that came to him openly through the post? And who settled Schulte? And who settled the other man? Who contrived the traps that sent them to their doom? It was *I*, Grundt, *I*, the cripple, *I*, the Clubfoot, that had these traitors despatched as an example to the six thousand of us who serve our Emperor and empire in darkness! You dog, I'll smash you!"

He was gibbering like an angry ape: his frame was shaking with fury: every hair in the tangle on his face and hands seemed to bristle with his Berserker frenzy.

But he kept away from me, and I saw that he was still fighting to preserve his self-control.

I maintained a bold front.

"This may do for your own people," I said contemptuously, "but it doesn't impress me. I'm an American citizen!"

He was calmer now, but his eyes glittered dangerously.

"An American citizen?" he said in an icy tone. Then he fairly hissed at me:

"You fool! Blind, besotted fool! Do you think you can trifle with the might of the German Empire? Ah! I've played a pretty game with you, you dirty English dog! I've watched you squirming and writhing whilst the stupid German told you his pretty little tale and plied you with his wine and his cigars. You're in our power now, you miserable English hound! Do you understand that? Now call on your fleet to come and save you!

"Listen! I'll be frank with you to the last. I've had my suspicions of you from the first, when they telephoned me that you had escaped from the hotel, but I wanted to make *sure*. Ever since you have been in this room it has been in my power to push that bell there and send you to Spandau, where they rid us of such dirty dogs as you.

"But the game amused me. I liked to see the Herr Englander playing the spy against *me*, the master of them all. Do you know, you fool, that old Schratt knows English, that she spent years of her harlot's life in London, and that when you allowed her a glimpse of that passport, your own passport, the one you so cleverly burned, she remembered the name? Ah! you didn't know that, did you?

"Shall I tell you what was in that telegram they just brought me? It was from Schratt, our faithful Schratt, who shall have a bangle for this night's work, to say that the corpse at the hotel has a chain round its neck with an identity disc in the name of Semlin. Ha! you didn't know that either, did you?

"And *you* would bargain and chaffer with me! *You* would dictate your terms, you scum! *You* with your head in a noose, a spy that has failed in his mission, a miserable wretch that I can send to his death with a flip of my little finger! You impudent hound! Well, you'll get your deserts this time, Captain Desmond Okewood... but I'll have that paper first!"

Roaring "Give it to me!" he rushed at me like some frenzied beast of the jungle. The veins stood out at his temples, his hairy nostrils opened and closed as his breath came faster, his long arms shot out and his great paws clutched at my throat.

But I was waiting for him. As he came at me, I heard his clubfoot stump once on the polished floor, then, from the radiator behind me, I raised high in my arms the heavy marble slab, and with every ounce of strength in my body brought it crashing down on his head.

He fell like a log, the blood oozing sluggishly from his head on to the parquet. I stopped an instant, snatched the cigar-case from the pocket where he had placed it, extracted the document and fled from the room.

11

MISS MARY PRENDERGAST RISKS HER REPUTATION

The rooms of our suite were intercommunicating so that you could pass from one to the other without going into the corridor at all. Schmalz had retired this way, going from my room through the bathroom to his own room. In the excitement of the moment I forgot all about this, else I should not have omitted such an elementary precaution as slipping the bolt of the door communicating between my room and the bathroom.

As I stepped out into the corridor, with the crash of that heavy body still ringing in my ears, I thought I caught the sound of a light step in the bathroom; the next moment I heard a door open and then a loud exclamation of horror in the room I had just left.

The corridor was dim and deserted. The place seemed uninhabited. No boots stood outside the rooms, and open doors, one after the other, were sufficient indication that the apartments they led to were untenanted.

I didn't pause to reason or to plan. On hearing that long drawn out cry of horror, I dashed blindly down the corridor at top speed, followed it round to the right and then, catching sight of a small staircase, rushed up it three steps at a time. As I reached the top I heard a loud cry somewhere on the floor below. Then a door banged, there was the sound of running feet and... silence.

I found myself on the next floor in a corridor similar to the one I had just left. Like it, it was desolate and dimly lit. Like it, it showed room after room silent and empty. Agitated as I was, the contrast with the bright and busy vestibule and the throng of uniformed servants below was so marked that it struck me with convincing force. Even the hotels, it seemed, were part and parcel of the great German publicity bluff which I had noted in my reading of the German papers at Rotterdam.

I had no plan in my head, only a wild desire to put as much distance as possible between me and that ape-man in the room below. So, after pausing a moment to listen and draw breath, I started off again. Suddenly a door down the corridor, not ten paces away from me, opened and a woman came out. I stopped dead in my headlong course, but it was too late and I found myself confronting her.

She was young and very beautiful with masses of thick brown hair clustering round a very white forehead. She was in evening dress, all in white, with an ermine wrap.

Even as I looked at her I knew her and she knew me.

"Monica," I whispered.

"Why! Desmond!" she said.

A regular hubbub echoed from below. Voices were crying out, doors were banging, there was the sound of feet.

The girl was speaking, saying in her low and pleasant voice phrases that were vague to me about her surprise, her delight at seeing me. But I did not listen to her. I was straining my ears towards that volume of chaotic noises that came swelling up from below.

"Monica!" I interrupted swiftly, "Have you any place to hide me? This place is dangerous for me... I must get away. If you can't save me, don't stay here but get away yourself as fast as you can. They're after me and if they catch you with me it will be bad for you!"

Without a word the girl turned round to the room she had just left. She beckoned to me, then knocked and went in. I followed her. It was a big, pleasant bedroom, elegantly furnished with a soft carpet and silk hangings, and I know not what, with shaded lights and flowers in profusion. Sitting up in bed was a stout, placid-looking woman in a pink silk kimono with her hair coquettishly braided in two short pigtails which hung down on either side of her face.

Monica closed the door softly behind her.

"Why, Monica!" she exclaimed in horror—and her speech was that of the United States—"What on earth...?"

"Not a word, Mary, but let me explain..."

"But for land's sake, Monica..."

"Mary, I want you to help..."

"But say, child, a man... in my bedroom... at this time o'night..."

"Oh, shucks, Mary! Let me talk."

The distress of the woman in bed was so comic that I could scarcely help laughing. She had dragged the bed-clothes up till only her eyes could be seen. Her pigtails bobbed about in her emotion.

"Now, Mary dear, listen here. You're a friend of mine. This is Desmond Okewood, another, a very old and dear friend of mine too. Well, you know, Mary, this isn't a healthy country these times for an English officer. That's what Desmond here is. I didn't know he was in Germany. I don't know a thing about him except what he's told me and that's that he's in danger and wants me to help him. I met him outside and brought him right in here, as I know you would want me to, wouldn't you, dear?"

The lady poked her nose over the top of the bedclothes.

"Present the gentleman properly, Monica!" she said severely.

"Captain Okewood... Miss Mary Prendergast," said Monica.

The lady's head, pigtails and all, now appeared. She appeared to be somewhat mollified.

"I can't say I approve of your way of doing things, Monica," she observed, but less severely than before, "and I can't think what an English officer wants in my bedroom at ten minutes to two in the morning, but if those Deutschers want to find him, perhaps I can understand!"

Here she smiled affectionately on the beautiful girl at my side.

"Ah! Mary, you're a dear," replied Monica. "I knew you'd help us. Why, a British officer in Germany... isn't it too thrilling?"

She turned to me.

"But, Des," she said, "what do you want me to do?"

I knew I could trust Monica and I resolved I would trust her friend too... she looked a white woman all right. And if she was a friend of Monica's, her heart would be in the right place. Francis and I had known Monica all our lives almost. Her father had lived for years... indeed to the day of his death... in London as the principal European representative of a big American financial house. They had lived next door to us in London and Francis and I had known Monica from the days when she was a pretty kid in short skirts until she had made her début and the American ambassadress had presented her at Buckingham Palace. At various stages of our lives, both Francis and I had been in love with her, I believe, but my life in the army had kept me much abroad, so Francis had seen most of her and had been the hardest hit.

Then the father died, and Monica went travelling abroad in great state, as befits a young heiress, with a prodigiously respectable American chaperon and a retinue of retainers. I never knew the rights of the case between her and Francis, but at one of the German embassies abroad—I think in Vienna—she met the young Count Rachwitz, head of one of the great Silesian noble houses, and married him.

It was not on the usual rock—money—that this German-American marriage was wrecked, for the Count was very wealthy himself. I had supposed that the German man's habitual attitude of mind towards women had not suited the girl's independent spirit on hearing that Monica, a few years after her marriage, had left her husband and gone to live in America. I had not seen her since she left London, and, though we wrote to one another at intervals, I had not heard from her since the war started and had no idea that she had returned to Germany. Monica Rachwitz was, in fact, the last person I should ever have expected to meet in Berlin in war-time.

So, as briefly as I could and listening intently throughout for any sounds in the corridor, I gave the two women the story of the disappearance of Francis and my journey into Germany to look for him. At the mention of my brother's name, I noticed that the girl stiffened and her face grew rigid, but when I told her of my fears for his safety her blue eyes seemed to me to grow dim. I described to them my adventure in the hotel at Rotterdam, my reception in the house of General von Boden, and my interview at the Castle, ending with the experiences of that night, the trap laid for me at the hotel and my encounter with Clubfoot in the room below. Two things only I kept back: the message from Francis and the document. I decided within myself that the fewer people in those secrets the safer they would be. I am afraid, therefore, that my account of my interview with the Emperor was a trifle garbled, for I made out that I did not know why I was bidden to the presence and that our conversation was interrupted before I could discover the reason.

The two women listened with grave faces. Only once did Monica interrupt me. It was when I mentioned General von Boden.

"I know the beast," she said. "But, oh, Des!" she exclaimed, "you seem to have fallen right among the top set in this country. They're a bad lot to cross. I fear you are in terrible danger."

"I believe you, Monica," I answered, dolefully enough. "And that's just where I feel such a beast for throwing myself upon your mercy in this way. But I was pretty desperate when I met you just now and I didn't know where to turn. Still, I want you to understand that if you can only get me out of this place I shall not trouble you further. I came to this country on my own responsibility and I'm going through with it alone. I have no intention of implicating anybody else along with me. But I confess I don't believe it possible to get away from this hotel. They're watching every door by now. Besides..."

I stopped abruptly. A noise outside caught my listening ear. Footsteps were approaching along the corridor. I heard doors open and shut. They were hunting for me, floor by floor, room by room.

"Open that wardrobe," said a voice from the bed: a firm, business-like voice that was good to hear. "Open it and get right in, young man; but don't go mussing up my good dresses whatever you do! And you, Monica, quick! Switch off those lights all but this one by the bed. Good! Now go to the door and ask them what they mean by making this noise at this time of the night and me ill and all!"

I got into the wardrobe and Monica shut me in. I heard the bedroom door open, then voices. I waited patiently for five minutes, then the wardrobe door opened again.

"Come out, Des," said Monica, "and thank Mary Prendergast for her cleverness."

"What did they say?" I asked.

"That reception clerk was along. He was most apologetic — they know me here, you see. He told me how a fellow had made a desperate attack upon a gentleman on the floor below and had got away. They thought he must be hiding somewhere in the hotel. I told him I'd been sitting here for an hour chatting with Miss Prendergast and that we hadn't heard a sound. They went away then!"

"You won't catch any Deutschers fooling Mary Prendergast," said the jovial lady in the bed; "but, children, what next?"

Monica spoke—quite calmly. She was always perfectly self-possessed.

"My brother is stopping with me in our apartment in the Bendler-Strasse," she said. "You remember Gerry, Des—he got all smashed up flying, you know, and is practically a cripple. He's been so much better here that I've been trying to get an attendant to look after him, to dress him and so on, but we couldn't find anybody; men are so scarce nowadays! You could come home with me, Des, and take this man's place for a day or two... I'm afraid it couldn't be longer, for one would have to register you with the police—every one has to be registered, you know—and I suppose you have no papers that are any good—now."

"You are too kind, Monica," I answered, "but you risk too much and I can't accept."

"It's no risk for a day or two," she said. "I am a person of consequence in official Germany, you know, with my husband A.D.C. to Marshal von Mackensen: and I can always say I forgot to send in your papers. If they come down upon me afterwards I should say I meant to register you but had to discharge you suddenly... for drink!"

"But how can I get away from here?" I objected.

"I guess we can fix that too," she replied. "My car is coming for me at two—it must be that now—I have been at a dance downstairs—one of the Radolin girls is getting married tomorrow—it was so deadly dull I ran up here and woke up Mary Prendergast to talk. You shall be my chauffeur! I know you drive a car! You ought to be able to manage mine... it's a Mercédès."

"I can drive any old car," I said, "but I'm blessed..."

"Wait there!" cried this remarkable girl, and ran out of the room.

For twenty minutes I stood and made small talk with Miss Prendergast. They were the longest twenty minutes I have ever spent. I was dead tired in any case, but my desperate position kept my thoughts so busy that, for all my endeavours to be polite, I fear my conversation was extremely distraught.

"You poor boy!" suddenly said Miss Mary Prendergast, totally ignoring a profound remark I was making regarding Mr Wilson's policy, "Don't you go on talking to me! Sit down on that chair and go to sleep! You look just beat!"

I sat down and nodded in the arm-chair.

Suddenly I was awake. Monica stood before me. She drew from under her cape a livery cap and uniform.

"Put these things on," she said," and listen carefully. When you leave here, turn to the right and take the little staircase you will find on the right. Go down to the bottom, go through the glass doors, and across the room you will find there, to a door in a corner which leads to the ballroom entrance of the hotel. I will give you my ermine wrap to carry. I shall be waiting there. You will help me on with my cloak and escort me to the car. Is that clear?"

"Perfectly."

"Now, pay attention once more, for I shall not be able to speak to you again. I shall have to give you your directions for finding the way to the Bendler-Strasse."

She did so and added:

"Drive carefully, whatever you do. If we had a smash and the police intervened, it might be most awkward for you."

"But your chauffeur," I said, "what will he do?"

"Oh, Carter," she answered carelessly, "he's tickled to death... he's American, you see... he drove me out into the Tiergarten just now and took off his livery, then drove me back here, hopped off and went home."

"But can you trust him?" I asked anxiously.

"Like myself," she said. "Besides, Carter's been to Belgium... he drove Count Rachwitz, my husband, while he was on duty there. And Carter hasn't forgotten what he saw in Belgium!"

She gave me the key of the garage and further instructions how to put the car up. Carter would give me a bed at the garage and would bring me round to the house early in the morning as if I were applying for the job of male attendant for Gerry.

"I will go down first," Monica said, "so as not to keep you waiting. My, but they're rattled downstairs—all the crowd at Olga von Radolin's dance have got hold of the story and the place is full of policemen. But there'll be no danger if you walk straight up to me in the hall and keep your face turned away from the crowd as much as possible."

She kissed Miss Prendergast and slipped away. What a splendid pair of women they were: so admirably cool and resourceful: they seemed to have thought of everything.

"Good night, Miss Prendergast," I said. "You have done me a good turn. I shall never forget it!' And as the only means at my disposal for showing my gratitude, I kissed her hand.

She coloured up like a girl.

"It's a long time since any one did that to a silly old woman like me," she said musingly. "Was it you or your brother," she asked abruptly, "who nearly broke my poor girl's heart?

"I shouldn't like to say," I answered; "but I don't think, speaking personally, that Monica ever cared enough about me for me to plead guilty."

She sniffed contemptuously.

"If that is so," she said, "all I can say is that you seem to have all the brains of your family!"

With that I took my leave.

* * *

I reached the ballroom vestibule without meeting a soul. The place was crowded with people, officers in uniform, glittering with decorations, women in evening dress, coachmen, footmen, chauffeurs, waiters. Everybody was talking sixteen to the dozen, and there were such dense knots of people that at first I couldn't see Monica. Two policemen were standing at the swing-doors leading into the street, and with them a civilian who looked like a detective. I caught sight of Monica, almost at the detective's elbow, talking to two very elegant-looking officers. I pushed my way across the vestibule, turned my back on the detective and stood impassively beside her.

"Ah! there you are, Carter!" she said. "Gute Nacht, Herr Baron! Auf wiedersehen, Durchlaucht!"

The two officers kissed her hand whilst I helped her into her wrap. Then I marched straight out of the swing-doors in front of her, looking neither to right nor to left, past the detective and the two policemen. The detective may have looked at me: if so, I didn't perceive it. I had made up my mind not to see him.

Outside Monica took the lead and brought me over to a chocolate-covered limousine drawn up at the pavement. I noted with dismay that the engine was stopped. That might mean further delay whilst I cranked up. But a friendly chauffeur standing by seized the handle and started the engine whilst I assisted Monica into the car, and the next moment we were gliding smoothly over the asphalt under the twinkling arc-lamps.

The Bendler-Strasse is off the Tiergarten, not far from the Esplanade, and I found my way there without much difficulty. I flatter myself that both Monica and I played our parts well, and I am sure nothing could have been more professional than the way I helped her to alight. It was an apartment house and she had the key to the front door, so, after seeing her safely within doors, I returned to the car and drove it round to the garage by a carriage-way leading to the rear of the premises.

As I unlocked the double doors of the garage, a man came down a ladder outside the place leading to the upper room.

"Did it work all right, sir?" he asked.

"Is that Carter?" I said.

"Sure that's me," came the cheery response. "Stand by now and we'll run her in. Then I'll show you where you are to sleep!"

We stowed the car away and he took me upstairs to his quarters, a bright little room with electric light, a table with a red cloth, a cheerful open fire and two beds. The walls were ornamented with pictures cut from the American Sunday supplements, mostly feminine and horsy studies.

"It's a bit rough, mister," said Carter, "but it's the best I can do. Gee! But you look that dawggorn tired I guess you could sleep anywheres!"

He was a friendly fellow, pleasant-looking in an ugly way, with a button nose and honest eyes.

"Say, but I like to think of the way we fooled them Deutschers," he chuckled. He kept on chuckling to himself whilst I took off my boots and began to undress.

"That there is your bed," he said, pointing; "the footman used to sleep there but they grabbed him for the army. There's a pair of Mr Gerry's pyjamas for you and you'll find a cup of cocoa down warming by the fire. It's all a bit rough, but it's the best we can do. I guess you want to go to sleep mortal bad, so I'll be going down. The bed's clean... there are clean sheets on it..."

"But I won't turn you out of your room," I said." There are two beds. You must take yours."

"Don't you fret yourself about me," he answered. "I'll make myself comfortable down in the garage. I don't often see a gentleman in this dawggorn country, and when I do I know how to treat him."

He wouldn't listen to me, but stumped off down the stairs. As he went I heard him murmuring to himself:

"Gee! But we surely fooled those Deutschers some!"

I drank this admirable fellow's cocoa; I warmed myself at his fire. Then with a thankful heart I crawled into bed and sank into a deep and dreamless sleep.

12

HIS EXCELLENCY THE GENERAL IS WORRIED

I sat with Monica in her boudoir, which, unlike the usual run of German rooms, had an open fireplace in which a cheerful fire was burning. Monica, in a ravishing kimono, was perched on the leather railed seat running round the fireplace, one little foot in a satin slipper held out to the blaze. In that pretty room she made a charming picture, which for a moment almost made me forget the manifold dangers besetting me.

The doughty Carter had acquitted himself nobly of his task. When I awoke, feeling like a giant refreshed, he had the fire blazing merrily in the fireplace, while on the table a delicious breakfast of tea and fried eggs and biscuits was spread.

"There ain't no call to mess yourself up inside with that dam' war bread of theirs," he chirped. "Miss Monica, she lets me have biscuits, same like she has herself. I always calls her Miss Monica," he explained, "like what they did over at her uncle's place in Long Island, where I used to work."

After breakfast he produced hot water, a safety razor and other toilet requisites, a clean shirt and collar, an overcoat and a Stetson hat—all from Gerry's wardrobe, I presumed. My boots, too, were beautifully polished, and it was as a new man altogether, fresh in mind and clean in body, that I presented myself, about ten o'clock in the morning, at the front door and demanded the "Frau Gräfin." By Carter's advice I had removed my moustache, and my clean-shaven countenance, together with my black felt hat and dark overcoat, gave me, I think, that appearance of rather dour respectability which one looks for in a male attendant.

Now Monica and I sat and reviewed the situation together.

"German servants spend their lives in prying into their masters' affairs," she said, "but we shan't be interrupted here. That door leads into Gerry's room: he was asleep when I went in just now. I'll take you in to him presently. Now tell me about yourself... and Francis!"

I told her again, but at greater length, all I knew about Francis, his mission into Germany, his long silence.

"I acted on impulse," I said, "but, believe me, I acted for the best. Only, everything seems to have conspired against me. I appear to have walked straight into a mesh of the most appalling complications which reach right up to the Throne."

"Never mind, Des," she said, leaning over and putting a little hand on my arm, "it was for Francis; you and I would do anything to help him, wouldn't we?... if he is still alive. Impulse is not such a bad thing, after all. If I had acted on impulse once, maybe poor Francis would not now be in the fix he is..."

And she sighed.

"Things look black enough, Des," she went on. "Maybe you and I won't get the chance of another chat like this again and that's why I'm going to tell you something I have never told anybody else. I am only telling you so as you will know that, whatever happens, you will always find in me an ally in your search... though, tied as I am, I scarcely think I can ever help you much.

"Your brother wanted me to marry him. I liked him better than anybody else I had ever met... or have ever met since, for that matter... Daddy was dead, I was absolutely free to please myself, so no difficulties stood in the way. But your brother was proud... his pride was greater than his love for me, I told him when we parted... and he wouldn't hear of marriage until he had made himself independent, though I had enough for both of us. He wanted me to wait a year or two until he had got his business started properly, but his pride angered me and I wouldn't.

"So we quarrelled and I went abroad with Mrs. Rushwood. Francis never wrote: all I heard about him was an occasional scrap in your letters. Mrs. Rushwood was crazy about titles, and she ran me round from court to court, always looking for what she called a suitable *parti* for me. At Vienna we met Rachwitz... he was very good looking and very well mannered and seemed to be really fond of me.

"Well, I gave Francis another chance. I wrote him a friendly letter and told him about Rachwitz wanting to marry me and asked his advice. He wrote me back a beastly letter, a wicked letter, Des. 'Any girl who is fool enough to sell herself for a title,' he said, 'richly deserves a German husband.' What do you think of that?"

"Poor old Francis," I said. "He was terribly fond of you, Monica!"

"Well, his letter did it. I married Rachwitz... and have been miserable ever since. I'm not going to bore you with a long story about my matrimonial troubles. No! I'm not going to cry either! I'm not crying! Karl is not a bad man, as German men go, and he's a gentleman, but his love affairs and his drunken parties and his attitude of mind towards me... it was so utterly different from everything I had been used to. Then you know, I left him..."

"But, Monica," I exclaimed, "what are you doing here then?"

She sighed wearily.

"I'm a German by marriage, Des," she said, "you can't get away from that. My husband's country... my country... is at war and the wives must play their part, wherever their heart is. Karl never asked me to come back, I'll give him credit for that. I came of my own accord because I felt my place was here. So I go round to needlework parties and sewing bees and Red Cross matinées and try to be civil to the German women and listen to their boasting and bragging about their army, their hypocrisy about Belgium, their vilification of the best friends Daddy and I ever had, you English! But doing my duty by my husband does not forbid me to help my friends when they are in danger. That's why you can count on me, Des."

And she gave me her hand.

"I want to be frank with you, too," I said, "so, whatever happens to me, you won't feel I have deceived you about things. I can't say much because my secret is not healthy for anyone to share, and, should they trace any connection between you and me, if they get me, it will be better for you not to have known anything compromising. But I want to tell you this. There is a consideration at stake which is higher than my own safety, higher even than Francis'. I don't believe I am afraid to die: if I escape here, I shall probably get killed at the front sooner or later: it is because of this consideration I speak of that I want to get away with my life back to England."

Monica laughed happily.

"Why do men always take us women to be fools?" she said. "You're a dangerous man to have around, Des, I know that, without worrying my head about any old secret. But you are my friend and Francis' brother and I'm going to help you.

"Now, listen! Old von Boden was at that party last night: he came in late. Rudi von Boden, he told me, is going to take despatches to Rumania, to Mackensen's headquarters. Well, I telephoned the old man this morning and asked him if Rudi would take a parcel for me to Karl. He said he would and the General is coming here to lunch today to fetch it.

"Von Boden is an old beast and runs after every woman he meets. He is by way of being partial to me, if you please, sir. I think I should be able to find out from him what are the latest developments in your case. There's nothing in the paper this morning about the affair at the Esplanade. But then, these things are always hushed up."

"He'll hardly say much in the circumstances," I objected. "After all, the Kaiser is involved..."

"My dear Des, opinion of feminine intelligence in military circles in this country is so low that the women in the army set at Court are very often far better informed than the General Staff. Von Boden will tell me all I want to know."

What a girl she was!

"About your friend, the clubfooted man," she went on, "I'm rather puzzled. He must be a person of considerable importance to be fetched by special train straight into the Emperor's private apartments, where very few people ever penetrate, I assure you. But I've never heard of him. He's certainly not a Court official. Nor is he the head of the Political Police... that's Henninger, a friend of Karl's. Still, there are people of great importance working in dark places in this country and I guess Clubfoot must be one of them.

"Now, I think I ought to take you in to Gerry. I want to speak to you about him, Des. I daren't tell him who you are. Gerry's not himself. He's been a nervous wreck ever since his accident and I can't trust him. He's a very conventional man and his principles would never hear of me harbouring a... a..."

"Spy?" I suggested.

"No, a friend," she corrected. "So you'll just have to be a male nurse, I guess. A German-American would be best, I think, as you'll have to read the German papers to Gerry—he doesn't know a word of German. Then, you must have a name of some kind..."

"Frederick Meyer," I suggested promptly, "from Pittsburg. It'll have to be Pittsburg: Francis went there for a bit, you know: he wrote me a lot about the place, and I've seen pictures of it, too. It's the only American city I know anything about."

"Let it be Meyer from Pittsburg, then," smiled Monica, "but you've got a terrible English accent, Des. I guess we'll have to tell Gerry you were years nursing in London before the war."

She hesitated a moment, then added:

"Des, I'm afraid you'll find Gerry very trying. He's awfully irritable and... and very spiteful. So you must be careful not to give yourself away."

I had only met the brother once and my recollection of him was of a good looking, rather spoilt young man. He had been brought up entirely in the States by the Long Island uncle whose great fortune he had inherited.

"You'll be quite safe up here for the present," Monica went on. "You'll sleep in the little room off Gerry's and I'll have your meals served there too. After I have found out from the General how things stand, we'll decide what's to be done next."

"I'll be very wary with Master Gerry," I said. "But, Monica, though he has only seen me once, he knows Francis pretty well and we are rather alike. Do you think he'll recognize me?"

"Why, Desmond, it's years since he saw you. And you're not much like Francis with your moustache off. If you're careful, it'll be all right! It isn't for long, either. Now we'll go in. Come along."

As we entered, a petulant voice cried:

"Is that you, Monica? Say, am I to be left alone all the morning?"

"Gerry dear," answered Monica very sweetly, "I've been engaging someone to look after you a bit. Come here, Meyer! This is Frederick Meyer, Gerry!"

I should never have recognized the handsome, rather indolent youth I had met in London in the pale man with features drawn with pain who gazed frowningly at me from the bed.

"Who is he? Where did you get him from? Does he know German?"

He shot a string of questions at Monica, who answered them in her sweet, patient way.

He was apparently satisfied, for, when Monica presently got up to leave us, he threw me an armful of German papers and bade me read to him.

I had not sat with him for ten minutes before I realized what an impossible creature the man was. Nothing I could do was right. Now he didn't want to hear the war news, then it was the report of the Reichstag debate that bored him, now I didn't read loud enough, then my voice jarred on him. Finally, he snatched the paper out of my hand.

"I can't understand half you say," he cried in accents shrill with irritability; "you mouth and mumble like an Englishman. You say you are an American?"

"Yes, sir," I answered meekly, "but I resided for many years in England."

"Well, it's a good thing you're not there now. Those English are just plumb crazy. They'll never whip Germany, not if they try for a century. Why, look what this country has done in this war? Nothing can stand against her! It's organization, that's what it is! The Germans lead the world. Take their doctors! I have been to every specialist in America about my back and paid them thousands of dollars. And what good did they do me? Not a thing. I come to Germany, they charge me a quarter of the fees, and I feel a different man already. Before tackling the Germans, the English..."

Thus he ran on. I knew the type well, the American who is hypnotized by German efficiency and thoroughness so completely that he does not see the reverse side of the medal.

He exhausted himself on the topic at last and bade me read to him again.

"Read about the affair at the Hotel Esplanade last night," he commanded.

I had kept an eye open for this very item but, as Monica had said, the papers contained no hint of it. I wondered how Gerry knew about it. Monica would I not have told him.

"What affair do you mean?" I said. "There is nothing about it in the papers."

"Of course there is, you fool. What is the use of my hiring you to read the papers to me if you can't find news that's spread all over the place? It's no use giving me the paper... you know I can't read it! Here, Josef will know!"

A man-servant had come noiselessly into the room with some clothes.

Gerry turned to him.

"Josef, where did you see that story you were telling me about an English spy assaulting a man at the Esplanade last night?"

"Dot ain't in de paper, sir. I haf heard dis from de chauffeur of de Biedermanns next door. He wass at de hotel himself wid hiss shentleman lars' night at de dance. Dey won't put dat in no paper, sir."

And the man chuckled.

I felt none too comfortable during all this and was glad to be told to read on and be damned.

I read to the young American all the morning. He went on exactly like a very badly brought up child. He was fretful and quarrelsome and sometimes abusive, and I had some difficulty in keeping my temper. He continually recurred to my English accent and jeered so offensively and so pointedly at what he called "your English friends" that I began to believe there was some purpose behind his attitude. But it was only part of his invalid's fractiousness, for when the valet, Josef, appeared with the luncheon tray, the American seemed anxious to make amends for his behaviour.

"I'm afraid I'm a bit trying at times, Meyer," he said with a pleasant smile. "But you're a good fellow. Go and have your lunch. You needn't come back till four: I always sleep after luncheon. Here, have a cigar!"

I took the cigar with all humility as beseemed my role and followed the valet into an adjoining room, where the table was laid for me. I am keenly sensitive to outside influences, and I felt instinctively distrustful of the man Josef. I expect he resented my intrusion into a sphere where his influence had probably been supreme and where he had doubtless managed to secure a good harvest of pickings.

He left me to my luncheon and went away. After an excellent lunch, washed down by some first-rate claret, I was enjoying my cigar over a book when Josef reappeared again.

"The Frau Gräfin will see you downstairs!" he said.

Monica received me in a morning-room (the apartment was on two floors). She was very much agitated and had lost all her habitual calm.

"Des," she said, "von Boden has been here!"

"Well!" I replied eagerly.

"I wasn't very successful," she went on; "I'm in deep water, Des, and that's the truth. I have never seen the old General as he was today. He's a frightful bully and tyrant, but even his worst enemy never accused him of cowardice. But, Des, today the man was cowed. He seemed to be in terror of his life and I had the greatest difficulty in making him say anything at all about your affair.

"I made a joking allusion to the escapade at the hotel last night and he said:

"'Yesterday may prove the ruin of not only my career but that of my son's also. Yesterday gained for me as an enemy, Madam, a man whom it spells ruin, perhaps death, to offend.'

"'You mean the Emperor?' I asked.

"'The Emperor!' he said. 'Oh! of course he's furious. No, I was not speaking of the Emperor!' Then he changed the subject and it took me all my tact to get back to it. I asked him if they had caught the author of the attack at the Esplanade. He said, no, but it was only a question of time: the fellow couldn't escape. I said I supposed they would offer a reward and publish a description of the assailant all over the country. He told me they would do nothing of the sort.

"'The public will hear nothing about the affair,' he said, 'and if you will take my advice, Countess, you will forget all about it. In any case, the Princess Radolin is writing to all her guests at the ball last night to urge them strongly to say nothing about the incident. The employees of the hotel will keep their mouths shut. The interests at stake forbid that there should be any attempt whatsoever made in public to throw light on the affair.'

"That is all I could get out of him. But I have something further to tell you. The General went away immediately after lunch. Almost as soon as he had gone I was called to the telephone. Dr Henninger was there: he is the head of the Political Police, you know. He gave me the same advice as the General, namely, to forget all about what occurred at the Esplanade last night. And then the Princess Radolin rang me up to say the same thing. She seemed very frightened: she was quite tearful. Someone evidently had scared her badly."

"Monica," I said, "it's quite clear I can't stay here. My dear girl, if I am discovered in your house, there is no knowing what trouble may not come upon you."

"If there is any risk," she answered, "it's a risk I am ready to take. You have nowhere to go to in Berlin, and if you are caught outside they might find out where you had been hiding and then we should be as badly off as before. No, you stay right on here, and maybe in a day or two I can get you away. I've been thinking something out.

"Karl has a place near the Dutch frontier, Schloss Bellevue, it is called, close to Cleves. It's an old place and has been in the family for generations. Karl, however, only uses it as a shooting-box: we had big shoots up there every autumn before the war.

"There has been no shooting there for two years now and the place is overstocked with game. The Government has been appealing to people with shooting preserves to kill their game and put it on the market, so I had arranged to go up to Bellevue this month and see the agent about this. I thought if I could prevail on Gerry to come with me, you could accompany him and you might get across the Dutch frontier from there. It's only about fifteen miles away from the Castle. If I can get a move on Gerry, there is no reason why we shouldn't go away in a day or two. In the meantime you'll be quite safe here."

I told her I must think it over: she seemed to be risking too much. But I think my mind was already made up. I could not bring destruction on this faithful friend.

Then I went upstairs again to Gerry, who was in as vile a temper as before. His lunch had disagreed with him: he hadn't slept: the room was not hot enough... these were a few of the complaints he showered at me as soon as I appeared. He was in his most impish and malicious mood. He sent me running hither and thither: he gave me an order and withdrew it in the same breath: my complacency seemed to irritate him, to encourage him to provoke me.

At last he came back to his old sore subject, my English accent.

"I guess our good American is too homely for a fine English gentleman like you," he said; "but I believe you'll as lief speak as you were taught before you're through with this city. An English accent is not healthy in Berlin at present, Mister

Meyer, sir, and you'd best learn to talk like the rest of us if you want to keep on staying in this house.

"I'm in no state to be worried just now and I've no notion of having the police in here because some of their dam' plain-clothes men have heard my attendant saying 'charnce' and 'darnce' like any Britisher—especially with this English spy running round loose. By the way, you'll have to be registered? Has my sister seen about it yet?"

I said she was attending to it.

"I want to know if she's done it. I'm a helpless cripple and I can't get a thing done for me. Have you given her your papers? Yes, or no?"

This was a bad fix. With all the persistence of the invalid, the man was harping on his latest whim.

So I lied. The Countess had my papers, I said.

Instantly he rang the bell and demanded Monica and had fretted himself into a fine state by the time she appeared.

"What's this I hear, Monica?" he cried in his high-pitched, querulous voice. "Hasn't Meyer been registered with the police yet?"

"I'm going to see to it myself in the morning, Gerry," she said.

"In the morning. In the morning!" he cried, throwing up his hands. "Good God, how can you be so shiftless? A law is a law. The man's papers must be sent in today... this instant."

Monica looked appealingly at me.

"I'm afraid I'm to blame, sir," I said. "The fact is, my passport is not quite in order and I shall have to take it to the embassy before I send it to the police."

Then I saw Josef standing by the bed, a salver in his hand.

"Zom letters, sir," he said to Gerry.

I wondered how long he had been in the room.

Gerry waved the letters aside and burst into a regular screaming fit. He wouldn't have things done that way in the house; he wouldn't have unknown foreigners brought in, with the city thick with spies—especially people with an English accent—his nerves wouldn't stand it: Monica ought to know better, and so on and so forth. The long and short of it was that I was ordered to produce my passport immediately. Monica was to ring up the embassy to ask them to stretch a point and see to it out of office hours, then Josef should take me round to the police.

I don't know how we got out of that room. It was Monica, with her sweet womanly tact, who managed it. I believe the madman even demanded to see my passport, but Monica scraped me through that trap as well.

I had left my hat and coat in the entrance hall downstairs. I put on my coat, then went to Monica in the morning-room.

There was much she wanted to say—I could see it in her eyes—but I think she gathered from my face what I was going to do, so she said nothing.

At the door I said aloud, for the benefit of Josef, who was on the stairs:

"Very good, my lady. I will come straight back from the embassy and then go with Josef to the police."

The next moment I was adrift in Berlin.

13

I FIND ACHILLES IN HIS TENT

Outside darkness had fallen. I had a vague suspicion that the house might be watched, but I found the Bendler-Strasse quite undisturbed. It ran its quiet, aristocratic length to the tangle of bare branches marking the Tiergarten-Strasse with not so much as a dog to strike terror into the heart of the amateur spy. Even in the Tiergarten-Strasse, where the Jewish millionaires live, there was little traffic and few people about, and I felt singularly unromantic as I walked briskly along the clean pavements towards Unter den Linden.

Once more the original object of my journey into Germany stood clearly before me. An extraordinary series of adventures had deflected me from my course, but never from my purpose. I realized that I should never feel happy in my mind again if I left Germany without being assured as to my brother's fate. And now I was on the threshold either of a great discovery or of an overwhelming disappointment.

For the street called In den Zelten was my next objective. I knew I might be on the wrong track altogether in my interpretation of what I was pleased to term in my mind the message from Francis. If I had read it falsely—if, perhaps, it were not from him at all—then all the hopes I had built on this mad dash into the enemy's country would collapse like a house of cards. Then, indeed, I should be in a sorry pass.

But my luck was in, I felt. Hitherto, I had triumphed over all difficulties. I would trust in my destiny to the last.

I had taken the precaution of turning up my overcoat collar and of pulling my hat well down over my eyes, but no one troubled me. I reflected that only Clubfoot and Schmalz were in a position to recognize me and that, if I steered clear of places like hotels and restaurants and railway stations, where criminals always seem to be caught, I might continue to enjoy comparative immunity. But the trouble was the passport question. That reminded me.

I must get rid of Semlin's passport. As I walked along I tore it into tiny pieces, dropping each fragment at a good interval from the other. It cost me something to do it, for a passport is always useful to flash in the eyes of the ignorant. But this passport was dangerous. It might denounce me to a man who would not otherwise recognize me.

I had some difficulty in finding In den Zelten. I had to ask the way, once of a postman and once of a wounded soldier who was limping along with crutches. Finally, I found it, a narrowish street running off a corner of the great square in front of the Reichstag, No. 2 was the second house on the right.

I had no plan. Nevertheless, I walked boldly upstairs. There was but one flat on each floor. At the third story I halted, rather out of breath, in front of a door with a small brass plate inscribed with the name "Eugen Kore." I rang the bell boldly.

An elderly man-servant opened the door.

"Is Herr Eugen Kore at home?" I asked.

The man looked at me suspiciously.

"Has the gentleman an appointment?" he said.

"No," I replied.

"Then the Herr will not receive the gentleman," came the answer, and the man made as though to close the door.

I had an inspiration.

"A moment!" I cried, and I added the word "Achilles" in a low voice.

The servant opened the door wide to me.

"Why didn't you say that at once?" he said. "Please step in. I will see if the Herr can receive you."

He led the way through a hall into a sitting-room and left me there. The place was a perfect museum of art treasures, old Dutch and Italian masters on the walls, some splendid Florentine chests, a fine old dresser loaded with ancient pewter. On a mantel shelf was an extraordinary collection of old keys, each with its label. "Key of the fortress of Spandau, 1715."

"Key of the Postern Gate of the Pasha's Palace at Belgrade, 1810,"

"House Key from Nuremberg, 1567," were some of the descriptions I read.

Then a voice behind me said:

"Ah! you admire my little treasures!"

Turning, I saw a short, stout man, of a marked Jewish appearance, with a bald head, a fat nose, little beady eyes and a large waist.

"Eugen Kore!" he introduced himself with a bow.

"Meyer!" I replied, in the German fashion.

"And what can we do for Herr... Meyer?" he asked in oily tones, pausing just long enough before he pronounced the name I gave to let me see that he believed it to be a pseudonym.

"I believe you know a friend of mine, whose address I am anxious to find," I said.

"Ah!" sighed the little Jew, "a man of affairs like myself meets so many people that he may be pardoned... What did you say his name was, this friend of yours?"

I thought I would try the effect of the name "Eichenholz" upon this enigmatic creature.

"Eichenholz? Eichenholz?" Kore repeated. "I seem to know the name... it seems familiar... now let me see again... Eichenholz, Eichenholz..."

While he was speaking he unlocked one of the oak cabinets and a safe came to view. Opening this, he brought out a ledger and ran his finger down the names. Then he shut the book, replaced it, locked the safe and the cabinet, and turned to me again.

"Yes," he said, "I know the name."

His reticence was disconcerting.

"Can you tell me where I can find him?" I asked.

"Yes," was the reply.

I was getting a trifle nettled.

"Well, where?" I queried.

"This is all very well, young sir," said the Jew. "You come in here from nowhere, you introduce yourself as Meyer; you ask me 'Who?' and 'What?' and 'Where?'—questions that, mark you, in my business, may have valuable answers. We private enquiry agents must live, my dear sir, we must eat and drink like other men, and these are hard times, very hard times. I will ask you a question if I may. Meyer? Who is Meyer? Everybody in this country is called Meyer!"

I smiled at this bizarre speech.

"This Eichenholz now," I said, "... supposing he were my brother."

"He might congratulate himself," Kore said, blinking his little lizard eyes.

"And he sent me word to call and see you to find out his whereabouts. You seem to like riddles, Herr Kore... I will read you one!"

And I read him the message from Francis... all but the first two lines.

The little Jew beamed with delight.

"Ach! that is bright!" he cried, "Oi, oi, oi, but he is smart, this Herr Eichenholz! Who'd have thought of that? Brilliant, brilliant!"

"As you say, Herr Kore, enquiry agents must live, and I am quite prepared to pay for the information I require..."

I pulled out my portfolio as I spoke.

"The matter is quite simple," Kore replied. "It is already arranged. The charge is five hundred marks. My client said to me the last time I saw him, 'Kore,' he said, 'if one should come asking news of me you will give him the word and he will pay you five hundred marks.'"

"The word?" I said.

"The word," he repeated.

"You must take Dutch money," I said. "Here you are... work it out in gulden... and I'll pay!"

He manipulated a stump of pencil on a writing block and I paid him his money.

Then he said:

"Boonekamp!"

"Boonekamp?" I echoed stupidly.

"That's the word," the little Jew chuckled, laughing at my dumbfounded expression, "and, if you want to know, I understand it as little as you do."

"But... Boonekamp," I repeated. "Is it a man's name, a place? It sounds Dutch. Have you no idea?... come, I'm ready to pay."

"Perhaps..." the Jew began.

"What? Perhaps what?" I exclaimed impatiently.

"Possibly..."

"Out with it, man!" I cried, "And say what you mean."

"Perhaps if I could render to the gentleman the service I rendered to his brother, I might be able to throw light..."

"What service did you render to my brother?" I demanded hastily. "I'm in the dark."

"Has the gentleman no little difficulty perhaps?... about his military service, about his papers? The gentleman is young and strong... has he been to the front? Was life irksome there? Did he ever long for the sweets of home life? Did he never envy those who have been medically rejected? The rich men's sons, perhaps, with clever fathers who know how to get what they want?"

His little eyes bored into mine like gimlets.

I began to understand.

"And if I had?"

"Then all old Kore can say is that the gentleman, has come to the right shop, as his gracious brother did. How can we serve the gentleman now? What are his requirements? It is a difficult, a dangerous business. It costs money, much money, but it can be arranged... it can be arranged."

"But if you do for me what you did for my brother," I said, "I don't see how that helps to explain this word, this clue to his address!"

"My dear sir, I am as much in the dark as you are yourself about the significance of this word. But I can tell you this, your brother, thanks to my intervention, found himself placed in a situation in which he might well have come across this word..."

"Well?" I said impatiently.

"Well, if we obliged the gentleman as we obliged his brother, the gentleman might be taken where his brother was taken, the gentleman is young and smart, he might perhaps find a clue..."

"Stop talking riddles, for Heaven's sake!" I cried in exasperation, "And answer my questions plainly. First, what did you do for my brother?"

"Your brother had deserted from the front—that is the most difficult class of business we have to deal with—we procured him a *permit de séjour* for fifteen days and a post in a safe place where no enquiries would be made after him."

"And then?" I cried, trembling with curiosity.

The Jew shrugged his shoulders, waving his hands to and fro in the air.

"Then he disappeared. I saw him a few days before he went, and he gave me the instructions I have repeated to you for anybody who should come asking for him."

"But didn't he tell you where he was going?"

"He didn't even tell me he was going, Herr. He just vanished."

"When was this?"

"Somewhere about the first week in July... it was the week of the bad news from France."

The message was dated July 1st, I remembered.

"I have a good set of Swedish papers," the Jew continued, "very respectable timber merchant... with those one could five in the best hotels and no one say a word. Or Hungarian papers, a party rejected medically... very safe those, but perhaps the gentleman doesn't speak Hungarian. That would be essential."

"I am in the same case as my brother," I said. "I must disappear."

"Not a deserter, Herr?" The Jew cringed at the word.

"Yes," I said. "After all, why not?"

"I daren't do this kind of business any more, my dear sir, I really daren't! They are making it too dangerous."

"Come, come!" I said, "You were boasting just now that you could smooth out any difficulties. You can produce me a very satisfactory passport from somewhere, I am sure!"

"Passport! Out of the question, my dear sir! Let once one of my passports go wrong and I am ruined. Oh, no! No passports where deserters are concerned! I don't like the business... it's not safe! At the beginning of the war... ah! that was different! Oi, oi, but they ran from the Yser and from Ypres! Oi, oi, and from Verdun! But now the police are more watchful. No! It is not worth it! It would cost you too much money, besides."

I thought the miserable cur was trying to raise the price on me, but I was mistaken. He was frightened: the business was genuinely distasteful to him.

I tried, as a final attempt to persuade him, an old trick: I showed him my money. He wavered at once, and, after many objections, protesting to the last, he left the room. He returned with a handful of filthy papers.

"I oughtn't to do it; I know I shall rue it; but you have overpersuaded me and I liked Herr Eichenholz, a noble gentleman and free with his money—see here, the papers of a waiter, Julius Zimmermann, called up with the Landwehr but discharged medically unfit, military pay-book and *permis de séjour* for fifteen days. These papers are only a guarantee in case you come across the police: no questions will be asked where I shall send you."

"But a fifteen days' permit!" I said. "What am I to do at the end of that time?"

"Leave it to me," Kore said craftily. "I will get it renewed for you. It will be all right!"

"But in the meantime..." I objected.

"I place you as waiter with a friend of mine who is kind to poor fellows like yourself. Your brother was with him."

"But I want to be free to move around."

"Impossible," the Jew answered firmly. "You must get into your part and live quietly in seclusion until the enquiries after you have abated. Then we may see as to what is next to be done. There you are, a fine set of papers and a safe, comfortable life far away from the trenches—all snug and secure—cheap (in spite of the danger to me), because you are a lad of spirit and I liked your brother... ten thousand marks!"

I breathed again. Once we had reached the haggling stage, I knew the papers would be mine all right. With Semlin's money and my own I found I had about £550, but I had no intention of paying out £500 straight away. So I beat the fellow down unmercifully and finally secured the lot for 3,600 marks—£180.

But, even after I had paid the fellow his money, I was not done with him. He had his eye on his perquisites.

"Your clothes will never do," he said; "such richness of apparel, such fine stuff—we must give you others." He rang the bell.

The old man-servant appeared.

"A waiter's suit—for the Linien-Strasse!" he said.

Then he led me into a bedroom where a worn suit of German shoddy was spread out on a sofa. He made me change into it, and then handed me a threadbare green overcoat and a greasy green felt hat.

"So!" he said. "Now if you don't shave for a day or two, you will look the part to the life!"—a remark which, while encouraging, was hardly complimentary.

He gave me a muffler to tie round my neck and lower part of my face and, with that greasy hat pulled down over my eyes and in those worn and shrunken clothes, I must say I looked a pretty villainous person, the very antithesis of the sleek, well-dressed young fellow that had entered the flat half an hour before.

"Now, Julius," said Kore humorously," come, my lad, and we will seek out together the good situation I have found for you."

A horse-cab was at the door and we entered it together. The Jew chatted pleasantly as we rattled through the darkness. He complimented me on my ready wit in deciphering Francis' message.

"How do you like my idea?" he said, "'Achilles in his Tent'... that is the device of the hidden part of my business—you observe the parallel, do you not? Achilles holding himself aloof from the army and young men like yourself who prefer the gentle pursuits of peace to the sterner profession of war! Clients of mine who have enjoyed a classical education have thought very highly of the humour of my device."

The cab dropped us at the corner of the Friedrich-Strasse, which was ablaze with light from end to end, and the Linien-Strasse, a narrow squalid thoroughfare of dirty houses and mean shops. The street was all but deserted at that hour save for an occasional policeman, but from cellars with steps leading down from the street came the jingle of automatic pianos and bursts of merriment to show that the Linien-Strasse was by no means asleep.

Before one of these cellar entrances the Jew stopped. At the foot of the steep staircase leading down from the street was a glazed door, its panels all glistening with moisture from the heated atmosphere within. Kore led the way down, I following.

A nauseous wave of hot air, mingled with rank tobacco smoke, smote us full as we opened the door. At first I could see nothing except a very fat man against a dense curtain of smoke, sitting at a table before an enormous glass goblet of beer. Then, as the haze drifted before the draught, I distinguished the outline of a long, low-ceilinged room, with small tables set along either side and a little bar, presided over by a tawdry female with chemically tinted hair, at the end. Most of the tables were occupied, and there was almost as much noise as smoke in the place.

A woman's voice screamed: "Shut the door, can't you, I'm freezing!" I obeyed and, following Kore to a table, sat down. A man in his shirt-sleeves, who was pulling beer at the bar, left his beer-engine and, coming across the room to Kore, greeted him cordially, and asked him what we would take.

Kore nudged me with his elbow.

"We'll take a Boonekamp each, Haase," he said.

14

CLUBFOOT COMES TO HAASE'S

Kore presently retired to an inner room with the man in shirt-sleeves, whom I judged to be the landlord, and in a little the flaxen-haired lady at the bar beckoned me over and bade me join them.

"This is Julius Zimmermann, the young man I have spoken of," said the Jew; then turning to me:

"Herr Haase is willing to take you on as waiter here on my recommendation, Julius. See that you do not make me repent of my kindness!"

Here the man in shirt-sleeves, a great, fat fellow with a bullet head and a huge double chin, chuckled loudly.

"Kolossal!" he cried. "Herr Kore loves his joke! Ausgezeichnet!" And he wagged his head roguishly at me.

On that Kore took his leave, promising to look in and see how I was faring in a few days' time. The landlord opened a low door in the corner and revealed a kind of large cupboard, windowless and horribly stale and stuffy, where there were two unsavoury-looking beds.

"You will sleep here with Otto," said the landlord. Pointing to a dirty white apron lying on one of the beds, he bade me take off my overcoat and jacket and put it on.

"It was Johann's," he said, "but Johann won't want it any more. A good lad, Johann, but rash. I always said he would come to a bad end." And he laughed noisily.

"You can go and help with the waiting now," he went on. "Otto will show you what to do!"

And so I found myself, within twenty-four hours, spy, male nurse and waiter in turn.

I am loth to dwell on the degradation of the days that followed. That cellar tavern was a foul sink of iniquity, and in serving the dregs of humanity that gathered nightly there I felt I had indeed sunk to the lowest depths. The place was a regular thieves' kitchen... what is called in the hideous Yiddish jargon that is the criminal slang of modern Germany a "Kaschemme." Never in my life have I seen such brutish faces as those that leered at me nightly through the smoke haze as I shuffled from table to table in my mean German clothes. Gallows' birds, sneak thieves, receivers, bullies, prostitutes and harpies of every description came together every evening in Herr Haase's beer-cellar. Many of the men wore the soiled and faded field-grey of the soldier back from the front, and in looking at their sordid, vulpine faces, inflamed with drink, I felt I could fathom the very soul of Belgium's misery.

The conversation was all of crime and deeds of violence. The men back from the front told gloatingly of rapine and feastings in lonely Belgian villages or dwelt ghoulishly on the horrors of the battlefield, the mounds of decaying corpses, the ghastly mutilations they had seen in the dead. There were tales, too, of "vengeance" wreaked on "the treacherous English." One story, in particular, of the fate of a Scottish sergeant... "der Hochländer" they called him in this oft-told tale... still makes me quiver with impotent rage when I think of it.

One evening the name of the Hotel Esplanade caught my ear. I approached the table and found two flashily dressed bullies and a bedraggled drab from the streets talking in admiration of my exploit.

"Clubfoot met his match that time," the woman cried. "The dirty dog! But why didn't this English spy make a job of it and kill the scum? Pah!"

And she spat elegantly into the sawdust on the floor.

"I wouldn't be in that fellow's shoes for something," muttered one of the men. "No one ever had the better of Clubfoot yet. Do you remember Meinhardt, Franz? He tried to cheat Clubfoot, and we know what happened to him!"

"They're raking the whole city for this Englishman," answered the other man. "Vogel, who works for Section Seven, you know the man I mean, was telling me. They've done every hotel in Berlin and the suburbs, but they haven't found him. They raided Bauer's in the Favoriten-Strasse last night. The Englishman wasn't there, but they got three or four others they were looking for—Fritz and another deserter included. I was nearly there myself!"

I was always hearing references of this kind to my exploit. I was never spoken of except in terms of admiration, but the name of Clubfoot—der Stelze—excited only execration and terror.

I lived in daily fear of a raid at Haase's. Why the place had escaped so long, with all that riff-raff assembled there nightly, I couldn't imagine. It was one of those defects in German organization which puzzle the best of us at times. In the meantime, I was powerless to escape. The first thing Haase had done was to take away my papers—to send them to the police, as he explained—but he never gave them back, and when I asked for them he put me off with an excuse.

I was a virtual prisoner in the place. On my feet from morning till night, I had indeed few opportunities for going out; but once, during a slack time in the afternoon, when

I broached the subject to the landlord, he refused harshly to let me out of his sight.

"The street is not healthy for you just now. You would be a danger to yourself and to all of us!" he said.

My life in that foul den was a burden to me. The living conditions were unspeakable. Otto, a pale and ill-tempered consumptive, compelled, like me, to rise in the darkness of the dawn, never washed, and his companionship in the stuffy hole where we slept was offensive beyond belief. He openly jeered at my early morning journeys out to a narrow, stinking court, where I exulted in the ice-cold water from the pump. And the food! It was only when I saw the mean victuals—the coarse and often tainted horseflesh, the unappetizing war-bread, the coffee substitute, and the rest—that I realized how Germany was suffering, though only through her poor as yet, from the British blockade. That thought used to help to overcome the nausea with which I sat down to eat.

Domestic life at Haase's was a hell upon earth. Haase himself was a drunken bully, who made advances to every woman he met, and whose complicated intrigues with the feminine portion of his clientèle led to frequent scenes with the fair-haired Hebe who presided at the bar and over his household. It was she and Otto who fared daily forth to take their places in the long queues that waited for hours with food cards outside the provision shops.

These trips seemed to tell upon her temper, which would flash out wrathfully at meal-times, when Haase began his inevitable grumbling about the food. As Otto took a malicious delight in these family scenes, I was frequently called upon to assume the rôle of peace-maker. More than once I intervened to save Madame from the violence she had called down upon herself by the sharpness of her tongue. She was a poor, faded creature, and the tragedy of it all was that she was in love with this degraded bully. She was grateful to me for my good offices,

I think, for, though she hardly ever addressed me, her manner was always friendly.

These days of dreary squalor would have been unbearable if it had not been for my elucidation of the word Boonekamp, which was said to hold the clue to my brother's address. On the wall in the cubby-hole where I slept was a tattered advertisement card of this *apéritif*—for such is the preparation—proclaiming it to be "Germany's Best Cordial." As I undressed at night, I often used to stare at this placard, wondering what connection Boonekamp could possibly have with my brother. I determined to take the first opportunity of examining the card itself. One morning, while Otto was out in the queue at the butcher's, I slipped away from the cellar to our sleeping-place and, lighting my candle, took down the card and examined it closely. It was perfectly plain, red letters on a green background in front, white at the back.

As I was replacing the card on the nail I saw some writing in pencil on the wall where the card had hung. My heart seemed to stand still with the joy of my discovery. For the writing was in my brother's neat, artistic hand, the words were English, and, best of all, my brother's initials were attached. This is what I read:

(Facsimile.) 5.7.16.
"You will find me at the Cafe Regina, Dusseldorf.—F. O."

After that I felt I could bear with everything. The message awakened hope that was fast dying in my my heart. At least on July 5th, Francis was alive. To that fact I clung as to a sheet-anchor. It gave me courage for the hardest part of all my experiences in Germany, those long days of waiting in that den of thieves. For I knew I must be patient. Presently, I hoped, I might extract my papers from Haase or persuade Kore, when he came back, to see me, to give me a permit that would enable me to get to Dusseldorf. But the term of my permit was fast running out and the Jew never came.

There were often moments when I longed to ask Haase or one of the others about the time my brother had served in that place. But I feared to draw attention to myself. No one asked any questions of me (questions as to personal antecedents were discouraged at Haase's), and, as long as I remained the unpaid, useful drudge I felt that my desire for obscurity would be respected. Desultory questions about my predecessors elicited no information about Francis. The Haase establishment seemed to have had a succession of vague and shadowy retainers.

Only about Johann, whose apron I wore, did Otto become communicative.

"A stupid fellow!" he declared. "He was well off here. Haase liked him, the customers liked him, especially the ladies. But he must fall in love with Frau Hedwig (the lady at the bar), then he quarrelled with Haase and threatened him—you know, about customers who haven't got their papers in order. The next time Johann went out, they arrested him. And he was shot at Spandau!"

"Shot?" I exclaimed. "Why?"

"As a deserter."

"But was he a deserter?"

"Ach! was! But he had a deserter's papers in his pockets... his own had vanished. Ach! it's a bad thing to quarrel with Haase!"

I made a point of keeping on the right side of the landlord after that. By my unfailing diligence I even managed to secure his grudging approval, though he was always ready to fly into a passion at the least opportunity.

One evening about six o'clock a young man, whom I had never seen among our regular customers, came down the stairs from the street and asked for Haase, who was asleep on the sofa in the inner room. At the sight of the youth, Frau Hedwig jumped off her perch behind the bar and vanished. She came back directly and, ignoring me, conducted the young man into the inner room, where he remained for about half an hour. Then he reappeared again, accompanied by Frau Hedwig, and went off.

I was shocked by the change in the appearance of the woman. Her face was pale, her eyes red with weeping, and her eyes kept wandering towards the door. It was a slack time of the day within and the cellar was free of customers.

"You look poorly, Frau Hedwig," I said. "Trouble with Haase again?"

She looked up at me and shook her head, her eyes brimming over. A tear ran down the rouge on her cheek.

"I must speak," she said. "I can't bear this suspense alone. You are a kind young man. You are discreet. Julius, there is trouble brewing for us!"

"What do you mean?" I asked. A foreboding of evil rose within me.

"Kore!" she whispered.

"Kore?" I echoed. "What of him?"

She looked fearfully about her.

"He was taken yesterday morning," she said.

"Do you mean arrested?" I exclaimed, unwilling to believe the staggering news.

"They entered his apartment early in the morning and seized him in bed. Ach! it is dreadful!" And she buried her face in her hands.

"But surely," I added soothingly, though with an icy fear at my heart, "there is no need to despair. What is an arrest today with all these regulations..."

The woman raised her face, pallid beneath its paint, to mine.

"Kore was shot at Moabit Prison this morning," she said in a low voice. "That young man brought the news just now." Then she added breathlessly, her words pouring out in a torrent:

"You don't know what this means to us. Haase had dealings with this Jew. If they have shot him, it is because they have found out from him all they want to know. That means our ruin, that means that Haase will go the same way as the Jew.

"But Haase is stubborn, foolhardy. The messenger warned him that a raid might be expected here at any moment. I have pleaded with him in vain. He believes that Kore has split; he believes the police may come, but he says they daren't touch him: he has been too useful to them: he knows too much. Ach, I am afraid! I am afraid!"

Haase's voice sounded from the inner room.

"Hedwig!" he called.

The woman hastily dried her eyes and disappeared through the door.

The coast was clear, if I wanted to escape, but where could I go, without a paper or passport, a hunted man?

The news of Kore's arrest and execution haunted me. Of course, the man was in a most perilous trade, and had probably been playing the game for years. But suppose they had tracked me to the house in the street called In den Zelten.

I crossed the room and opened the door to the street. I had never set foot outside since I had come, and, hopeless as it would be for me to attempt to escape, I thought I might reconnoitre the surroundings of the beer-cellar for the event of flight.

I lightly ran up the stairs to the street and nearly cannoned into a man who was lounging in the entrance. We both apologized, but he stared at me hard before he strolled on. Then I saw another man sauntering along on the opposite side of the street. Further away, at the corner, two men were loitering.

Every one of them had his eyes fixed on the cellar entrance at which I was standing.

I knew they could not see my face, for the street was but dimly lit, and behind me was the dark background of the cellar stairway. I took a grip on my nerves and very deliberately lit a cigarette and smoked it, as if I had come up from below to get a breath of fresh air. I waited a little while and then went down.

I was scarcely back in the cellar when Haase appeared from the inner room, followed by the woman. He carried himself erect, and his eyes were shining. I didn't like the man, but I must say he looked game. In his hand he carried my papers.

"Here you are, my lad," he said in quite a friendly tone, "put 'em in your pocket—you may want 'em tonight."

I glanced at the papers before I followed his advice.

He noted my action and laughed.

"They have told you about Johann," he said. "Never fear, Julius, you and I are good friends."

The papers were those of Julius Zimmermann all right.

We were having supper at one of the tables in the front room—there were only a couple of customers, as it was so early—when a man, a regular visitor of ours, came down the stairs hurriedly. He went straight over to Haase and spoke into his ear.

"Mind yourself, Haase," I heard him say. "Do you know who had Kore arrested and shot? It was Clubfoot. There is more in this than we know. Mind yourself and get out! In an hour or so it may be too late."

Then he scurried away, leaving me dazed.

"By God!" said the landlord, bringing a great fist down on the table so that the glasses rang, "They won't touch me. Not the devil himself will make me leave this house before they come, if coming they are!"

The woman burst into tears, while Otto blinked his watery eyes in terror. I sat and looked at my plate, my heart too full for words. It was bitter to have dared so much to get this far and then find the path blocked, as it seemed, by an insuperable barrier. They were after me all right: the mention of Clubfoot's name, the swift, stern retribution that had befallen Kore, made that certain—and I could do nothing. That cellar was a cul-de-sac, a regular trap, and I knew that if I stirred a foot from the house I should fall into the hands of those men keeping their silent vigil in the street.

Therefore, I must wait, as calmly as I might, and see what the evening would bring forth. Gradually the cellar filled up as people drifted in, but many familiar faces, I noticed, were missing. Evidently the ill tidings had spread. Once a man looked in for a glass of beer and drifted out again, leaving the door open. As I was closing it, I heard a muffled exclamation and the sound of a scuffle at the head of the stairs. It was so quietly done that nobody below, save myself, knew what had happened. The incident showed me that the watch was well kept.

The evening wore on—interminably, as it seemed to me. I darted to and fro from the bar, laden with mugs of beer and glasses of schnaps, incessantly, up and down. But I never failed, whenever there came a pause in the orders, to see that my journey finished somewhere in the neighbourhood of the door. A faint hope was glimmering in my brain.

Until the end of my life, that interminable evening in the beer-cellar will remain stamped in my memory. I can still see the scene in its every detail, and I know I shall carry the picture with me to the grave; the long, low room with its blackened ceiling, the garish yellow gaslight, the smoke haze, the crowded tables, Otto, shuffling hither and thither with his mean and sulky air, Frau Hedwig, preoccupied at her desk, red-eyed, a graven image of woe, and Haase, presiding over the beer-engine, silent, defiant, calm, but watchful every time the door opened.

When at last the blow fell, it came suddenly. A trampling of feet on the stairs, a great blowing of whistles... then the door was burst open just as everybody in the cellar sprang to their feet amid exclamations and oaths from the men and shrill screams from the women. Outlined in the doorway stood Clubfoot, majestic, authoritative, wearing some kind of little skull-cap, such as duelling students wear, over a black silk handkerchief bound about his head. At the sight of the man the hubbub ceased on the instant. All were still save Haase, whose bull-like voice roaring for silence broke on the quiet of the room with the force of an explosion.

I was in my corner by the door, pressed back against the coats and hats hanging on the wall. In front of me a frieze of frightened faces screened me from observation. Quickly, I slipped off my apron.

Clubfoot, after casting a cursory glance round the room, strode its length towards the bar where Haase stood, a crowd of plain-clothes men and policemen at his heels. Then quite suddenly the light went out, plunging the place into darkness. Instantly the room was in confusion; women screamed; a voice, which I recognized as Clubfoot's, bawled stentorianly for lights... the moment had come to act.

I grabbed a hat and coat from the hall, got into them somehow, and darted to the door. In the dim light shining down the stairs from a street lamp outside, I saw a man at the door. Apparently he was guarding it.

"Back!" he cried, as I stepped up to him.

I flashed in his eyes the silver star I held in my hand. "The Chief wants lanterns!" I said low in his ear. He grabbed my hand holding the badge and lowered it to the light.

"All right, comrade," he replied. "Drechsler has a lantern, I think! You'll find him outside!"

I rushed up the stairs right into a group of three policemen.

"The Chief wants Drechsler at once with the lantern," I shouted, and showed my star. The three dispersed in different directions calling for Drechsler.

I walked quickly away.

15

THE WAITER AT THE CAFÉ REGINA

I calculated that I had at least two hours, at most three, in which to get clear of Berlin. However swiftly Clubfoot might act, it would take him certainly an hour and a half, I reckoned, from the discovery of my flight from Haase's to warn the police at the railway stations to detain me. If I could lay a false trail I might at the worst prolong this period of grace; at the best I might mislead him altogether as to my ultimate destination, which was, of course, Düsseldorf. The unknown quantity in my reckonings was the time it would take Clubfoot to send out a warning all over Germany to detain Julius Zimmermann, waiter and deserter, wherever and whenever apprehended.

At the first turning I came to after leaving Haase's, tram-lines ran across the street. A tram was waiting, bound in a southerly direction, where the centre of the city lay. I jumped on to the front platform beside the woman driver. It is fairly dark in front and the conductor cannot see your face as you pay your fare through a trap in the door leading to the interior of the tram. I left the tram at Unter den Linden and walked down some side streets until I came across a quiet-looking café. There I got a railway guide and set about reviewing my plans.

It was ten minutes to twelve. A man in my position would in all probability make for the frontier. So, I judged, Clubfoot must calculate, though, I fancied, he must have wondered why I had not long since attempted to escape back to England. Dusseldorf was on the main road to Holland, and it would certainly be the more prudent course, say, to make for the Rhine and travel on to my destination by a Rhine steamer. But time was the paramount factor in my case. By leaving immediately—that very night—for Dusseldorf I might possibly reach there before the local authorities had had time to receive the warning to be on the lookout for a man answering to my description. If I could leave behind in Berlin a really good false clue, it was just possible that Clubfoot might follow it up *before* taking general dispositions to secure my arrest if that clue failed. I decided I must gamble on this hypothesis.

The railway guide showed that a train left for Dusseldorf from the Potsdamer Bahnhof—the great railway terminus in the very centre of Berlin—at 12.45 a.m. That left me roughly three-quarters of an hour to lay my false trail and catch my train. My false trail should lead Clubfoot in a totally unexpected direction, I determined, for it is the unexpected that first engaged the notice of the alert, detective type of mind. I would also have to select another terminus.

Why not Munich? A large city on the high road to a foreign frontier—Switzerland—with authorities whose easy-going ways are proverbial in Germany. You leave Berlin for Munich from the Anhalter Bahnhof, a terminus which was well suited for my purpose, as it is only a few minutes' drive from the Potsdamer station.

The railway guide showed there was a train leaving for Munich at 12.30 a.m.—an express. That would do admirably. Munich it should be then.

Fortunately I had plenty of money. I had taken the precaution of getting Kore to change my money into German notes before we left In den Zelten... at a preposterous rate of exchange, be it said. How lost I should have been without Semlin's wad of notes!

I paid for my coffee and set forth again. It was 12.15 as I walked into the hall of the Anhalt station.

Remembering the ruse which the friendly guide at Rotterdam had taught me, I began by purchasing a platform ticket. Then I looked about for an official upon whom I could suitably impress my identity. Presently I espied a pompous-looking fellow in a bright blue uniform and scarlet cap, some kind of junior stationmaster, I thought.

I approached him and, raising my hat, politely asked him if he could tell me when there was a train leaving for Munich.

"The express goes at 12.30," he said, "but only first and second class, and you'll have to pay the supplementary charge. The slow train is not till 5.49."

I assumed an expression of vexation.

"I suppose I must go by the express," I said. "Can you tell me where the booking-office is?"

The official pointed to a pigeon-hole and I took care to speak loud enough for him to hear me ask for a second-class ticket, single, to Munich.

I walked upstairs and presented my Munich ticket to the collector at the barrier. Then I hurried past the main-line platforms over the suburban side, where I gave up my platform ticket and descended again to the street.

It was just on the half-hour as I came out of the station. Not a cab to be seen! I hastened as fast as my legs would carry me until, breathless and panting, I reached the Potsdam terminus. The clock over the station pointed to 12.39.

A long queue, composed mostly of soldiers returning to Belgium and the front, stood in front of the booking-office. The military were getting their warrants changed for tickets. I chafed at the delay, but it was actually this circumstance which afforded me the chance of getting my ticket for Düsseldorf without leaving any clue behind.

A big, bearded Landsturm man with a kind face was at the pigeon-hole.

"I am very late for my train, my friend," I said, "would you get me a third-class single for Dusseldorf?" I handed him a twenty-mark note.

"Right you are," he answered readily.

"There," he said, handing me my ticket and a handful of change, "and lucky you are to be going to the Rhine. I'm from the Rhine myself and now I'm going back to guarding the bridges in Belgium!"

I thanked him and wished him luck. Here at least was a witness who was not likely to trouble me. And with a thankful heart I bolted on to the platform and caught the train.

Third-class travel in Germany is not a hobby to be cultivated if your means allow the luxury of better accommodation. The travelling German has a habit of taking off his boots when he journeys in the train by night—and a carriageful of lower middle-class Huns, thus unshod, in the temperature at which railway compartments are habitually kept in Germany, is an environment which makes neither for comfort nor for sleep.

The atmosphere, indeed, was so unbearable that I spent most of the night in the corridor. Here I was able to destroy the papers of Julius Zimmermann, waiter... I felt I was in greater danger whilst I had them on me... and to assure myself that my precious document was in its usual place—in my portfolio. It was then I made the discovery, annihilating at the first shock, that my silver badge had disappeared. I could not remember what I had done with it in the excitement of my escape from Haase's, I remembered having it in my hand and showing it to the police at the top of the stairs, but after that my mind was a blank. I could only imagine I must have carried it unconsciously in my hand and then dropped it unwittingly.

I looked at the place where it had been clasped on my braces: it was not there and I searched all my pockets for it in vain.

I had relied upon it as a stand-by in case there were trouble at the station in Düsseldorf. Now I found myself defenceless if I were challenged. It was a hard knock, but I consoled myself by the reflection that, by now Clubfoot knew I had this badge... it would doubtless figure in any description circulated about me.

It was a most unpleasant journey. There was some kind of choral society on the train, occupying seven or eight compartments of the third-class coach in which I was travelling. For the first few hours they made night hideous with part-songs, catches and glees chanted with a volume of sound that in that confined place was simply deafening. Then the noise abated as one by one the singers dropped off to sleep. Presently silence fell, while the train rushed forward in the darkness bearing me towards fresh perils, fresh adventures.

* * *

A gust of fresh air in my face, the trample of feet, loud greetings in guttural German, awoke me with a start. It was broad daylight and through my compartment, to which I had crept in the night, weary with standing, filed the jovial members of the choral society, with bags in their hands and huge cockades in their buttonholes. There was a band on the platform and a huge choir of men who bawled a stentorian-voiced hymn of greeting. "Düsseldorf" was the name printed on the station lamps.

All the passengers, save the members of the choral society, had left the train, apparently, for every carriage door stood open. I sprang to my feet and let myself go with the stream of men. Thus I swept out of the train and right into the midst of the jostling crowd of bandsmen, singers and spectators on the platform. I stood with the new arrivals until the hymn was ended and thus solidly *encadrés* by the Düsseldorfers, we drifted out through the barrier into the station courtyard. There brakes were waiting into which the jolly choristers, guests and hosts, clambered noisily. But I walked straight on into the streets, scarcely able to realize that no one had questioned me, that at last, unhindered, I stood before my goal.

Düsseldorf is a bright, clean town with a touch of good taste in its public buildings to remind one that this busy, industrial city has found time even while making money to have called into being a school of art of its own. It was a delightful morning with dazzling sunshine and an eager nip in the air that spoke of the swift, deep river that bathes the city walls. I revelled in the clear, cold atmosphere after the foulness of the drinking-den and the stifling heat of the journey. I exulted in the sense of liberty I experienced at having once more eluded the grim clutches of Clubfoot. Above all, my heart sang within me at the thought of an early meeting with Francis. In the mood I was in, I would admit no possibility of disappointment now. Francis and I would come together at last.

I came upon a public square presently and there facing me was a great, big café, white and new and dazzling, with large plate-glass windows and rows of tables on a covered verandah outside. It was undoubtedly a *"kolossal"* establishment after the best Berlin style. So that there might be no mistake about the name it was placarded all over the front of the place in gilt letters three feet high on glass panels—Café Regina.

It was about nine o'clock in the morning and at that early hour I had the place to myself. I felt very small, sitting at a tiny table, with tables on every side of me, stretching away as it were into the *Ewigkeit*, in a vast white room with mural paintings of the crassest school of impressionism.

I ordered a good, substantial breakfast and whiled away the time while it was coming by glancing at the morning paper which the waiter brought me.

My eyes ran down the columns without my heeding what I read, for my thoughts were busy with Francis. When did he come to the café? How was he living at Düsseldorf?

Suddenly, I found myself looking at a name I knew... it was in the personal paragraphs.

"Lieut.-General Count von Boden," the paragraph ran, "Aide-de-Camp to H.M. the Emperor, has been placed on the retired list owing to ill-health. General von Boden has left for Abbazia, where he will take up his permanent residence." There followed the usual biographical notes.

Of a truth, Clubfoot was a power in the land.

I ate my breakfast at a table by the open door, and surveyed the busy life of the square where the pigeons circled in the sunshine. A waiter stood on the verandah idly watching the birds as they pecked at the stones. I was struck with the profound melancholy depicted in his face. His cheeks were sunken and he had a pinched look which I had observed in the features of most of the customers at Haase's. I set it down to the insufficient feeding which is general among the lower classes in Germany today.

But in addition to this man's wasted appearance, his eyes were hollow, there were deep lines about his mouth and he wore a haggard look that had something strangely pathetic about it. His air of brooding sadness seemed to attract me, and I found my eyes continually wandering back to his face.

And then, without warning, through some mysterious whispering of the blood, the truth came to me that this was my brother. I don't know whether it was a passing mood reflected in his face or the shifting lights and shadows in his eyes that lifted the veil. I only know that through those features ravaged by care and suffering and in spite of them I caught a glimpse of the brother I had come to seek.

I rattled a spoon on the table and called softly out to the verandah.

"*Kellner!*"

The man turned.

I beckoned to him. He came over to my table. He never recognized me, so dull was he with disappointment... me with my unshaven, unkempt appearance and in my mean German shoddy... but stood silently, awaiting my bidding.

"Francis," I said softly... and I spoke in German... "Francis, don't you know me?"

He was magnificent, strong and resourceful in his joy at our meeting as he had been in his months of weary waiting.

Only his mouth quivered a little as instantly his hands busied themselves with clearing away my breakfast.

"*Jawohl!*" he answered in a perfectly emotionless voice.

And then he smiled and in a flash the old Francis stood before me.

"Not a word now," he said in German as, he cleared away the breakfast. "I am off this afternoon. Meet me on the river promenade by the Schiller statue at a quarter past two and we'll go for a walk. Don't stay here now but come back and lunch in the restaurant... it's always crowded and pretty safe!"

Then he called out into the void:

"Twenty-six wants to pay!"

* * *

Such was my meeting with my brother.

16

A HAND-CLASP BY THE RHINE

That afternoon Francis and I walked out along the banks of the swiftly flowing Rhine until we were far beyond the city. Anxious though I was that he should reveal to me that part of his life which lay hidden beneath those lines of suffering in his face, he made me tell my story first. So I unfolded to him the extraordinary series of adventures that had befallen me since the night I had blundered upon the trail of a great secret in that evil hotel at Rotterdam.

Francis did not once interrupt the flow of my narrative. He listened with the most tense interest but with a growing concern which betrayed itself clearly on his face. At the end of my story, I silently handed to him the half of the stolen letter I had seized from Clubfoot at the Hotel Esplanade.

"Keep it, Francis," I said. "It's safer with a respectable waiter like you than with a hunted outcast like myself!"

My brother smiled wanly, but his face assumed the look of grave anxiety with which he had heard my tale. He scrutinized the slips of paper very closely, then tucked them away in a letter-case, which he buttoned up in his hip pocket.

"Fortune is a strange goddess, Des," he said, his weary eyes roving out over the turgid, yellow stream, "and she has been kind to you, though, God knows, you have played a man's part in all this. She has placed in your possession something for which at least five men have died in vain, something that has filled my thoughts, sleeping and waking, for more than half a year. What you have told me throws a good deal of light upon the mystery which I came to this cursed country to elucidate, but it also deepens the darkness which still envelops many points in the affair.

"You know there are issues in this game of ours, old man, that stand even higher than the confidence that there has always been between us two. That is why I wrote to you so seldom out in France—I could tell you nothing about my work: that is one of the rules of our game. But now you have broken into the scramble yourself, I feel that we are partners, so I will tell you all I know.

"Listen, then. Some time about the beginning of the year a letter written by a German interned at one of the camps in England was stopped by the Camp Censor. This German went by the name of Schulte: he was arrested at a house in Dalston the day after we declared war on Germany. There was a good reason for this, for our friend Schulte—we don't know his real name—was known to my Chief as one of the most daring and successful spies that ever operated in the British Isles.

"Therefore, a sharp eye was kept on his correspondence, and one day this letter was seized. It was, I believe, perfectly harmless to the eye, but the expert to whom it was eventually submitted soon detected a conventional code in the chatty phrases about the daily life of the camp. It proved to be a communication from Schulte to a third party relating to a certain letter which, apparently, the writer imagined the third party had a considerable interest in acquiring. For he offered to sell this letter to the third party, mentioning a sum so preposterously high that it attracted the earnest attention of our Intelligence people. On half the sum mentioned being paid into the writer's account at a certain bank in London, the letter went on to say, the writer would forward the address at which the object in question would be found.

"It was a simple matter to send Schulte a letter in return, agreeing to his terms, and to have the payment made, as desired, into the bank he mentioned. His communication in reply to this was duly stopped. The address he gave was that of a house situated on the outskirts of Cleves.

"We had no idea what this letter was, but its apparent value in the eyes of the shrewd Mr Schulte made it highly desirable that we should obtain possession of it without delay. Four of us were selected for this dangerous mission of getting into Germany and fetching it, by hook or by crook, from the house at Cleves where it was deposited. We four were to enter Germany by different routes and different means and to converge on Cleves (which is quite close to the Dutch frontier).

"It would take too long to tell you of the very exact organization which we worked out to exclude all risk of failure and the various schemes we evolved for for keeping in touch with one another though working separately and in rotation. Nor does it matter very much how I got into Germany. The fact is that, at my very first attempt to get across the frontier, I realized that some immensely powerful force was working against me.

"I managed it, with half a dozen hairbreadth escapes, and I set down my success solely to my knowledge of German and to that old trick of mine of German imitations. But I felt everywhere the influence of this unseen hand, enforcing a meticulous vigilance which it was almost impossible to escape. I was not surprised, therefore, to learn that two of my companions came to grief at the very outset."

My brother lowered his voice and looked about him.

"Do you know what happened to those two gallant fellows?" he said. "Jack Tracy was found dead on the railway: Herbert Arbuthnot was discovered hanging in a wood. 'Suicide of an

Unknown Individual' was what the German papers called it in each case. But I heard the truth... never mind how. They were ambushed and slaughtered in cold blood."

"And the third man you spoke of?" I asked.

"Phillip Brewster? Vanished, Des... vanished utterly. I fear he, too, has gone west, poor chap!"

"Of the whole four of us I was the only one to reach our objective. There I drew blank. The letter was not in the hiding-place indicated. I think it never had been or the Huns would have got it. I felt all the time that they didn't know exactly where the letter was but that they anticipated our attempt to get it, hence the unceasing vigilance all along the frontier and inside it, too.

"They damned nearly got me at Cleves: I escaped as by a miracle, and the providential thing for me was that I had never posed as anything but a German, only I varied the type I represented almost from day to day. Thus I left no traces behind or they would have had me long since."

The sadness in my brother's voice increased and the shadows deepened in his face.

"Then I tried to get out," he continued. "But it was hopeless from the first. They knew they had one of us left in the net and they closed every outlet. I made two separate attempts to cross the line back into Holland, but both failed. The second time I literally had to flee for my life. I went straight to Berlin, feeling that a big city, as remote from the frontier as possible, was the only safe hiding-place for me as long as the hue and cry lasted.

"I was in a desperate bad way, too, for I had had to abandon the last set of identity papers left to me when I bolted. I landed in Berlin with the knowledge that no roof could safely shelter me until I got a fresh lot of papers.

"I knew of Kore—I had heard of him and his shirkers' and deserters' agency in my travels—and I went straight to him. He sent me to Haase's... this was towards the end of June. It was when I was at Haase's that I sent out that message to van Urutius that fell into your hands. That happened like this.

"I was rather friendly with a chap that frequented Haase's, a man employed in the packing department at the Metal Works at Steglitz. He was telling us one night how short-handed they were and what good money packers were earning. I was sick of being cooped up in that stinking cellar, so, more by way of a joke than anything else, I offered to come and lend a hand in the packing department. I thought I might get a chance of escape, as I saw none at Haase's. To my surprise, Haase, who was sitting at the table, rather fancied the idea and said I could go if I paid him half my wages: I was getting nothing at the beercellar.

"So I was taken on at Steglitz, sleeping at Haase's and helping in the beer-cellar in the evenings. One day a package for old van Urutius came to me to be made up and suddenly it occurred to me that here was a chance of sending out a message to the outside world. I hoped that old van U., if he tumbled to the 'Eichenholz,' would send it to you and that you would pass it on to my Chief in London."

"Then you expected me to come after you?" I said.

"No," replied Francis promptly. "I did not. But the arrangement was that, if none of us four men had turned up at Headquarters by May 15th, a fifth man should come in and be at a given rendezvous near the frontier on June 15th. I went to the place on June 15th, but he never showed up and, though I waited about for a couple of days, I saw no sign of him. I made my final attempt to get out and it failed, so, when I fled to Berlin, I knew that I had cut off all means of communication with home. As a last hope, I dashed off that cipher on the spur of the moment and tucked it into old van U's invoice."

"But why 'Achilles' with one 'l'?" I asked.

"They knew all about Kore's agency at Headquarters, but I didn't dare mention Kore's name for fear the parcel might be opened. So I purposely spelt 'Achilles' with one 'l' to draw attention to the code word, so that they should know where news of me was to be found. It was devilish smart of you to decipher that, Des!"

Francis smiled at me.

"I meant to stay quietly in Berlin, going daily between Haase's and the factory and wait, for a month or two, in case that message got home. But Kore began to give trouble. At the beginning of July he came to see me and hinted that the renewal of my *permis de séjour* would cost money. I paid him, but I realized then that I was absolutely in his power and I had no intention of being blackmailed. So I made use of his cupidity to leave a message for the man who, I hoped, would be coming after me, wrote that line on the wall under the Boonekamp poster in that filthy hovel where we slept and came up here after a job I had heard of at the Café Regina.

"And now, Des, old man," said my brother, "you know all that I know!"

"And Clubfoot?"

"Ah!" said Francis, shaking his head, "there I think I recognize the hand that has been against us from the start, though who the man is, and what his power, I, like you, only know from what he told you himself. The Germans are clever enough, as we know from their communiqués, to tell the truth when it suits their book. I believe that Clubfoot was telling you the truth in what he said about his mission that night at the Esplanade.

"You and I know now that the Kaiser wrote that letter... we also know that it was addressed to an influential English friend of William II. You have seen the date... Berlin, July 31st, 1914... the eve of the outbreak of the world war. Even from this half in my pocket... and you who have seen both halves of the letter will confirm what I say... I can imagine what an effect on the international situation this letter would have had if it had reached the man for whom it was destined. But it did not... why, we don't know. We do know, however, that the Emperor is keenly anxious to regain possession of his letter... you yourself were a witness of his anxiety and you know that he put the matter into the hands of the man Clubfoot."

"Well," I observed thoughtfully, "Clubfoot, whoever he is, seems to have made every effort to keep my escapades dark..."

"Precisely," said Francis, "and lucky for you too. Otherwise Clubfoot would have had you stopped at the frontier. But obviously secrecy is an essential part of his instructions, and he has shown himself willing to risk almost anything rather than call in the aid of the regular police."

"But they can always hush these things up!" I objected.

"From the public, yes, but not from the Court. This letter looks uncommonly like one of William's sudden impulses... and I fancy anything of the kind would get very little tolerance in Germany in war-time."

"But who is Clubfoot?" I questioned.

My brother furrowed his brows anxiously.

"Des," he said, "I don't know. He is certainly not a regular official of the German Intelligence like Steinhauer and the others. But I *have* heard of a clubfooted German on two occasions... both were dark and mysterious affairs, in both we played a leading rôle and both ended in the violent death of one of our men."

"Then Tracy and the others...?" I asked.

"Victims of this man, Des, without any doubt," my brother answered. He paused a moment reflectively.

"There is a code of honour in our game, old man," he said, "and there are lots of men in the German secret service who live up to it. We give and take plenty of hard knocks in the rough-and-tumble of the chase, but ambush and assassination are barred."

He took a deep breath and added:

"But the man Clubfoot doesn't play the game!"

"Francis," I said, "I wish I'd known something of this that night I had him at my mercy at the Esplanade. He would not have got off with a cracked skull... with one blow. There would have been another blow for Tracy, one for Arbuthnot, one for the other man... until the account was settled and I'd beaten his brains out on the carpet. But if we meet him again, Francis... as, please God, we shall!... there will be no code of honour for *him*... we'll finish him in cold blood as we'd kill a rat!"

My brother thrust out his hand at me and we clasped hands on it.

Evening was falling and lights were beginning to twinkle from the further bank of the river.

We stood for a moment in silence with the river rushing at our feet. Then we turned and started to tramp back towards the city. Francis linked his arm in mine.

"And now, Des," he said in his old affectionate way, "tell me some more about Monica!"

Out of that talk germinated in my head the only plan that seemed to offer us a chance of escape. I was quite prepared to believe Francis when he declared that the frontier was at present impassable: if the vigilance had been increased before it would be redoubled now that I had again eluded Clubfoot. We should, therefore, have to find some cover where we could lie doggo until the excitement passed.

You remember that Monica told me, the last time I had seen her, that she was shortly going to Schloss Bellevue, a shooting-box belonging to her husband, to arrange some shoots in connection with the Governmental scheme for putting game on the market. Monica, you will recollect, had offered to take me with her, and I had fully meant to accompany her but for Gerry's unfortunate persistence in the matter of my passport.

I now proposed to Francis that we should avail ourselves of Monica's offer and make for Castle Bellevue. The place was well suited for our purpose as it lies near Cleves, and in its immediate neighbourhood is the Reichswald, that great forest which stretches from Germany clear across into Holland. All through my wanderings, I had kept this forest in the back of my head as a region which must offer facilities for slipping unobserved across the frontier. Now I learnt from Francis that he had spent months in the vicinity of Cleves, and I was not surprised to find, when I outlined this plan to him, that he knew the Reichswald pretty well.

"It'll be none too easy to get across through the forest," he said doubtfully, "it's very closely patrolled, but I do know of one place where we could lie pretty snug for a day or two waiting for a chance to make a dash. But we have no earthly chance of getting through at present: our clubfooted pal will see to that all right. And I don't much like the idea of going to Bellevue either: it will be horribly dangerous for Monica!"

"I don't think so," I said. "The whole place will be overrun with people, guests, servants, beaters and the like, for these shoots. Both you and I know German and we look rough enough: we ought to be able to get an emergency job about the place without embarrassing Monica in the least. I don't believe they will ever dream of looking for us so close to this frontier. The only possible trail they can pick up after me in Berlin leads to Munich. Clubfoot is bound to think I am making for the Swiss frontier."

Well, the long and the short of it was that my suggestion was carried, and we resolved to set out for Bellevue that very night. My brother declared he would not return to the café: with the present shortage of men, such desertions were by no means uncommon, and if he were to give notice formally it might only lead to embarrassing explanations.

So we strolled back to the city in the gathering darkness, bought a map of the Rhine and a couple of rucksacks and laid in a small stock of provisions at a great department store, biscuits, chocolates, some hard sausage and two small flasks of rum. Then Francis took me to a little restaurant where he was known and introduced me to the friendly proprietor, a very jolly old Rheinlander, as his brother just out of hospital. I did my country a good service, I think, by giving a most harrowing account of the terrible efficiency of the British army on the Somme!

Then we dined and over our meal consulted the map.

"By the map," I said, "Bellevue should be about fifty miles from here. My idea is that we should walk only at night and lie up during the day, as a room is out of the question for me without any papers. I think we should keep away from the Rhine, don't you? As otherwise we shall pass through Wesel, which is a fortress, and, consequently, devilish unhealthy for both of us."

Francis nodded with his mouth full.

"At present we can count on about twelve hours of darkness," I continued, "so, leaving a margin for the slight detour we shall make, for rests and for losing the way, I think we ought to be able to reach Castle Bellevue on the third night from this. If the weather holds up, it won't be too bad, but if it rains, it will be hellish! Now, have you any suggestions?"

My brother acquiesced, as, indeed, he had in everything I had proposed since we met. Poor fellow, he had had a roughish time: he seemed glad to have the direction of affairs taken out of his hands for a bit.

At half-past seven that evening, our packs on our backs, we stood on the outskirts of the town where the road branches off to Crefeld. In the pocket of the overcoat I had filched from Haase's I found an automatic pistol, fully loaded (most of our customers at the beer-cellar went armed).

"You've got the document, Francis," I said. "You'd better have this, too!" and I passed him the gun.

Francis waved it aside.

"You keep it," he said grimly, "it may serve you instead of a passport."

So I slipped the weapon back into my pocket.

A cold drop of rain fell upon my face.

"Oh, hell!" I cried, "It's beginning to rain!" And thus we set out upon our journey.

* * *

It was a nightmare tramp. The rain never ceased. By day we lay in icy misery, chilled to the bone in our sopping clothes, in some dank ditch or wet undergrowth, with aching bones and blistered feet, fearing detection, but fearing, even more, the coming of night and the resumption of our march. Yet we stuck to our programme like Spartans, and about eight o'clock on the third evening, hobbling painfully along the road that runs from Cleves to Calcar, we were rewarded by the sight of a long massive building, with turrets at the corners, standing back from the highway behind a tall brick wall.

"Bellevue!" I said to Francis, with pointing finger.

We left the road and climbing a wooden palisade, struck out across the fields with the idea of getting into the park from the back. We passed some black and silent farm buildings, went through a gate and into a paddock, on the further side of which ran the wall surrounding the place. Somewhere beyond the wall a fire was blazing. We could see the leaping light of the flames and drifting smoke. At the same moment we heard voices, loud voices disputing in German.

We crept across the paddock to the wall. I gave Francis a back and he hoisted himself to the top and looked over. In a moment he sprang lightly down, a finger to his lips.

"Soldiers round a fire," he whispered. "There must be troops billeted here. Come on... we'll go further round!"

We ran softly along the wall to where it turned to the right and followed it round. Presently we came to a small iron gate in the wall. It stood open.

We listened. The sound of voices was fainter here. We still saw the reflection of the flames in the sky. Otherwise, there was no sign or sound of human life.

The gate led into an ornamental garden with the Castle at the further end. All the windows were in darkness. We threaded a garden path leading to the house. It brought us in front of a glass door. I turned the handle and it yielded to my grasp.

I whispered to Francis:

"Stay where you are! And if you hear me shout, fly for your life!"

For, I reflected, the place might be full of troops. If there were any risk it would be better for me to take it since Francis, with his identity papers, had a better chance than I of bringing the document into safety.

I opened the glass door and found myself in a lobby with a door on the right.

I listened again. All was still. I cautiously opened the door and looked in. As I did so the place was suddenly flooded with light and a voice—a voice I had often heard in my dreams— called out imperiously:

"Stay where you are and put your hands above your head!"

Clubfoot stood there, a pistol in his great hand pointed at me.

"Grundt!" I shouted but I did not move.

And Clubfoot laughed.

17

FRANCIS TAKES UP THE NARRATIVE

I saw the lights flash up in the room. I heard Desmond cry out: "Grundt!" Instantly I flung myself flat on my face in the flower bed, lest Desmond's shout might have alarmed the soldiers about the fire. But no one came; the gardens remained dark and damp and silent, and I heard no sound from the room in which I knew my brother to be in the clutches of that man.

Desmond's cry pulled me together. It seemed to arouse me from the lethargy into which I had sunk during all those months of danger and disappointment. It shook me into life. If I was to save him, not a moment was to be lost. Clubfoot would act swiftly, I knew. So must I. But first I must find out what the situation was, the meaning of Clubfoot's presence in Monica's house, of those soldiers in the park. And, above all, was Monica herself at the Castle?

I had noticed a little estaminet place on the road, about a hundred yards before we reached the Schloss. I might, at least, be able to pick up something there. Accordingly, I stole across the garden, scaled the wall again and reached the road in safety.

The estaminet was full of people, brutish-looking peasants swilling neat spirits, cattle drovers and the like. I stood up at the bar and ordered a double noggin of *Korn*—a raw spirit made in these parts from potatoes, very potent but at least pure. A man in corduroys and leggings was drinking at the bar, a bluff sort of chap, who readily entered into conversation. A casual question of mine about the game conditions elicited from him the information that he was an under-keeper at the Castle. It was a busy time for them, he told me, as four big shoots had been arranged. The first was to take place the next day. There were plenty of birds, and he thought the Frau Grahn's guests ought to be satisfied.

I asked him if there was a big party staying at the Castle. No, he told me, only one gentleman besides the officer billeted there, but a lot of people were coming over for the shoot the next day, the officers from Cleves and Goch, the Chief Magistrate from Cleves, and a number of farmers from round about.

"I expect you will find the soldiers billeted at the Castle useful as beaters," I enquired with a purpose.

The man assented grudgingly. Gamekeepers are first-class grumblers. But the soldiers were not many. For his part he could do without them altogether. They were such terrible poachers to have about the place, he declared. But what they would do for beaters without them, he didn't know... they were very short of beaters... that was a fact.

"I am staying at Cleves," I said, "and I'm out of a job. I am not long from hospital, and they've discharged me from the army. I wouldn't mind earning a few marks as a beater, and I'd like to see the sport. I used to do a bit of shooting myself down on the Rhine where I come from."

The man shrugged his shoulders and shook his head. "That's none of my business, getting the beaters together," he replied. "Besides, I shall have the head gamekeeper after me if I go bringing strangers in..."

I ordered another drink, for both of us, and won the man round without much difficulty. He pouched my five mark note and announced that he would manage it... the Frau Gräfin was to see some men who had offered their services as beaters after dinner at the Castle that evening. He would take me along.

Half an hour later I stood, as one of a group of shaggy and bedraggled rustics, in a big stone courtyard outside the main entrance to the Castle. The head gamekeeper mustered us with his eye and, bidding us follow him, led the way under a vaulted gateway through a massive door into a small lobby which had apparently been built into the great hall of the Castle, for it opened right into it.

We found ourselves in a splendid old feudal hall, oak-lined and oak-raftered, with lines of dusty banners just visible in the twilight reigning in the upper part of the vast place. The modern generation had forborne to desecrate the fine old room with electric light, and massive silver candlesticks shed a soft light on the table set at the far end of the hall, where dinner, apparently, was just at an end.

Three people were sitting at the table, a woman at the head, who, even before I had taken in the details I have just set down, I knew to be Monica, though her back was towards me. On one side of the table was a big, heavy man whom I recognized as Clubfoot, on the other side a pale slip of a lad in officer's uniform with only one arm... Schmalz, no doubt.

A servant said something to Monica, who, asking permission of her companions by a gesture, left the table and came across the hall. To my surprise, she was dressed in deepest black with linen cuffs. Her face was pale and set, and there was a look of fear and suffering in her eyes that wrung my very heart.

I had shuffled into the last place of the row in which the head keeper had ranged us. Monica spoke a word or two to each of the men, who shambled off in turn with low obeisances. Directly she stopped in front of me I knew she had recognized me—I felt it rather, for she made no sign—though the time I had had in Germany had altered my appearance, I dare say, and I must have looked pretty rough with my three days' beard and muddy clothes.

"Ah!" she said with all her languor *de grande dame*, "you are the man of whom Heinrich spoke. You have just come out of hospital, I think?"

"Beg the Frau Grahn's pardon," I mumbled out in the thick patois of the Rhine which I had learnt at Bonn, "I served with the Herr Graf in Galicia, and I thought maybe the Frau Gräfin..."

She stopped me with a gesture.

"Herr Doktor!" she called to the dinner-table.

By Jove! this girl had grit: her pluck was splendid.

Clubfoot came stumping over, all smiles after his food and smoking a long cigar that smelt delicious.

"Frau Gräfin?" he queried, glancing at me.

"This is a man who served under my husband in Galicia. He is ill and out of work, and wishes me to help him. I should wish, therefore, to see him in my sitting-room, if you will allow me..."

"But, Frau Gräfin, most certainly. There surely was no need..."

"Johann!" Monica called the servant I had seen before, "Take this man into the sitting-room!"

The servant led the way across the hall into a snugly furnished library with a dainty writing-desk and pretty chintz curtains. Monica followed and sat down at the desk.

"Now tell me what you wish to say..." she began in German as the servant left the room, but almost as soon as he had gone she was on her feet, clasping my hands.

"Francis!" she whispered in English in a great sob, "Oh, Francis! What have they done to you to make you look like that?"

I gripped her wrist tightly.

"Frau Gräfin," I said in German, still in that hideous patois, "you must be calm." And I whispered in English in her ear:

"Monica, be brave! And talk German whatever you do."

She regained her self-possession at once.

"I understand," she answered, sitting down at her desk again; "it is more prudent."

And for the rest of the time we spoke in German.

"Desmond?" I asked.

"Locked up in Grundt's bedroom," she replied. "I met them pushing him along the corridor—it was horrible! Grundt won't let him out of his sight. Oh, it was madness to have come. If only I could have warned you!"

"What is Grundt doing here?" I asked. "And those soldiers and that officer?"

"My dear," she answered, and her eyes flashed mischief in a sudden change of mood, "I'm in preventive arrest!"

"But, Monica..."

"Listen! Gerry and that spying man-servant of his made trouble. When Des went off that evening and didn't come back, Gerry insisted that we should notify the police. He made an awful scene, then the valet chipped in, and from what he said I knew he meant mischief. I didn't dare trust Gerry with the truth, so I let him send a note to the police. They came round and asked a lot of questions and went away again, so I thought we'd heard the last of it and came up here. Gerry wouldn't come. He's gone off to Baden-Baden on some new cure.

"About a week ago the Chief Magistrate at Cleves, who is an old friend of ours, motored over, and after a lot of talk, blurted out that I was to consider myself under arrest, and that an officer and a detachment of men from Goch were coming over to guard the house. The magistrate man would have told me anything I wanted to know, but he knew nothing: he simply carried out his orders. Then the lieutenant and his men arrived, and since that time I have been a prisoner in the house and grounds. I was terribly scared about Des until Grundt arrived suddenly, two nights ago, and I saw at once by his face that Des was still at large. But, Francis, that Clubfoot man came here to catch Des... and he has simply walked into the trap."

"And Desmond?" I asked. "What is Clubfoot going to do about him?"

"He was with Des for about an hour in his room, and I heard him tell Schmalz he would 'try again' after dinner. Oh, Francis, I am frightened of that man... not a word has he said to me about my knowing Desmond—not a word about my harbouring Des in Berlin... but he knows everything, and he watches me the whole time."

I glanced through the open door into the hall. The candles still burnt on the dinner-table, where Clubfoot and the officer sat conversing in low tones.

"I have been here long enough," I said. "But before I go, I want you to answer one or two questions, Monica. Will you?"

"Yes, Francis," she said, raising her eyes to mine.

"What time is the shoot tomorrow?"

"At ten o'clock."

"Are Grundt and Schmalz going?"

"Yes."

"You too?"

"Yes."

"Could you get away back to the house by 12.30?"

"Not alone. One of them is always with me out of doors."

"Could you meet me alone anywhere outside at that time?"

"There is a quarry outside a village called Quellen-burg... it is on the edge of our preserves... just off the road. We ought to be as far as that by twelve. If it is necessary, I will try and give them the slip and hide in one of the caves there. Then, when you came, if you whistled I could come out."

"Good. That will do excellently. We will arrange it so. Now, another question... how many soldiers have you here?"

"Sixteen."

"Are they all going beating?"

"Oh, no! Only ten of them. The other six and the sergeant remain behind."

"Have you a car here?"

"No, but Grundt has one."

"How many servants will there be in the house tomorrow?"

"Only Johann, the butler, and the maids... a woman cook and two girls."

"Can you contrive to have Johann out of the house between 10 and 12.30 tomorrow morning?"

"Yes, I can send him to Cleves with a note."

"The maids too?"

"Yes, the maids too."

"Good. Now will you do one thing more—the hardest of all? I want you to send a message to Desmond. Can you arrange it?"

"Tell me what your message is, and I may be able to answer you."

"I want you to tell him that he must at all costs contrive to keep Grundt from going to that shoot tomorrow... at any rate between ten and twelve. He must manage to let Grundt believe that he is going to tell him where Grundt may find what he is after... but he must keep him in suspense during those hours."

"And after?"

"There will be no after," I said.

"I will see that Des gets your message," Monica replied, "for I will take it myself."

"No, Monica," I said, "I don't want..."

"Francis,"... she spoke almost in a whisper... "my life in this country is over,"... and she touched her widow's weeds... "Karl was killed at Predeal three weeks ago...You know as well as I do that I am involved in this affair as much as you and Des... and I will share the risk if only you will take me away with you... that is, if you..." She faltered.

I heard the chairs scrape in the corner of the hall where the dinner-party was breaking up.

"The Frau Gräfin has only to command," I said, "The Frau Gräfin knows I have been waiting for years..."

Clubfoot was crossing towards the open door.

"...I never expected to find the Frau Gräfin so gracious... I had never hoped that the Frau Gräfin would be willing to do so much for me... the Frau Gräfin has made me very happy."

Clubfoot stood on the threshold and listened to my halting speech.

"You can bring your things in when you come tomorrow..." Monica said. "The keeper will tell you what time you must be here."

Then she dismissed me, but as I went I heard her say:

"Herr Doktor! Can I have a word with you?"

18

I GO ON WITH THE STORY

I was in the billiard-room of the Castle, a dusty place, obviously little used, for it smelt of damp. A fire was burning in the grate, however, and on a table in the corner, which was littered with papers, stood a dispatch box.

Clubfoot wore a dinner-coat and, as he laughed, his white expanse of shirt-front heaved to the shaking of his deep chest. For a moment, however, I had little thought of him or the ugly-looking Browning he held in his fist. My ears were strained for any sound that might betray Francis' presence in the garden. But all remained silent as the grave.

Clubfoot, still chuckling audibly, walked over to me. I thought he was going to shoot me, he came so straight and so fast, but it was only to get behind me and shut the door, driving me, as he did so, farther into the room.

The door by which he had entered stood open. Without taking his eyes off me or deflecting his weapon from its aim, he called out:

"Schmalz!"

A light step resounded, and the one-armed lieutenant tripped into the room. When he saw me, he stopped dead. Then he softly began to circle round me with a mincing step, murmuring to himself: "So! So!"

"Good evening, Dr Semlin!" he said in English. "Say, I'm mighty glad to see you! Well, Okewood, dear old boy, here we are again. What? Herr Julius Zimmermann..." and he broke into German, "*es freut mich!*"

I could have killed him where he stood, maimed though he was, for his fluency in the American and English idiom alone.

"Search him, Schmalz!" commanded Clubfoot curtly.

Schmalz ran the fingers of his one arm over my pockets, flinging my portfolio on the billiard-table towards Clubfoot, and the other articles as they came to light... my pistol, watch, cigarette-case and so forth... on to a leather lounge against the wall. In his search he brushed me with his severed stump... ugh, it was horrible!

Clubfoot had snatched up the portfolio and hastily examined it. He shook the contents out on the billiard-table and examined them carefully.

"Not there!" he said. "Run him upstairs, and we'll strip him," he ordered; "and let not our clever young friend forget that I'm behind him with my little toy!"

Schmalz gripped me by the collar, spitefully digging his knuckles into my neck, and propelled me out of the room... almost into the arms of Monica.

She screamed and, turning, fled away down the passage. Clubfoot laughed noisily, but I reflected mournfully that in my present sorry plight, unwashed and unshaven, in filthy clothes, haled along like a common pickpocket, even my own mother would not have recognized me.

There was a degrading scene in the bedroom to which they dragged me, where the two men stripped me to the skin and pawed over every single article of clothing I possessed. Physically and mentally, I cowered in my nudity before the unwholesome gaze of these two sinister cripples. Of all my experiences in Germany, I still look back upon that as almost my worst ordeal.

Of course, they found nothing, search as they might, and presently they flung my clothes back at me and bade me get dressed again, "for you and I, young man," said Clubfoot, with his glinting smile, "have got to have a little talk together!"

When I was once more clothed—

"You can leave us, Schmalz!" commanded Clubfoot, "And send up the sergeant when I ring: he shall look after this tricky Englishman whilst we are at dinner with our charming hostess."

Schmalz went out and left us alone. Clubfoot lighted a cigar. He smoked in silence for a few minutes. I said nothing, for really there was nothing for me to say. They hadn't got their precious document, and it was not likely they would ever recover it now. I feared greatly that Francis in his loyalty might make an attempt to rescue me, but I hoped, whatever he did, he would think first of putting the document in a place of safety. I was more or less resigned to my fate. I was in their hands properly now, and whether they got the document or not, my doom was sealed.

"I will pay you the compliment of saying, my dear Captain Okewood," Clubfoot remarked in that urbane voice of his which always made my blood run cold, "that never before in my career have I devoted so much thought to any single individual, in the different cases I have handled, as I have to you. As an individual, you are a paltry thing: it is rather your remarkable good fortune that interests me as a philosopher of sorts... I assure you it will cause me serious concern to be the instrument of severing your really extraordinary strain of good luck. I don't mind telling you, as man to man, that I have not yet entirely decided in my mind what to do with you now that I've got you!"

I shrugged my shoulders.

"You've got me, certainly," I replied, "but you would vastly prefer to have what I have not got."

"Let us not forget to be always content with small mercies," answered the other, smiling with a gleam of his golden teeth... "that is a favourite maxim of mine. As you truly remark, I would certainly prefer the... the jewel to the infinitely less precious and... interesting... casket. But what I have, I hold. And I have you... and your accomplice as well."

"I have no accomplice," I denied stoutly.

"Surely you forget our gracious hostess, our most charming Countess? Was it not thanks to the interest she deigned to take in your safety that I came here? Had it not been for that circumstance, I should scarcely have ventured to intrude upon her widowhood..."

"Her widowhood?" I exclaimed.

Clubfoot smiled again.

"You cannot have followed the newspapers in your... retreat, my dear Captain Okewood," he replied, "or surely you would have read the afflicting intelligence that Count Rachwitz, A.D.C. to Field-Marshal von Mackensen, was killed by a shell that fell into the Brigade Headquarters where he was lunching at Predeal. Ah, yes," he sighed, "our beautiful Countess is now a widow, alone..." he paused, then added, "...and unprotected!"

I understood his allusion and went cold with fear. Why, Monica was involved in this affair as much as I. Surely they wouldn't dare to touch her...

Clubfoot leaned forward and tapped me on the knee.

"You will be sensible, Okewood," he said confidentially. "You've lost. You can't save yourself. Your life was forfeit from the moment you crossed the threshold of his Majesty's private apartments... but you can save *her*."

I shook his huge hand off my leg.

"You won't bluff me," I answered roughly. "You daren't touch the Countess Rachwitz, an American lady, niece of an American ambassador, married into one of your leading families... no, Herr Doktor, you must try something else."

"Do you know why Schmalz is here?" he asked patiently, "and those soldiers?... You must have passed through the cordon to come here. Your little friend is in preventive arrest. She would be in gaol (she doesn't know it), but that His Majesty was unwilling to put this affront on the Rachwitz family in their great affliction."

"The Countess Rachwitz has nothing whatever to do with me,"... rather a foolish lie, I thought to myself too late, as I was in her house.

But Clubfoot remained quite unperturbed.

"I shall take you into my confidence, my dear sir," he said, "to show that I know you to be stating an untruth. The Countess, on the contrary, is, to use a vulgar phrase, in it up to the neck. Thanks to the amazing imbecility of the Berlin police, I was not informed of your brief stay at the Bendler-Strasse, even after they were called in by the invalid American gentleman in the matter of your hasty flight when asked to have your passport put in order. But we are systematic, we Germans; we are painstaking; and I set about going through every possible place that might afford you shelter.

"In the course of my investigations I came across our mutual friend, Herr Kore. A perusal of his very business-like ledgers showed me that on the day following your disappearance from the Esplanade he had received 3,600 marks from a certain E. 2... all names in his books were in cipher. Under the influence of my winning personality, Herr Kore told me all he knew; I pursued my investigations and then discovered what the asinine police had omitted to tell me, namely, that on the date in question an alleged American had made a hurried flight from the Countess Rachwitz's apartment in the Bendler-Strasse. An admirable fellow... Max or Otto, or some name like that... anyhow, he was valet to Madame's invalid brother, was able to fill in all the lacunæ, and I was thus enabled to draw up a very strong case against your well-meaning but singularly ill-advised hostess. By this time the lady had left Berlin for this charming old-world seat, and I promptly took measures to have her placed in preventive arrest whilst I tracked *you* down.

"You got away again. Even Jupiter nods, you know, my dear Captain Okewood, and I frankly admit I overlooked the silver badge which you had in your possession. I must compliment you also on your adroitness in leaving us that false trail to Munich. It took me in to the extent that I dispatched an emissary to hunt you down in that delightful capital, but, for myself, I have a certain flair in these matters, and I thought you would sooner or later come to Bellevue. You will admit that I showed some perspicacity?"

"You're wasting time with all this talk," I said sullenly.

Clubfoot raised a hand deprecatingly.

"I take a pride in my work," he observed half-apologetically. Then he added:

"You must not forget that your pretty Countess is not an American. She is a German. She is also a widow. You may not know the relations that existed between her and her late husband, but they were not, I assure you, of such warmth that the Rachwitz family would unduly mourn her loss. Do you suppose we care a fig for all the American ambassadors that ever left the States? My dear sir, I observe that you are still lamentably ignorant of the revolution that war brings into international relations. In war, where the national interest is concerned, the individual is nothing. If he or she must be removed, puff! you snuff the offender out. Afterwards you can always pay or apologize, or do what is required."

I listened in silence; I had no defence to offer in face of this deadly logic, the logic of the stronger man.

Clubfoot produced a paper from his pocket.

"Read that!" he said, tossing it over to me. "It is the summons for the Countess Rachwitz to appear before a court-martial. Date blank, you see. You needn't tear it up... I've got several spare blank forms... one for you, too!"

I felt my courage ebbing and my heart turning to water. I handed him back his paper in silence. The booming of a dinner gong suddenly swelled into the stillness of the room. Clubfoot rose and rang the bell.

"Here's my offer, Okewood!" he said. "You shall restore that letter to me in its integrity, and the Countess Rachwitz shall go free provided she leaves this country and does not return. That's my last word! Take the night to sleep on it! I shall come for my answer in the morning."

A sergeant in field-grey with a rifle and fixed bayonet stood in the doorway.

"I make you responsible for this man, Sergeant," said Clubfoot, "until I return in an hour or so. Food will be sent up for him and you will personally assure yourself that no message is conveyed to him by that or any other means."

* * *

I had washed, I had brushed my clothes, I had dined, and I sat in silence by the table, in the most utter dejection of spirit, I think, into which it is possible for a man to fall. I was so totally crushed by the disappointment of the evening that I don't think I pondered much about my own fate at all. But my thoughts were busy with Monica. My life was my own, and I knew I had a lien on my brother's if thereby our mission might be carried through to the end. But had I the right to sacrifice Monica?

And then the unexpected happened. The door opened, and she came in, Schmalz behind her. He dismissed the sergeant with a word of caution to see that the sentries round the house were vigilant, and followed the man out, leaving Monica and me alone.

The girl stopped the torrent of self-reproach that rose to my lips with a pretty gesture. She was pale, but she held her head as high as ever.

"Schmalz has given me five minutes alone with you, Des," she said, "to plead with you for my life, that you may betray your trust. No, don't speak... there is no time to waste in words. I have a message for you from Francis... Yes, I have seen him here, this very night... He says you must contrive at all costs to keep Grundt from going to the shoot at ten o'clock tomorrow, and to detain him with you from ten to twelve. That is all I know about it... But Francis has planned something, and you and I have got to trust him. Now, listen... I shall tell Clubfoot I have pleaded with you and that you show signs of weakening. Say nothing tonight, temporize with him when he comes for his answer in the morning, and then send for him at a quarter to ten, when he will be leaving the house with the others. The rest I leave to you. Good night, Des, and cheer up!"

"But, Monica," I cried, "what about you?"

She reddened deliciously under her pallor.

"Des," she replied happily, "we are allies now, we three. If all goes well, I'm coming with you and Francis!"

With that she was gone. A few minutes after, a couple of soldiers arrived with Schmalz and took me downstairs to a dark cellar in the basement, where I was locked in for the night.

* * *

I was dreaming of the front... again I sniffed the old familiar smells, the scent of fresh earth, the fetid odour of death; again I heard outside the trench the faint rattle of tools, the low whispers of our wiring party; again I saw the very lights soaring skyward and revealing the desolation of the battlefield in their glare. Someone was shaking me by the shoulder. It was my servant come to wake me... I must have fallen asleep. Was it stand-to so soon? I sat up and rubbed my eyes and awoke to the anguish of another day.

The sergeant stood at the cellar door, framed in the bright morning light.

"You are to come upstairs!" he said.

He took me to the billiard-room, where Clubfoot, sleek and washed and shaved, sat at the writing-table in the sunshine, opening letters and sipping coffee. A clock on a bracket above his head pointed to eight.

"You wish to speak to me, I believe," he said carelessly, running his eye over a letter in his hand.

"You must give me a little more time, Herr Doktor," I said. "I was worn out last night and I could not look at things in their proper light. If you could spare me a few hours more..."

I put a touch of pleading into my voice, which struck him at once.

"I am not unreasonable, my dear Captain Okewood," he replied, "but you will understand that I am not to be trifled with, so I give you fair warning. I will give you until..."

"It is eight o'clock now," I interrupted. "I tell you what, give me until ten. Will that do?"

Clubfoot nodded assent.

"Take this man upstairs to my bedroom," he ordered the sergeant. "Stay with him while he has his breakfast, and bring him back here at ten o'clock. And tell Schmidt to leave my car at the door: he needn't wait, as he is to beat: I will drive myself to the shoot."

I don't really remember what happened after that. I swallowed some breakfast, but I had no idea what I was eating, and the sergeant, who was a model of Prussian discipline, declined with a surly frown to enter into conversation with me.

My morale was very low: when I look back upon that morning I think I must have been pretty near the breaking-point.

As I sat and waited I heard the house in a turmoil of preparation for the shoot. There was the sound of voices, of heavy boots in the hall, of wheels and horses in the yard without. Then the noises died away and all was still. Shortly afterwards, the clock pointing to ten, the sergeant escorted me downstairs again to the billiard-room.

Grundt was still sitting there. A hot wave of anger drove the blood into my cheeks as I looked at him, fat and soft and so triumphant at his victory. The sight of him, however, gave me the tonic I needed. My nerve was shaken badly, but I was determined it must answer to this last strain, to play this uncouth fish for two hours. After that... if nothing happened...

Clubfoot sent the sergeant away.

"I can look after him myself now," he said, in a blithe tone that betrayed his conviction of success. So the sergeant saluted and left the room, his footsteps echoing down the passages like the leaden feet of Destiny, relentless, inexorable.

19

WE HAVE A RECKONING WITH CLUBFOOT

I looked at Clubfoot.

I must play him with caution, with method, too.

Only by acting on a most exact system could I hope to hold him in that room for two hours. I had four points to argue with him and I would devote half an hour to each of them by the clock on the bracket above his head. If only I could keep him confident in his victory, I might hope to prevent him finding out that I was playing with him... but two hours is a long time... it would be a near thing.

One point in my favour... my manner gave him the assurance of success from the start. There was nothing counterfeit about my tone of humility, for in truth I was very near despair. I was making this last effort at the bidding of my brother, but I felt it to be a forlorn hope: in my heart of hearts I knew I was down and out.

So I went straight to the point and told Clubfoot that I was beaten, that he should have his paper. But there were difficulties about the execution of both sides of the bargain. We had deceived one another. What mutual guarantees could we exchange that would give each of us an assurance of fair play?

Clubfoot settled this point in characteristic fashion. He protested his good faith elaborately, but the gist of his remarks was that he held the cards and that consequently, it was he who must be trusted, whilst I furnished the guarantee.

Whilst we were discussing this point the clock chimed the half-hour.

I switched the conversation to Monica. I was not at all concerned about myself, I said, but I must feel sure in my mind that no ill should befall her. To this Clubfoot replied that I might set my mind at ease; the moment the document was in his hands he would give orders for her release: I should be there and might see it done myself.

What guarantee was there, I asked, that she would not be detained before she reached the frontier.

Clubfoot was getting a little restless. With his eye on the clock but in a placid voice he again protested that his word was the sole guarantee he could offer.

We discussed this too. My manner was earnest and nervous, I know, and I think he enjoyed playing with me. I told him frankly that his reputation belied his protestations of good faith. At this he laughed and cynically admitted that this was quite possibly the case.

"Nevertheless, it is I who give the guarantee," he said in a tone that brooked no contradiction.

The clock struck eleven.

One hour to go!

"Come, Okewood," he added good-naturedly, "we waste time. Up to this you've had all the sport, you know. You wouldn't have me miss the first day's shooting I've had this year. Where have you got this letter of ours?"

He was an extraordinary man. To hear him address me, you would never have supposed that he was sending me to my death. He appeared to have forgotten this detail. It meant so little to him that he probably had.

I turned to my third point. He made things very hard for me, I said, but I was the vanquished and must give way. The trouble was that the document was still in two portions and neither half was here.

"You indicate where the halves are hidden," said Clubfoot promptly. "I will accompany you to the hiding-places and you will hand them to me."

"But they are nowhere near here," I replied.

"Then where are they?" answered Clubfoot impatiently. "Come, I'm waiting and it's getting late!"

"It will take several days to recover both portions," I muttered unwillingly.

"That does not matter," retorted the other; "there is no particular hurry... now!"

And he smiled grimly.

I dared not raise my eyes to the clock, for I felt the German's gaze on me. An intuitive instinct told me that his suspicions had been awakened by my reluctance. I was very nearly at the end of my resources.

Would the clock never strike?

"I tell you frankly, Herr Doktor," I said in a voice that trembled with anxiety, "I cannot leave the Countess unprotected whilst we travel together to the hiding-places of the document. I only feel sure of her safety whilst she is near me..."

Clubfoot bent his brows at me.

"What do you suggest then?" he said very sternly.

"You go and recover the two halves at the places I indicate," I stammered out, "and... and..."

A faint whirr and the silver chime rang out.

Half an hour more!

How still the house was! I could hear the clock ticking—no, that thudding must be my heart. My wits failed me, my mind had become a blank, my throat was dry with fear.

"I've wasted an hour and a half over you, young man," said Clubfoot suddenly, "and it's time that this conversation was brought to a close. I warn you again that I am not to be trifled with. The situation is perfectly clear: it rests with you whether the Countess Rachwitz goes free or is court-martialled this afternoon at Cleves and shot this evening. Your suggestion is absurd. I will be reasonable with you. We will both stay here. I will wire for the two portions of the letter to be fetched at the places you indicate, and as soon as I hold the entire letter in my hands the Countess will be driven to the frontier. I will allow her butler here to accompany her, and he can return and assure you that she is in safety."

He stretched out his hand and pulled a block of telegraph forms towards him.

"Where shall we find the two halves?" he said.

"One is in Holland," I murmured.

He looked up quickly.

"If you dare play me false..."

He broke off when he saw my face.

The room was going round with me. My hands felt cold as ice. I was struggling for the mastery over myself, but I felt my body swaying.

"Ah!" exclaimed Clubfoot musingly, "that would be Semlin's half... I might have known... Well, never mind, Schmalz can take my car and fetch it. He can be back by tomorrow. Where is he to go?"

"The other half is in Berlin," I said desperately. My voice sounded to me like a third person speaking.

"That's simpler," replied Clubfoot. "Ten minutes to twelve now... if I wire at once, that half should be here by midnight... I'll get the message off immediately..."

He looked up at me, pencil in hand.

It was the end. I had kept faith with Francis to the limit of my powers, but now my resistance was broken. He had failed me... not me, but Monica, rather... I could not save her now. Like some nightmare film, the crowded hours of the past few weeks flashed past my eyes, a jostling procession of figures — Semlin with his blue lips and livid face, Schratt with her bejewelled hands, the Jew Kore, Haase with his bullet head, Francis, sadly musing on the café verandah... and Monica, all in white, as I saw her that night at the Esplanade... my thoughts always came back to her, a white and pitiful figure in some dusty courtyard at lamplight facing a row of levelled rifles...

"I am waiting!"

Clubfoot's voice broke stridently upon the silence. Should I tell him the truth now?

It was three minutes to the hour.

"Come! The two addresses!"

I would keep faith to the last.

"Herr Doktor!" I faltered.

He dashed the pencil down on the table and sprang to his feet. He caught me by the lapels of my coat and shook me in an iron grip.

"The addresses, you dog!" he said.

The clock whirred faintly. There was a knock at the door.

"Come in!" roared Clubfoot and resumed his seat.

The clock was chiming twelve.

An officer stepped in briskly and saluted.

It was Francis!... Francis, freshly shaved, his moustache neatly trimmed, a monocle in his eye, in a beautifully waisted grey military overcoat, one white-gloved hand raised in salute to his helmet.

"Hauptmann von Salzmann!"... he introduced himself, clicking his heels and bowing to Clubfoot, who glared at him, frowning at the interruption. He spoke with the clipped, mincing utterance of the typical Prussian officer. "I am looking for Herr Leutnant Schmalz," he said.

"He is not in," answered Clubfoot in a surly voice. "He is out and I am busy... I do not wish to be disturbed."

"As Schmalz is out," the officer returned suavely, advancing to the desk, "I must trouble you for an instant, I fear. I have been sent over from Goch to inspect the guard here. But I find no guard... there is not a man in the place."

Clubfoot angrily heaved his unwieldy bulk from his chair.

"Gott im Himmel!" he cried savagely. "It is incredible that I can never be left in peace. What the devil has the guard got to do with me? Will you understand that I have nothing to do with the guard! There is a sergeant somewhere... curse him for a lazy scoundrel... I'll ring..."

He never finished the sentence. As he turned his back on my brother to reach the bell in the wall, Francis sprang on him from behind, seizing his bull neck in an iron grip and driving his knee at the same moment into that vast expanse of back.

The huge German, taken by surprise, crashed over backwards, my brother on top of him.

It was so quickly done that, for the instant, I was dumbfounded.

"Quick, Des, the door!" my brother gasped. "Lock the door!"

The big German was roaring like a bull and plunging wildly under my brother's fingers, his clubfoot beating a thunderous tattoo on the parquet floor. In his fall Clubfoot's left arm had been bent under him and was now pinioned to the ground by his great weight. With his free right hand he strove fiercely to force off my brother's fingers as Francis fought to get a grip on the man's throat and choke him into silence.

I darted to the door. The key was on the inside and I turned it in a trice. As I turned to go to my brother's help my eye caught sight of the butt of my pistol lying where Schmalz had thrown it the evening before under my overcoat on the leather lounge.

I snatched up the weapon and dropped by my brother's side, crushing Clubfoot's right arm to the ground. I thrust the pistol in his face.

"Stop that noise!" I commanded.

The German obeyed.

"Better search him, Francis," I said to my brother. "He probably has a Browning on him somewhere."

Francis went through the man's pockets, reaching up and putting each article as it came to light on the desk above him. From an inner breast pocket he extracted the Browning. He glanced at it: the magazine was full with a cartridge in the breach.

"Hadn't we better truss him up?" Francis said to me.

"No," I said. I was still kneeling on the German's arm. He seemed exhausted. His head had fallen back upon the ground.

"Let me up, curse you!" he choked.

"No!" I said again and Francis turned and looked at me.

Each of us knew what was in the other's mind, my brother and I. We were thinking of a handclasp we had exchanged on the banks of the Rhine.

I was about to speak but Francis checked me. He was trembling all over. I could feel his elbow quiver where it touched mine.

"No, Des, please..." he pleaded, "let me... this is my show..."

Then, in a voice that vibrated with suppressed passion, he spoke swiftly to Clubfoot.

"Take a good look at me, Grundt," he said sternly. "You don't know me, do you? I am Francis Okewood, brother of the man who has brought you to your fall. You don't know me, but you knew some of my friends, I think. Jack Tracy? Do you remember him? And Herbert Arbuthnot? Ah, you knew him, too. And Philip Brewster? You remember him as well, do you? No need to ask you what happened to poor Philip!"

The man on the floor answered nothing, but I saw the colour very slowly fade from his cheeks.

My brother spoke again.

"There were four of us after that letter, as you knew, Grundt, and three of us are dead. But you never got me. I was the fourth man, the unknown quantity in all your elaborate calculations... and it seems to me I spoiled your reckoning... I and this brother of mine... an amateur at the game, Grundt!"

Still Clubfoot was silent, but I noticed a bead of perspiration tremble on his forehead, then trickle down his ashen cheeks and drop splashing to the floor.

Francis continued in the same deep, relentless voice.

"I never thought I should have to soil my hands by ridding the world of a man like you, Grundt, but it has come to it and you have to die. I'd have killed you in hot blood when I first came in but for Jack and Herbert and the others... for their sake you had to know who is your executioner."

My brother raised the pistol. As he did so the man on the floor, by a tremendous effort of strength, rose erect to his knees, flinging me headlong. Then there was a hot burst of flame close to my cheek as I lay on the floor, a deafening report, a thud and a sickening gurgle.

Something twitched a little on the ground and then lay still.

We rose to our feet together.

"Des," said my brother unsteadily, "it seems rather like murder."

"No, Francis," I whispered back, "it was justice!"

20

CHARLEMAGNE'S RIDE

The hands of the clock pointed to a quarter past twelve. Funny, how my eyes kept coming back to that clock! There was a smell of warm gunpowder in the room, and the autumn sunshine, struggling feebly through the window, caught the blue edges of a little haze of smoke that hung lazily in the air by the desk in the corner. How close the room was! And how that clock seemed to stare at me! I felt very sick...

Lord? What a draught! A gust of icy air was raging in my face. The room was still swaying to and fro...

I was in the front seat of a car beside Francis, who was driving. We were fairly flying along a broad and empty road, the tall poplars with which it was lined scudding away into the vanishing landscape as we whizzed by. The surface was terrible, and the car pitched this way and that as we tore along. But Francis had her well in hand. He sat at the wheel, very cool and deliberate and very grave, still in his officer's uniform, and his eyes had a cold glint that told me he was keyed up to top pitch.

We slackened speed a fraction to negotiate a turn off to the right down a side road. We seemed to take that corner on two wheels. A thin church spire protruded from the trees in the centre of the group of houses which we were approaching so furiously. The village was all but deserted: everybody seemed to be indoors at their midday meal, but Francis slowed down and ran along the dirty street at a demure pace. The village passed, he jammed down the accelerator and once more the car sprang forward.

The country was flat as a pancake, but presently the fields fell away a bit from the road with boulders and patches of gorse here and there The next moment we were slackening speed. We drew up by a rough track which led off the road and vanished into a tangle of stunted trees and scrub growing across the yellow face of a sand-pit.

Francis motioned me to get out, and then sprang to the ground himself, leaving the engine throbbing. His face was grey and set.

"Stay here!" he whispered to me. "You've got your pistol? Good. If anybody attempts to interfere with you, shoot!" He dashed into the tangle and was swallowed up. I heard a whistle, and a whistle in answer, and a minute later he appeared again helping Monica through the thick undergrowth.

Monica looked as pretty as a picture in her dark green shooting suit and her muffler. She was as excited as a child at its first play.

"A car!" she exclaimed. "Oh, Francis, I'll sit beside you!"

My brother glanced at his watch.

"Twenty to one!" he murmured. He had a hunted look on his face. Monica saw it and it sobered her.

They got up in front, and I sat in the body of the car.

"Hang on to that!" said Francis, handing me over a leather case. I recognised it at a glance. It was Clubfoot's dispatch-box. Francis was thorough in everything.

Once more we dashed out along the desolate country roads. We saw hardly a soul. Houses were few and far between and, save for an occasional greybeard hoeing in the wet fields or an old woman hobbling along the road, the countryside seemed dead. In the cold air the engine ran splendidly, and Francis got every ounce of horse-power out of it.

On we rushed, the wind in our ears, the cold air in our faces, until we found ourselves racing along an avenue of old trees that led straight as an arrow right into the heart of the forest. It was as silent as the grave: the air was dank and chill and the trees dripped sorrowfully into the brimming ruts of the road.

We whizzed past many tracks leading into the depths of the forest, but it was not until the car had eaten up some five kilometres of the main road that Francis slowed to a halt. He consulted a map he pulled from his pocket, then glanced at his watch with puckered brow.

"I had hoped to take the car into the forest," he said, "but the roads are so soft we shan't get a yard. Still we can but try."

We went forward again, very slowly, to where a track ran off to the left. It was badly ploughed up, and the ruts were fully a foot deep. Monica and I got out to lighten the car, and Francis ran her in. But he hadn't gone five yards before the car was bogged up to the axles.

"We'll have to leave it," he said, jumping out. "It's ten minutes to two... we haven't a second to lose."

He pulled a cloth cap from the pocket of his military overcoat, then stripped off the coat, showing his ordinary clothes underneath, and very shiny black field-boots up to his knees. He put his helmet in the overcoat and made a roll of it, tucking it under his arm, and then donned his cap.

"Now," he said, "we'll have to run for it, Monica, I'm afraid: we must reach our cover while the light lasts or I shan't be able to find it and it will be dark in these woods in about two hours from now. Are you ready?"

We struck off the track into the forest. There was not much undergrowth, and the trees were not planted very close, so our way was not impeded. We jogged on over a carpet of wet leaves, stumbling over the roots of trees, tearing our clothes on the brambles, bringing down showers of raindrops from the branches of pine or fir we brushed on our headlong course. Now a squirrel bolted up his tree, now a rabbit frisked back into his hole, now a soft-eyed deer crashed away into the bushes on our approach. The place was so still that it gave me confidence. There was not a trace of man now that we were away from the marks of his carts on the tracks, and I began to feel, in the presence of the stately, silent trees, that at last I was safe from the menace that had hung over me for so long.

We rested frequently, breathless and panting, a hand to the side. Monica was a marvel of endurance. Her boots were sopping, her skirt wet to the waist, her face was scratched, and her hair was coming down, but she never complained. Francis was seemingly tireless and was always the one to lead the way when we started afresh.

It was heavy going, for at every step our feet sank deep in the leaves. The forest was undulating with deep hollows and steep banks, which tried us a good deal. It soon became evident that we could not keep up the pace. Monica was tiring visibly, and I had had about enough; Francis, too, seemed done up. We slackened to a walk. We were toiling painfully up one of these steep banks when Francis, who was leading, held up his hand.

"Charlemagne's Ride!" he whispered as we came up. We looked down from the top of the bank and saw below us a broad forest glade, canopied by the thick branches of the ancient trees that met overhead, and leading up a slope, narrowing as it went, to a path that lost itself among the shadows that were falling fast upon the forest.

Francis clambered down the bank and we followed. Twilight reigned below in the glade under the lofty roof of branches and our feet rustled softly as we trod the leaves underfoot. It was a ghostly place, and Monica clutched my arm as we went quickly after Francis, who, striding rapidly ahead, threatened to be swallowed up in the shadows of the autumn evening. He led us up the slope and along the narrow path. A path struck off it, and he took it. It led us into a thicker part of the forest than we had yet struck, where there were great boulders protruding from the dripping bushes, and brambles grew so thick that in places they obscured the track.

The forest sloped up again, and in front of us was a steep bank, its sides dotted with great rocks and a tangle of brambles and undergrowth. Francis stooped between two boulders at the foot of the slope, then turning and beckoning us to follow, disappeared. Monica went in after him, and I came last. We were in a kind of narrow entrance, scooped out of the earth between the rocks, and it led down to a broad chamber, which had apparently been dug beneath some of the boulders, for, stretching out my hand, I found the roof was rock and damp to the touch.

Francis and Monica were standing in this chamber as I came down. Directly I entered I knew why they stood so still. A glimmer of light came from the farther end of the cave, and a strange sound, a sort of strangled sobbing, reached our ears.

I crept forward in the dark in the direction of the light. My outstretched hands came upon a low opening. I stooped and, crawling round a rock, saw another chamber illuminated by a guttering candle stuck by its wax to the earthen wall. On the floor a man was lying, sobbing as though his heart would break. He was wearing some kind of a military great-coat with a yellow stripe running down the back.

"Pst!" I called to him, drawing my pistol from my pocket. As I did so, Francis behind me touched my arm to let me know he was there.

"Pst!" I called again louder.

The man swung round on to his knees with a sudden, frightened spring. When he saw my pistol, he jerked his hands above his head. Dirty and unshaven, with the tears all wet on his face, he looked a woe-begone and tragic figure.

"Kamerad! Kamerad!" he muttered stupidly at me. "Napoo! Kaput! Englander!"

I gazed at the stranger, hardly able to believe my ears. That trench jargon in this place!

"Are you English?" I asked him.

At the sound of my voice he stared about him wildly.

"Ay, I be English, zur," he replied with a strong West Country burr, "God help me!" And, heedless of me and my pistol, he covered his face with his hands and burst into a wild fit of sobbing again, rocking himself to and fro in his grief.

"Go back to Monica!" I whispered to Francis. "I'll see to this fellow!"

I managed to pacify him presently. Habit is a tenacious ruler and, grotesque figures though we were, the "zur" he had addressed to me brought out the officer in me. I talked to him as I would have done to one of my own men, and he quietened down at last and looked up at me.

He was only a lad—I could tell that by the clearness of his skin and the brightness of his eyes—but his face was wan and wasted, and at the first glance he looked like a man of forty. Under his great-coat which was German, he was clad in filthy rags which once had been a khaki uniform, as the cut—and nothing else—revealed.

He told me his simple story in his soft Somersetshire accent, just the plain tale of the fate that had overtaken thousands of our fellow-countrymen since the war began. His name was Maggs, Sapper Ebenezer Maggs, of the Royal Engineers, and he was captured near Mons in August, 1914, when out laying a line with a party. With a long train of British prisoners—"zum of 'em was terrible bad, zur, dying, as you might say"—he had been marched off to a town and paraded to the railway station through streets thronged with jeering German soldiery. In cattle trucks, the fit, the wounded, the dying and the dead herded together, without food or water, they had made their journey into Germany with hostile mobs at every station, once the frontier was past, brutal men and shrieking women, to whom not even the dying were sacred.

It was a terrible tale that lost nothing of its horror from the simple, unadorned style of this West Country farmer's son. He had been one of the ragged, emaciated band of British prisoners of war who had shivered through that first long winter in the starvation camp of Friedrichsfeld, near Wesel. For two years he had endured the filthy food, the neglect, the harsh treatment, then a resourceful Belgian friend, whom he called John, in happier days a contraband runner on this very frontier, had shown him a means to escape. Five days before they had left the camp and separated, agreeing to meet at Charlemagne's Ride in the forest and try to force the frontier together. "John" had never come. For twenty-four hours Maggs had waited in vain, then his courage had forsaken him, and he had crept to that hole in his grief.

I went and fetched Francis and Monica. Maggs shrunk back as they came in.

"I bean't fit cumpany for no lady, zur," he whispered to me, "I be that durty, fair crawling I be... We couldn't keep clean nohow in that camp!"

All the good soldier's horror of dirt was in his voice.

"That's all right, Maggs," I answered soothingly, "she'll understand!"

We sat down on the floor in the light of Sapper Maggs' candle, and Francis and I reviewed our situation. The cave we were in... an old smuggler's *cache*... was where Francis had spent several days during his different attempts to get across the frontier. The border line was only about a quarter of a mile distant and ran right through the forest. There was no live-wire fencing in the forest, such as the Germans have erected along the frontier between Holland and Belgium. The frontier was guarded by patrols. These patrols were posted four men to every two hundred yards along the line through the forest, so that two men, patrolling in pairs, covered a hundred yards apiece.

It was now half-past five in the evening. We both agreed that we should certainly make the attempt to cross the frontier that night. Francis nudged me, indicating the sapper with his eyes.

"Maggs," I said, "we are all in a bad way, but our case is more desperate than yours. I shall not tell you more than this, that, if we are caught, any of us three, we shall be shot, and anyone caught with us will fare the same. If you will take my advice, you will leave us and start off by yourself; the worst that can happen to you is to be sent back to your camp. You will be punished for running away, but you won't lose your life!"

Sapper Maggs shook his yellow head.

"I'll stay," he answered stolidly; "it's more cumfortable-like for us four to 'old together, and it's a better protection for the lady. I bean't afear'd of no Gers, I bean't! I'll go along o' yew officers and the lady, if yew don't mind, zur!"

So it was settled, and we four agreed to unite forces. Before we set out Francis wanted to go and reconnoitre. I thought he had done more than his share that day, and said so. But Francis insisted.

"I know my way blindfold about the forest, old man," he said; "it'll be far safer for me than for you. I'll leave you the map and mark the route you are to follow, so that you can find the way if anything happens to me. If I'm not back by midnight, you ought certainly not to wait any longer, but make the attempt by yourselves."

My brother handed me back the document and went over the route we were to follow on the map. Then he deposited his bundle in the cave and declared himself ready.

"And don't forget old Clubfoot's box," he said by way of a parting injunction.

Monica took him out to the entrance of our refuge. She was dabbing her eyes with her handkerchief when she returned. To divert her thoughts, I questioned her about the events that led to my rescue, and she told me how, at Francis' request, she had got all the servants out of the Castle on different pretexts. It was Francis who had got rid of the soldiers remaining as a guard.

"You remember the Captain of Köpenick trick?" she said. "Well, Francis played it off on the sergeant and those six men. He slept at Cleves, had himself trimmed up at the barber's, bought those field-boots he is wearing, and stole that helmet and great-coat off the pegs in the passage at Schmidt's Café, where the officers always go and drink beer after morning parade. Then he drove out to the Castle—he knew that the place would be deserted once the shoot had started—and told the sergeant he had been sent from Goch to inspect the guard. I think he is just splendid! He inspected the men and cursed everybody up and down, and sent the sergeant out to the paddock with orders to drill them for two hours. Francis was telling me all about it as we came along. He says that if you can get hold of a uniform and hector a German enough, he will never call your bluff. Can you beat it?"

The hours dragged wearily on. We had no food, and Maggs, who had eaten the last of his provisions twenty-four hours before—the British soldier is a bad hoarder—soon consumed the last of my cigarettes. It was past ten o'clock when I heard a step outside. The next moment Francis came in, white and breathless.

"They're beating the forest for us," he panted. "The place is full of men. I had to crawl the whole way there and back, and I'm soaked to the skin."

I pointed to Monica, who was fast asleep, and he lowered his voice.

"Des," he said, "I've hoped as long as I dared, but now I believe the game's up. They're beating the forest in a great circle, soldiers and police and customs men. If we set out at once we can reach the frontier before they get here, but what's the use of that... every patrol is on the look-out for us... the forest seems ablaze with torches."

"We must try it, Francis," I said. "We haven't a dog's chance if we stay here!"

"I think you're right," he answered. "Well, here's the plan. There's a deep ravine that runs clear across the frontier. I spent an hour in it. They've built a plank bridge across the top just this side of the line, and the patrol comes to the ravine about every three minutes. It is practically impossible to get out of sight and sound along that ravine in three minutes, but..."

"Unless we could drar the patrol's attention away!" said Sapper Maggs.

But Francis ignored the interruption.

"...We can at least try it. Come on, we must be starting! Thank God, there's no moon; it's as dark as the devil outside!"

We roused up Monica and groped our way out of the cave into the black and dripping forest. Somewhere in the distance a faint glare reddened the sky. From time to time I thought I heard a shout, but it sounded far away.

We crawled stealthily forward, Francis in front, then Monica, Maggs and I last. In a few minutes we were wet through, and our hands, blue and dead with cold, were scratched and torn. Our progress was interminably slow. Every few yards Francis raised his hand and we stopped.

At last we reached the gloomy glade where, as Francis had told us, according to popular belief, the wraith of Charlemagne was still seen on the night of St. Huber's Day galloping along with his ghostly followers of the chase. The rustling of leaves caught our ears; instantly we all lay prone behind a bank.

A group of men came swinging along the glade. One of them was singing an ancient German soldier song:

"Die Vöglein im Walde
Sie singen so schön
In der Heimat, in der Heimat,
Da gibt's ein Wiederseh'n."

"The relief patrol!" I whispered to Francis, as soon as they were past.

"The other lot they relieve will be back this way in a minute. We must get across quickly." My brother stood erect, and tiptoed swiftly across Charlemagne's Ride, and we followed.

We must have crawled for an hour before we came to the ravine. It was a deep, narrow ditch with steep sides, full of undergrowth and brambles. Now we could hear distinctly the voices of men all around us, as it seemed, and to right and to left and in front we caught at intervals glimpses of red flames through the trees. We could only proceed at a snail's pace lest the continual rustle of our steps should betray us. So each advanced a few paces in turn; then we all paused, and then the next one went forward. We could no longer crawl; the undergrowth was too thick for that; we had to go forward bent double.

We had progressed like this for fully half an hour when Francis, who was in front as usual, beckoned us to lie down. We all lay motionless among the brambles Then a voice somewhere above us said in German: "And I'll have a man at the plank here, sergeant: he can watch the ravine."

Another voice answered:

"Very good, Herr Leutnant, but in that case the patrols to right and left need not cross the plank each time; they can turn when they come to the ravine guard."

The voices died away in a murmur. I craned my neck aloft. It was so dark, I could see nothing save the fretwork of branches against the night sky. I whispered to Francis, who was just in front of me:

"Unless we make a dash for it now that man will hear us rustling along!"

Francis held up a finger. I heard a heavy footstep along the bank above us.

"Too late!" my brother whispered back. "Do you hear the patrols?"

Footsteps crashing through the undergrowth resounded on the right and left.

"Cold work!" said a voice.

"Bitter!" came the answer, just above our heads.

"Seen anything?"

"Nothing!"

The rustling began again on the right, and died away.

"They're closing in on the left!" Another voice this time.

"Heard anything, you?" from the voice above us.

"Not a thing!"

The rustling broke out once more on the left, and gradually became lost in the distance.

Silence.

I felt a hot breath in my ear. Sapper Maggs stood by my side.

"There be a feller a-watching for us up there," he whispered.

I nodded.

"If us could drar his 'tention away, yew could slip by, next time the patrols is past, couldn't 'ee?"

Again I nodded.

"It'd be worse for yew than for me, supposin' yew'd be ca-art, that's what t'other officer said, warn't it?"

And once more I nodded.

The hot whisper came again.

"I'll drar 'un off for ee, zur, nex' time the patrols pass. When I holler, yew and the others, yew run. Thirty-one forty-three Sapper Maggs, R.E., from Chewton Mendip... that's me... maybe yew'll let us have a bit o' writing to the camp."

I stretched out my hand in the darkness to stop him. He had gone.

THE MAN WITH THE CLUBFOOT

I leant forward to Francis:

"When you hear a shout, we make a dash for it!"

I felt him look at me in surprise—it was too dark to see his face.

"Right!" he whispered back.

Now to the left we heard voices shouting and saw torches gleaming red among the trees. To right and rear answering shouts resounded.

Again the patrols met at the plank above our heads, and again their departing footsteps rustled in the leaves.

The murmur of voices grew nearer. We could fairly smell the burning resin of the torches.

Then a wild yell rent the forest. The voice above us shouted "Halt!" but the echo was lost in the deafening report of a rifle.

Francis caught Monica by the wrist and dragged her forward. We went plunging and crashing through the tangle of the ravine. We heard a second shot and a third, commands were shouted, the red glare deepened in the sky...

Monica collapsed quite suddenly at my feet. She never uttered a sound, but fell prone, her face as white as paper. Without a word we picked her up between us and went on, stumbling, gasping, coughing, our clothes rent and torn, the blood oozing from the deep scratches on our faces and hands.

At length our strength gave out. We laid Monica down in the ravine and drew the undergrowth over her, then we crawled in under the brambles exhausted, beat.

* * *

Dawn was streaking the sky with lemon when a dog jumped sniffing down into our hiding-place. Francis and Monica were asleep.

A man stood at the top of the ravine looking down on us. He carried a gun over his shoulder.

"Have you had an accident?" he said kindly.

He spoke in Dutch.

21

RED TABS EXPLAINS

From the Argyllshire hills winter has stolen down upon us in the night. Behind him he has left his white mantle, and it now lies outspread from the topmost mountain peaks to the softly lapping tide at the black edges of the loch. Yet as I sit adding the last words to this plain account of a curious episode in my life, the wintry scene dissolves before my eyes, and I see again that dawn in the forest... Francis and Monica, sleeping side by side, like the babes in the wood, half covered with leaves, the eager, panting retriever, and myself, poor, ragged scarecrow, staring open-mouthed at the Dutchman whose kindly enquiry has just revealed to me the wondrous truth... that we are safe across the frontier.

What a disproportionate view one takes of events in which one is the principal actor! The great issues vanish away, the little things loom out large. When I look back on that morning I encounter in my memory no recollection of extravagant demonstrations of joy at our delivery, no hysteria, no heroics. But I find a fragrant remembrance of a glorious hot bath and an epic breakfast in the house of that kindly Dutchman, followed by a whirlwind burst of hospitality on our arrival at the house of van Urutius, which was not more than ten miles from the fringe of the forest.

Madame van Urutius took charge of Monica, who was promptly sent to bed, whilst Francis and I went straight on to Rotterdam, where we had an interview at the British Consulate, with the result that we were able to catch the steamer for England the next day.

As the result of various telegrams which Francis dispatched from Rotterdam, a car was waiting for us on our arrival at Fenchurch Street the next evening. In it we drove off for an interview with my brother's Chief. Francis insisted that I should hand over personally the portion of the document in our possession.

"You got hold of it, Des," he said, "and it's only fair that you should get all the credit. I have Clubfoot's dispatch-box to show as the result of my trip. It's only a pity we could not have got the other half out of the cloak-room at Rotterdam."

We were shown straight in to the Chief. I was rather taken aback by the easy calm of his manner in receiving us.

"How are you, Okewood?" he said, nodding to Francis. "This your brother? How d'ye do?"

He gave me his hand and was silent. There was a distinct pause. Feeling distinctly embarrassed, I lugged out my portfolio, extracted the three slips of paper and laid them on the desk before the Chief.

"I've brought you something," I said lamely.

He picked up the slips of paper and looked at them for a moment. Then he lifted a cardboard folder from the desk in front of him, opened it and displayed the other half of the Kaiser's letter, the fragment I had believed to be reposing in a bag at Rotterdam railway station. He placed the two fragments side by side. They fitted exactly. Then he closed the folder, carried it across the room to a safe and locked it up. Coming back, he held out his two hands to us, giving the right to me, the left to Francis.

"You have done very well," he said. "Good boys! Good boys!"

"But that other half..." I began.

"Your friend Ashcroft is by no means such a fool as he looks," the Chief chuckled. "He did a wise thing. He brought your two letters to me. I saw to the rest. So, when your brother's telegram arrived from Rotterdam, I got the other half of the letter out of the safe; I thought I'd be ready for you, you see!"

"But how did you know we had the remaining portion of the letter?" I asked.

The Chief chuckled again.

"My young men don't wire for cars to meet 'em at the station when they have failed," he replied. "Now, tell me all about it!"

So I told him my whole story from the beginning.

When I had finished, he said:

"You appear to have a very fine natural disposition for our game, Okewood. It seems a pity to waste it in regimental work..."

I broke in hastily.

"I've got a few weeks' sick leave left," I said, "and after that I was looking forward to going back to the front for a rest. This sort of thing is too exciting for me!"

"Well, well," answered the Chief, "we'll see about that afterwards. In the meantime, we shall not forget what you have done... and I shall see that it is not forgotten elsewhere."

On that we left him. It was only just outside that I remembered that he had told me nothing of what I was burning to know about the origin and disappearance of the Kaiser's letter.

* * *

It was my old friend, Red Tabs, whom I met on one of our many visits to mysterious but obviously important officials, that finally cleared up for me the many obscure points in this adventure of mine. When he saw me be burst out laughing.

"'Pon my soul," he grinned, "you seem to be able to act on a hint, don't you?"

Then he told me the story of the Kaiser's letter.

"There is no need to speak of the contents of this amazing letter," he began, "for you are probably more familiar with them than I am. The date alone will suffice... July 31st, 1914... it explains a great deal. The last day of July was the moment when the peace of Europe was literally trembling in the balance. You know the Emperor's wayward, capricious nature, his eagerness for fame and military glory, his morbid terror of the unknown. In that fateful last week of July he was torn between opposing forces. On the one side was ranged the whole of the Prussian military party, led by the Crown Prince and the Emperor's own immediate entourage; on the other, the record of prosperity which years of peace had conferred on his realms. He had to choose between his own megalomania craving for military laurels, on the one hand, and, on the other, that place in history as the Prince of Peace for which, in his gentler moments, he has so often hankered.

"The Kaiser is a man of moods. He sat down and penned this letter in a fit of despondency and indecision, when the vision of Peace seemed fairer to him than the spectre of War. God knows what violent emotion impelled him to write this extraordinary appeal to his English friend, an appeal which, if published, would convict him of the deepest treachery to his ally, but he wrote the letter and forthwith dispatched it to London. He did not make use of the regular courier: he sent the letter by a man of his own choosing, who had special instructions to hand the letter in person to Prince Lichnowski, the German ambassador. Lichnowski was to deliver the missive personally to its recipient.

"Almost as soon as the letter was away, the Kaiser seems to have realised what he had done, to have repented of his action.

Attempts to stop the messenger before he reached the coast appear to have failed. At any rate, we know that all through July 31st and August 1st Lichnowski, in London, was bombarded with dispatches ordering him to send the messenger with the letter back to Berlin as soon as he reached the embassy.

"The courier never got as far as Carlton House Terrace. Someone in the War party at the Court of Berlin got wind of the fateful letter and sent word to someone in the German embassy in London—the Prussian jingoes were well represented there by Kuhlmann and others of his ilk—to intercept the letter.

"The letter was intercepted. How it was done and by whom we have never found out, but Lichnowski never saw that letter. Nor did the courier leave London. With the Imperial letter still in possession, apparently, he went to a house at Dalston, where he was arrested on the day after we declared war on Germany.

"This courier went by the name of Schulte. We did not know him at the time to be travelling on the Emperor's business, but we knew him very well as one of the most daring and successful spies that Germany had ever employed in this country. One of our people picked him up quite by chance on his arrival in London, and shadowed him to Dalston, where we promptly laid him by the heels when war broke out.

"Schulte was interned. You have heard how one of his letters, stopped by the Camp Censor, put us on the track of the intercepted letter, and you know the steps we took to obtain possession of the document. But we were misled... not by Schulte, but through the treachery of a man in whom he confided, the interpreter at the internment camp.

"To this man Schulte entrusted the famous letter, telling him to send it by an underground route to a certain address at Cleves, and promising him in return a commission of twenty-five per cent on the price to be paid for the letter. The interpreter took the letter, but did not do as he was bid. On the contrary, he wrote to the go-between, with whom Schulte had been in correspondence (probably Clubfoot), and announced that he knew where the letter was and was prepared to sell it, only the purchaser would have to come to England and fetch it.

"Well, to make a long story short, the interpreter made a deal with the Huns, and this Dr Semlin was sent to England from Washington, where he had been working for Bernstorff, to fetch the letter at the address in London indicated by the interpreter. In the meantime, we had got after the interpreter, who, like Schulte, had been in the espionage business all his life, and he was arrested.

"We know what Semlin found when he reached London. The wily interpreter had sliced the letter in two, so as to make sure of his money, meaning, no doubt, to hand over the other portion as soon as the price had been paid. But by the time Semlin got to London the interpreter was jugged and Semlin had to report that he had only got half the letter. The rest you know... how Grundt was sent for, how he came to this country and retrieved the other portion. Don't ask me how he set about it: I don't know, and we never found out even where the interpreter deposited the second half or how Grundt discovered its hiding-place. But he executed his mission and got clear away with the goods. The rest of the tale you know better than I do!"

"But Clubfoot," I asked, "who is he?"

"There are many who have asked that question," Red Tabs replied gravely, "and some have not waited long for their answer. The man was known by name and reputation to very few, by sight to even fewer, yet I doubt if any man of his time wielded greater power in secret than he. Officially, he was nothing, he didn't exist; but in the dark places, where his ways were laid, he watched and plotted and spied for his master, the tool of the Imperial spite as he was the instrument of the Imperial vengeance.

"A man like the Kaiser," my friend continued, "monarch though he is, has many enemies naturally, and makes many more. Head of the Army, head of the Navy, head of the Church, head of the State—undisputed, autocratic head—he is confronted at every turn by personal issues woven and intertwined with political questions. It was in this sphere, where the personal is grafted on the political, that Clubfoot reigned supreme... here and in another sphere, where German William is not only monarch, but also a very ordinary man.

"There are phases in every man's life, Okewood, which hardly bear the light of day. In an autocracy, however, such phases are generally inextricably entangled with political questions. It was in these dark places that Clubfoot flourished... he and his men... 'the G gang' we called them, from the letter 'G' (signifying *Garde* or *Guard*) on their secret-service badges.

"Clubfoot was answerable to no one save to the Emperor alone. His work was of so delicate, so confidential a nature, that he rendered an account of his services only to his Imperial master. There was none to stay his hand, to check him in his courses, save only this neurotic, capricious cripple who is always open to flattery..."

Red Tabs thought for a minute and then went on.

"No one may catalogue," he said, "the crimes that Clubfoot committed, the infamies he had to his account. Not even the Kaiser himself, I dare say, knows the manner in which his orders to this blackguard were executed—orders rapped out often enough, I swear, in a fit of petulance, a gust of passion, and forgotten the next moment in the excitement of some fresh sensation.

"I know a little of Clubfoot's record, of innocent lives wrecked, of careers ruined, of sudden disappearances, of violent deaths. When you and your brother put it across 'der Stelze,' Okewood, you settled a long outstanding account we had against him, but you also rendered his fellow-Huns a signal service."

I thought of the comments I had heard on Clubfoot among the customers at Haase's, and I felt that Red Tabs had hit the right nail on the head again.

"By the way? "said Red Tabs, as I rose to go, " would you care to see Clubfoot's epitaph? I kept it for you."He handed me a German newspaper—the *Berliner Tageblatt*, I think it was— with a paragraph marked in red pencil. I read:

"We regret to report the sudden death from apoplexy of Dr Adolf Grundt, an inspector of secondary schools. The deceased was closely connected for many years with a number of charitable institutions enjoying the patronage of the Emperor. His Majesty frequently consulted Dr Grundt regarding the distribution of the sums allocated annually from the Privy purse for benevolent objects."

"Pretty fair specimen of Prussian cynicism?" laughed Red Tabs. But I held my head... the game was too deep for me.

* * *

Every week a hamper of good things is dispatched to 3143 Sapper Ebenezer Maggs, British Prisoner of War, Gefangenen-Lager, Friedrichsfeld bei Wesel. I have been in communication with his people, and since his flight from the camp they have not had a line from him. They will let me know at once if they hear, but I am restless and anxious about him.

I dare not write lest I compromise him: I dare not make official enquiry as to his safety for the same reason. If he survived those shots in the dark, he is certainly undergoing punishment, and in that case he would be deprived of the privilege of writing or receiving letters...

But the weeks slip by and no message comes to me from Chewton Mendip. Almost daily I wonder if the gallant lad survived that night to return to the misery of the starvation camp, or whether, out of the darkness of the forest, his brave soul soared free, achieving its final release from the sufferings of this world... Poor Sapper Maggs!

Francis and Monica are honeymooning on the Riviera. Gerry, I am sure, would have refused to attend the wedding, only he wasn't asked. Francis is getting a billet on the Intelligence out in France when his leave is up.

I have got my step, antedated back to the day I went into Germany. Francis has been told that something is coming to him and me in the New Year's Honours.

I don't worry much. I am going back to the front on Christmas Eve.

The Return of Clubfoot

22

DOÑA LUISA

As I was sitting on the verandah of John Bard's bungalow, glancing through a two-month old copy of *The Sketch*, I heard the clang of the iron gate below where I sat. I raised my eyes from the paper and looked down the gardens. At my feet was stretched a dark tangle of palms and luxuriant tropical verdure, beyond them in the distance the glass-like surface of the sea, on which a great lucent moon threw a gleaming path of light.

The night was very tranquil. From the port at the foot of the hill, on which my old friend, John Bard, had built his bungalow in this earthly paradise, the occasional screech of a winch was wafted with astonishing clearness over the warm air. Somewhere in the distance there was the faint monotonous thrumming of guitars. To these night noises of the little Central American port the sea murmured faintly a ceaseless accompaniment.

I heard voices in the garden. Within the house a door swung to with a thud; there was the patter of slippered feet over the matting in the living-room and Akawa, Bard's Japanese servant, was at my elbow. His snow-white drill stood out against the black shadows which the moon cast at the back of the verandah. He did not speak; but his mask-like face waited for me to notice him.

"Well, Akawa?" said I; "What is it?"

"Doña Luisa ask for the *Senor Commandants*, excuse me!" announced the Jap stolidly.

Comfortably stretched out in a cane chair, a cold drink frosting its long glass in the trough at my side, I turned and stared at the butler. I was undoubtedly the *Señor Commandante*, for thus, in the course of a lazy, aimless sort of holiday on the shores of the Pacific, had my rank of Major been hispaniolised.

But what lady wanted me? Who could possibly know me here, seeing that only the day before one of John Bard's fruit ships had landed me from San Salvador?

Doña Luisa! The name had an alluring, romantic ring, especially on this gorgeous night, the velvety sky powdered with glittering stars, the air heavy with perfumes exhaled from the scented gardens. That broad strain of romance in me (which makes so much trouble for us Celts) responded strongly to the appeal of my environment. Doña Luisa! The distant strains of music seemed to thrum that soft name into my brain.

I swung my feet to the ground, stood up and stretched myself.

"Where is the lady?" I demanded. "In the sitting-room?"

"No, sir," replied the Japanese. "In the garden!"

More and more romantic! Had some lovely senorita, in high comb and mantilla, been inflamed by a chance sight of the *Inglez* as I had walked through the grass-grown streets of the city with John Bard that morning, and pursued me to my host's gardens to declare her love? The thought amused me and I smiled. Yet I don't mind admitting that, on my way through the sitting-room in Akawa's wake, I glanced at a mirror and noted with satisfaction that my white drill was spotless, and my hair smooth. I adjusted my tie and with that little touch of swagger which the prospect of a romantic rendezvous imparts to the gait of the most modest of us men, I passed out of the room to the corridor which led to the door into the gardens.

THE RETURN OF CLUBFOOT

The passage was brightly lit so that, on emerging into the darkness again, my eyes were dazzled. At first I could only discern a vast black shape. But presently I made out the generous proportions of an enormouslly stout, black woman.

She was wearing a torn and filthy cotton dress and about her head was bound a spotted pink and white handkerchief. With her vast bosom and ample span of hip she looked almost as broad as she was long. On seeing me she bobbed.

"You're *Señor Commandante?*" she asked in English in her soft Black womanly voice.

"Yes," I replied, rather taken aback by this droll apparition. "What did you want with me?"

"I has a letter for you, suh!"

She plunged a brown hand into the unfathomable depths of her opulent corsage.

"From Doña Luisa?" I asked expectantly.

The black woman stopped her groping and grinned up at me with flashing teeth. Her eyeballs glistened white as her face lit up with a broad smile. Then she tapped herself with a grimy paw.

"*I* is Doña Luisa!" she announced with pride.

I staggered beneath the shock of this revelation. My vision of a sloe-eyed damsel in a mantilla vanished in smoke.

"I has a fine Spanish name," remarked the lady resuming her spasmodic searchings of her person, "but I wus riz in N'Awleans. That's how I talks English so good! Ah!"

With a grunt she fished out a folded sheet of dirty note-paper and handed it to me.

"You're certain this is meant for me?" I asked, racking my brains to recall who was likely to send me messages by such an intermediary and at such an hour.

"I sure is!" responded Doña Luisa with authority.

Stepping back into the lighted corridor I unfolded the note and read:—

"To Major Desmond Okewood, D.S.O.

"Do you remember the beach-comber to whom you did a good turn at San Salvador a few weeks back? I now believe I am in a position to repay it if you will accompany the bearer of this note, I wish to see you *most urgently* but I am too ill to come to you. Don't dismiss this note as merely an ingenious attempt on my part to raise the wind. Perhaps, by the time you have received it, I shall have already escaped from the disgrace and infamy of my present existence. Therefore come at once, I beg you.

"And *make haste*."

The note was written in pencil in rather a shaky hand. There was no signature. But I remembered the writer perfectly and his signature would have availed me nothing; for I never knew his name.

Our meeting happened thus. I was visiting the jail at San Salvador and in the prison-yard I remarked among the shambling gang of prisoners taking exercise a pallid, hollow-eyed creature whose twitching mouth and fluttering hands betrayed the habitual drunkard recovering from a bout. I should have dismissed this scarecrow figure from my mind only that, suddenly evading the little brown warder, he plucked me by the coat and cried:—

"If you're a *sahib*, man, you'll get me out of this hell!"

He spoke in English and there was a refined note in his voice which, coupled with the haggard expression of his face, decided me to inquire into his case. I discovered that the man, as, indeed, he had avowed himself in the letter, was a beach-comber, a drunken wastrel, a dope fiend. In short, he was one of the unemployable, and every Consulate in the Central Americas was closed to him. But he was an Englishman; more, by birth an English gentleman. One of the officials at our Consulate told me that he was, undoubtedly, of good family.

Well, one doesn't like to think of one of one's own kith and kin locked up with a lot of coffee-coloured cut-throats among the cockchafers and less amiable insects of a Dago calaboose. So I interested myself in Friend Beach-comber and he was set free. His incarceration was the result of a tradesman's plaint and a few dollars secured his release. A few more, as it appeared in the upshot, had ensured his lasting gratitude; for I gave him a ten dollar bill to see him on his way, the State stipulating, as a condition of his liberation, that he should leave the city forthwith.

The outcast's letter was in my hand. I looked at Doña Luisa and hesitated. Would it not be simpler to give the woman a couple of dollars and send her about her business? Surely this note was nothing more than a subterfuge to obtain a further "loan" with which to buy drink or drugs—the dividing line between the two is none too clearly defined in the Central Americas.

But I found myself thinking of the beach-comber's eyes. I recalled a certain wistfulness, a sort of lonely dignity, in their mute appeal. I glanced through the note a second time. I rather liked its independent tone. So in the end I bade the woman wait while I fetched my hat. But as I took down my panama from its peg I paused an instant, then, running into my room, picked my old automatic out of my dressing-case and slid it into my jacket pocket. I had long since learnt the lesson of the Secret Service that a man may only once forget to carry arms.

As soon as I stepped out into the gardens the old black woman waddled off down the path, her bare feet pattering almost noiselessly on the hard earth. She made no further effort at conversation; but, with a swiftness surprising in one of her prodigious bulk, paddled rapidly through the scented night down the hill towards the winking lights of the port. As we left the pleasant height on which John Bard's bungalow stood, I missed the cooling night breeze off the Pacific. The air grew closer. It was steamy and soon I was drenched in perspiration.

Doña Luisa skirted the quays softly lapped by the sluggish, phosphorescent water, and plunged into a network of small streets fringed by the little yellow houses. Most of them were in darkness; for it was getting late, but here and there a shaft of golden light, shining through a heart-shaped opening cut in the shutters, fell athwart the cobbled roadway. There was something subtly evil, something *louche*, about the quarter. From behind the barred and bolted windows of one such shuttered house came strains of music, fast and furious, endlessly repeated accompanied by the rhythmic stamp of a Spanish dance and the smart click of castanets. Over the door a red light glowed dully...

But presently we left the purlieus of the port and after passing a long block of warehouses, black and forbidding, came upon a kind of township of tumbledown wooden cabins on the outskirts of the city. The stifling air was now heavy with all manner of evil odours; and heaps of refuse, dumped in the broken roadway, reeked in the hot night. The houses were the merest shanties, most of them in a dilapidated condition.

But the place swarmed with life. Black faces grinned at the unglazed casements; dark figures hurried to and fro; while from many cabins came chattering voices raised high in laughter or dispute. In the distance a native drum throbbed incessantly. To me it was like entering an African village. I knew we were in the African quarter of the city.

Suddenly Doña Luisa stopped and when I was beside her said in a low voice:

"We're mos' there!"—and struck off down a narrow lane.

Somewhere behind one of the shacks, in a full, mellow tenor, a man, hidden by the night, was singing to the soft tinkling accompaniment of a guitar. He sang in Spanish and I caught a snatch of the haunting refrain:

> "Se murio, y sobre su car a
> "Un panuelito le heche..."

THE RETURN OF CLUBFOOT

But the next moment the woman, after fumbling with a key, pushed me through a big door and the rest of the song was lost in the slamming of a great beam she fixed across it. The door gave access to a little square yard with adobe walls, an open shed along one side, a low shanty along the other. Doña Luisa pushed at a small wooden door in the wall of the shanty. Instantly a thin, quavering voice called out in English:

"Have you brought him?"

The woman murmured some inaudible reply and the voice went on:

"Have you barred the door? Then send him in! And you, get out and leave us alone!"

With a little resigned shrug of the shoulders the woman stepped back into the yard and pushed me into the cabin.

23

IN WHICH A GENTLEMAN PAYS HIS DEBT

The first thing I saw on entering the room was my beach-comber. For the rushlight, which was the cabin's sole illuminant, stood on a soap-box beside the couch on which the outcast lay. Dressed in a shrunken and dirty cotton suit, he was propped up against the rough mud wall, a grimy and threadbare wrap thrown across his knees. Despite the awful stuffiness of the place, he shivered beneath this ragged coverlet, although his face and chest glistened with perspiration.

Once upon a time, I judged as I measured him with my eye, he must have been a fine figure of a man. Though now coarse and bloated, with white and flabby flesh, it would easily be seen that he was tall beyond the ordinary with the narrow hips of the athlete. His eyes were deeply sunk in his head; and in them flickered wanly that strange, restless light which one sees so often in the faces of those whom Death is soon to claim. Even amid the ravages which undernourishment, drink and drugs had made in his features, the influence of gentle birth might yet be marked in the straight, firm pencilling of the eyebrows and the well-shaped aquiline nose. I thought the man looked dreadfully ill and I noted about nose and mouth that pinched look which can never deceive.

The whole shack appeared to consist of the one room in which I found myself. It was pitiably bare. A table on which stood some unappetising remnants of food was set against the wall beneath the unglazed window which faced the sick man's couch. A broken stool and a couple of soap-boxes, one furnished with a tin basin and a petrol can of water, completed the furniture.

"There's a bar to go across the door," said a weak voice from the corner where the sick man lay; "would you be good enough to put it down? I don't want us to be disturbed..."

He cast an apprehensive glance at the window. I fitted the rough beam across the door and approached the couch. It was merely a bed of maize stalks.

"You're very ill, I'm afraid," I said pulling over one of the boxes and seating myself by the Englishman. "Have you seen a doctor?"

The vagrant waved his hand in a deprecatory manner.

"My dear fellow," he said—and again I noted the refinement in his voice—"no sawbones can help *me*. I never held with them much anyway. Luisa got paid today—she washes at Bard's, you know (it was she who told me you were here)—and so I've got some medicine..."—he touched a little pannikin which stood on the floor at his side— "it's all that keeps me alive now that I can't get the 'snow!'"

I recognised the name which the drug traffic gives to cocaine.

The sick man was rent by a spasm of coughing.

"It's paradoxical," he gasped out presently, "but the more I take of my life-giving elixir here the quicker the end. will come. All I live for now, it seems to me, is to shorten as much as possible the intervals between the bouts."

I've seen something in my time of the cynical resignation of your chronic drunkard. So I wasted no good advice on the poor devil, but held my peace while he swallowed a mouthful from the pannikin at his elbow.

"You went out of your way to do me a good turn once, Okewood," he said, setting the vessel down and wiping his mouth on his soiled sleeve. "I know your name, you see. I made some inquiries about you before they ran me out of San Salvador. You got a D.S.O. in the war, I think?"

"They gave away so many!" I said idiotically. But that sort of remark always engenders an idiotic reply.

"No, no," he insisted. "Yours was one of the right ones, Okewood; I can see that by looking at you. You're the real type of British officer. And, although you may not think it to see me now, I know what I'm talking about. You fellows had your chance in the war and by Gad, sir, some of you took it..."

I knew he was an army man and said so.

He nodded.

"Cavalry," he answered. "You might be in the cavalry, too, by your build!"

I told him I was a field-gunner—or used to be, and then I asked him his name.

He smiled wanly at that.

"No names, no court-martials!" he quoted.

He drank from his pannikin again.

"Call me Adams!" he said.

There was a moment's silence. The sick man moved restlessly on his rustling couch and I heard his teeth rattle in his head. Outside, the pulsating life of the black quarter shattered the brooding stillness of the tropical night. The sound of low, full-throated laughter, mingling with the jangling of guitars, drifted up from the lane.

"Broken as a major," the sick man said abruptly. "A bad business, very. Yes, they jailed me over it. And when I came out it was to find every man's hand against me. It's been against me ever since! Ah, it's a bad thing to make an enemy of England! When I think of the humble pie I've eaten from some of these blasted counter-jumping finnicking consuls of ours along this coast only to be thrown out of doors at last by their dago servants! Once go down and out in England, and God help you. You'll never come back! Ah! It's not your own folk who'll lend you a hand then. It's the humble people, like Luisa here on whom I sponge, who keeps me, Okewood, who is proud to keep me..."

His voice quavered and broke. Tears welled up in his sunken eyes. One hates to see a man break down, so I looked away. And the beach-comber went to his pannikin for solace.

"That day at the calaboose at San Salvador," he said presently, "I wanted to tell you who I was. Twenty-five years ago I buried my real name. But what you did for me... well, it was a white thing to do. I wanted to say to you: 'Race tells, sir! You have helped one of your own breed and upbringing.' It shall be written in our family records that 'Such-a-one (meaning myself) of Blank in the County of So-and-so, being in sore distress in the hands of the foreigner, was succoured by the chivalrous intervention of Major Desmond Okewood.'"

He sighed, then added:

"But I doubt if you would have understood my meaning!"

I found myself becoming extraordinarily interested in this grotesque wastrel who, though sunk to the lowest depths a man may touch, managed to cling so desperately to his pride of birth.

The outcast spoke again.

"I mustn't waste your time. But it's so rare to find one of my own world to talk to. Listen to me, now! You stood up for me at San Salvador and in return... You're not a rich man, Okewood?"

I laughed.

"I have to work for my living, Adams," I answered.

"Good, good! Then you will appreciate the more the fortune I am going to put in your way. An Eldorado to make you rich beyond the dreams of..."

He broke off, racked by a terrible fit of coughing. The spasm left him weak and gasping.

His talk about fortunes and the rest made me think he was a trifle light-headed. So I made to rise from my seat.

"You're talking too much," I said soothingly. "I think I'll leave you now and come back another day!"

But the beach-comber thrust out a hand—such a thin and wasted hand!—and clutched my sleeve. He could not speak for the moment, but he cast me a despairing look eloquent in its appeal to me to stay.

"A fortune," he gasped out when his breath began to come back to him. "I'll make you rich! I want to show my gratitude to the man who knows what is due to a... a... a gentleman!"

He fell back with livid face. I raised his head and held the pannikin to his lips. It was half full of some terrible-looking, dark-brown liquor. He drank a little, then lay back with closed eyes. He lay so still that, with his sunken eyes and hollow cheeks, you might have taken him for a corpse.

In a little while he was better and spoke again.

"Okewood," he said—and this time his voice was hardly above a whisper, "I believe I know where treasure's hid. For more than a year now I've carried my secret round with me, for the chance to get back there, waiting to find the partner I could trust. And now Fate (with whom I've quarrelled all my life) has played me a dirty trick to finish up. I've found my partner when it's too late for me to share!"

He relapsed into silence again. His head drooped and his eyes were closed so that for the moment I thought he had fainted. But presently he asked abruptly:

"Have you ever heard of Cock Island?"

"Cock Island?" I repeated. "No, I don't think so. Where is it?"

"In the Pacific, about 400 miles out at sea. Many months ago—the summer after the Armistice it was—I was serving before the mast in a Dutch schooner—the *Huis-ten-Bosch*, her name was. I signed on at Papeete to run to Callao with a cargo of copra. The crew were all Kanakas, natives, you know, except for one other man who signed on with me—Dutchey, they called him. We were on the beach together in Tahiti..."

His fit of weakness seemed to have passed and his voice grew stronger and his eyes brighter as he proceeded with his tale.

"Well, something went amiss with our fresh water supply," he went on, "so we laid off at Cock Island to replenish our casks. It was a jolly little place—you know the sort of thing, all wavy, coconut palms and wooded peaks running up steeply from the foreshore. And, of course, the very dickens of a surf bar. The skipper sent me and Dutchey with a gang of Kanakas to fill up with water. We found a way in through the bar and having landed, set the Kanakas to work to fill the casks at a fine spring of water, cold and clear, which fell from the hillside. Then Dutchey and I had a look round.

"I had asked our old man—the captain, you know—about Cock Island. He had told me, that according to the Sailing Directions, it was uninhabited. Therefore, as Dutchey and I were pushing our way through the undergrowth to get to the high central upland, we were a bit taken aback to come upon a grave in a clearing.

"It was a regular grave cut out of the rough grass with a mound and a cross all shipshape and proper. The cross, which was merely two bits of stout deal lashed together with wire, was a bit weatherbeaten and polished smooth by the sand blown against it. It had no inscription. Against the cross a small mirror was propped up, while in front of it stood a bottle half embedded in the earth. The bottle contained some writing on a piece of folded oilsilk."

"We used to bury fellows that way in France," I remarked. "One stuck the name and particulars on a piece of paper and shoved it in a bottle until they had time to put a cross up, don't you know?"

"I had no idea what this was," said the beachcomber, "the writing was a fearful scrawl and rather faint at that. I couldn't make head or tail of it. I just slipped it into my pocket, meaning to have a look at it another time. While I had been examining the grave, the fellow with me, the man we called Dutchey, had been rooting about in the clearing. Presently he emerged from behind a bush with a whole collection of junk which he laid on the ground at my feet. There was an old newspaper, a piece of dirty packing paper and a cigar-box.

"He was a queer chap, this Dutchey. We never could quite make him out. Personally, I thought he wasn't all there. He spoke very rarely but, when he opened his lips, he talked some kind of German-American double Dutch. He was very taciturn; the sort of man you know, who gives no confidences and invites none. That was really what attracted him to me when we chummed up on the beach at Papeete. We went through a rough time there together, too!..."

The sick man broke off musingly. Then the cough took him again and it was some minutes before he resumed speaking.

"Dutchey laid all this junk out in front of me rather like a dog bringing you a stick you've thrown it. Then he said: —

"'Dat bunch o' toughs from San Salvador bin here!'

"Dutchey's conversational bursts generally opened enigmatically and I knew from experience that it was no use interrupting him to ask for enlightenment. One could only hope it might come in due course.

"Dutchey lifted up the newspaper.

"'De *Heraldo* of San Salvador of nineteen eighteen—you see de date March Seventeen?'

"He raised up the piece of wrapping paper.

"'You savvy José Garcia's store at San Salvador?'

"(I should say I did, Okewood. He was the swine that jugged me over his rotten bill!)

THE RETURN OF CLUBFOOT

"'Dis from Garcia's store! You see de name printed on it?'

"Finally he picked up the cigar-box and opening it displayed a row of mouldy cigars with a yellow band.

"'Black Pablo!' he said.

"'How do you mean, Dutchey?' I asked.

"'Dere ain't but the one man in San Salvador smoke dese ceegyars,' he answered, 'and dat's Black Pablo. Jose Garcia smuggles dem in express for him. Dis sure is fonny!'

"He broke into a fit of laughter, dribbling a good deal.

"'Dis um de l'il island!' he exclaimed and went off again.

"'But who is Black Pablo?' I demanded. 'Is he the head of this gang?'

"'Is he... hell?' cried Dutchey. 'Dere ain't no one amounts to a row o' beans since El Cojo come along. Black Pablo, Neque, Mahon... dere's not one of them dawg-gorn four-flushers dare open deir face when El Cojo's round. Dey shoot off deir mouth tome 'bout deir l'il island. Pretty goddam mysterious 'bout it, too. No blab to Dutchey, dey say. El Cojo won't have it. But Dutchey knows. Blarst me sowl...'

"Dutchey had a great flow of language. And he let it rip as he told me the way he meant to crow over El Cojo and his gang when he got back to San Salvador."

Adams had warmed to his story and a little red had crept into his cheeks. He was an excellent *raconteur* and he seemed to enjoy reproducing the extraordinary lingo of his friend Dutchey.

"We rowed over to the ship again," he resumed, "and as soon as I had a moment alone I had another look at the writing on the oilsilk. But I could make nothing of it. I thought I'd keep it, though, just for luck, so I strung it round my neck and forgot all about it until one day in the calaboose at San Salvador I overheard a very curious conversation. Can you reach the pannikin? Thanks!"

The outcast drank and wiped his mouth on the back of his dirty white cuff.

"You know the way they lock one up in these dago jails—all in a common room together. Well, a day or two after I got in I was sitting on the floor with my back against the wall taking a bit of a siesta when suddenly I heard the name 'Neque.' I recollected at once that Dutchey had spoken of 'Neque' as one of El Co jo's gang because once, years ago, I had a Spanish, pal whose nickname was 'Neque'—I used to play polo with him in Madrid—and the name was familiar to me.

"I opened my eyes and saw two of the prisoners sitting on the floor within a yard of me talking together in Spanish. Everybody else was asleep. The one whom I discovered to be Neque was a young fellow of about twenty-five, very slim and wiry. His companion was a dark man with a yellow face, a broken nose, and a patch over one eye. I closed my eyes quickly again and pretended to be asleep.

"'Such accursed luck!' the younger man said,' five hundred thousand dollars in gold and you and I will not be there to share it!'

"'*Caraco!*' replied the fat man,' but who shall say it is there?'

"'Imbecile!' exclaimed Neque. 'I was with El Cojo when he examined the Kanaka. Did not this Kanaka sail in the ship which brought the foreigner and the gold to Cock Island? He was one of those, this Kanaka, who survived the influenza sickness that swept the vessel. He told El Cojo—I, Neque, heard it with my own ears—how the foreigner was landed alone with the gold, how he remained by himself on the island for two days and how, when the Kanakas rowed in from the ship to fetch him, they found him with death on his face—the mauve death, you and I have seen it, per Dios, eh? And the boxes of gold gone! The foreigner gave them a bottle with a writing in it, bidding them swear that they would put it on his grave or he would haunt them. Then he died and the Kanakas buried him and having placed this object on the grave as he had ordered, fled from the island in the ship!'

"The fat man spat.

"'Who shall believe a Kanaka?' he said contemptuously.

"'The foreigner was the only white man with these natives,' argued Neque. 'They feared him and they did as he bade them lest his spirit should torment them. Besides the grave has been seen on the island since...'

"At that the fat man woke up and became interested.

"'Never!' he exclaimed in astonishment.

"And then Neque told him of a conversation El Cojo had had with a 'mad seaman,' in whom it was not difficult to recognise Dutchey, who had landed with a companion from a Dutch schooner and had seen the grave and on it a bottle. The other man, the 'loco' (madman) had said, had taken out of the bottle a piece of writing.

"'This other man,' questioned his companion. 'Who was he?'

"'An Inglez,' replied Neque, 'but the mad seaman did not know his name and had not seen him since they had landed.'

"At that the fat man spat again.

"'Bah!' he said, 'these *locitos* are cunning. There was no *Inglez*. The mad seaman has that writing which tells where the gold lies as sure as men call me Black Pablo...'

"The name brought back to me Cock Island in a flash; I seemed to see Dutchey, with his puzzled, woe-begone expression, holding a handful of mouldy cigars, the cigars that Jose Garcia imported for Black Pablo. And looking at the fellow with his single eye and his hideous twisted nose I couldn't help feeling glad, my friend, that he doubted my existence..."

The beach-comber stopped and looked at me. Then he thrust a lean hand inside the bosom of his ragged jacket.

"You've now heard the tale for what it's worth, Okewood," said he, "and here's that dead man's message! Take good care of it! It may mean a fortune for you...!"

He pulled out a greasy package which hung on a cord round his neck. He unfastened the cord and handed me a flat, narrow parcel. I was going to open it; but he stayed my hand.

"Not here," he enjoined in a low whisper. Then, with a wistful smile, he added:

"I'm afraid it's a dangerous present I'm making you, old man!"

"Why do you say that?" I demanded.

The sick man turned his head and looked at the unglazed window protected only by a pair of rough-carpentered wooden shutters. In the street outside someone was lightly thrumming a guitar. Now and then came the sound of soft laughter. Otherwise the black village had sunk to rest. All was still without and the plaintive chords resounded distinctly through the hot night.

"A week after I was shipped from San Salvador," he said, "they found Dutchey's body in the dock with a noose round his neck. Poor old Dutchey who never harmed anybody! Listen!"

The rich, full-throated tenor voice, which I had heard as I was following Doña Luisa through the black quarter, suddenly burst into song quite close at hand. On a sad and plaintive melody it sang with a liquid enunciation which made every chord distinct:

> "Se murio, y sobre su cara
> Un fanuelito le heche
> Por que no toque la tierra
> Esa bocca que yo bese!"

The beach-comber held up his hand as the melody died away on a minor key.

"It is time for you to go!" he whispered. "The door over there, opposite the one by which you came in, leads to the yard at the back. Cross the yard, take the path through the plantation, bear always to the right and you will strike the main road to the docks. Go as quietly as you can and don't dawdle on the way... Ah!"

Again the singer in the lane sent his plaintive melody soaring to the stars. He chanted his little verse through once more. Feebly, the sick man beat time with his hand.

"He's been singing on and off all the evening, Okewood," he murmured. "Always the same song. I Englished it while I was waiting for you. Listen!" In a soft, quavering voice he whispered rather than sang:

> *"She died, and on her face*
> *I laid a napkin fine*
> *Lest the cold earth should touch*
> *Those lips I pressed to mine...*

"Ah!" he sighed as the song died away and silence fell on us once more; "When the hour strikes for me, Okewood, there'll be no one, except, maybe, old Mammie Luisa there, to lay a pretty thought like that in my coffin!"

He held out his hand.

"Now go!" he bade me. "And good luck go with you!"

I took his proffered hand.

"I will come again and see you, Adams," said I. "I expect you'll want to hear what I've made of the message!"

He was looking at me whimsically.

"No, Okewood," he said, shaking his head, "I'm thinking we shan't meet again!"

I was thinking the same; for, in truth, the man looked at death's door.

The unseen singer had attacked another verse.

"Mira si seria bella..."

The opening words came resonantly to me as I quietly stole from the room. At the door I turned for a last look at the beachcomber. The candle was guttering away and its trembling light illuminated only the pinched, worn features and the sombre, suffering eyes. The grossness of that broken body was mercifully swallowed up in the shadows. To and fro across the candle's feeble gleam the hands moved in cadence with the song...

24

THE MESSAGE

I was loth to leave him. What he had told me of the fate of his friend, the man called Dutchey, made me feel a trifle apprehensive of his own safety. And I had had a kind of feeling that, for all his apparent calm, he was frightened. On looking back at my interview that night with the beach-comber in his wretched shack, I realise there must have been something unusually sweet about his personality. Its flavour seemed to linger; for I left him, as I have said, reluctantly, and I have thought of him many times since.

The back door led straight into a kind of open shed which, from the stove and stacked-up wood pile, I judged to be Doña Luisa's cooking-place. The shed gave on a dusty yard, small and narrow, smelling horribly of poultry, with a high mud wall. In this wall I saw—for the moonlight made everything as bright as day—a wooden door. On reaching it I found that it was locked.

For a moment I had a mind to go back to the front and home by the way I had come. But I felt doubtful as to whether I should be able to follow in the opposite direction the intricate route by which Doña Luisa had brought me, and I had no desire to be lost in the black quarter at night. So without more ado I scaled the mud wall and, dropping to earth on the other side, found myself in the plantation of which the beachcomber had spoken.

Here I was alone with the noises of the tropical night. Of human being there was neither sound nor sign. However, I had Adams's directions firmly in my head; and by following them to the letter came back at last without incident, but very hot and sticky, to John Bard's bungalow.

The verandah was empty, the house very quiet. I looked at my watch. It was half-past eleven. Bard had gone down to the club for his usual evening rubber of bridge but I had excused myself for I had meant to write letters. I knew it would be at least an hour before Bard returned; for he was a late bird. So I went through to my room, had a sponge down and changed into pyjamas and made my way to the living-room.

It was a delightfully airy apartment, one side, glazed, opening on to the verandah, the other walls distempered a pale green. There were native mats on the floor and comfortable chairs stood about the room. I went over to the writing desk in the corner, switched on the reading-lamp and lit a cigar. Then I pulled out of my pocket the package which I had received from the beach-comber.

The outer covering was a piece of greasy flannel which looked as if it had been torn off an old shirt. With my knife I slit up the stitches—it had been lightly tacked across with thread—and pulled out a narrow pad of oilskin folded once across. Spread out it made a piece roughly about nine inches long by six wide. Across it stood written some lines hastily scribbled in indelible pencil. The hand was crabbed and irregular, the writing indistinct and, in some places, almost completely effaced. But I could distinguish enough to recognise that both the hand and the words were German.

At this I felt my pulse quicken. A faint instinct of the chase began to stir in my blood. For three long months I had dawdled deliciously; for, in turning my face towards the sunshine of the

New World, I had deliberately turned my back on the thrills and disappointments, the dangers and the *ennuis* of the Secret Service. This almost undecipherable scrawl, with here and there a German word clearly protruding itself (I could read *"Kiel"* and *"siehst Du"*) and, above all, the indelible pencil, in whose pale mauve character gallant young men wrote the real history of the war, brought back to me with vivid clearness, memorable moments of those half-forgotten campaigning days. I fumbled in a drawer of the desk for Bard's big magnifying glass, drew up my chair and set myself stolidly—as I had so often done in the past!—to the deciphering of what is, in all circumstances, easily the most illegible handwriting in the world.

In truth, no writing is harder to read than the German. In his intercourse with the foreigner, the brother Boche, it is true, not infrequently employs the Latin character. But, for communications among themselves, the Germans continue to use their own damnable hieroglyphics. I have often wondered to see how the most unintelligent German will read off with ease a closely written scrawl of German handwriting looking as though a spider, after taking an ink-bath, had jazzed up and down the page.

This particular specimen of the Hun fist was a proper Chinese puzzle. Where in places it was beginning to be decipherable, the heavy indelible ink had run (under the influence of damp, I suppose) and where the writing was not a mass of smears it was illegible in a degree to make one despair.

Well, I got down to it properly. My knowledge of German (which I know about as well as English) was a great help. Finally, with the assistance of Bard's magnifying-glass, a deduction here and a guess there, after nearly an hour's hard work, I produced what was, as nearly as I could make it, an accurate version of the original. My greatest triumph lay, I think, in establishing the fact that an unusually baffling row of cryptic signs at the bottom of the thing was, in reality, four bars of music.

But when I had set it all down (on a sheet of John Bard's expensive glazed note-paper), I scratched my head and, despite my aching eyes, took another good look at the original. For I could make no sense of the writing at all.

The message (for such it seemed to be) was signed with the single letter "U." And this is what I got:

> "Mittag. 18/11/18.
> "Flimmer', flimmer' viel
> Die Garnison von Kiel
> Mit Kompass dann am besten
> Denk' an den Ordensfesten
> Am Zuckerhut vorbei
> Siehst Du die Lorelei
> Und magst Du Schatzchen gern.

> U."

(Reproduced by permission of B. Fieldman & Co.)

Blankly I stared at this doggerel. Then I took down from the rack another sheet of paper and jotted down a rough English translation:—

> "Noon. *18/11/18.*
> "Flash, flash much
> The garrison of Kiel
> Then with the compass is best
> Think of the Feast of Orders
> Past the Sugar-Loaf
> You'll see the Lorelei
> And if you desire the sweetheart.
> U."

Leaning back in my chair I cast my mind over the strange tale I had heard that night from Adams, the story, whispered in the fierce noonday heat of the calaboose of San Salvador, of the ship which had brought the solitary white man and his gold out of the Unknown to Cock Island, of the Unknown's death and of the message he had left so oddly behind him. And, lest anyone should think that I was paying too much heed to a rambling yarn told me at second-hand by a drunken outcast, a yarn, moreover, based on a statement by a Kanaka deckhand, let me say that my whole training in the Intelligence had taught me never to reject any statement, however improbable it sounded until it had failed to withstand an elaborate series of tests. Indeed, the major satisfaction of this poorly paid and sometimes dangerous profession of ours is the rare delight of seeing emerge out of some seemingly impossible tale a solid basis of fact.

And, behind the beach-comber's rambling story, there *were* certain solid facts which, from the moment of discovering that the message was in German, I could not afford to neglect. When William the Second launched the world war, like a big stone dropped in a pond, the ripples reached to the uttermost ends of the earth. In many a lonely island of the Seven Seas there had been, I knew, mysterious comings and goings, connected with gun-running, submarine work and dark conspiracies of all kinds. Did this scrap of stained oilsilk, picked off a lonely grave in the Southern Seas, lead back to a secret adventure of this kind? I decided that it might.

I turned to the message again. It was obviously written *by* a German and *for* a German, it was fair to presume... for some specific German, furthermore, who would hold the key to the conventional code in which this message was almost certainly written. Consequently, the solitary stranger of Cock Island had expected to meet a German on the island, *ergo*, the island was a meeting-place, some secret rendezvous of the busy German conspirators in the war. This was borne out by the remarkable evidence laid before Adams by Dutchey on their visit to Cock Island to prove that some gang of desperadoes from San Salvador had previously been there. The names mentioned by Dutchey were undoubtedly Spanish—Black Pablo and Neque, for instance—but there might have been Germans with them. El Cojo was also Spanish, to judge by the name; but apparently he had put in an appearance later and had not visited the island.

To what did the message refer? What would the solitary German, with the hand of Death at his throat, wish to tell the man whom he was to have met? Might it not be, as Adams had said, the whereabouts of the gold, brought to the island by the Unknown, which, from the observation of Adams' fellow prisoners at the calaboose, was apparently still on the island? Various geographical indications in the message—the Sugar-Loaf, the Lorelei (the latter the well-known crag on the Rhine) seemed to confirm this.

But the message had remained in its bottle on the grave until, months later, Adams and Dutchey had found it. It was, therefore, to be presumed that the unknown German's friend, probably someone in El Cojo's gang, had not kept the appointment. Why?

I stared in perplexity at the dead man's scrawl. Every one of my deductions, I perceived all too clearly, led to a question to which I was unable to supply an answer. I began to regret that I had not read the message at Adams' hut and cross-examined him on it before I left. But I realized I should never have been able to decipher the scrawl by the flickering light of the oil-lamp in the shack. I resolved to go down to the black quarter and see Adams again in the morning.

I suddenly began to feel restless and rather unhappy. I knew the symptoms. In me they always presage a burst of activity after a spell of idleness. This infernal riddle had altogether upset me. I had no desire to go to bed; the very idea of sleep was repugnant to me.

I measured myself out a "peg" of whisky and splashed the soda into it. My eyes, roaming round the room, fell on the upright piano in the corner. I crossed to the instrument and opening the lid, put on the music rest the little square of oilskin. Then, summoning back to my mind with an effort the hazy musical knowledge of my early school days, with considerable deliberation I picked out on the piano the notes indicated in the four bars of music appended to the end of the message.

I got the melody at once, or rather one movement of a melody which was dimly familiar to me. It fitted itself to no words or voice in my mind; but as I hummed it over, a silly little jingle, I suddenly had a mental picture of a cheap German dance-hall such as you find in the northern part of Berlin, with a blaring orchestra and jostling couples redolent of perspiration and beer. I *knew* the tune; but it was, I thought, the words that were wanted to complete the dead man's message. And they came not.

I was laboriously pounding the piano with one finger when I heard Bard's heavy step on the verandah. The next moment, he came into the room, a big figure of a man in a tussore silk suit with a panama hat. Somehow the sight of him made me feel easier in my mind. That sublime sense of superiority, which we British suck in with our mother milk, is a heartening thing when you find it in your fellow Britisher abroad, thousands of miles from home. And John Bard, though, with his small pointed beard and rather pallid face, he looked like a Spaniard, was through and through British. Trader, merchant, financier and, on occasion, statesman, his massive body bore scars which told of thrilling years spent among the cannibals and head-hunters of the Pacific islands.

But long years of exile had only served to make John Bard more resolutely British. An uncompromising bachelor, abstemious in his habits and puritanical in his outlook, his mental attitude towards his fellow-man in this tiny republic of the Spanish Main was exactly what it would have been had he been a London suburbanite suddenly translated from his native Brixton to these distant shores. He was an eminently common-sensible person who was generally reputed to run the miniature republic of Rodriguez in which he had elected to settle down after his adventurous life.

His unshakable phlegm lent him a reposeful air which I believe was the first thing that drew me to him when, a few months before, for the first time for many years, I had met him again in a New York hotel. Six months' leave, unexpectedly offered, found me at a loose end and I gladly accepted his invitation to travel down by one of his ships and visit him in his Central American home. His cheery self-possession, as he stepped through the open doors of the verandah, seemed to put to flight the unpleasant shape which my mind's eye had seen rising from the little piece of oilsilk.

Bard crossed the room without speaking and filled himself a glass of soda-water from a syphon on the side-table. He tossed his soft panama hat on a chair and brushed back his closely cut crop of iron-grey hair from his temples. With his glass in his hand he dropped into a seat at my side.

"There's a yacht in the harbour," he said. "That's what made me late. She's called for some stuff they've got waiting for her at the Consulate. Fordwich—that's the Consul, you know—is down with a go of fever so I went round with his clerk to see about this consignment. Whew! But it's warm walking!"

"What's the yacht? I asked.

"Name of *Naomi*. She's come through the Canal"... "the Canal" in these parts, of course, the Panama Canal... "and is going across to Hawaii, I believe!"

He yawned and stretched his big frame, drained his glass and stood up.

"Heigho," he said, "it's after two. I'm for bed"

Now between John Bard and me exists that sort of uncommunicative friendship which is often found between two men who have knocked about the world a good deal. Though I could tell by Bard's elaborate of nonchalance that he noticed I was preoccupied, I knew he would never demand the cause of this. If I wanted his advice I should have to ask for it.

"John," said I, "just a minute. Who's El Cojo?"

I pronounced it in the English fashion but Bard gave the word its rasping Spanish aspirate as he repeated it.

"El Cojo?" he queried. "That's a nickname, isn't it? What is he? A bull-fighter, or a cigar?"

"I gather," I remarked, "that he's a gentleman of fortune!"

Bard laughed.

"The production of that type is an old industry in these parts, my boy," he riposted. "And even I don't know 'em all. I never heard of your pal. Is he a citizen of this illustrious republic?"

I shook my head.

"I haven't an idea," I answered. "I only know that a man called Black Pablo is mixed up with him..."

John Bard whistled softly.

"*Dime con quien andas, decirte de quien eres,*" he quoted. "That is to say, tell me whom you go with and I'll tell you who you are. If your pal is a friend of Black Pablo then he's 'no freend o'mine'!"

"Why?"

"Because," said John Bard slowly, and I noticed that his mocking air had altogether disappeared, "because Black Pablo is the greatest scoundrel on this coast... and that's going some! During the war, when, after a good deal of pressure, our most illustrious President ultimately kicked out Schwanz, the German Consul, Black Pablo became Germany's unofficial agent. He was mixed up with running guns for the Mexicans to annoy the Yanks, and supplies for the Hun commerce raiders to worry the British and every other kind of dirty work. As long as he was merely a smuggler, a cut-throat and a hired assassin, as he was before the war... Bien! I had nothing to say to him. But when the fellow had the blasted impudence to come butting into our war on the wrong side, by George! one had to do something. The Americans were devilish decent about it, I must say, and, with their support, we ran the skunk out of here P.D.Q. That was around January, 1918, and I have never heard of our friend since. But I'll give you a word of advice, young fellow my lad. If you come across Black Pablo, give him a wide berth. And mind his left! He keeps his knife in that sleeve!"

I pointed at the open cigar-box.

"Light up, John Bard," said I, "for I want to tell you a story and get your advice!"

So, while in the garden, trees and bushes stirred lazily to a little breeze before dawn, I told him, as briefly as might be, the story I had heard from Adams. My host never once interrupted me but sat and smoked in silence till my tale was done. Even after I had finished he remained silent for a spell.

At length he said musingly:

"Cock Island, eh? Yes, it surely would be a good spot for a quiet rendezvous."

"You know it then?" I asked eagerly.

"Aye," he averred. "I know it by name. But I was never there. It lies off the beaten trade routes, you see. But I remember hearing once that it had been a port of call for some of the old buccaneers like Kidd and Roberts who plied their trade in these parts. And so you think there's German gold hidden there, eh?"

"This"—I held up the fragment of oilsilk—"looks as if it might answer that question. If only one could read it," I said. And I spread it out before him. We put our heads together, under the lamp, while I read out my rough translation. Then

Bard, shrugging his shoulders, leaned back in his chair and blew out a cloud of smoke.

"What are you going to do about it, Desmond?"

"Well," I said slowly, "if there were any sort of certainty about it not being absolutely a wild goose chase..."

"You'd go after it, eh?"

"It'd be a devilish amusing way of finishing up my leave."

John Bard smiled indulgently.

"It might be more exciting than amusing," he said, "if Black Pablo has anything to do with this affair."

"Do you think there is anything in it?" I asked.

"In the latter stages of the war," my host replied, "I heard vague rumours about some island off the coast where German commerce-raiders used to rendezvous for supplies. But I never heard this island named. It seems to me that the first thing to be done is to see your friend, Adams, again. After all, he's been to the island. He might be able to tell us more about it. Besides..."

He broke off and flicked the ash from his cigar. His manner had suddenly become grave.

"Besides what?" I demanded.

"If Black Pablo and his friends are after that plan or whatever it is, Adams is in pretty considerable danger."

"He knows it himself, I believe," I replied. "I didn't like leaving him tonight, and that's a fact. He seemed to be frightened about something. There was a man in the lane outside the hut who was singing and..."

"A man singing?" Bard queried sharply.

"Yes, to a guitar," I answered, surprised by his tone. "He sang very well, too!"

John Bard rose to his feet suddenly. He stepped to the verandah and held up his hand for silence.

"Were you followed when you came back from Adams's?" he asked me.

"No, not as far as I know."

Bard was listening intently. All was quiet in the gardens below, save for the murmurings of the sea breeze in the palms.

"Get into your clothes and come along, Okewood," he said, turning away from the window. "And leave that damned plan behind."

"Why, what..."

"Hurry, man, or we shall be too late."

"But, damn it, John, explain! "I cried in exasperation.

"Black Pablo is renowned all along the coast for his exquisite singing to the guitar. Be quick, be quick, old man, and don't forget your gun!..."

25

A FOOTSTEP IN THE LANE

The moon had paled and a greyness in the sky, as we hurried down the hill, betokened the approach of day. At length the city had sunk to rest; the port slumbered and in the red light quarter behind the docks the laughter and the guitars were stilled. How through that maze of mean streets and lanes I found the way back to Doña Luisa's cabin I don't know; but I expect that a kind of instinct for marking a route once traversed, which, with me, is inborn, stood me in good stead.

The black quarter was wrapped in silence. The swift rustling of a rat, a distant cock-crow from the sleeping city, were the only sounds to break the stillness of the night. At length we reached the narrow lane in which the shanty stood. It was almost dark; for the moon had gone in behind a bank of clouds and the day was not yet come.

The big wooden door stood wide. Across the little yard dimly we saw the dark outline of the shack. The mud surface of the court was wet and sticky and my rubber-soled shoes slipped on it as we crossed the threshold of the enclosure. John Bard touched my arm.

"Man alive," he whispered, "look at your shoes!"

I did as I was bid and recoiled in horror.

The white buckskin was deeply smeared with crimson.

We dashed across the yard. The shanty door stood open.

Within, amid a scene of hideous confusion, the body of the beach-comber hung head downwards from the rough couch, the throat cut from ear to ear. And behind the door in another welter of blood lay the corpse of Doña Luisa.

The place was a shambles. The hut had been turned upside-down and the few poor belongings of the outcast were scattered all over the floor. The very maize cane on which his dead body lay had been tossed about. And the blood was smeared everywhere as though the murderer or murderers had brought it in on their boots.

John Bard's face was anxious.

"We'll do well to clear out of here," he said, "before it gets light. They mustn't find us here. Let's go out by the back and return by the way you came..."

I gladly acquiesced in his suggestion. To tell the truth, I was feeling a little sick. The fetid odours of the black quarter reeked to heaven in the freshening morning air, and mingled with them was a suspicion of some unutterably horrid taint arising from the two corpses which had lain there all through the warm night.

We had reached the threshold of the back door when suddenly a heavy footstep sounded from the front. In the absolute stillness all round the sound rang out clearly. It was as though a heavy man were stumping slowly across the hard pounded earth of the front yard. He came with a step and a stump, a step and a stump, like a lame man walking with a stick or crutches.

John Bard made as though to bolt. But I restrained him. I felt I must see this mysterious visitant. And John Bard, loyal friend as he is, though he had nothing to gain by my rashness, stopped dead in his tracks and with me drew behind the cover of the back door. Through the chink between the door and the jamb we surveyed the entrance to the shack.

A huge black shape stood on the threshold. It was too dark within the hut to note the newcomer's features or his dress. One had only the sensation of a great form that bulked largely, immensely, in the doorway.

I turned noiselessly to Bard. He divined the unspoken proposal on my lips for he shook his head curtly and his grip on my sleeve tightened. At the same moment the great form in the doorway moved and the next instant was swallowed up in the shadows of the courtyard. We heard the clip-clop of his limping step as he crossed the enclosure and, little by little, die away as he stumped up the lane.

"Smear some earth over your shoes!"

John Bard was speaking to me. Blindly I did as he bade me and rubbed dust over the damp, dark stains on the white buckskin. Then gripping me by the arm my friend ran me through the backyard and out by the door which now stood open.

In the freshness of the plantation, away from the stenches of the village and the nameless taint of that house of slaughter, my senses came back to me and I felt ashamed of the rashness which might have had disastrous consequences for both of us. But, when at length we stood once more in the bungalow and Bard poured me out a stiff dose of brandy, I noticed that, contrary to his invariable rule, he had one himself as well.

"And now," said he, and in his voice was a note of decision, "the sooner you leave Rodriguez, Desmond, the better for you. I don't want to appear inhospitable or I might add, the better for me too. That poor devil, Adams, is dead and you can do nothing for him by staying. You are sufficiently acquainted, I take it, with the mentality of my distinguished fellow-citizens to realize that very little fuss will be made over the untimely demise of Adams and his coloured lady. In the meantime you are in the greatest danger here..."

"I don't see why I should worry," I argued. "If they had known of my visit to Adams they would have raided the hut and butchered the three of us to get hold of the document. But they didn't; and they don't even know me by sight..."

"They evidently didn't know of your visit *at the time*," remarked John Bard gravely. "But obviously something happened after your departure to put them wise. Hence the attack on the house. You were either seen going to the house or Doña Luisa gave you away. It looks to me as though they had only just traced the document to Adams. Black Pablo was set to watch but, after the happy-go-lucky fashion of Latin America, he whiled away the time by serenading some of the dusky belles in the vicinity and failed to observe your arrival."

I recalled the soft laughter I had heard, mingling with the strains of the guitar in the lane, and nodded.

"You think that this fellow Black Pablo was put on guard to see that Adams did not leave the house?..."

"Precisely," agreed my friend, "while El Cojo was sent for..."

"El Cojo, the head of the gang?"

"Himself and no other... the lame man who came to the door of the shack after the crime had been committed. In Spanish 'El Cojo' means 'the lame man,' 'he who goes with a limp'..."

John Bard went on talking but I have no recollection of what he said. For my thoughts had flown back to another "lame man "who had dominated the most thrilling episode in the whole of my life, the giant and ape-like cripple, head of the Kaiser's personal Secret Service in the days of Germany's greatness, who had dogged my brother Francis and myself until he had met his end at our hands in the chateau on the German-Dutch frontier. Old Clubfoot, as men called him in his heyday, had been in his grave these four years past; yet once again I found the path of adventure barred at its outset by a great lame man. I thought of that huge figure blocking up the narrow doorway of the reeking hut and, as so often in the past, I felt welling up within me admiration for the extraordinary ingenuity of old man Destiny...

"...This gang of El Cojo's," John Bard was saying impressively, leaning across the table at me, hands palms downwards before him, "is a tremendous organisation with a network of spies as widespread and efficient as the Camorra and Mafia in Italy or the Carbonarios in Portugal and Brazil. I have long suspected that there was at the head of it a man much bigger and abler than that murdering ruffian, Black Pablo, and now we have proof of it. I know a bit about men, Desmond, and that hulking dot-and-carry-one scoundrel we saw tonight gives me a damned unpleasant feeling. You mark my words; whether you were actually spotted or not they'll trace that plan to you and if you stay here, they'll get you! And I *know!*"

He appeared to reflect for a moment whilst I considered him with attention; for I had never before seen old John so worked up. But there is nothing like the Unknown for getting on a fellow's nerves.

Then he drove his fist into his palm as if a sudden idea had struck him.

"The *Naomi*," he said; "the very thing for you!"

"The *Naomi?*" I repeated.

"Yes. The yacht that came in last evening. She's going down to Honolulu. We ought to be able to fix it for you so they'll take you with them..."

"What is this yacht?" I asked.

"She belongs to Sir Alexander Garth. By George! She's a beauty, Desmond! White paint and a gold line, green and white deck awnings, everything slap up. He's a millionaire, they say!"

"I don't know the name."

"We looked him up in the 'Who's Who' at the club tonight. He's a baronet, and a big man in cotton. J.P. and D.L. of the county. What brings him here I don't know, except that cruising to the Southern Seas seems to be a fashionable rest-cure for millionaires whose nerves have been jaded by piling up money during the war."

"But, see here, John," I expostulated, "I can't go butting into a private pleasure cruise like this, I really can't. It isn't done, you know! And you can't expect these prosaic English folk to swallow a long yarn about my life being in danger!"

"Desmond," said Bard—and now his voice was very stern. "You can take it from me that if you don't clear out at once, you'll get your throat cut and probably mine into the bargain. There won't be a steamer for Colon for at least a fortnight. This yacht is a heaven-sent opportunity for making your lucky. If you wait for the steamer it's a ten to one chance you'll go up the gangway in your coffin neatly packed in ice! Do you get that? For the Lord's sake, burn that damned rigmarole and beat it!"

We Celts have a broad strain of contrariness in our nature which probably accounts for my strong inclination to disregard Bard's advice. But his manner was so impressive for one of his unemotional disposition that I could not but feel convinced.

"Perhaps you're right, old man," I said. "I won't burn the 'rigmarole' as you call it, but otherwise I will follow your suggestion. But it will be on one condition and one condition only. That is, that we part here and now and that, should by any chance your plan for my forcing my company upon the excellent cotton-spinner and his party fail, you will not associate with me or in any way acknowledge me as long as I am in the city..."

I held out my hand. But Bard laughed and put his two hands on my shoulders.

"No, no," he protested, "it's not so bad as all that. I'm coming down to the harbour to fix it up with Garth for you. He will probably call at the Consulate this morning any way to fetch the stores we are holding for him."

"John," said I, "I've dragged you far enough into this mess. It's early enough yet for me to go down to the harbour and on to that yacht without attracting much attention. So let's part here and ever so many thanks again for all your kindness..."

"Desmond"—John Bard's voice trembled a little—"I wouldn't hear of it..."

"My dear old man," I said. "I'm in a proper mess and I've no intention of pulling you into it after me. And I'd like to say one thing more. You might have rubbed it in that the whole of this trouble was brought on us by my initial folly in accompanying an unknown messenger to the purlieus of the city in the middle of the night. You have never alluded to it; but I'd like you to know that your forbearance did not escape me..."

I stretched forth my hand again. This time John Bard took it.

"I'll send your things down to the Consulate," he said; "they can go on board with Garth's stores."

And so, in perfect understanding, we settled it. At the verandah door I turned and said:

"And do you think now that there's anything in Adams's story?"

"Yes," my host replied, "I do!"

Then he added, with his little indulgent smile:

"Are you going after it?"

I shrugged my shoulders.

"I might!" said I.

But already fermenting in my brain was the germ of a great idea. The next moment the iron gate of the gardens clanged behind me and I was off at a good pace down the hill.

26

THE GIRL IN THE SMOKE-ROOM

The sun was up; but the air was still delightfully fresh and the verdure yet glistened with the heavy night dews. Beyond the fringe of wavy palms which marked the shore the sea glittered and sparkled, its deep blue melting to a paler shade where on the horizon sea mingled with sky. Past the tangle of white and yellow houses where the city stood, a creamy dead-white edging of foam, like ermine laid on an azure mantle, marked the intricate windings of the coast until once more ocean, shore and sky imperceptibly blended in the glorious blue.

It was a morning on which one was glad to be alive. The champagne-like quality of the air sent a zest for action thrilling through my veins. The world seemed very fair and, as I crossed the marketplace, I paused an instant to gaze with utter satisfaction on that brilliant mass of colour, the scarlet umbrellas of the stalls, the country-women with their heads enveloped in kerchiefs of flaming hues, the bold reds and greens and yellows of the masses of fruit and vegetables set forth in magnificent profusion for sale.

I felt that I was standing on the threshold of a great adventure. The strain of romance which Celtic blood bestows leaped to answer its appeal. In my head ran the mysterious jingle in which, as I was now convinced, a treasure lay concealed.

THE RETURN OF CLUBFOOT 263

So engrossed was I with my thoughts that, on mounting the broad flight of steps which led to the long, cool verandah of the British Consulate, I collided violently with a man who was coming out.

He was a short, stocky fellow, enormously strongly built, so massive in bulk, indeed, that one might almost say of him that he was as broad as he was long. His clean-shaven face, big and smooth and freckled, was tanned a deep brick-red and, especially about the good-natured, firm mouth, was lined with innumerable creases. The hair visible beneath his rather battered yachting-cap was close-cropped and a flaming red tint and his tufted eyebrows were of the same shade. A pair of brave and honest eyes shone very bluely out of his sunburnt face. He was wearing a clean but somewhat creased suit of white drill and in his hand he carried a sheaf of papers.

The mere sight of him carried me straight away back to Southsea or Plymouth or one of those queer steep little towns of the Isle of Wight where so many masters of our merchant marine have their homes. From the crown of his head to the sole of his foot he was British, a type that, I imagine, has scarcely changed through the ages.

"Sorry!" he said, as though realising that in the impact it could only be my less substantial frame which could suffer, and, taking a step back, scrutinised me.

"My fault!" said I, rubbing my head, for I felt as if I had butted it against a stone wall.

"If you're going to see the Consul," said the big man—and in his speech was a pleasant touch of the Hampshire burr—"you'll not find him. And the Vice-Consul's not in, either! He don't come to the office before 9 o'clock; leastwise that's what I figured out the Dago within was tryin' to tell me! They don't overwork in the Government offices!"

With the perfect complacency of the Britisher he addressed me in English, probably assuming, were I a foreigner, that I would understand him.

He stood on the steps and mopped his brow.

"I wonder whether you could tell me," I said, "where the steam yacht *Naomi* is lying?"

The big man smiled and crinkled his face into a thousand fresh creases.

"Aye," he replied. "That I can! She's lying about a hundred yards off the Customs House jetty—a white craft flying the Thames Yacht Club burgee. You can't mistake her! Do you know anybody aboard?"

"Not exactly," said I. "But I wanted to call on Sir Alexander Garth, the owner."

"Then you come right along with me." Placidly observed the big man. "I'm captain of the *Naomi*—I sail her for Sir Alexander. I've got our mail here and I'm going straight back on board. I left the launch at the steps! And, by the way, my name is Lawless—Harvey Lawless..."

"I should be delighted to come with you," I replied. "My name is Okewood!"

We turned our backs on the Consulate and crossing the Cathedral Square, followed a shabby, grass-grown street which rejoiced in the grandiose name of the Avenida de la Liberacion. As we strolled along in the shade Captain Lawless entertained me to some of his ideas on the shortcomings of the Central American republics and, in particular, of the State whose hospitality we were then enjoying. But with becoming reticence he did not question me as to the object of my desire to call upon his employer nor, on the other hand, did he volunteer any information about that gentleman or his friends.

Presently we emerged into a great white square on the sea, a place of blinding glare and whirling dust. Here at the foot of some white stone steps a trim motor launch was heaving to and fro in the bright green swell under the silent gaze of a knot of loafers. Two men were in the launch, one wearing a white jersey with "S.Y. Naomi" embroidered in blue and a round sailor's cap with the yacht's name on the ribbon. The other was in a blue suit and wore a yachting cap.

"You'll want to bring the launch back in a couple of hours' time, Parsons," said the captain, addressing the man in the yachting cap. "The Vice-Consul won't be there till then. You'll have to get a move on him about those fittings. Mr Mackay will not be very pleased, I'm thinking! He expected me to bring 'em back with me."

I stood a little to one side during the brief dialogue which ensued and feasted my eyes on the picturesque scene. Viewed from the water the city presented a beautiful spectacle. The houses rose in tiers amid masses of greenery which rested the eye from the pitiless glare of the sea. In the distance I noted the pleasant green hill where the long low line of John Bard's bungalow was just discernible among the trees. The square in which we stood was in itself a wonderful picture with its great white warehouses, public buildings and the like built over deep high arcades where with shrill cries newspaper boys and boot-blacks plied their trade and lemonade sellers and beggars drowsed in the cool shadows.

The little knot of spectators fringing the quayside were as picturesque a bunch of picaroons as I have ever set eyes on. Their complexions ran through the whole series of shades from light coffee to Brunswick black. Their attire was as varied as their colour; but for the most part it consisted in a ragged panama hat, a dirty vest and a pair of thin striped cotton trousers.

I noticed one unusually striking figure, a stunted black with a pock-marked face who wore a gaudy yellow handkerchief bound about his head and heavy gold rings in his ears. I observed this sportsman looking hard at me, and was a little nonplussed to see him ostensibly draw the attention of the man at his side to my appearance. The black companion was a swarthy lissom young fellow with handsome features and a pair of bold black eyes. The black nudged him and broke into a torrent of words. I was not near enough to make out what was said (and, if I had been, I doubt if I should have understood their rapidly-spoken lingo). But I felt tolerably certain that the black man was speaking about me; for twice he nodded his head in my direction. The upshot of it was that the swarthy young man turned and—a remarkable thing in this indolent population—sprinted hard away in the direction of the city.

I must say I felt disquietened. Since I had left John Bard's house that morning, I had kept a careful watch to see if I were followed. But no one had appeared to take any notice of me whatsoever and I felt reasonably sure that I was not shadowed. But now it distinctly looked as though I had been recognised. And in that moment, I believe, there hardened into determination in my mind the great resolve which had come into my head as I was taking leave of John Bard.

But the captain was summoning me to step into the launch. I dropped in, he followed, and in a moment we were "teuf-teufing" through the rolling green swell of the harbour towards the long and graceful shape of the *Naomi* as she tugged at her moorings over against the battered white bulk of the Customs House. It was with feelings of profound satisfaction that I saw the square with its fringe of loafers, the white houses and the tufted palms recede as the natty little boat cleaved a foaming path through the green water. I had got clear away. It was up to me to secure for myself an invitation to join the party on Sir Alexander Garth's yacht.

She was a beautiful craft, with a good turn of speed, to judge by her design. As we drew nearer, I could see, by the many evidences of comfort displayed, that her owner must be a man of wealth. The snowy decks, the burnished brass and copper fittings, the clean, well turned-out sailors who were busy on the deck beneath the striped sun-awnings, the neat gangway let down over the side with its clean white hand-rope—the whole impression given was one of luxury regardless of cost.

As we turned to run alongside, I found myself wondering what manner of man this Sir Alexander Garth was. Was he a wealthy industrialist of pre-war England or merely one of the new rich? If the latter he would be less easy to handle than the former, I reflected; besides, I reckoned, a war profiteer would not wear well on a long cruise to the South Seas! The next moment I stood on the deck of the *Naomi* in the modulated light which penetrated through the green-and-white awning.

The captain bade the man he had addressed as Parsons, whom I found to be the head steward, take me to the smoke-room while he asked "Sir Alexander" if he would receive me. Treading almost noiselessly on his rubber soles the steward led me along the deck to the back of the bridge where a door hooked back revealed a glimpse of a long low-ceilinged saloon set about with comfortable settees and club chairs in soft green Morocco leather, the port-holes screened against the blinding light from without.

Even below the awning the light outside was so much stronger than the comparative obscurity within the smoke-room that at first I could not distinguish much. Parsons left me at the door and I was about to sit down when I discovered to my surprise that I was not alone. At a desk set in one of the two recesses which flanked a doorway a girl was sitting. She was dressed in a plain white silk tennis shirt and white pique skirt and her panama hat lay on a chair by her side. She was writing letters. In the stillness of the room I could hear her pen scratching across the paper. So engrossed was she in her writing that she did not turn round.

I felt a little embarrassed. I felt it would be too farcical to cough mildly, in the manner of a stage comedian, in order to announce my presence; while, on the other hand, to make some violent noise like dropping on the floor one of the books which were lying around might, I conceived, unduly frighten the young lady. So I sat where I was, enjoying the pleasant half-light of the room after the heat and glitter outside, and amused myself by guessing at the appearance of the stranger from her back.

She had beautiful hair of a glossy golden brown, "bobbed" after the modern fashion, but so exquisitely brushed and tended that I decided she must have a good maid. Her figure was admirable, her neck very white and slender and matchless in the grace of its poise as she inclined her head to the paper. Her clothes, simple as they were, were faultless both in their cut and the way she wore them. I suppose there are fashions in a tennis blouse and skirt the same as there are in other kinds of women's clothes. At any rate, there was a flawless *chic* about this girl's appearance which told me that she was Paris-clad.

Presently the scratching of the pen stopped. A white hand stole up and patted the golden brown hair.

Then some intuitive sense told me that the girl knew there was someone in the room. It was as though our two minds communed in that still, cool place. At the same moment she swung round on her chair and, seeing me, rose abruptly to her feet.

As she confronted me I realised that I must have divined her beauty; for it came as no surprise to me to find her extremely good-looking. I have met many women in my time and, as is not uncommon in my profession, many were of the "charmer" order.

But the girl who stood facing me, a little perturbed, somewhat nonplussed by the unexpected apparition, had an indefinite quality of beauty which would have made her remarkable in any society. A beautifully shaped head, an oval face, delicately pencilled eyebrows throwing into relief the large grey eyes, a fine white skin and unusually good teeth—all these attributes of beauty she possessed. But with them went a curiously strong attraction, some quality of magnetism, which, to speak quite personally, made me want to see her radiantly happy, to conjure up a smile which I felt must be unusually sweet.

THE RETURN OF CLUBFOOT

"Oh," she exclaimed and blushed very prettily, "I didn't hear you come in. How do you do? I am Marjorie Garth. Does Daddy know you're here?"

With the *empressement* of the exiled Briton, to whom the vision of a fresh young English girl is as the first violets of spring or the fragrance of the forest after summer rain, I took the slim, cool hand she offered me.

"The steward," I said, "has gone to tell him!"

"I'm afraid," she went on, scrutinising me dispassionately after the manner of the modern young girl, "that you're in for a very slow time. There's nobody but just Daddy and me. Of course, that was the idea of this cruise. Daddy overworked terribly in the war and the doctors told him he'd never get his nerves right unless he dropped business absolutely for a whole year."

I wondered how she had divined the nature of my mission to her father. Perhaps the captain had jumped to conclusions and had imparted them to her. But her next remark puzzled me horribly.

"Of course, I'm perfectly fit," she observed, and smiled with a glint of white teeth. "But Daddy is very difficult to handle. He has cables sent to him at every port, and when we're in harbour his cabin looks like his office at the Manchester Cotton Exchange. You'll have to be very severe with him about it..."

"I don't know really," I replied, very puzzled, "whether I should feel justified..."

"Oh," laughed the girl, "that's no way to handle Daddy. He's from the North, remember! He made his money by knowing when to say 'No'; at least, that's what he says. And *you'll* have to say 'No' to him. And to me, as well. I'm like Daddy. I adore having my own way. And I usually get it..."

"That I'm fully prepared to believe!" I answered, and we both laughed. It was as though we were old friends. Then, growing serious on a sudden, the girl very deliberately started rolling up the left sleeve of her blouse. I gazed at her in bewilderment.

What was coming now? I asked myself. With the utmost composure she unbared to the shoulder a firm, round and very white arm.

"Don't give me away to Daddy," she observed confidentially. "But my idiotic French maid burnt my arm the day before yesterday with the electric tongs and it's rather sore. I wish you would just have a look at it. I haven't said a word to Daddy, for, if he knew, he would insist on dismissing Yvonne. Would you mind...?"

She extended her left arm to me whilst I, like an idiot, blushed furiously in my embarrassment and vainly cudgelled my brains to discover who this charming girl thought I was. And why the devil should I look at the burn on her arm?

A calm voice at the doorway delivered me from my dilemma.

"Sir Alexander will see you, sir!"

The steward, Parsons, was there. Marjorie Garth pulled her sleeve down.

"Don't keep Daddy waiting!" she warned, and added: "You shall dress my arm afterwards!"

I said "Oh, *rather!*" or something equally idiotic and followed the steward out. As I passed the girl, she leant forward and whispered:

"Mind you stand up to him!"

As we crossed the blinding sunshine of the deck and went down a companion-way Parsons confided to me that the owner was at breakfast. My heart sank rather. It is poor tactics to ask a man for favours before noon.

The saloon, which was panelled in some light-coloured wood, maple or birch, resembled, with its little domed skylight, the restaurant of a liner in miniature. It was a small, snug little place with rose-coloured silk curtains and carpet and a profusion of silver and flowers. At the far end was a door which, I imagined led to the cabins.

At the sound of my entrance Sir Alexander Garth looked up from his egg. As he stood up to greet me, I saw he was a tall, heavily-built man in the fifties with a heavy iron-grey moustache. He had about him an air I have noticed in other prosperous business people—a sort of "moneyed manner" which reveals itself in a great deal of self-confidence with just a touch of parade. The hard grey eyes and the firm chin denoted the man of action; but the physiognomist in me (which my work has considerably developed) took mental stock of the arched nostril and the downward dip to the corners of the mouth which are the unmistakable signals of a violent temper.

These and other little details I noticed about him as we shook hands and he asked me if I had breakfasted. And because I was really pretty peckish and because I believe one can always do business best over a meal, I accepted his invitation and started in on a luscious grape-fruit. When he had poured out my coffee, pushed the toast-rack at me and generally put me at my ease, Sir Alexander Garth, who had been scrutinising me rather closely, remarked:

"I should never have taken you for a doctor!"

"I'm not a doctor, sir!" I answered.

"I see—not taken your degree, eh? Well, well, I told our New York office in my cable to do the best they could; indeed, I wasn't at all sure that our manager could manage it in the time. But Lowry's a spry chap—he don't come from Bolton for nothing—and he knows that when th'oud man gives an order he expects it to be carried out. Did you meet Lowry, doctor?"

Now I understood Miss Garth's inexplicable and embarrassing desire to show me her burnt arm.

"I'm afraid you've made a mistake, Sir Alexander," I said. "I'm not a doctor..."

"Eh?" ejaculated the baronet, sitting back in his chair and looking at me. "Then who the devil are you?"

"My name is Okewood, Major Desmond Okewood," I replied as boldly as might be, though my host's countenance was hoisting all manner of storm signals in the shape of a reddening of the cheeks and a twitching of the nostrils, "and I have rather a strange request to make..."

But I got no farther for Garth exploded.

"Damn it!" he exclaimed, pounding the table with his big, sun-burnt hand, "I knew it. You're from Allan's. My Manchester office turned their proposition down without reference to me, and as soon as I heard about it, I wrote and confirmed the decision. And they've done nothing but badger me about it ever since. At every port there's been a cable. And now you have the brass to come interfering with my holiday, asking yourself to breakfast under false pretences... Parsons!"

He yelled for the steward, at the same time putting forth his hand to pound a bell that stood on the table at his side.

"Stop!" I said.

"Will you stop me from ringing for my own servants?" he demanded truculently.

"I'll stop you from making yourself look a fool before your own steward," I retorted, "if you'll quit shouting and listen to me for a minute. I have nothing to do with Allan's or any other business concern..."

At the first glimpse of this resolute-looking cotton-spinner I knew that, to achieve my end, I should have to take him more fully into my confidence than either my inclination allowed or my instructions warranted. I took my letter-case from my pocket and extracting a folded blue paper, laid it before Sir Alexander on the white damask table-cloth. These were my credentials which we are only supposed to show in moments of direst necessity.

"Will you read that?" I said.

The baronet looked questioningly at me, then slowly put on a pair of horn-rimmed spectacles which he took from a case in his pocket. He carefully perused my blue paper and then handed it back to me.

"Eh," he remarked without a trace of apology in his manner, "and we all thought you were the doctor I ordered our New York office to send to join the yacht at Rodriguez. Well, young man, and what can I do for you?"

With the utmost candour I told him. Thereafter for ten minutes or more, our heads were close together. Then he rang the bell.

"My compliments to Captain Lawless," he said to the steward, "and I should be obliged if he could spare me a few minutes! We will come to him in the charthouse!"

He gave the steward the start of us by lingering to offer me a cigar and to light one for himself. Then we made our way up on deck and presently entered the chart-house, a room abaft the bridge and above the smoke-room. Here the captain, looking very red and shaggy without his cap, awaited us.

"Ah, captain!" said our host, "Let me make you acquainted with Major Okewood, who is coming on a cruise with us. I want you to show me on the chart Cock Island in the Eastern Pacific. And let's hear, too, what the 'Sailing Directions' have to say about it!"

Thus I learnt that my pleading had prevailed with him and that, behind a hard and business-like exterior, there flickered a little spark of romance that had burst into flame at the magic tale of treasure trove I had poured into his ears. As the skipper spread out upon the mahogany top of the chart-locker the section in which, amid weird whorls and lines signifying tides and depths, Cock Island figured, I felt once more the strong tug at my heart from that secluded islet whence at the foot of volcanic peaks an enigmatic grave seemed to beckon...

27

I RECEIVE AN INVITATION

Garth appeared to be a seaman of no mean order. With the charts spread out before them he and the skipper promptly became immersed in a maze of technicalities. My ignorance of matters nautical is abysmal; and I listened in some bewilderment to talk of winds and tides and channels, of soundings and of reefs. I can reconstruct the scene now—the prelude to so many strange adventures I—as the three of us pored over the chart; the long, low chart-house with its clean smell of paint, the holland sun-blinds rattling smartly in the breeze which blew in through the open port-holes, Garth in his loose tussore suit, with his eager face and keen eyes, a fragrant cigar thrust in his mouth, Lawless, rather awed by the other and consequently a trifle formal, stubbing the chart with a huge and podgy thumb.

When they pulled down the big orange-coloured volume of "Sailing Directions" for the Eastern Pacific and opened the page at Cock Island, I could better follow them.

"'The island is mountainous,'" Garth read out in his pleasant, deep voice, "'and entirely volcanic, rising to several peaks, of which the highest reaches 2,856 feet. These peaks are probably volcanoes, but the interior is unexplored and almost impenetrable owing to its steep, rugged and often precipitous nature, the many rushing streams and the dense vegetation. There are small areas of comparatively level ground surrounding Sturt and Horseshoe Bays...'"

He turned the page and skipped a mass of detail.

"'There are only two harbours,'" he read, "'Sturt and Horseshoe Bays. Horseshoe Bay is larger than Sturt Bay but is less sheltered, as it opens to the west and so has a heavy swell during the early months of the year. Moreover, the slopes surrounding the bay are much more abrupt and the area of level land in its neighbourhood is much less considerable.'"

Adams, I recollected, had spoken of the man Dutchey and himself coming upon the grave in a clearing in the undergrowth close to the shore. He had mentioned, too, that their ship's boat had had to find a way in through the bar. It looked to me, therefore, as though they had landed in Horseshoe Bay where the upward slopes began closer to the shore than in Sturt Bay.

We read on. The island, it seemed, had never had any permanent population. It was "the resort of buccaneers in the seventeenth century, and later was a watering-place for whalers." It had "little animal life"; but there were wild pigs, descendants of those left by Captain Martin of the frigate *Rover* in 1774, and rats, introduced by calling ships. Mention had been made, we were told, by various explorers of huge carved images reputed to exist in the interior of the island, similar to those for which Easter Island is famous; but there was no certain knowledge of their existence.

There were a lot of particulars about attempts to colonise the island, of stray parties of mariners who had landed, with the intention of settling there; but in a year or two had gone away in a passing ship or died off. And there was a string of names, British and foreign, of naval men or of explorers who, landing to fill up with water or to kill some fresh meat, had jotted down a few observations about the island and then sailed away again across the boundless Pacific.

"And now, Okewood," said Garth pleasantly, "you and I and all of us, you know, are merely passengers on the high seas of Captain Lawless here, and with your permission I propose that we should tell him who you are and what you have just confided to me. You have no objection, I take it?"

"None whatever," said I.

"Then tell him yourself!" urged Garth, dropping on to the leather settee. So, sitting between the two on the softly padded seat, I unfolded my plan while the yacht gently swayed at her moorings, and the awnings without cracked like a whip in the breeze.

When I had finished, Garth said:

"You'll agree, I'm sure, that we can spare a week!"

"I'm entirely in your hands, Sir Alexander!" returned the captain. "But there is one condition I should like to make, and that is that this matter remains strictly between us three. I have a very decent lot of men as crew, Sir Alexander, hard-working, reliable chaps and every one personally known to me for years. I'd go so far as to say you've got the pick of the Solent in the *Naomi*. But this isn't a man-o'-war, gentlemen, nor yet even a merchant vessel. In a pleasure yacht like this there isn't rightly speaking the discipline that you'd find in either, and, to be plain-spoken, I don't want the major here to go upsetting the men with his treasure tales. Lay off at Cock Island, go ashore by all means, and have a 'look see' but don't, for God's sake, blab about it or you'll rot the finest crew that ever shipped! Let's keep this thing to ourselves; indeed I'll go further than that. Leave me out of it! Then the men, should they hear anything, can't say that I'm in it while they are not! And to tell you the truth, gentlemen, I've had a strict upbringing, my people being chapel-goers, and I was taught to believe that no blessing rests on money that we have not earned with the sweat of our brow and the work of our strong right hand. You two gentlemen take your week ashore and I'll look after the ship!"

Garth turned to me.

"I don't want to leave Captain Lawless out," he said, "but I can't help feeling he's right about the crew!"

"And about everybody else on board, Sir Alexander!" Lawless broke in.

"You mean the women?"

"I mean *everybody* else on board, just as I said, sir!" reiterated the skipper very firmly and with meaning. "What everybody's secret is nobody's secret! Mum's the word or you'll have trouble! Mum's the word, I say!"

"Well!" said Garth, "So be it! Mum's the word!" Then came an unlooked-for interruption.

"Why 'mum'? What's the secret?"

A clear young voice rang out from the door. The three of us scrambled hastily to our feet. On the threshold stood the girl of the smoke-room.

"Morning, Marjie!" said Garth.

He wore something of a hang-dog look. So did I, I think, as I did my best to secrete myself behind them. I was wondering what the girl would think of me when she discovered my involuntary deception. Fortunately Lawless's huge frame completely obliterated me.

"What are you two talking secrets about?" she demanded bluntly. "And why 'mum's the word'?"

Garth looked at Lawless and Lawless looked at Garth; but neither answered her question. Then she looked at the skipper. His air reminded me of a pickpocket caught red-handed.

"Good morning, Miss Garth!" he mumbled and made a stiff little bow. That bow was my undoing; for the captain disclosed me behind him.

"Oh!" cried the girl with a little gurgle of amusement, "It's the doctor! Well, did you take my advice?"

"Yes," I answered. Then, taking the plunge, I faltered:

"But I'm not the doctor..."

On that the girl coloured up a little. I knew what she was thinking of and our eyes met. I felt relieved to see the glint of humour creep into them.

Then Garth who had turned to speak to the captain, broke in.

"I should have introduced you. Major, this is my daughter—Marjie, Major Okewood, who is coming as far as Honolulu with us. Would you see Carstairs about getting a cabin ready for him?"

With a graceful little nod to her father and a smile to me which had its hidden meaning for us two alone, Marjorie Garth went out again on to the sunlit deck. We three men plunged into our deliberations again and when at length the gong sounded for luncheon we had evolved a rough plan of campaign.

I told Garth quite frankly that the message found on the grave at Cock island was so far unintelligible to me that I had no certainty of ever being able to decipher it. What I proposed to do, was to examine the grave and the island generally to see whether I could find anything on the spot to throw any light on the message. We arranged, therefore, that in reaching Cock Island, Garth and I should take a camping outfit and go ashore for a period not to exceed a week; that if at the end of that time, my investigations had led to no result I should abandon the enterprise and return with him to the yacht.

It was settled that we should sail that night, as soon as ever the spare parts required by Mr Mackay, the engineer, were aboard; for I informed Garth of Bard's advice to me to make myself scarce without delay. The captain reckoned that, taking things easy, we should make Cock Island on the fifth day out. We finally decided to put ashore at Horseshoe Bay, as both Lawless and Garth agreed with me that this landing tallied best with the beach-comber's description.

As we crossed the deck to go down to the saloon the spare parts were being hoisted into the yacht from a barge. A hard-faced little man with a rasping Scottish accent, whom I took to be Mr Mackay, the engineer, was in charge of the operation which was accompanied by some fine, full-flavoured swearing in broad Clydebank and a torrent of epileptic Latin-American blasphemy from various parties unseen in the lighter. Small boats piled up to their thwarts with poultry, fruit, vegetables and bread, were bobbing about in a wide semi-circle about the yacht and the air rang with the shrill cries of the vendors.

As we passed the engineer the captain said:

"You'll let none of this scum aboard, Mr Mackay!"

"But the steward was wishful..."

"I don't give a hoot for the steward. I'll have none of these dagoes aboard my ship. Have you got that clear?"

"Verra guid, sir!" replied the Scotsman resignedly.

I appreciated the skipper's motive and looked at him gratefully. I was beginning to have an admiration for Captain Lawless. Besides being a man of character he was plainly a person of quick perception.

It was now very hot. The pitch was soft in the seams of the deck and the broken white line of the port buildings on shore swam in a tremor of heat. It was a relief to escape from the dazzling sunlight into the shaded seclusion of the saloon, where two purring electric fans kept the atmosphere cool and ice tinkled melodiously in crystal jugs of cider cup.

The girl Marjorie was already seated at the table. With her demurely cropped brown hair gleaming golden where the sunshine touched it, her serene beauty and her white dress, she reminded me of some Florentine Madonna, the shining white port-hole like a halo framing her face against a background of deep azure sky.

"*Le Medecin malgre Lui!*" she exclaimed as I came in, "Come and sit by me and tell me how you managed to captivate Daddy so completely! And I promise," she added, smiling up at me deliciously, "that I won't ask you for any more medical advice!"

The girl's attractive presence, the pleasant cool of the saloon, the quiet efficient service made it difficult for me to realise that, only a very few hours before, I had stumbled through blood into a dark and perilous adventure. As I looked into Marjorie Garth's friendly grey eyes, I found the present so attractive that it was no effort to me to thrust into the background the enigma of the future.

My adventure, I decided, was opening under the most pleasant auspices.

28

THE VICE-CONSUL'S WARNING

The *Naomi* was fitted out with the greatest luxury imaginable. She was not a large vessel, but she was so well designed that every inch of space was utilised. The cabin allotted to me was small but beautifully compact and tastefully furnished. There was a proper brass bedstead, not a bunk; pile carpet, silk curtains, silver-plated toilet fittings and an electric fan. My traps had been unpacked and my clothes stowed away in a cunningly contrived wardrobe. Carstairs, Garth's man, showed me where everything was. He was a nice, fresh-faced young fellow, of smart military appearance. He told me he had served in the war with the Royal Engineers.

Luncheon ended, Marjorie Garth left us to go and write letters to be sent ashore in the launch for posting. I repaired to my cabin to snatch a little sleep in the siesta hour; for I was very tired after our disturbed night. But though the gently whirring fan kept the atmosphere nicely cool and my bed invited repose, I could not sleep. Now that I was alone again, I found my thoughts continually recurring to the slip of oilsilk with its enigmatic message.

I have always found that short commons of sleep is an excellent mental tonic. Though I was physically worn out, my brain was alive and active and, pulling from my pocket the dead man's message (for so I designated it to myself) I fell to studying it with renewed zest.

I had it already by heart even to the bars of music (though for music I have little ear); but I read it over again. What absolute rot it sounded!

"Noon. 18/11/18."

I considered the date for an instant. Why, by November 18th, 1918, the war was over! The Armistice had been signed seven days earlier. And at once a light dawned on me. The dead man, I had surmised, had an appointment with someone at Cock Island, probably with El Cojo's gang. Realising that he was about to die the Unknown had left this message for his friends; but, probably knowing that an occasional ship touched at the island, he had coded his instructions to prevent them from falling into the wrong hands. The date of the message seemed to give the clue as to why his friends had failed to keep their appointment, so that the message had remained on the grave until it was found months later by Adams. The Armistice had been signed; Germany was beaten; and consequently the services of such obliging "neutrals" as El Cojo and Co. had abruptly ceased.

With growing excitement, for I felt certain that, this time, my deductions were not at fault, I read on:

"Flash, flash, much.
The garrison of Kiel"

This absolutely defeated me and I passed on.

"With the compass is best
Think of the Feast of Orders"

Der Ordensfest! Unconsciously, as I repeated the words to myself, the clean white panels of the cabin melted away, and there rose before my mind a dim picture, a study in grey, an outdoor scene across which swept the wintry wind with biting blast... A leaden sky, grey buildings, their roofs deep-thatched with snow, and grey-clad troops, masses of them, set about a vast square. It was a blurred picture with, here and there, a detail clear, the rime glistening on an officer's *pelisse*, the plume of a helmet blown out in the icy breeze... Ah! I had it! Berlin... The Feast of Orders, with the annual ceremony of the so-called nailing of the Colours. I had seen it once, that famous winter parade, as a boy when my brother Francis and I had been on a visit to a cousin of ours, who was secretary at the Berlin Embassy...

But what did it mean in this connection? What had the Feast of Orders, the annual bestowal on the old Prussian bureaucracy of thousands of crosses and stars and medals, as an economical substitute for increases in salary, what had it to do with a compass?

Then it came to me with a flash... A compass argued a compass bearing, and this bearing was there concealed in this phase! "Der Ordensfest!" Stay! The date. What was the date? And that came back to me too... January 27th, "Kaisers Geburtstag," the Emperor's birthday.

By jove! At last a beam of light was piercing the darkness.

Those two lines meant indubitably: "Take a compass bearing of 27 degrees!"

The next two lines:

> "Past the Sugar-Loaf
> You'll see the Lorelei"

obviously referred to those "peaks" of which the "Sailing Directions" had spoken.

"If you desire the sweetheart."

Schätzchen was the German word. But, ye gods, *Schatz* of which *Schätzchen* is the diminutive, properly speaking, means" treasure"! By what form of physical and mental blindness had I been smitten to have failed to see this direct reference to treasure in the cipher?

The four bars of music brought me up with a jerk. I hummed the tune which I had strummed out on John Bard's piano. It seemed, as I said, vaguely familiar as a German ditty of the popular sort but what or where... I...

On this I must have fallen asleep. I awoke with a start, as one does from an afternoon nap, and stared round blankly, trying to recollect where I was. There was a little sidelong motion in the cabin as the yacht rose and fell at anchor to the swell and the electric fan purred gently as it revolved. Someone was tapping at the door.

"Come in!" I cried and Carstairs put his face in.

"Sir Alexander begs pardon for disturbing you, sir," the man said, "but could you make it convenient to go to him at once in his cabin? He said as how it was urgent..."

"Of course. Tell Sir Alexander I'll be with him immediately."

Garth had a little suite at the far end of the saloon consisting of a small state-room, very handsomely furnished, with sleeping apartment and bath off it. I found him seated in a swivel-chair at his desk in conversation with a dark young man, his face yellowed from the tropics, in a creased white duck suit.

"Ah, major," said the baronet, "I'm sorry to have had to spoil your forty winks. But a rather curious thing has happened. They're getting a warrant out against you for murder. The British Vice-Consul here has been good enough to come off and give us the tip..."

"It's a most singular thing," said the Vice-Consul. "Last night a poor white, a drunken Englishman who lived with a coloured woman in the native quarter, had his throat cut. He was a worthless creature, called himself Adams; I knew him well. In fact, it's only about a fortnight ago that we threw him out of the Consulate. Well, an information has been laid against you by two citizens who swear that they saw you leave this man Adams's shack in the early hours of the morning.

"Now in the ordinary way nobody in Rodriguez makes any bones about a plain murder like this. But our friend Adams — or his black lady who, incidentally, was also killed — seemed to have had some amazing political pull. The Procurator-General of the Republic in person came down to the office half an hour ago to see me about it. He seemed scared out of his life, told me he would certainly lose his job unless he could produce you for trial. Now—" the Vice-Consul cleared his throat and drew hard on the black cigar he was smoking, "I don't know anything about you, major, or your business," he looked sharply at me, "and I'm not inquiring. But I do know that, while straightforward murder in Rodriguez is scarcely a penal offence, dabbling in politics is a very serious matter. What I came off to tell you was to beat it while the going's good... That's all!"

"It's extremely kind of you to have taken the trouble," I replied, "and I highly appreciate your discretion in the matter. But surely, if the warrant is out, it will be served at once. After all, we're within the three-mile limit..."

The Vice-Consul waved his hand.

"In this illustrious Republic," he remarked dryly, "no business of any description is ever done in the siesta hours. Even during our periodical revolutions there's a truce every day between noon and 4 p.m. But you'll want to hurry; for, as soon as it cools off, you'll have a bunch of coffee-coloured dons alongside in the harbour-master's launch!"

"I'll see about getting under way at once!" said Garth, and hastened out.

The Vice-Consul picked up his panama and approached me. He looked cautiously about him and lowered his voice as he spoke.

"I'm risking my job by doing this," he said, "for the Consul's down with fever and I'm acting on my own responsibility. But Bard was telling us about you at the Club, about your D.S.O. and that in the war, and it's the least a fellow can do who didn't fight—I'm rotten through and through with malaria, you know—to help a chap who did. Now, listen! You're in great danger. You've run up against the biggest bunch of crooks in Central America..."

"You mean El Cojo and his gang?"

"Aye..."

"Who is this man, El Cojo?"

"No one knows. No one ever sees him. No one knows where he lives. Some say he is a Mexican. But his power is tremendous and his vengeance swift and terrible. I could tell you stories... You should be safe on this yacht. But take my advice and don't leave it until you can go ashore under the American or the British flag!"

He gave me his hand.

"I shan't forget this service," I said warmly, "if there's anything I can ever do in return..."

"Well," he answered slowly, "I was recommended for the M.B.E. once. But the F.O. turned it down. If you had any influence..."

"If Sir Robert is still my friend," I assured him, "you shall have it. And perhaps it might be an O.B.E. Write me down your name and address..."

As we emerged on the deck the crew were busy getting the yacht ready for sea. There was a bit of commotion at the gangway. Garth and Captain Lawless stood at the head of the ladder in animated conversation with a very trim young man, beautifully dressed in spotless white drill.

"Hullo," said the Vice-Consul, "it's Custrin, your new doctor!"

"It's no good," Garth was saying as we approached the group," we'll have to be away in ten minutes, doctor, and there's so much work going forward on deck that your friends would only be in the way..."

"But, sir," the young man urged, "they need only stay for a minute. As distinguished residents of Rodriguez they wished to have the honour of meeting you, of showing you courtesy. They set great store by such things here and if you refuse I'm very much afraid they'll take it amiss..."

I glanced over the side. In a row-boat at the foot of the ladder sat three swarthy gentlemen in frockcoats, their large dark eyes turned appealingly up to the deck of the *Naomi*.

"You'll tell your friends," said the baronet, "how much I appreciate their great attention and how much I regret that circumstances prevent me from receiving their visit on board. Captain Lawless, the Vice-Consul's launch!"

Lawless gave an order and while the doctor descended the ladder and spoke to the party in the boat, the Vice-Consul took his leave and boarded his launch.

Five minutes later the *Naomi*, curtseying to the long green swell, pointed her bows towards the fronded headlands which marked the entrance to the harbour. As we passed out between the buffs, the dull report of a gun drifted out to us over the freshening breeze. At the same moment, in a smother of spray, a launch came tearing out of the port, a mere speck in the shimmering green sea far astern.

At my side on the bridge, Garth laughed.

"Here comes the warrant!" he said. "Captain, is that launch back yonder going to overhaul us?"

Lawless took his freckled hand off the engine-room telegraph and looked back.

"Huh!" he grunted, "not on this side of hell. Or any other!"

29

DR CUSTRIN

It was not until dinner that evening that I had the opportunity of meeting Dr Custrin. The *Naomi* was steaming along amid the gorgeous pageantry of sunset and the warm glow of the dying day was warring with the soft lights of the electric candles on the dinnertable when I came in to the saloon.

Garth introduced me to the doctor. He was a sleek, smooth young man with hair like black satin and a beautifully trained small black moustache. His hands and feet were small and well-made and there would have been a touch of effeminacy about him but for his otherwise manly bearing, his bold black eyes and pleasant voice. A certain narrowness of the eyes and a curl of the nostrils told me, who have an eye for such things, that, probably, as his name indicated, he was of Jewish extraction. In conversation I elicited that he had been born in Mauritius, educated at Cape Town, and had taken his degree at King's College Hospital in London. Garth's New York office it appeared, had picked him up at Colon where he was studying Colonel Goethals' wonderful arrangements for the extermination of yellow fever and malaria.

Lawless and Mackay, the chief engineer, a sententious Scot, who opened his mouth only to utter a platitude or to put food or drink into it, dined with us. Garth made me sit next to Marjorie who looked ravishing in a white lace evening frock.

"Put the two war veterans together!" the baronet commanded. "My little girl here," he explained to me, "drove a car at the front. She has the Military Medal."

"Daddy!" expostulated Marjorie and a warm flush coloured her cheeks.

"I would never have given my consent," Garth added, "but she just didn't ask me for it!"

"My dear old thing," said the girl. "You make me look ridiculous by bragging about my silly little trips around the bases when I'm sure Dr Custrin or Major Okewood saw a hundred times more of the war than I ever did!"

"I never got out of the base at the Cape," said the doctor. "The East African campaign kept us too busy for anybody to be spared."

"And I," was my retort, "never went back to France after the Somme!"

"Were you wounded?" asked Garth.

"Badly?" questioned Marjorie in reply to my nod.

"Nothing to write home about," I answered. "When I came out of hospital I went into the Intelligence."

"How fearfully thrilling!" exclaimed the girl. "Wasn't it frightfully exciting?"

"It wasn't the front," I replied.

After dinner on the deck under a vast span of velvet sky spangled with stars I found myself alone with Marjorie Garth. A broad band of yellow light shone out from the smoke-room where the others sat and talked over their coffee. Above us on the bridge the form of the man at the wheel bulked black.

We strolled up and down in silence. For myself I was quite overcome by the majesty of the tropical night at sea.

"The Intelligence," asked Marjorie suddenly, "that's the Secret Service, isn't it?"

"Yes," I agreed.

"You were very modest about it at dinner," she remarked.

I shrugged my shoulders.

"I only stated the plain truth," I returned. "In the fighting troops, remember, every fifth man became a casualty and three months was the average run of the platoon officer!"

"Yet," commented the girl, "you seem like a man who has been in tight places. I shouldn't say to look at you that you've had a placid or easy existence. Like mine, for instance. Sometimes I think it's only men of action like you who know how to grapple with life. Can you imagine me in an emergency for instance?"

"Yes," I said. "I believe I can. You've got a brave eye, Miss Garth. I think one can judge people's temperaments, as one judges horses, by the eye."

She shook her head and laughed.

"What does this sort of life teach anybody? This beautiful ship, these well-trained sailors, the splendid service that Daddy's money can buy? My dear man, it's no good flattering me about my brave eye. Money makes a solid barrier between my life and any really thrilling crisis! I shall be kept in cotton-wool till the end of the chapter."

"What a strange person you are!" I exclaimed. "Girls of your age with your position and your... your... attractions don't find time for philosophising as a rule. You ought to be enjoying your youth instead of meditating about life. I don't mean to be inquisitive; but... are you unhappy?"

We had halted near the rail. We were standing very close together and I felt the touch of her warm young body against my arm.

She turned and looked at me. Again I told myself that this girl was the most beautiful, the most unspoiled creature I had ever met.

"I've only once been thoroughly happy," she answered rather wistfully, "and that was when I was with the army in

France. I loved the romance, the adventure of it all, the good comradeship not only between the women but also between the men and the women. Money wasn't everything then. I was an individual with my own personality, my own friends. But what am I now? The daughter of Garth, the millionaire. And they print my picture in the weekly papers because one day I shall have a great deal of money which Daddy has worked all his life to make. I've never had any brothers and sisters and my mother has been dead for years. I've had to live my whole life with money as my companion. And money's not a bit companionable!"

She smiled whimsically at me, then gazed down abstractedly at the phosphorescent water thumping against the side of the ship.

"This yacht!" she went on. "I have everything a girl could possibly require here—everything except my freedom!"

"Good Lord!" I observed, "You'll have that too, when you marry! You've plenty of time for that!"

Marjorie Garth laughed.

"My dear man," she protested, "don't you know it's easier to marry off a girl with no money than one who will have as much as I shall? To Daddy every young man I meet is a fortune-hunter. If I run a boy home from the golf-club in my car I am cross-questioned regarding his 'intentions'; if a man takes me out dancing in the afternoon there's a scene. And Daddy's taste in men is vile; I'm not alluding to you—I mean at home! But I've no use for the second generation of millionaires and I've told Daddy so. I'd rather marry a beggar than some of the rich men's sons he tries to throw in my way..."

Lucky beggar, I thought.

"I don't know why I've told you all this," the girl concluded. "You seem to draw me out. Or perhaps it's the night. Oh, look! Wish!"

A star fell gleaming across the sky.

"I have," I said (it was one of those idle wishes which a poor man must not admit even to himself).

"Was it about your trip to Cock Island?"

"I'll lose my wish if I tell!" I replied. "As a matter of fact it was not!"

Suddenly she put a warm soft hand on mine. Her touch made my heart beat faster.

"Is it a Secret Service mission?" she asked.

Caution is second nature to a man who has served his apprenticeship in the silent corps. In that balmy air, beneath a brilliant moon hanging like some great lamp in the sky, it was hard to refuse a woman's pleading, especially a girl like this, bending forward with sparkling eyes and parted lips so close to me that I could detect the fragrance of her hair. I put my other hand over hers as it rested on mine on the rail.

"You can trust me," she pleaded. "I am sure there is something mysterious about your trip to this tiny island. I know you are not going on Government survey" (this was the pretext which Garth had given out for my visit to Cock Island) "for the Navy always do that sort of work. Tell me your secret!"

I had to catch hold of myself; for she was almost irresistible. I looked away from her, steeling myself to a refusal. What I might have done I cannot say for what man can account for actions performed under the magic of the tropical moon? But at that moment my nose detected the scent of a cigarette quite close.

I glanced quickly round. To all appearances we were alone. Behind us the white smoke stack of the *Naomi* reared itself into the night; on either hand the deck was quite deserted; the only human being visible was the black form of the man at the wheel silhouetted against the faint glow of the binnacle light. But the acrid fragrance of Turkish tobacco stole up my nostrils and the possibility of a listener within earshot brought me swiftly back to earth.

"I'm afraid there's no mystery about my little jaunt," said I, turning to the girl, "you know all there is to know!"

I spoke as nonchalantly as possible. But I would not meet the reproachful gaze she turned upon me. Then she snatched her hand away.

"I'm afraid you must think me horribly inquisitive!" she observed coldly.

There was a footstep on the deck. Dr Custrin stood behind us. Between his fingers a cigarette sent up a little spiral of blue smoke; across his arm he carried a shining silver wrap.

"Sir Alexander asked me to tell you to put this round your shoulders," he said to Marjorie and unfolded the silver scarf. "The wind is freshening."

The girl drew the wrap about her shoulders. The doctor looked at the two of us.

"What a wonderful night!" he remarked. "In these latitudes the moon seems to exercise a strange influence upon us. For example, your father has been telling me the whole story of his early life, Miss Garth, and I believe I have been unbosoming my aspirations and ambitions to him. But confidences under the moon one is apt to regret in the morning, eh, major?"

He spoke perfectly suavely and with no trace of impertinence in his manner. But there was a hint of double meaning in his words (which clearly indicated that he had overheard at any rate the end of our conversation) that jarred on me.

"You need have no fears about Major Okewood," replied Marjorie with just the faintest touch of scorn in her voice. "I am sure he is the pattern of discretion. I think," she added, "I am feeling the tiniest bit chilly. You promised to play for me, doctor. Won't you come into the saloon? There is a piano there!"

Her gaze travelled proudly past me as she turned to Custrin. She made it as clear as was compatible with the laws of hospitality that her invitation did not include me. It was her woman's way of getting her own back. I loved her for it; but I took a violent dislike to Custrin.

I mumbled some excuse about having to go to the chart-room and they left me. Presently from the saloon came the rhythmic strains of the *Rosen-Kavalier*, most sensual, most entrancing, of all Strauss's music, played with a master-hand. The *Liebestod*, Grieg, Massenet's *Air des Larmes*, Schumann— Custrin ran from one to the other while the *Naomi* stolidly thumped her way through the hissing sea. And always, curse his impudence! the fellow played love-music...

One by one members of the crew drifted to the head of the companion-way until there was quite a company of them outlined against the yellow light that shone up from the cosy saloon. I remained leaning against the rail, my chin on my chest, my pipe in my mouth, and let my thoughts drift... Adams coughing over his pannikin, John Bard, his honest face troubled, looking round that house of death, the yellow-faced Vice-Consul pulling on his black cigar.

But always I found my mind harking back to that ungainly silhouette framed in the doorway of the hut and to the sinister echo of his footsteps in the yard as the stranger turned his back on the scene of slaughter which, I doubted not, had been of his contriving. What had the Vice-Consul said? "His power is tremendous, his vengeance swift and terrible!" Who was this lame man whom nobody saw yet whom everybody feared? There was something of the insistence of a nightmare in the way in which the glimpse I had had of him hung in my thoughts, confounding itself with the ineffaceable image of that clubfooted man whom I had seen fall lifeless— how many years ago it seemed now!—before my brother's smoking automatic.

Well, whoever El Cojo was, Mexican or South American, I was out of his clutches now. The rail of the *Naomi*, quivering beneath my hand to the leap of the seas, gave me confidence. I knocked the ashes out of my pipe and went below.

30

CONCERNING A LONG DRINK

The weather continued magnificent. The barometer on the chart-house wall was high and steady, the sea like a sheet of painted glass. On board the *Naomi* the perfect luxury, the admirable efficiency of the service might have led one to fancy oneself at Cowes but for the boundless expanse of the Pacific surrounding us. The sun-burnt faces, the natty white caps and the spotless white drill of the crew, the brasswork polished until the blaze of the fierce sun upon it made the eyes ache, the long chairs set out invitingly under the striped deck awnings—it all brought back Regatta Week to me so vividly that I sometimes imagined one had only to look over the ship's side to see the boats setting down the visitors at the Squadron steps.

There were deck quoits, shuffleboard and various other ship's games for our amusement. But it was too hot for violent exercise. The men rigged up a huge canvas bath, contrived out of a mainsail, in the bows forward, and here, each morning before breakfast, Garth, Custrin and I used to disport ourselves like young seals in their tank at the Zoo. For the rest, the day passed very pleasantly with a little gossip, a little music, a little bridge. We three men, following a custom which Garth had established, took our trick at the wheel and when Custrin had finished his watch, Marjorie reported for duty and proved herself the best helmsman of us all.

As a matter of fact, I had no time to be bored. I spent many hours in the chart-house with Garth and Lawless settling the details of our contemplated expedition. There was, in truth, much to plot out and arrange. The captain was more emphatic than ever against the idea of anybody beyond us three being let into the secret of the treasure-hunt. In fact, as our discussions proceeded, he showed himself increasingly reluctant to grant us as long as a week on the island.

"It's asking too much, Sir Alexander," he said, shaking his red head, "to expect the crew to remain cooped up in the yacht in sight of green land and not a man allowed ashore. I might hold 'em in hand for a couple of days; but after that it will be difficult, very difficult, as well you and the major here must know!"

It was Garth, with his quick business mind, who made the suggestion which solved the problem. Raising his head from the chart which he had been studying while Lawless, in an aggrieved tone, was presenting his case, he said:

"I've got it. You can maroon us!"

"Maroon you?" repeated the captain in a puzzled voice.

"Aye! Dump us ashore and then take the yacht to Alcedo!"

Alcedo, he explained to us with chart and "Sailing Directions," was an islet lying some ninety miles west of Cock Island, a small, uninhabited rock, the home of seabirds of all kinds.

"You can get some shooting," Sir Alexander added, "and, if the 'Sailing Directions' speak true, good fishing. There's a fair landing on the north face, it says here, and a run ashore will do the men all the good in the world. You won't have above two or three days at the most at the rock before it will be time to put about and sail back and fetch us off!"

Lawless raised various objections, all of which did him the greatest credit. He didn't like leaving us. Suppose something happened to the *Naomi P* But Garth swept all objections aside. Then Lawless played his last trump.

"And what about Miss Garth?" he queried. "How will she like leaving you ashore on an uninhabited island? Or do you propose to take her with you?"

Garth rubbed his nose rather sheepishly.

"H'm," he mused. Then, "Okewood," he remarked, "this will be a little difficult. How about taking Marjie ashore at Cock Island with us?"

But I promptly negatived this idea.

"Out of the question," I retorted. "We're going to rough it, Sir Alexander. And it will be no life for your daughter. Why, we aren't even taking a servant!"

Garth jibbed at that. It would be bad enough leaving Marjie, he grumbled, and how he would face her he didn't know. But he must have his man with him. He must have Carstairs. In that I was inclined to support him. I had taken a fancy to Carstairs. I liked his honest, sensible face; he knew Garth and his ways; besides, he seemed a knowledgeable sort of sort of chap and I had an idea that his experience with the sappers in the war might prove uncommonly useful when we pitched our little camp. It was ultimately decided that Carstairs should accompany us.

Then Garth suggested that we should take Custrin as well.

"Capital fellow, the doctor," he remarked, "what the Americans call a good mixer. I like Custrin. And he'll be useful, you know, Okewood, in the case of snakebite or anything like that, eh?"

Now, as I have explained, I hadn't particularly cottoned to Custrin. Since that first night out he had made famous progress with Marjorie and while Garth and I were sweltering in the hold, assembling equipment and supplies for our expedition, she and the doctor had sat for hours at the piano in the saloon. I have always tried to be honest with myself and I may as well admit that I was envious of Custrin's delightfully easy manner. He was never *gauche* or sheepish with Marjorie and I knew what a boor she had set me down in her estimation.

So I demurred from the proposal of Sir Alexander. The party was big enough, I urged; to add another mouth would mean seriously increasing the amount of supplies we should have to take with us.

"But Custrin's a first-class geologist as well," pleaded the baronet, "and his knowledge should prove most valuable in our quest!"

I felt a very unpleasant suspicion dawn within me. Was it possible that Garth had told Custrin about the grave on the island and the clue that lay in my lettercase?

"Have you told Custrin about the treasure?" I asked bluntly.

Garth looked decidedly uncomfortable.

"The doctor's a most reliable fellow and highly recommended, very highly recommended to me. You can see his references if you wish, major. He is quite one of us, you know, and I did not think there was any harm... Really, I think he'd be a distinct asset. Besides, he'll be horribly disappointed now if we don't take him!"

Then, of course, I knew that Garth had told Custrin the whole story and had definitely promised him into the bargain that he should join our party. I remembered now that the two had been in the smoke-room alone together for an hour or more after lunch. I breathed a little prayer of thanksgiving that in my almost wholly Irish nature a little store, an isolated stronghold, as it were, of caution, legacy of some unknown ancestor, was included. Throughout my career in the Secret Service I have made it a practice, when disclosure is necessary, to disclose only as much as is absolutely essential to the business in hand. My brother Francis, probably the greatest secret agent our country has ever had, gave me this tip.

Accordingly, I had told Garth nothing of El Cojo, the man of mystery, of his appearance at Adams's hut or of the Vice-Consul's warning. Apart altogether from this cautious instinct of mine, I knew next to nothing of this romantic cut-throat, and until I did I had no intention of jeopardising my chances of sailing with Garth by alarming the owner of the *Naomi*. I now realised that everything I might have told Garth about El Cojo, the baronet would have inevitably passed on to the doctor.

As for Custrin, I had nothing whatever against him. But he was a stranger—and in our job, if we don't necessarily "'eave 'arf a brick" at the stranger, we are exceedingly cold to him. Custrin was a perfectly civil, unassuming Englishman; but in my career I have refused confidence to many a fellow-countryman far more patently trustworthy than he. His rather mixed upbringing would, for one thing, have prompted me to wariness and Garth's ready confidence in him really rather horrified me. I was quite determined not to have him on the island with me and I said so as frankly as possible. On that, with rather an ill-grace, Garth capitulated.

The *Naomi* carried a small camp equipment with two light and portable Armstrong huts in sections. There was a fold-up camp bedstead for Garth, while I had my battered old Wolseley valise and my flea-bag from France. In addition to our provisions, such as biscuits, tinned food of all kinds, groceries and a suitable stock of drinks including a case of soda-water, we added, as general stores, some electric torches, a couple of ship's lamps and a good supply of candles, a large picnic basket, some mosquito netting, a medicine chest, a couple of axes, and two spades and two picks which Lawless extracted from the stokehold. There were kitchen utensils for Carstairs, who, it appeared, was an excellent cook. Garth had a pair of shot-guns and a Winchester and the three of us had an automatic pistol apiece. This constituted our armoury. I thought of those "volcanic peaks" of which the "Sailing Directions" spoke and sighed for a box of gun-cotton, a tube of primers and some lengths of fuse such as we used to carry with the battery in France. But well-equipped as she was, the *Naomi* did not run to H.E.

This happened on our third day out of Rodriguez. At dinner that evening the captain announced that, if all went well, we ought to sight Cock Island about dawn two days hence.

* * *

In the chart-house that evening Custrin pleaded with me to reconsider my decision not to take him ashore with us. I told him as nicely as possible that all our arrangements were made and could not now be altered. He then asked me to let him see the message. Now I had not shown this to Garth (nor to anybody else except Bard) nor had I vouchsafed to our host any information whatever on the subject. I was still very largely in the dark as to its meaning and I was appreciative of Garth's tact in not pressing me on the subject. So I told Custrin that I was still working on the message and was not showing it to anybody just then.

"I'm sorry," he said at once, "I didn't mean to be tactless, Okewood. But I'm a pretty fair hand at languages, French or Spanish or Dutch or German and that kind of thing, you know. I thought I might be useful. Or perhaps it's in cipher?"

Custrin's affectation of nonchalance was very well done. But I have had so much of this kind of spellbinding tried on me in my time that I detected without difficulty a little note of anxiety in his voice. A very inquisitive young man, was my mental note. But aloud I said;

"Thanks for the offer, doctor. I'll bear it in mind. When I think two heads are better than one on this thing I'll let you know!"

That was straight enough, one would have thought. But he was a persistent beggar, was Custrin. I'm dashed if he didn't get Garth to tackle me. Our worthy host's rather elephantine attempts at diplomacy, however, were not difficult to counter and I had my way about keeping the message to myself without, I think, offending his *amour propre*. I should have dismissed the incident from my mind but for a strange and rather disquietening event which took place the following night.

I had gone below, preparatory to turning in, after another disastrous encounter with Marjorie. When I came off the bridge after taking my turn at the wheel, I found her standing alone at the rail. Since our little passage at arms the first night out, while she had not ostensibly avoided me, she had not given me the opportunity of another *tête-à-tête*. Her father, it appeared, had told her that she could not go ashore with us on Cock Island and she wanted me, as leader of the expedition, to intercede with him.

We were going to rough it on the island and a woman would have been impossible. And so I told her. I also thought it quite likely that the surf-bar mentioned by Adams (one always finds something of the sort round isolated islets like this) would make landing dangerous and we should be lucky, I surmised, if we escaped with nothing worse than a good soaking.

Marjorie was at first pleading, then indignant and at last angry. There was a good deal of the plethoric temperament of her father in the toss of her head with which, in disgust at my obstinacy, she turned and left me on the deck. And I, feeling the criminal every man feels when he has displeased a charming girl, slunk below to my bunk.

I had changed into pyjamas when Custrin, who had the cabin next to mine, put his head in the door.

"I'm just going up to get a 'peg,'" he said. "You look as though you could do with one yourself. Shall I bring you one down?"

A drink was emphatically what I needed in the frame of mind in which I found myself, so I gratefully accepted his offer.

"And make it a stiff one!" I called out after him. Then Carstairs, who had been working like a Trojan all the evening, packing, oiling guns and greasing boots, fetched me away to the little sort of pantry-place at the end of the flat which was his especial domain, to consult me about the clothes I was taking. When I got back to my cabin my drink in a long glass stood on the chest of drawers. There was no sign of Custrin.

Carstairs, in shirt and trousers, was simply dripping with perspiration. He looked absolutely all in. "Here" I said, "you seem to be more in need of a 'peg' than I am, Carstairs. Suppose you take hold of that glass and show what you can do with it!"

The offer was scarcely in accordance with the discipline of the *Naomi* and Carstairs glanced cautiously up and down the corridor before he seized the glass and with a whispered "Here's luck, sir!" drained it.

I don't know how long I had been asleep when I awoke with the impression that my cabin door had opened. Then I remembered, with a flash, that on going to lock it as usual before getting into my bunk I had found the key to be missing. I had searched the floor of the cabin and the corridor for it in vain. Carstairs had turned in and I was loath to disturb him after his heavy day.

There was no moon on this night and my cabin was quite dark. The *Naomi* trembled to the thump of the propeller and at the wash-basin some fitting or other rattled a merry little jig. Otherwise, all was still. I was about to turn over on my side and go to sleep again when a slight noise caught my ear. My hand flashed instantly to the electric switch and the cabin was flooded with light.

Custrin stood in the doorway. He was in his pyjamas, barefooted. His eyes were closed and one hand rested on the chest of drawers just inside the door. He was muttering to himself. As I sprang out of my bunk he turned round and, still muttering, made his own way back to his room next door.

I dashed after him. The corridor was quite dark and by the time I had found the switch in Custrin's cabin, the doctor was in his berth, to all intents and purposes sleeping peacefully.

"Trust all men; but cut the pack!" is a favourite saying of my brother Francis. With that document in my possession I had no desire to be disturbed by surprise visitors, even though they walked in their sleep. I now blamed myself for my slackness in not making Carstairs find the key of my door. I went straight off to his bunk.

Carstairs was asleep on his back, snoring merrily. I tapped on the side of the bunk and finding that this failed to awaken him, shook him by the arm. He never budged. The snoring stopped; but he slept on.

I shook him violently again. Never had I seen a man sleep like this! I put my two hands under his shoulders, raised him up and jerked him to and fro. But he remained a dead weight in my grip, sunk in deep sleep.

There was a step in the corridor outside. I put my head out. Mackay, the engineer, was there on his way to his bunk.

"Hsst!" I whispered. "Mackay, what do you make of this? I can't wake Carstairs..."

Mackay thrust his grizzled head into the cabin. He bent down over the sleeping man and sniffed audibly.

"The man's drunk!" he remarked casually.

My conscience smote me. But then I reflected. Could one "peg" have reduced the model Carstairs to this state? Unless, of course, he had already been drinking that evening. I had detected no signs of it about him...

"I wonder if I should fetch the doctor..." I began.

"Hoots!" broke in the engineer, "let the man bide. He's a gude lad but, mon, he'll have a sore heid tomorrow! I'm thinkin' Sir Alec wull gie him all the doctorin' he wants!"

"After all," said I, "I don't think we need disturb the doctor!"

Custrin's curiosity about the message, the inexplicable disappearance of my key, the drink the doctor had prepared for me which I had given to Carstairs and the servant's drunken stupor, Custrin's visit to my cabin... my mind sprang from rung to rung in this ladder of curious happenings. What had John Bard told me about El Cojo's gang?... "a tremendous organisation with an immense network of spies as widespread and efficient as the Mafia of Italy!"

My hand went instinctively to the inside pocket of my pyjamas, a pocket with a button-up flap specially designed, which has rendered me good service in sleeping-cars and cabins half round the world. I felt beneath my fingers the crackle of the oilskin in its flannel cover.

I held my secret still guarded. I congratulated myself on my firmness in refusing to let this persistent Master Custrin accompany the expedition. But we had not yet reached the island. I must be watchful, watchful...

* * *

Half an hour later, as I sat on the edge of my bunk smoking a cigarette, there came a tap at the door. Garth, looking strangely big and unwieldy in his pyjamas, stood outside.

"Come up at once!" he whispered. "Don't trouble to dress. There's no one about!"

He glided away. When I emerged on deck the eastern sky was streaked with light. Lawless was on the bridge, Garth at his side.

Silently the captain pointed to the horizon. Away on the port bow a faint grey blur rested lightly on the straight edge of the ocean like a wisp of mist on a lake at dawn.

"Cock Island!" said the skipper.

31

THE GRAVE IN THE CLEARING

"Till Monday then!" said Garth as Lawless stepped into the launch.

"Today week it is, sir!" returned the captain as Carstairs cast him the painter.

"You might fire the gun to let us know you're back," cried the baronet.

"Right-o!"

Lawless turned to bend over the engine. Then he looked round quickly and grinned.

"Good luck!" he cried, "and good hunting!" and waved a friendly hand. With that he pushed over the lever and with a mighty flurry of propeller and vast bustle among the sea-birds on the foreshore, the *Naomi's* launch throbbed her way out into the bay towards where, spanning as it seemed the harbour's narrowest part, a creamy band of white spume marked the surf-line. Silently we watched the pretty craft, her paint and brass-work flashing in the morning sun, gliding through the green water. Then Lawless raised an arm in a parting greeting, and the white launch melted into the spume and spray of the open sea.

We stood on a long sloping beach of gleaming white sand shut in on all sides save the sea by lofty grey rocks. Their jagged points out-topped the bright-green fronds of the waving palm-trees which grew almost down to the water's edge. Their column-like appearance, coupled with the singular silence of the island, gave me a sort of solemn feeling, like being in a cathedral.

Some three hundred yards from where the foam-crested rollers beat their thunderous measure on the beach, the ground rose abruptly. The sand ended and became emerged in a tangle of coarse grass. Alternating with a wild and luxuriant undergrowth of a great variety of tree ferns and other plants, it formed a kind of tasselling to a great curtain of greenery which rose, as it seemed, sheer from the sea.

The verdure was so dense that it completely hid the bases of the pointed cliffs which, clustered together like a bundle of faggots, formed the high central part of the island. From some hidden source a clear cold stream of water came plunging down from the cliff, rushing and gurgling until it lost itself in the sea.

It was the first time I had ever set foot on an uninhabited shore. It was a curious sensation. The sea-birds wheeled aloft with their harsh melancholy cries; among the trees above the beach there was sometimes the flash of a brilliantly-plumaged bird and here and there some animal rustled in the undergrowth. But otherwise a deep silence brooded over the island. There was an atmosphere of expectancy about the place which rather intrigued me.

I lost no time in setting about choosing a site for our camp. The appearance of the foreshore, exposed to the full force of the wind in unfavourable weather, did not impress me favourably, nor, owing to the danger from lightning in the thunderstorms that spring up so suddenly in these climes, did the obvious solution of erecting our huts under the shelter of the trees higher up on the shore commend itself. Moreover, I knew very little about conditions on Cock Island and, were there any wild animals about, it would be as well, I reflected, to pitch our camp in some spot not easily accessible to attack.

After exploring round a bit I came, behind a mantle of hanging creeper, upon the mouth of a cave. Set in the lofty grey rocks dominating the beach, it was well clear of high-tide level and clean and dry into the bargain. The roof sloped somewhat, but there was ample clearance for Garth's six feet when he stood erect and the cave ran back for some twenty feet into the rock.

So we plumped for the cave. Having stripped to vest and trousers, Garth and I started carrying up our stores from where the launch of the *Naomi* had deposited them on the beach. While we stacked the various boxes neatly at the back of the cave, Carstairs was busy fitting up what he called his "field-kitchen." Higher up the rocks, in a little cavity well-sheltered from the wind, he installed his Primus stove, cook-pots and other impedimenta.

It was with the utmost reluctance that I spared the time for this tiring but necessary fatigue. I was on fire to be off into the interior of the island and locate the grave. Garth, too, was as keen as mustard, and fairly jumped at my proposal that, as soon as the stores were stowed away, we should set forth on a voyage of discovery.

It was a long job; for the cases were heavy and the going was bad, but when I stood on the beach below and, with the roar of the ocean in my ears, looked up at our temporary home, I felt rather pleased. Absolutely no trace of our presence was discernible. Though I was aware that perhaps not one vessel in two years called at the island, I have always had a very healthy respect for the long arm of coincidence. I did not wish my investigations at Cock Island to become the mark of prying eyes.

It was past three o'clock and the sun very warm when Garth and I set out. We took with us a flask of cold tea apiece, some biscuits and some dates and a shot-gun each. With a wave of the hand to Carstairs, our guns slung across our backs, we plunged into the tangle of steep woods growing down to the shore.

The climate of the island seemed to be temperate enough. The air was a little steamy but mild and at first there was a pleasant breeze off the sea to cool us. To be equipped for the rocky nature of the island both of us had brought stout hob-nailed boots, and we praised our circumspection when we realised that only by boulder-climbing should we gain access to the higher parts of the island.

The climbing was arduous (for neither of us was in form) but not too difficult. I kept a sharp look-out for any traces of former visitors. Once I found some sheep droppings and again a large bleached bone which looked as if it might have come from a sheep. But of man there was no trace.

The scrub soon gave way to forest and for a good half hour we toiled up the jungle-clad slopes. Great trees formed an almost impenetrable roof over our heads through which the sunshine fell but sparsely. We went forward in a dim and mysterious twilight with no sound in our ears other than the swift rushing of the stream which gave us our direction, our laboured breathing and the rattle of our nailed boots on the boulders. It was an eerie place which somehow filled me with misgivings.

Suddenly Garth, who was leading, gave a shout. He stood on the flat top of a rock, a dozen feet above my head, and pointed excitedly in front of him. I scrambled to his side.

We were looking down into a deep circular depression shaped like a basin. It reminded me of a quarry, but I imagine it was in reality the crater of some small extinct volcano. What had brought the shout to Garth's lips was the sight of a ruined hut which thrust its broken roof from out of a tangle of gigantic ferns.

So breathless were we with our climb that we were past speech. In silence we slithered and scrambled down into the hollow, the long tendrils of the plants twisting themselves round our legs and the thorns catching in our coats.

It was a rude timber shack with a door and a window, the interior choked roof-high with growing ferns. The timber flooring had rotted away and through the mouldering planks the jungle had thrust its shoots profusely as though to claim its own. But in one corner, where a roughly-carpentered bedstead of timber stood, some attempt had apparently been made to thin out the ferns for a space. On the bed there lay a rotting blanket; on the floor close by some empty canned beef tins red with rust. The blanket practically fell to pieces at the touch. It was not marked and, though we groped pretty thoroughly among the ferns, that was all we found in the hut.

"There's nothing here," I said at last. "Let's have a look round outside. I am wondering..."

The words died away on my lips. I had reached the hut door, my face turned towards the farther edge of the crater, the opposite side from that by which we had descended. A hundred and fifty yards from where I stood a large timber cross was planted in the ground. Between it and the hut lay a great isolated boulder which had probably concealed the cross from our view when we had climbed down into the hollow.

For a moment I could hardly speak. I have seen the proud loneliness of Cecil Rhodes' resting-place in the Matoppos; I have stood (like everybody else) in the amber light that bathes Napoleon's tomb "on the banks of the Seine among this French people I have loved so well." But I have never seen a sight more impressive than that solitary grave on that desert island set down beneath the little round canopy of blue sky which seemed to be borne by the lofty frowning cliffs towering all around. Beneath that plain wooden cross, I told myself, in a silence unbroken by Man, lies the Unknown. It was a mighty impressive thought.

A rudimentary path, still to be discerned through the all-pervading undergrowth, led, round the boulder of which I have spoken, to the cross. The grave lay out in the open in a little patch which had been cleared of ferns. As we came up to it I noted, with an odd little trick of memory, that the grey and weather-beaten surface of the cross was highly polished, even as the beachcomber had described, by the action of the sand grains blown by the wind from the seashore.

Fashioned out of two baulks of timber wired together and solidly implanted in the ground, the cross stood at the head of a long hillock of earth. On the grave lay, face upwards, a small round mirror and, a little beyond it, an empty bottle, uncorked, which had fallen on its side.

"You see," I remarked to Garth, "It's just as Adams said!"

I stooped to pick up the mirror. Then to my surprise I saw that it was wired to a timber cross-piece which ran out from the cross as a support. It was a little glass set in a metal frame.

"It looks like a shaving-glass!" said Garth.

I did not undeceive him. I am not a secretive person by nature but by training. The very character of Intelligence work—the careful sifting of every apparently insignificant scrap of evidence, the lengthy process of surmise and deduction—tends to make one discreet, even when dealing with one's familiars, until a plain statement of fact can be drawn up. So I did not tell my host that, the moment I saw that the glass was attached to the cross, my brain leaped at the first clear clue to the Unknown's baffling cipher.

For the sight of the mirror, loosely wired so that it faced the foot of the grave, immediately brought into my mind the first line of that bewildering doggerel:

"Flimmer', flimmer' viel."

The reference to flashing surely indicated that the mirror was to be used as a heliograph. The next line—that about "the garrison of Kiel"—still utterly floored me; but, I reflected, since we had a heliograph, the following lines which I surmised to give a compass bearing of 27 degrees ("The Feast of Orders," *i.e.*, Jan. 27), might well furnish the direction in which—for reasons still unknown to me—the sun's rays were to be flashed. The wiring of the mirror to the timber indicated the direction in which the bearing was to be taken. It looked to me as though the Unknown must have set up his own cross and wired the mirror to it before he died.

I opened the little leathern case which hung at my belt and drew out my prismatic compass, trusty friend of my campaigning days in France. The grave faced practically due north. I laid the compass on the mirror and took a bearing of 27 degrees. The white arrow on the floating centre of the compass swung round. The mark of the 27th degree pointed towards a gaunt and barren pile of rock on the far side of the crater. I took as my line of direction a tall bush aflame with some gorgeous flower on the edge of the clearing.

Some cautious instinct made me detach the mirror. Holes had been bored on either side of the frame through which strands of copper wire were passed and knotted to holes bored in the timber cross-piece. I removed wire and all and slipped the mirror into my pocket. Garth did not notice the action; for he was busy pottering about the clearing. From the luxuriant undergrowth he ultimately collected a cigar box which, I made no doubt, was the identical one from which the man Dutchey had established the fact that Black Pablo and his friends had visited the island. It was curious to find everything in the same state as it had been left more than a year ago. I felt rather like a man must feel who violates a grave.

"There's a path beyond," Garth said, pointing over to the left. "It leads to the spring. I found an old bucket on the bank. But otherwise there's no sign of our unknown friend here. In fact the whole place looks as if it had been undisturbed since the flood. Whew! but it's hot! Okewood, I believe we're going to have a storm!"

The air was indeed strangely oppressive. The patch of sky which thatched the clearing was now flecked with daubs of white cloud and there was a curiously menacing stillness in the atmosphere. On trees and bushes the leaves hung motionless without a tremor. We sat down to cool off a bit.

"It doesn't look too good to me," I answered.

"Garth, I shouldn't wonder if we were in for a soaking tonight!"

Sir Alexander Garth, Bart., who had never slept out in the rain in his life, smiled in rather superior fashion.

"I shouldn't wonder," he returned. "As a matter of fact, I rather like roughing it. It's a devilish healthy life, my boy! What's the next move? Has the grave given you any ideas for the location of the treasure?"

I pointed at the scarlet bush.

"Do you see that plant with the red flowers?" said I. "I have a fancy to take a stroll in that direction and see how far we can get up the cliff."

Garth struck his palm with his clenched fist.

"Okewood!" he exclaimed. "By Jove! I believe you're on to something!"

"I am!" I answered rashly and cursed myself for a babbling fool. For Garth, his curiosity afire, forthwith plied me with questions.

"Don't press me just yet!" I countered. "I'm still groping in the dark. You shall know all in good time!"

But he would not be pacified. Two heads were better than one, he argued, and very often a clear-sighted, shrewd man of business could see a deal farther than an expert.

"Well," I said, "for all that, I think I'll keep my own counsel until we've looked round a bit more!"

At that Garth became huffy. We were partners in this venture, he reminded me, and we must have no secrets. He did not think he should have to recall that fact to my mind.

The stifling heat and the fatigue of our long climb had made us both a bit cross, I suppose. At any rate I was pretty short with him.

"My dear fellow," I said, and rose to my feet by way of putting an end to the conversation, "all in good time. In this sort of work one must work alone, at any rate in the initial stages. Give me a little breathing space!"

Garth followed my example and stood up.

"Shall we go on?" he asked.

He spoke without heat, but there was a look in his face which reminded me that at our first meeting, I had noticed signs of temper about his nose and mouth. Garth was a man who obviously did not like to be thwarted. Now I thought I knew where Marjorie got her proud temper from.

A little puff of hot wind came whirling into the hollow. The trees swayed to it as it rustled through the leaves with a melancholy sound.

"We don't want to go too far," remarked Garth, cocking an eye at the sky, "or we shall have this storm on us before we can get under cover at the camp."

At the first blush the cliff on the far side of the hollow looked perfectly inaccessible. But handy to my bush with the red flowers a succession of flat boulders, like a giant's staircase, enabled us to scramble up until we found ourselves on a plateau of rock dominated on one side by an immense crag which towered above our heads in a succession of shelving ledges. In front of us the ground dropped to a steep nullah from which rose a sheer wall of rock and barred the way.

It was a desolate scene. Neither tree nor shrub nor anything green grew in this barren landscape of grey and friable volcanic rock. The bare and frowning heights oppressed me. I turned to Garth.

"This looks like the end of things," said I, "unless we can find a way up by these terraces. What do you say? Shall we have a try?"

"If we could manage to reach that first shelf," my companion answered, "we could at any rate get a view. There's nothing to be seen from here."

I had to give Garth a back to do it and his sixteen stone, I felt convinced, punched a pretty pattern of his hobnails into my skin. However, at the cost of my back and sundry abrasions of his hands and knees, Garth at last gained a footing on the sheer face of the rock and then, giving me a hand, swung me up beside him. After a vertiginous climb, which at one time brought us on to a ledge a hundred feet above the nullah, we struck something like a steep track that eventually landed us on the first terrace.

The view was disappointing. We were still too low to clear the frowning cliffs encircling the nullah and we looked forth on the same gloomy prospect of grey volcanic peaks that had confronted us from below. The shelf on which we stood was only about thirty feet wide and ran for a distance of sixty yards across the face of the cliff and then stopped abruptly. It had obviously been cut by the hand of man out of the friable rock; for a number of caves scooped out of the back wall showed that cave-dwellers must have lived here in that remote period when the island had been inhabited. The ledge was in fact nothing but a street for communication between the different cave-houses. The caves were low-roofed and empty. By craning our necks upward we saw that the whole face of the cliff was thus honeycombed with cave-dwellings in a succession of terraces. At the far end the steep track, by which we had gained access to the first terrace, wound its way upward to the higher levels. There were three terraces in all.

We rested for a while on our rocky shelf and ate some biscuits and chocolate. From our post of vantage we looked down on to the grave in the clearing. The sun had gone in but it was still oppressively sultry. The sky had assumed a forbidding leaden tinge. It looked like some great furnace door radiating a fierce heat from the fire within.

Whilst we ate our frugal lunch we discussed our plans. We decided that, in view of the weather, we would break off our exploration for the day, return to camp and get comfortably installed and make an early start the next morning in order to visit the upper ledges of the rock. Garth had apparently quite recovered his equanimity after our little breeze.

The descent from the rock was a thrilling business. In places the track had crumbled away and more than once we found ourselves, held only by the nails of our boots, on a slippery slope overhanging a sheer deep drop. I have a poor head for heights and to me it was a nightmare experience. The result was that our progress was slow and it took us a full hour to make the descent. By the time we had reached the rocky plateau the wind was whirling the grey volcanic dust in great pillars about our heads. The sky had grown perceptibly darker with an eerie yellow glow and a few big drops of rain splashed down on the bushes. With startling suddenness a long drawn-out rumble of thunder awakened a thousand echoes as it reverberated among the lonely island peaks.

"By George," said Garth turning up his coat collar, "we're going to catch it, Okewood. We'll have to steer clear of these trees."

"We'd better make a bolt for the hollow," I counselled. "The hut is out in the open. If it stands the wind it will give us some shelter!"

We started to run while the light perceptibly diminished, like a lighting effect on the stage. We were actually crossing the hollow when the storm broke. There was a blinding glare of lightning, a deafening peal of thunder and the light went out while, with a whooshing and rushing and crashing, the rain suddenly descended in what seemed to be a dense sheet of water.

"The hut!" I shouted in Garth's ear.

Well it was that we were just upon it or in that inky darkness we should never have found it. Over the wooden bedstead in the corner the roof was whole and solid and it kept the worst part of the rain off us, though we were splashed by the cataract of water which poured off the roof into the centre of the hut. The air was so highly charged that one could almost smell the electricity in the atmosphere as the lightning rent the sky in blinding flashes which illuminated the whole clearing and the trees and cliffs all round with the brightness of daylight.

The storm was at its height; the thunder was echoing in and out of the rocky hollows of the island and in the moments of stillness the gurgling and splashing of the rain filled our ears. Then came a blinding lightning flash, brighter and more enduring than the rest. It lit up the whole clearing and revealed the cross over the grave of the Unknown standing out hard and black against a fantastic background of bending, straining tree-trunks with branches and leaves blown out in the wind. And by its light, before the brightness died, I saw the figure of a man standing with bowed head at the grave.

32

A VOICE IN THE FOREST

I saw only him for the fraction of a second, a young man, tall and slim and very blond, in a shirt open at the neck and riding-breeches, his head bared to the storm. The water streamed off his face and clothing; but he stood perfectly still in an attitude of reverence. In that wild setting of tempest-swept rocks the apparition seemed like some spectre of the Brocken. Or one might have thought that the storm had summoned forth the Unknown himself from his grave.

The vision fairly staggered me; for my mind was imbued with the idea that the island was uninhabited. But my brain keyed up by the events of the day, did not dwell for an instant on any supernatural explanation of the apparition. I promptly asked myself whether, after all, there were people living on the island or whether the man I had seen had, like ourselves, landed from some passing ship.

But then, without warning, there came an ear-shattering metallic crash, as though a big shell had exploded beside us, the earth shook and a perfect tornado of wind and water descended upon the clearing, clawing and tearing at the hut until it seemed as though the beams of the flimsy structure to which we desperately clung would be wrenched from our grasp. The inky-black sky appeared to split across in a jagged band of light which again showed up the clearing as bright as day. But now the tall wooden cross stood aloft in solitary majesty once more. The figure at the graveside had vanished and the clearing was entirely deserted. I asked myself whether the apparition had not, after all, been the figment of my imagination. Garth had seemingly remarked nothing so I resolved to say nothing about it unless he should ask me.

But now, amid the grumbling and rumbling of the thunder receding into the distance, the storm was passing. The air reeked with the stench of sulphur and I guessed that the appalling crash we had heard had marked the fall of a thunderbolt. Slowly the light was coming back and, though the rain yet descended in torrents, the downpour was much less heavy.

We were in a sorry plight, the pair of us. Our thin garments clung to us like wet swimming suits and our teeth chattered in our heads.

"We appear to have timed things very badly," grumbled Garth, wringing the water out of a corner of his tussore jacket. "We had plenty of warning of this storm. I should have thought we might have managed to have got back to the camp in time to escape it..."

I wiped the water out of my eyes and grinned.

"Oh," I said lightly, "a ducking won't hurt us! Look, the rain's stopping already..."

"I am not complaining about getting wet," observed Garth with an air of dignity which went ill with his bedraggled appearance—he was squatting on his hunkers squeezing out his hat—"I can, I believe, put up with the hardships of an expedition like this as well as any man. But I do think the—er, staff work this afternoon leaves something to be desired. To be wet to the skin an hour's tramp from camp may amuse you, Major Okewood, but the prospect of a heavy chill does not strike *me* as being funny in the least!"

In high dudgeon he placed upon his head the shapeless mass of soggy felt which had once been a hat.

"I vote we make a move for the camp," he proposed. "That is, if anything is left of it. I should not be in the least surprised to find the cave under water, our stores ruined and Carstairs drowned—or struck by lightning, as like as not. I don't wish to seem inquisitive, Major Okewood, but might I inquire what progress this afternoon's unfortunate jaunt has brought to your investigations?"

I was rather nettled by the line he was taking, and the way he manhandled my name irritated me.

"You needn't worry," I retorted curtly. "I'm perfectly satisfied so far!"

"Indeed," replied the baronet—he was struggling to free himself from a giant creeper which had firmly fixed itself about his sodden clothes. "I am sorry I cannot share your optimism. But then I'm wholly in the dark—maybe, it's just as well—about this infernal wildgoose chase. Damn it," he cried suddenly, "can't you lend me a hand to get this blasted root off my legs?"

I hastened to release him, fuming and fretful.

"We shall be home in no time," I said soothingly to humour him, for he was like a spoilt child, "and you'll see what marvels Carstairs has accomplished in the way of making us comfortable. And you needn't worry about the cave. It's splendidly sheltered. Not a drop of water will get in!"

Night was falling by the time we emerged from the steamy atmosphere of the sopping woods and made for the faint glow of light which shone from our cave. Carstairs met us at the entrance. He had fully justified my prophecy to Garth.

Our beds were made up, one on either side of the cave, and our washing and shaving kit laid out on toilet tables improvised out of boxes neatly covered with clean white paper. Hot water steamed in our wash-basins and a dry change of clothing was laid out on the beds. In the centre of the cave, on packing-cases covered by a white damask cloth, the table was set for dinner. A hurricane lamp, placed in the centre, was flanked by enamel cups from the picnic basket filled with bright flowers and on the ground a bottle of Garth's excellent champagne was cooling in a bucket of spring-water.

We lost no time in changing, and within a quarter of an hour were sitting down to what was, in the circumstances, an extraordinarily well-cooked meal. Garth's ill-temper melted perceptibly and it was with the utmost cordiality that he raised his glass and pledged the success of the expedition. The ingenuity of the incomparable Carstairs had so completely reproduced the atmosphere of civilisation that it was difficult to believe we three were dining on a lonely islet in the middle of the Pacific.

After dinner Garth yawned expansively and opined that he would turn in. The unwonted exercise of the afternoon, he declared, had fagged him out. But I had no mind for bed. My brain, stimulated by the unaccustomed environment, was active. The apparition at the graveside during the storm had profoundly disquieted me and I wanted to think. So I strolled outside for a solitary pipe beneath the stars.

On the shore I found Carstairs, pipe in mouth, contemplating the sea. I love the old-time Regular, such as Carstairs, with his twelve years' service in the Sappers, was; his loyalty, his quiet efficiency, his eminent common sense. And as between two professional soldiers a bond of silent sympathy had established itself between Carstairs and me. We had not even discussed the incident of the drink I had given him that night on board the yacht. Having ascertained that Carstairs was practically a total abstainer, I gave Mackay a hint to forget all about his nocturnal diagnosis. I had my own theory about that drink and perhaps Carstairs had his; anyway, we did not discuss it.

"Grand night, sir!" said Carstairs, taking his pipe out of his mouth as I approached over the sand.

"Wonderful!" I commented. "Good spot this, Carstairs!"

The man did not reply. He was sucking on his pipe which did not seem to be drawing well.

"It's a uncanny kind o' place, as you might say, sir!" he remarked presently.

"Well," I observed, "it's a bit lonesome, I suppose. But all desert islands are that!"

"Lonesome?" retorted the man. "I wouldn't have nothing to say agin it if it were lonesome. I'm partial to the moors and such-like places meself. I never was a one for the towns, sir. But I don't like all these tall rocks and all these quiet trees at the back of one. They give me the fair 'ump!"

I laughed.

"You want the desert, Carstairs," I said. "Nothing but sand and then some. No trees looking at you there!"

"It ain't altogether the trees an' the cliffs!"

The man paused and scratched his head with the stem of his pipe.

"There's something sort o' creepy about this place, sir!"

"How do you mean?"

"Well," he said slowly, "it's a funny thing, but all the blessed evening I've had a kind o' feeling as if I was being watched. You know how it was in the war, sir—w'en you was workin' out in No Man's Land on a pitch-black night, scared to death you was walkin' into Fritz's line, tellin' yerself all through 'If you can't see him, he can't see you' but feelin'—well, as though there was nothin' but eyes starin' at you all around!"

He shook himself.

"It fair gives me the creeps!" he finished.

Now Carstairs was a plain honest-to-God Englishman from the New Forest, the very incarnation of the soldier from the English shires whose sheer lack of imagination and consequent inability to accept defeat in any circumstances clear broke the German spirit in the war. There was no associating that good-humoured face, that big mouth and button nose, with the idle fears of a overheated imagination. There are some people — I am one — who, even though they see nothing, have the faculty of detecting the presence of human beings in their vicinity. I recalled the eerie sensation I myself had had on landing but, of course, above all I thought of that bowed figure which the lightning had shown me standing by the grave in the clearing.

I was filled with the deepest foreboding. If there were people on the island, surely they must have remarked the arrival of the *Naomi*. Would they not have announced themselves to us? What object could they have, supposing Carstairs was not mistaken, in slinking round the camp?

Well, it was no part of my plans as yet to communicate my fears to Carstairs. So I rallied him gently.

But Carstairs stuck to his guns.

"It come over me so strong w'en you and the guv'nor was away this evening," Carstairs said, "that no less than four times I left my cook-pots to have a look round..."

"Well, and did you see anybody?"

"Not a blessed soul!"

"Did you hear anything?"

"No, sir!"

Yet the man was not to be shaken.

"W'en I was servin' dinner jes' now," he persisted, "I was as sure as sure there was a chap watchin' me from just about there" — he turned and indicated the black shape of a palm on the fringe of the shore — "not doin' anything but jes' settin' there, spyin'!"

The man knocked out his pipe.

"I'm to call you gentlemen at four, sir. If you didn't mind, I think I'll get down to it!"

THE RETURN OF CLUBFOOT

This little bit of trench slang (which, being interpreted means to retire for the night), uttered in our romantic surroundings, amused me not a little.

"Goodnight, Carstairs!"

"Goodnight, sir!"

He plodded up the beach, his feet making no sound on the soft sand, a white, ghostly figure against the dark foliage. Then he was swallowed up in the mystery and silence of the night.

There was no moon, but in compensation such a prodigious display of stars as only the tropics can show, blazing and twinkling in their myriads till one could almost believe the heavens were in motion. On the open shore there was yet a kind of half-light but beyond, where the woods began, the blackness of the night was Stygian.

Carstairs was right. This island was an eerie place. The absolute stillness of the night, marred only by the mournful rhythm of the waves, seemed to accentuate that air of expectancy about it which I had already remarked. I found myself thinking of the island as of a stage set for the performance of some play.

Here, perhaps, I reflected, the Unknown, destined for that nameless grave I had come to seek, had landed, carried ashore, maybe, by his native crew. I tried to picture him, with death in his face, painfully scrawling the message which had so strangely come into my hands. What manner of man was this Unknown? A German officer, a naval officer probably (as the reference to Kiel seemed to indicate). And for whom did he write? For Germans, for a German. Yet there were no Germans, as far as I knew, in the gang that had taken two men's lives to get the message now reposing in my pocket. Black Pablo, Neque, El Cojo... these were Spanish names.

El Cojo? "He who goes with a limp." *Der Stelze*, Clubfoot, had been the nickname of that other cripple, the man of might in that Imperial Germany which sank to destruction in the fire and smoke of the Hindenburg Line, whose ways lay in dark places, whom everybody feared but whom so few had ever seen... If he could rise from his grave and seek me out on the island, then, indeed, might my imagination, like poor old Carstairs', people these darkling woods with hidden spies!

Sunk in my thoughts I had wandered on heedlessly, going ever deeper into the tangle of the forest. But now the undergrowth, growing thicker, barred my further progress and I came to an abrupt halt with the thick tendril of some creeping plant wound about my body. On it blossomed a gaudy flower with a heavy, musky scent. The touch of the creeper on my bare arm made me shrink.

It was as dark as pitch in that jungle-like forest. A phrase I had read somewhere about "opaque blackness" flashed into my mind. I realised I stood an extremely good chance of being lost, and cursed myself for a dreamy fool. Fortunately, I had the orientation of our camp—I had taken it that afternoon on the beach—and I knew that, by striking west, I should roughly hit Horseshoe Harbour where we had put ashore.

I took out my compass and opening the lid bent over the luminous needle. I stood absolutely still to allow the pointer to swing to rest. Then, from the black depths of the forest all about me, a gentle droning fell upon my ear.

I listened. No mistake was possible. It was undoubtedly a human voice. And it was softly humming, as a man might hum quietly to himself, to pass away the time. I listened again. The voice rose and fell, with now and then a break, but always on a muted note. Suddenly, I caught the melody, a melancholy, haunting refrain with a phrase, as in a folk-song, that came again and again. And I felt the perspiration break out on my brow, my heart grow cold within me, as I recognised the air...

> "*Se murio, y sobre su cara*
> "*Un panuelito le heche...*"

It was the song of Black Pablo, the singer in the lane.

33

I MEET AN OLD ACQUAINTANCE

I remained rooted to the spot. The droning chant went on. How far the singer was from me, it was impossible to estimate; for a voice carries far at night—he might be anything from twenty to a hundred yards away. There was nothing to do but retire... in that clammy, steamy darkness any idea of stalking a man was out of the question.

All the events of the past week came tumbling into my brain. They had tracked me down, then, and now I was at grips with El Cojo's famous organisation... But this was no time for speculation or surmise. I could think matters out afterwards; for the moment I must keep my mind clear and concentrate on getting out of this dense jungle quietly and quickly.

Now the humming had ceased. Did it mean that the singer was moving forward? I strained my ears but could catch no sound other than the rustle of the leaves as they dripped moisture. To move in silence through the clinging undergrowth was, I knew, a thing impossible. An old memory of capercailzie shooting in Russia came to my aid. One stalked the male bird perched on a tree-top as he uttered his love-call to the females at the foot. When he called one moved; when he stopped, one halted.

The droning recommenced. Did my ears mislead me? It certainly sounded nearer now. My compass lying flat in my left palm, I moved swiftly forward, heading for the west. When the humming ceased, I stood still and pushed on again as soon as it was resumed.

A horrid thought assailed me. Was the singer the spy whose unseen presence had impressed itself on Carstairs that evening? Or were there others? Had the cordon let me through only to draw in upon me as I returned? I had no weapon; for I had given Carstairs my revolver to clean and oil on our return from camp that evening after our wetting.

The crooning chant had grown much fainter. I must be drawing away from it. I paused an instant to wipe away the sweat which was pouring into my eyes. Then came a sudden crash in the undergrowth close to hand. I steeled myself to the encounter, getting my back to the tree and striving—but how vainly?—to pierce with my eyes that bewildering pall of darkness. Another heavy crash, a frightened squawk, and I breathed again. It was only one of the island pigs whose nocturnal rambles I had disturbed.

And now for full five minutes I had heard the singer no more. The forest was getting lighter, and like blissful music there came to my ears the distant surge of the sea. Presently, without further incident, I stepped out on the beach not more than twenty paces from our cave.

A black shape rose out of the darkness at my feet. It was Carstairs. I put my hand over his mouth and drew him into the cave. The place re-echoed with Garth's rhythmic snoring.

"You were quite right, Carstairs," I whispered. "There is someone in the woods back there! Have you heard or seen anything?"

"No, sir!" the man returned. "But I was that certain sure there was somebody round the place that I nipped in and got a pistol to sit up and wait for you..."

He showed me the automatic in his hand.

"I don't like the look of things at all, Carstairs," said I, "and that's a fact. I'm not getting the wind up over a lot of shadows; but I don't propose to risk having the camp rushed. You've got some bread-bags and the like, haven't you? Well, get one of the shovels and start filling 'em with sand, will you? If we can run up a bit of cover round the entrance to the cave, one man ought to be able to hold it against all-comers. Meanwhile, I'll wake Sir Alexander here!..."

It is a little embarrassing to rouse a man up out of his beauty sleep and tell him you have been keeping essential facts from his knowledge. However, I could at least honestly claim that, until that moment, I had nothing stronger than suspicions to go upon.

Propped up on his elbow, Garth heard my whole tale just as I have set it down here, from the moment that John Bard identified Black Pablo with the man who had kept watch outside Adams' hut down to the strange happenings in the woods that night.

"Just what we are up against, Sir Alexander," I concluded, "I don't know. But we're here for a specific purpose and I feel sure you will agree with me that we should not allow a band of filthy cutthroats to deter us from it!"

"Certainly not, my boy, certainly not!" declared the baronet. "As a matter of fact, I cannot really believe that these fellows really intend us any harm. After all, we're British subjects and a little of Britain goes the deuce of a long way in these parts..."

"Very possibly, sir," I replied, "but you must remember we do not know how strong this party is. Force is the ultimate sanction of the law, they say; but on this particular island British prestige is backed up by exactly three very imperfectly armed Britishers..."

"If you'll allow me to say so," Garth broke in pompously, "you go rather fast. From the accident that you overheard on an island which we previously believed to be uninhabited a song you heard sung (in peculiar circumstances, I grant you) at Rodriguez, you appear to assume that the men who murdered Adams have landed on this island. Your song may be a popular favourite in Rodriguez; everybody may be singing it. Have you thought of that?

"If this figure you saw at the grave and this man whom you heard humming in the forest belong to this mysterious gang led by El What's-his-name, then they must have followed us here. But how did they come? We have seen no steamer. If, on the other hand, the song incident is capable of some simple explanation such as I have suggested, your last valid link of evidence connecting these mysterious visitors of Cock Island with El Thingumybob's gang snaps."

This was very ingenious. But it didn't convince me. The intonation of the singer in the forest was identical with that of the man in the lane. Of that I was sure. Besides, in the back of my mind lurked a half-formed suspicion about Custrin which I had not as yet thought proper to communicate to the worthy cotton-spinner. And, as for having seen no steamer, I recollected that launch which had put out from Rodriguez after us.

"I'll tell you something else," Garth resumed, "that perhaps you don't know, major. Many of these Pacific islands do contain treasure; not doubloons but something almost equally valuable: phosphates. Adventurers are always roaming about the Pacific prospecting for guano deposits and mighty shy they are, many of 'em, of casual visitors. Now you mark my words, these chaps who have been behaving so oddly are in all probability just a band of shysters from Rodriguez—without any concession, of course—dropped here by a ship to look for phosphates. They think we've come to jump their claim..."

I felt very perplexed. Garth was a hard-headed Lancashire businessman and there seemed to be a good deal of horse sense in what he said. And yet somehow...

I walked to the entrance of the cave and looked out. In awe-inspiring majesty the sun came rolling up from the east and the glistening beach was dyed in the hues of the morning. A few paces away Carstairs was shovelling sand for dear life. Already he had filled a dozen stout cotton bags.

"You may be right, Sir Alexander," I said at length. "I hope you are. But even if these gentry are concession-hunters we have to bear in mind that they are a cut-throat lot. They are quite capable of shooting first and of asking your name afterwards. I'm going to run up a little sand-bag parapet at the mouth of this cave. It commands a fine field of fire and will allow you or Carstairs to challenge anybody who comes within thirty yards. As soon as we've put the place in a proper state of defence I'm going out to do a little reconnoitring on my own..."

"My dear fellow," remarked Garth, sitting up in bed and nursing his toes, "to hear you talk you'd think the blessed old British Empire had ceased to count in the world. Foreigners can't go about murdering British subjects, you know. They'd have the Foreign Office on them damned quick, send a cruiser and all that sort of thing. However," he finished indulgently, "I'm quite prepared to hold the fort while you have a look round. I'm not sorry to have a lazy morning for, to tell you the truth, I'm so stiff from our climb yesterday that I can scarcely move!"

Rather with the air of Daddy helping his little boy to build sand-castles, Garth assisted me to erect a parapet at the mouth of the cave. There were not many sand-bags, but we helped out with some cases of tinned provisions, putting the sand-bags on top and then a layer of sand scooped out from the foot of our fortification. The screen of creeper across the entrance to the cave, while it obscured the view from outside, was not so dense as to prevent anybody within from commanding the approach to our stronghold.

Carstairs brought coffee and sandwiches and at my request filled my flask with brandy and brought me my automatic pistol and a couple of charges of ammunition. Then, turning my back on the sea, I once more struck out into the woods.

My plan was to make for the grave in the clearing. This should be the test. If our mysterious visitors were after the treasure I made sure I would come upon them in the vicinity of the grave. For, as far as I knew, the grave was the only indication they had to guide them in their hunt. It was still very early, and if I could gain the clearing unobserved, I would post myself at some convenient point, perhaps on the high ground beyond the grave, and await events.

I went forward very cautiously, my pistol cocked in my hand. I stopped repeatedly and listened; but, save for the hubbub of the birds in the trees, all was still around me. The burbling stream that fell from the high ground of the island to the beach gave me my direction.

I had reached a narrow ravine at the end of which was that flat rock whence, on the previous evening, Garth had described the ruined hut. On a slab which formed a convenient step to mount the boulder something white caught my eye as I came down the nullah. To my unbounded surprise it proved to be one of those cheap cigar-holders made of cardboard which so many Germans use.

I stooped to examine it. The holder with its quill mouthpiece, was quite clean and obviously brand-new. Therefore, it was no relic of the former visitors to the island. *And it had not been there yesterday.* I had mounted by this very slab to stand by Garth on the flat rock and if the holder had been there, I could not possibly have failed to see it.

It looked as though it might have dropped out of a man's pocket as he was scrambling up the rock. The name of a popular firm of cigar-merchants, with branches all over Germany, was printed on it. "Loeser und Wolff, Berlin. S.W.

Friedrich-Strasse," I read. I knew the shop well. I had bought cigars there scores of times in the past...

A sudden feeling of uneasiness, an acute sense of danger, came over me. To be shadowed is an almost everyday experience on our job and one develops a kind of sixth sense in detecting it. I had the distinct impression that somebody was watching me.

My brain worked swiftly. I was in the open, without cover, liable to be shot down with impunity from the edge of the ravine. To keep perfectly calm, to show no signs of fluster and, above all things, to spot your man without his knowing that he has been seen, is the only safe course in moments like this. My grip tightened on my pistol as, very slowly, I began to raise my head...

The top of the rock above me was level with my eyes. As I lifted them my gaze fell upon a monstrous mis-shapen boot, projecting awkwardly over the edge. For the moment, I had no eyes for the huge figure that stood there resting on the rubber-shod stick. I could only stare, like one transfigured, at that sinister club-foot, as a voice, a well-remembered voice that for months had haunted me in dreams, cried out sharply:

"Stay as you are and raise your hands! Quick! And drop that gun!"

I glanced up and as I lifted my arms, my pistol rattled noisily on the slab below.

Over the barrel of a great automatic clasped in a huge hairy hand, the Man With the Clubfoot was looking at me.

34

EL COJO

Well, I was up against it now. In vain my memory protested against the credibility of the evidence which my eyes could not repudiate. Grundt was dead these four years; had I not seen him, dimly, through the blue haze of smoke from my brother's automatic, sink back lifeless on the carpet in the billiard-room of that frontier Schloss? Had I not even read his obituary in the German newspapers?

Yet here he stood before me again, the man as I had known him in the past, ruthless-looking, formidable, sinister in his clumsy, ill-fitting suit of black. Again I noted the immense bulk which, with the overlong sinewy arms, the bushy eyebrows and the black-tufted cheek-bones, irresistibly suggested some fierce and gigantic man-ape. Beneath the right eye a red and angry scar, a deep indentation in the cheek-bone, solved at a glance the mystery which had almost paralysed my brain. My brother's aim had failed. That hideous cicatrice, accentuating the leer of the bold menacing eyes and of the cruel mouth, told me beyond all possibility of doubt, that, out of the dim, dark past, Clubfoot had again arisen to confront me.

A sort of cold despair settled down upon me. That Clubfoot would, in his good time, shoot and shoot to kill I made no doubt; for we had been mortal enemies and quarter did not ever come into Grundt's reckoning. All kinds of odd scenes from my crowded life swarmed into my mind; dear old Francis serving in the tennis-court at Prince's; a juggler on the Maidan at Calcutta, when I was a subaltern in India; Doña Luisa, standing in Bard's garden and rolling her white eyeballs at me...

Then Clubfoot laughed, a dry mirthless chuckle. The sound was forbidding enough but it braced me like a tonic. I had beaten this man before; I would beat him again. I dropped my eyes, seeking to locate my pistol.

"Five paces back, if you please, Herr Major," rang out a commanding voice from the rock. "And, to save misunderstanding, let me say that it would add to the decorum of the proceedings if you renounced any attempt to find your weapon..." He spoke in German in accents of deadly suavity. "On the occasion of our last meeting you—or was it your brother?—showed that your hand is the prompt servant of your brain, an invaluable asset (let me add in parenthesis) to the big-game hunter, but disconcerting in civilised society..."

What a commanding presence this man had! Again I was conscious of it as, before his slow and searching gaze, I fell back as ordered. He seemed to fill that narrow glen. This effect was not produced by his bulk (which was considerable) but by his amazing animal vitality, the mental and physical vigour of some great beast of prey.

Keeping me covered with his pistol, he lowered himself to a sitting position on the rock and with surprising agility in one crippled as he was, dropped heavily on to the slab. In a lightning motion he stooped and whipped up my automatic which, with a whirling motion of the left hand, he sent flying away into the bush.

"Now, Okewood," he remarked, "you can sit down! But be good enough to keep your hands above your head!"

He gave me the lead by seating himself on the rocky slab. I followed his example and dropped on to the ground.

"Would you mind," I asked, "if I clasped my hands behind my head? Otherwise, the position is fatiguing..."

"Not in the least," retorted Clubfoot, baring his teeth with a gleam of gold, "as long as you remember that I shoot quickly—and straight!"

He measured the distance between us with his eye and then, as though in deliberate challenge, laid his pistol down on the rock beside him. He produced a cigar case from his pocket.

"I seem to recollect that you are a cigar-smoker!" he began.

"Thanks," I retorted, remembering the holder I had picked up, "I don't smoke German cigars!"

Clubfoot chuckled amiably.

"Nor do I! he rejoined. "I believe you will find these as good as any that ever came out of Havana. Not long ago I was a highly respected member of the Club there!"

And he tossed his case across to me, after selecting a cigar for himself. I let it lie. I was not taking favours from this man.

Grundt raised his eyebrows and shrugged his shoulders. But he made no comment on my ungraciousness.

"Herr Major!" he said as he bit off the end of his cigar, "I must once more congratulate you on the supreme excellence of your country's Secret Service! The intelligence system which located this remote island as the hiding-place, real or imaginary, of treasure, is remarkable! The resource you displayed in acquiring the document which now rests in the letter-case in your pocket does credit both to the service and yourself. My congratulations!"

Here he paused to light his cigar from a pocket-lighter and with lips pursed up, noisily exhaled a long puff of smoke, cocking his head to watch the smoke drift aloft. It was nonchalantly done. But I knew that in reality he was watching me.

I felt puzzled. Obviously, he was feeling his way; *ergo*, he was not sure of his ground. And he had no inkling, apparently, of the aimless way in which I had stumbled upon this amazing adventure. He seemed to believe that I was *en service commandé*. Well, I could put up a bit of bluff on that...

"You will at least do us the justice," he resumed, "of not withholding your admiration of the way in which, as the result of careful planning, this pleasant reunion of today was achieved. The luck was on your side that night at Rodriguez, Herr Major; if my orders had been carried out, we should have spared ourselves—and you—this cruise in the Pacific..."

"You mean," I retorted, "that, if your spy had done his work properly, he would have cut my throat as well as that other poor fellow's and the woman's..."

"I can honestly say," observed Clubfoot, blinking his eyes benignly at me, "that I should have sincerely deplored such an eventuality..."—he paused and smiled expansively—"at hands other than my own..."

My brain was working rapidly. Grundt was apparently alone. But, knowing the man, I guessed he had help in the vicinity to summon at need. Therefore, even if I could get past that gun of his, a frontal attack was out of the question. I wondered whether, if my return to camp were over-long delayed, Garth or Carstairs would come out in search of me. At best we were only three. Against how many? So far I only knew of two, the stranger at the graveside and Black Pablo. But to have brought a ship here from Rodriguez argued a crew. In any case we were hopelessly outnumbered...

Curiously enough, Clubfoot himself answered my unspoken question.

"Now, Okewood," he said leaning forward and looking sharply at me, "I don't have to tell a man of your intuition and... and imagination that the game is up. I shall be quite frank with you, *jawohl*. We are fourteen against you and your two companions. I am well acquainted with your movements, you see. And, to remove any misapprehension from your mind, let me say at once that I am not the only German in your company. You are not dealing exclusively with men of the calibre of Black Pablo whose minds are a confusion of murder and the soft allurements of love. You will be wise to capitulate gracefully and hand over that message which, incidentally, was never meant for you. And perhaps, since two heads are better than one—and, I have, as you know, the highest opinion of your "intelligence—I might consider allowing you to help in working out the clue..."

Again that note of doubt! Then I realised that I was, after all, the only man, barring Dutchey who was dead, who had spoken to Adams. Apparently Clubfoot believed that I might have information as to the hiding-place of the treasure additional to the indications in the message. Now I began to understand the meaning of his honeyed words, his deadly suavity. And I guessed that he could not *afford* to kill me—at least, not yet.

"Grundt," said I, speaking with all the decision I could command, "if you think I'm going to work in with you, you're making a big mistake. On the contrary, I'm going to show you what it means for a German, after the Armistice, to lay hands on an Allied subject. Your knowledge of our Intelligence Service will tell you that it does not leave its agents unprotected..."

I broke off significantly and looked at him. Mine were brave words enough, though, the Lord knows, my heart was in my boots. But bluff, I have often noticed, has a heartening effect upon the bluffer; and I was summoning all my strength to face whatever dark fate was in store for me. For I realised that, whether Grundt and his merry men found the treasure or not, either way my chances at long last of leaving the island alive were of the smallest.

Very coolly Clubfoot flicked the ash off his cigar.

"Quite, quite!" he observed carelessly. "But for the time being, my friend, let us not forget that you have to forgo that protection. An *Engländer* in the hand is worth two light cruisers in the Pacific. You take me?"

With his cigar thrust out at a defiant angle from his mouth, he planked his hairy hands palms downwards on his knees.

"I'll put the situation quite plainly before you!" he said. "You're in grave danger, Okewood. I've a rough lot of shipmates and they've got the treasure fever in their blood. My German companions have no liking for their dear English cousins. We have some survivors of von Spee's squadron; they are absurdly prejudiced against you and your race. The brother of the gentleman who wrote that message in your pocket is with me. He was an officer of the *Gneisenau* sunk by your Admiral Sturdee at the Falkland Islands..."

There came into my mind the picture of that blond youth as I had seen him in the storm standing with bowed head at the grave.

"...We have the bo'sun of the *Nürnberg*, her sister vessel, and a couple of *Blaujacken* of the *Dresden* who swam ashore after your Navy destroyed their ship off Juan Fernandez, besides various army veterans from France. And, my dear Okewood, I need scarcely tell you that, after the Somme and the Hindenburg Line, our brave 'eighty-fivers' dislike you British even as much as our sailormen do..."

A little tremor ran through me. My hands were shaking with excitement behind my head.

I shrugged my shoulders.

"You must let me take my hands down, Herr Doktor," I said.

He glanced sharply at me, then picked up his pistol.

"Why?" he demanded fiercely.

"To get out my letter-case!"

Clubfoot nodded sagely.

"*So, so!*" he murmured, and his fleshy lips bared his yellow teeth in a cunning smile. "You have taken my advice. *Gut, gut!*"

But then he flashed at me a look full of suspicion and menace.

"No tricks!" he warned in a harsh voice of command. "*Himmelkreuzsakrament nochmal!* If you play me false, you dog, I'll blow your brains all over the ravine! Now, bring your hands slowly down and remember, one suspicious gesture will cost you your life!"

"Calm yourself, Herr Doktor!" I rejoined. "I know when I am beaten!"

And I made to pitch the letter-case on to the slab at his side.

Ah, but he was the cautious one, was old Clubfoot... cautious with that deadly thoroughness of the Germans that gave a fellow who fell into their hands in the war such a very slender chance. He was taking no risks. With an imperious gesture he stopped me and made me take out the message from the case myself.

"Now throw it on the ground in front of you and turn about!"

I dropped the little flannel-encased package at his feet and swung round. I heard the cripple grunt with excitement as he stooped; I could picture to myself the eagerness with which he snatched up the message. A moment's silence—then he bade me face him again.

"I think you acted wisely," he said with his slow smile. "Bah! You hadn't a dog's chance. See...!"

He blew three short blasts on a silver whistle he drew from his waistcoat pocket. Immediately a little cloud of men broke out from the cover of the trees at his back.

There were, perhaps, half-a-dozen of them. They were a villainous-looking lot with the exception of a fresh-faced, clean-cut young man whose pink-and-white complexion and fair hair were in striking contrast with the swarthy features and stubbly chins of his companions. I knew him again for the man at the graveside. Another I particularly noticed was a squat, obese fellow with a patch over one eye, the other dull and malevolent. On his yellow jaundiced face a mass of blue-black stubble extended from the cheek-bones down to the loose folds of his double chin, while a twisted and flattened nose, which looked as though a heavy hand had tweaked it, lent a crowning touch of distortion to a face which was, I think, the vilest I have ever seen. From Adams's description I recognised Black Pablo.

Grundt halted them with an imperious gesture.

"Herr Major," he remarked sleekly, "I need not detain you further. A word of advice to you, however, the counsel of a friend. Now that you will have the leisure to devote yourself to that Government survey work on which, of course, you came to Cock Island, I would suggest that you confine your activities to the shores of... let me see, what was the name?... ah yes, of Horseshoe Bay. The interior of this delightful island, so they tell me, is most unhealthy and I should be desolated were any accident to befall you."

He paused and meditatively fingered his heavy chin.

"*Noch eins!* If you should be tempted by some slight feeling of irritation at anything I have said or done to contemplate reprisals or anything calculated to interfere with the... er, research work of myself and my companions, let me warn you that I have the means of very quickly bringing you..."—he stopped and added significantly—"*and* your friend to your senses! *Kinder!*"

His voice rang triumphantly as he turned to his companions. "*Ich hab's!*"

With a whoop of excitement the ragged band gathered about him. They had forgotten all about me, seemingly. I had a last glimpse of Grundt, leaning heavily on his stick, holding aloft in one great hairy paw the little square of oilsilk.

Dejectedly I slunk away.

35

"DIE FÜNF-UND-ACHTZIGER"

My back view, head sunk forward, shoulders humped up, gave, I believe, a convincing picture of utter abasement as I slowly retraced my steps down the ravine. But the moment I was out of sight of the ill-favoured group about the rock, I darted into the thickest part of the jungle and, after dragging myself painfully through the undergrowth for about a hundred yards, sank down hot and breathless.

I did not care whether I was followed or not. I wanted to be alone to compose my thoughts, to think. My brain was still reeling beneath the shock of my stupendous good fortune. Five minutes since I would scarcely have given a sixpence for my chances of life. Yet here I had regained my freedom of action, had lulled old Clubfoot, by giving him an easy victory, into a false sense of security and, at the same time, had obtained the solution of the knottiest point of the whole cipher message. At the thought that it was Grundt himself who had given me the clue which, till then, I had vainly sought, I leant back and laughed.

"After the Somme and the Hindenburg Line," he had said, "our brave 'eighty-fivers' dislike you British even as much as our sailormen do..."

"*Unsere braven Fünf-und-Achtziger*"... he had used the German phrase and in a flash brought back to my mind a bit of German naval slang which I had heard so long ago that I had forgotten it! "*Die Fünf-und-Achtziger!*" What memories of pre-war days the phrase awakened! Dinner at Kiel in the ward-room of the German flagship, the tables ablaze with blue and gold uniforms sparkling with decorations, guest night in the mess of the Kaiser Franz Hussars at Stettin... and always army and navy "shop" the staple theme of our table talk. To the Imperial Navy the German Army was (slightly superciliously, for the rivalry between the two was intense) "*die Fünf-und-Achtziger*" because the 85th Infantry Regiment composed the garrison of Kiel, Germany's premier war-harbour.

The garrison of Kiel! Clubfoot, like all his master's *entourage*, was in closest touch with the Fleet, the Kaiser's own creation. That scrap of navy slang came naturally to his lips and in uttering it, he had sent with a flash the cipher to my mind.

"Flimmer', flimmer' viel"
Die Garnison von Kiel

The garrison of Kiel represented the figure "85." How, then, did the cipher run *en clair*?

Heliograph
85
Compass bearing of 27 degrees.

Eighty-five, I realised at once, was the *angle* for the heliograph. The message, therefore, read:—

"Turn the heliograph at an angle of 85 degrees (*i.e.*, from the horizontal since it had been wired so as only to be raised or lowered) on a compass bearing of 27 degrees..."

The weight of the little mirror in my jacket pocket heartened me immensely. Clubfoot, I knew, would see the figure "85" in the allusion to the Kiel garrison. But the mirror was the starting-point for the whole cipher. *And he had never known that a mirror was on the grave!* The mirror, fixed in position as I had found it, made the first half of the message as clear as day. Without this essential pointer the cipher itself would be useless to Clubfoot. Even if his remarkably astute brain should divine the allusion to a heliograph in that first line, he would not have the mirror...

In any case, his investigations would be delayed. And I was playing for time. Six days must elapse, I reflected, before the yacht could return. For how many of these would I continue to enjoy my liberty? For as soon as Clubfoot realised that he had been fooled, I knew that he would once again stretch out that long arm of his to seize me. I should have to find a secure hiding-place—I thought of the high ground of the island, somewhere among those lofty volcanic peaks, in this connection—but the present need was for action. In the light of the fresh clue I had obtained, I must push on with my investigation at the grave itself and that without a moment's delay. For the rest of the cipher, notably those baffling bars of music, which were firmly fixed in my mind—well, sufficient for the day is the evil thereof!

I looked at my watch. It was twenty minutes past eleven. "Mittag"—noon—the message was dated, clearly an indication of the time at which the experiment with the heliograph was to be made. If I were to act, I must act at once. Fortunately, the grave could not be far from where I lay. But what of Clubfoot?

The sound of voices came as if in answer to my query—of voices close at hand. Parting the foliage in front of me, I saw a file of men winding their way through the forest not twenty paces away. They appeared to be following some kind of path; for they marched steadily, one behind the other.

I pressed myself flat behind my protecting bush, only my head raised to observe the men as they went by. Now scraps of German came to my ears. There was talk of someone they called "Red Itzig," a Jew, who was to read the cipher for them. Itzig was apparently ill for there was some chaff about "the Jew" being cured as soon as he could hear that the treasure was within their grasp.

Did this mean that they were going back to their camp? And that the coast was clear for that pressing work I had to do? Five minutes, I calculated, would suffice for my purpose.

I kept a sharp eye open for Clubfoot. Here he came, the eighth in the party, hobbling along in the rear, with set face, grim and silent. The line halted for a moment. The man in front of Clubfoot, a small, dark man, doffed his panama to sponge his face. To my amazement it was Custrin... Custrin, whom I had last seen, at the side of Marjorie Garth, standing at the head of the *Naomi's* ladder waving us farewell as the launch took us ashore...

Now I had the solution of something that had greatly puzzled me—Clubfoot's exact knowledge of where I kept the cipher message, his allusion to my "Government survey work" on Cock Island. Then Custrin *was* one of El Cojo's spies! With a little shiver I thought of that hocussed drink. What would have been my fate that night but for the merciful intervention of Providence? I could make a pretty shrewd guess. They would have found me insensible in my berth and Custrin gone in the morning—in one of the ship's boats. I wondered vaguely what had become of the doctor whose papers he must have appropriated...

The voices had died away now and Clubfoot, the last of the line, had disappeared from my sight. I had counted eight in the party. All, therefore, seemed to have passed. Softly I began to wriggle myself forward...

I reached the path which the party had followed. It was a well-marked track through the forest. The trees were not so dense here, and above my head I caught at intervals a glimpse of dazzling blue sky. The sun was very hot.

Quietly and quickly I went down the track, heading for the direction from which Clubfoot and his men had come. I went warily, bitterly conscious of my defenceless state. But I met no one and presently I stood on the edge of the clearing, the grave of the Unknown below me.

The clearing was all a-quiver with heat; gorgeous-hued butterflies danced from bush to bush amid flaming flowers; the drone of insects was in the air. I skirted the edge of the basin, then silently dropped down to the grave.

I took out the little mirror and gave it a good rub-up with my handkerchief. Then, going down on my knees, I laid it on the grave as I had originally found it—face upwards with the holes in the frame aligned with the holes in the timber baulk beneath. With my compass I took my bearing of 27 degrees, adjusted the mirror's position to the line it gave and then raised the glass on its base until it stood, as far as one might reckon by the eye, at an angle of 85 degrees from the horizontal.

I looked at my watch. It marked five minutes to twelve.

A gleaming speck of light flamed on the mirror's polished surface as it caught the sun, danced on fern and bush and boulder as I raised the glass and then, as I steadied it, came tremulously to rest on the topmost pinnacle of that terraced rock which Garth and I had climbed on the previous afternoon.

From where I stood I could see the edges of the three shelves which had been cut by some forgotten generation of cave-dwellers out of the friable volcanic rock. The speck of light trembled on the crag on a level with the topmost terrace. It rested on a tall, flat stone which stood out from the rest of the weather-beaten face of the rock because its surface was smooth while all the rest was jagged and serrated. Only the upper part of this pillar-like stone was visible to me; for the projecting edge of the terrace cut off the rest from my sight. As far as I could judge the pillar must have been hewn out of the face of the rock on the highest shelf.

The stone was easy to identify, I felt a little thrill of excitement. What should I find on scaling the rock? From the first terrace on which Garth and I had rested before the thunderstorm there had been, I now recalled, a little winding path leading aloft. What did the cipher say?

> "Past the Sugar-Loaf you see the Lorelei
> And if you want the little treasure"

I quoted to myself and realised, with a pang, that I was still without the key to the riddle of those four bars of music. Well, the next thing to do was to climb to that topmost shelf...

Suddenly Garth and Carstairs came into my mind. With a little twinge of conscience I became aware that, in the excitement of the morning's events, I had completely forgotten them. I was sorely tempted to push on with my quest. But I thrust the temptation aside. My encounter with Clubfoot had put an entirely new complexion on the situation. I should have to consider seriously with my companions what we were going to do. After all it was I who had brought Garth into this business... With a last regretful glance at that terraced crag where all my hopes were centred, I turned my back on the grave and set my face for the shore. When I emerged at the top of the beach, the first thing I saw was the *Naomi's* launch drawn up on the shining white sand.

Garth, followed by Carstairs, tumbled out of the cave at my approach.

"Okewood," cried the baronet and his face was very grave, "what does this mean?"

He pointed at the launch.

"It means," said I, "that Dr Custrin fooled us, Sir Alexander. You say he presented letters of recommendation?"

"Certainly. From my New York manager!"

"Well, they were stolen. I have just seen Custrin in the forest. He obviously took the yacht's launch to come ashore and join his employer..."

"His employer?"

"El Cojo!"

Then I told him about my meeting with Grundt and of the previous history of the man, of Custrin's attempts to get me to show him the message and of the opiate he had put in my drink. Garth listened without interruption but his eyes began to bulge and his cheeks to redden in an ominous way.

"Dang it!" he burst out at length, and the northern burr crept into his speech as it did when he got angry, "I'll see this clubfooted man and learn him to send his spies on to my yacht. A German, too! I'll talk to him. I'll..."

I observed that they were fourteen to three.

"It will be at least six days before the *Naomi* calls for us," I pointed out, "and for that time we are practically at their mercy..."

"And to think that those damned doctors wouldn't let me have the wireless on the yacht!" exclaimed the baronet. "Wait till I get to a cable-instrument. If I don't have a warship here within a week..."

"We've got to do something *now*, Sir Alexander!" I broke in. "If Grundt realises that he has been tricked before we are out of his clutches all a British warship can do is to give us a military funeral. Do you understand me? Now I had thought of withdrawing our guns and stores to the upper part of the island and trying to find a safe hiding-place there until the *Naomi* comes back. But the sight of the launch has given me a better idea than that. By the way, where did you find her?"

"About half a mile down the coast, under some branches she was!" said Carstairs. "I was having a bit of a look round and I came upon her. She'd had a rough time, by the look of her. There was a lot of water in her afore I baled her out. I brought her round and beached her..."

"Is there any petrol in her?" I asked him.

"She always carries a reserve of forty gallons," Garth replied. "And that's intact. And her tank's half-full!"

"Then," said I broaching my idea, "why shouldn't you and Carstairs take her and fetch the *Naomi* back? Alcedo is only a matter of a hundred miles or so. You could be back here with the yacht tomorrow or the next day. You've got the chart, haven't you?"

"Aye," rejoined Garth slowly, "I've got the chart and a compass. But we're not leaving you here?"

"Yes," I said, "you are."

And I drew him aside.

"With luck," I told him, "I may have twenty-four hours — not more — in which to work undisturbed on the clearing-up of the cipher. I have no right to throw this chance away. If I were to go with you and to find, on our return, that Clubfoot and his gang had stolen a march on us and found the treasure, I should never forgive myself... And there's another thing! I've brought you into this mess, Garth, and, believe me, I take it very kindly of you that you have never once reproached me, as was your right, with my responsibility in the matter. Knowing that you are out of the island I shall have my mind easy on that score. Besides, I shall be able to reckon on your being back within forty-eight hours and can lay my plans accordingly!"

I had a lot of trouble to overcome his resistance; for he was a stout-hearted fellow. But my mind was made up. All my life I have played a lone hand and I knew that I should face the future with greater confidence by myself. In the end I had my way and the three of us immediately set about filling up the launch with stores and water.

In half an hour all was ready. We pushed the launch down into the water and shook hands all round.

"If I don't show up when you land," was my parting injunction to Garth, "occupy the beach here and wait for me. I shall always have the cave to come back to. And fire a gun, when you sight the island, to let me know you're here!"

With that Carstairs started the engine and churning up the green water, the launch glided out into the harbour. I did not wait to see her fade out of sight in the spray of the surf-bar for I had not a moment to lose. I made at once for the cave to collect a few provisions for my change of camp.

* * *

I had filled a knapsack and was strapping it when a sudden sound brought me hastily to the mouth of the cave. The launch had disappeared and the bay lay deserted before me.

Somewhere in the woods behind me I had heard a woman scream.

36

MARJORIE'S ADVENTURE

It was the high-pitched cry of a woman in terror. It rang out sharply over the ominous silence resting on that quiet island. And it was not far away. Clapping my hand to my pocket to make sure I had the automatic pistol which Carstairs had pressed upon me before he left, I dropped the knapsack and darted from the cave.

I had no clear purpose in my mind, I think. Did not Edmund Burke tell us that the age of chivalry is dead? But half the battle in this curious work of ours is knowing what the other fellow is up to and I have never been able to sit down quietly under uncertainty.

Swiftly I mounted the rocky slope from the shore. Behind me the gulls uttered their mournful cries as they hung above the placid sea and in the woods around me there was the loud chatter of birds. But there was no sound of human voice.

Then suddenly I came upon Marjorie Garth in a little open space between two moss-grown boulders. Though I could hardly believe my own eyes there was no mistake about it; for her face was turned towards me. And she was struggling in the arms of Custrin. Her face was very pale and in her grey eyes was a look of despair which I shall not easily forget. She was wearing no hat and her gold-brown hair tossed to and fro as with one hand thrust in her opponent's face, she fought desperately to keep him off.

It all happened in a flash. The next thing I knew, I felt the bite of my knuckles in Custrin's damp neck as, my hand firmly clutching his collar, I tore him backwards. All my resentment against this false, sleek, smooth-spoken creature welled up within me and I exulted to feel him stagger and wilt, then crumple up in a grasp which I willed to be as violent and brutal as mind and muscle could make it.

Caught unawares he reeled backwards inert, for a fraction of a second a dead weight in my hold. But then he reacted. I felt his wiry frame stiffen as he struggled to elude me. But I held fast and swinging him round, gave him my fist in his face.

It was the force of my own blow that sent him from my hands—staggering against a rock which brought him up standing. A single word he spoke.

"*Herr!*" he cried and the word burst in a kind of sob from his throat. In the crisis his native tongue came to his lips and in that moment I knew Dr Custrin for a German.

There was murder in his quick, black eyes. His hand clawed for his hip-pocket but I was at him at once, driving for his face again. This time he dodged the blow and I felt my wrist rasp on the rough boulder behind him. For all his pretty drawing-room ways he was game enough, and with outstretched hands made at my throat.

But I drew back swiftly and as he came at me, let fly with my left to the point of the chin. He stopped dead, his eyes goggling, his head sagging on his shoulders. Then he crumpled up in a mass at my feet.

I turned to Marjorie. She stood, where I had found her, against the other boulder, dabbing at her lips with her handkerchief, her breath coming and going in quick gasps.

"The beast!" she said and her voice broke.

"The beast!"

THE RETURN OF CLUBFOOT

Then, plaintively like a little child, she cried:-

"Where is Daddy? Oh, please, will you take me to him..."

"Your father has gone to fetch the yacht," I answered and broke off in sheer perplexity. Where *was* the *Naomi*? The unexplained appearance of Marjorie on the island complicated matters horribly. Alone I was content to face the prospect of eluding Clubfoot and the vengeance he would surely try to wreak on me. But with a woman...!

There was nothing for it but to put into execution the plan I had already formed. I must find—and that without an instant's delay—a hiding-place and withdraw there with the girl. That must be my first care. The future must look after itself.

And the cipher? My intention had been to scale the terraced rock to follow up the next clue. There were caves there in which we could shelter and the topmost terrace would surely afford a view over the sea and enable us *to* sight the *Naomi* as soon as she appeared off the island.

We would make for the terraces and lie, snugly hidden there, until the yacht came back. And in this way I might also continue to follow up the clue to the treasure. But we must have food and arms. We should have to go back to the cave on the shore.

I looked at Custrin. He lay like a log.

"Come," I said to Marjorie, who was now looking at me curiously.

I glanced down at my clothes and realised that my appearance must be nothing less than forbidding—my face grimy and unshaven, my white drill torn and stained and my boots all soggy with sea-water.

"You look so tired... and so grave," she said. "What can have happened?"

"Let us go back to the camp," I rejoined, "and I'll tell you as we go."

"What about... him?" she asked and looked at the prone form of the doctor.

"He'll sleep it off!" said I, "And the longer his slumbers last the better I shall be pleased!"

"But we can't go away and leave him like this!" she expostulated.

"When you have heard my story," I rejoined, "you will think as I do. He'll be all right. He's stirring already. Come! Let's go back to the shore!"

As we turned in the direction of the beach, I said:

"But how on earth did you come to be here? What has happened to the *Naomi*?"

A little red crept into the girl's cheeks and she bit her lip.

"I wasn't going to be left behind. I told Captain Lawless so. I insisted on joining Daddy on shore. There was an awful row, but" — triumphantly — "I had my own way in the end. It was really Dr Custrin who managed it for me. He said he would take the responsibility of explaining to Daddy that I would come. And, as the captain was anxious to be off, he said he would let us keep the launch. The *Naomi* went on to Alcedo..."

"But," I said, "where have you been since yesterday?"

Marjorie laughed mischievously.

"Daddy will be out of his mind when I tell him," she replied. "I spent the night at a prospector's camp. Dr Custrin found that he knew some of the men there..."

I stared at her in astonishment.

"Was the leader a clubfooted man?" I asked.

"Yes!" rejoined the girl in a bubble of laughter. "Such a funny old thing... a German. There were lots of Germans there. It was quite extraordinary... like a dream!"

"But," I protested, "why didn't you land on our beach? Why was it necessary to spend the night with these people? A girl like you, alone!"

"Oh," she laughed back at me, "you needn't be so scandalised. I can take care of myself. I meant to bring Yvonne, my maid, you know, with me, but the silly creature lost her courage when it came to dropping into the launch and she wouldn't come. Just as we were through the surf-bar we were caught in that tremendous thunderstorm and we had to run straight for the shore. We tied up the launch and started to walk through the woods. Then we came upon this party of prospectors. Dr Custrin seemed very surprised to find them there. He said it would be impossible to locate your camp in the dark and we should have to stay the night. They were all very nice to me and I had a room in a sort of wooden hut just above the beach."

Mentally, I took off my hat to Custrin. Not only had he contrived to get ashore without arousing suspicions but he had brough with him a most valuable hostage. Grundt had spoken of having the means of bringing us to our senses. Now I knew what he had had in mind...

"When I woke up this morning," Marjorie continued, "I found that everybody, including Dr Custrin, had gone. A hideous-looking Coloured man was left in charge. There was some man ill, too, in one of the huts. The Coloured man seemed to be watching me all the time and I got horribly frightened. So, after waiting a long time for the doctor to come back, I decided to start off and find Daddy and you for myself. The sick man called the Coloured man into the hut for a moment and I got away. Then I met Dr Custrin in the woods and he tried to stop me. He wanted to kiss me, too..."

She paused and looked at me curiously.

"You hit him very hard, didn't you? she remarked.

"I'd have twisted his neck clean off," I answered savagely, "if I'd known then what I know now!"

"I thought you were going to kill him," said the girl. "You must have a very bad temper, Major Okewood," she added sedately.

After what I had already gone through that day, it galled me to think of the two of us chatting away as inconsequently as though we were on the lawns at Ascot. No man, I grant you, could have had a more charming companion than Marjorie Garth and she was as pretty as a picture in the plain tussore riding costume she wore with a rakish little brown felt hat.

But I was in no mood for badinage. I was haunted by the imminent peril of our position and weighed down by my responsibility for the safety of this girl. So bluntly, for my nerves were on edge and every flowering bush seemed to conceal an enemy, I told her how things stood. She listened very quietly but when I had finished I noticed that her little air of raillery had gone.

"If you only knew," I concluded, "how bitterly I reproach myself for bringing you into this..."

"When you came on board the *Naomi*," Marjorie said gently, "you could not tell that you would be followed to the island."

"That," I rejoined rather forlornly, "is my only excuse."

We halted in the woods on coming in sight of the sea. The beach was deserted, as we had left it, with the sea-birds wheeling ceaselessly over the bay and the tide lapping gently on the white sand.

The light was mellowing. My watch showed it to be five o'clock.

"We shall have to hurry," I warned, "for we must be in our new retreat before it is dark."

I bade her wait there while I fetched from the cave the knapsack I had packed and the Winchester.

I advanced cautiously down the shore. I wondered what Grundt was doing. How oppressive the island silence was! It unsettled me. I thought of the strange unnatural hush which is said to precede an earthquake.

I bent down and lifted the pall of creeper screening the mouth of the cave. As I entered a bulky form rose up from one of the beds. There was no mistaking that massive figure, its slow, deliberate movement. I sprang back but the creeper hampered my movements and before I could gain the open, my shoulders were firmly grasped, my arms pinioned. I sought to twist myself free but I was held by those who must have held a man before and I could barely struggle in that iron grip. As I thus stood helpless I heard Marjorie cry out.

37

BLACK PABLO MAKES HIS PREPARATIONS

They pushed me into the cool dimness of the cave. An odour of unwashed humanity, which blended gratefully with a searching smell of garlic, hung about my unseen captors.

"*Herrgott!*" cried Grundt, "it's as dark as pitch in this hole. Cut away this cursed plant, some of you, and let's have some light!"

The creeper fell away. The golden sunlight that flooded the cave showed me Clubfoot, his black-tufted hands folded across the crutch handle of his heavy stick, grim and lowering.

Black Pablo and a regular Hercules of a man, a broad-chested, yellow-bearded giant, a good type of the German bluejacket from the Frisian seaboard, were holding me. Grundt made a quick gesture of the hand.

"Take away his gun!" he ordered.

The fair young man I had seen at the graveside stepped forward. Roughly, vindictively, he ran his hands over me. He found Carstairs' automatic in my side pocket and transferred it to his own.

"You see these men," said Clubfoot, bending his bushy eyebrows at me. "Their orders are to shoot to kill in the event of any attempt on your part to escape. And whatever your private views on suicide may be you will probably bear in mind that

Miss Garth—the charming Miss Garth—will, in any case, be left to mourn you..."

This allusion to Marjorie frightened me. There was no suavity about Clubfoot now. He was in his blackest, most menacing mood. His face was positively baleful; and there was a twitching of his black-bristled nostrils which warned me that he was on the verge of a paroxysm of fury.

"Leave me alone with him!" he commanded brusquely—his voice was harsh and snarling—"but remain outside within call!"

I felt the blood rush back into my numbed arms as the men relaxed their grip and withdrew.

Nervously Grundt's great fist beat a little tattoo on his open palm. He appeared to be making an effort to control himself.

"You would play a double game with me, would you?" he said. "No man has ever double-crossed me and got away with it, do you hear? My master may be in exile, my country fallen from greatness; but *I* am king here. Do you understand that?"

His pale lips trembled and he stuttered as he strove to master his rising passion.

"This cipher message is useless, as well you know. Without the preliminary indication, it is unintelligible. So Itzig, who in his day was the greatest cipher expert the Russian Okhrana ever had, has reported to me. And you knew it, you... you..."

He pawed the air with his huge hand, the fingers outstretched.

"They have examined his grave again. There are signs that something was attached to the timber-work. What that was the drunken Englishman who first visited the grave must have known. And he confided it to you. 'I know when I'm beaten, Herr Doktor'; and 'I'll give you the cipher,' say you! You thought you were too clever for old Clubfoot, the cripple, the beaten Hun. But I'm master here, Herr Major, and you shall do my bidding!..."

"You are misinformed, Herr Doktor!" I said, trying to speak calmly. My lips were dry and my heart-beats thumped in my ears. But I was not thinking of myself. I was tormented with anxiety for Marjorie—Marjorie in the hands of those men.

"Don't answer hastily!" counselled Grundt changing to a tone of deadly calm that struck chill on my heart. "Ulrich von Hagel, who wrote that message left it for one who should come after him, who would be a naval officer like himself. He wrote it so that it should be unintelligible to the casual person into whose hands it might fall, yet as clear as day to one of his own caste. And you would tell me that the message as it stands is all he left behind! *Nein, nein, Herr Major, es geht nicht!* I know that you have this information"—he crashed his fist into his open hand—"and you are going to give it to me!"

I shrugged my shoulders. I would not speak yet. Sooner or later, I knew, they would use Marjorie to break my silence. Then it would be time to speak. Till then I must await developments. After all, time was on my side.

My gesture seemed to rekindle all Grundt's rage. Slowly the colour faded out of his face, leaving it livid save where that hideous scar beneath the cheekbone made an angry patch of red. His bushy eyebrows drew together and his mouth trembled.

"So you'd still play with me, would you, you scum?" he shouted, his voice rising to a roar. "You'd pit your wits against mine, would you? *Herrgott*, I have an account to settle with you and that brother of yours, and, by God! I'm going to settle it! And *you* shall pay double for the pair of you! Do you know..."—his voice dropped to a savage whisper—"that these German seamen of mine would cheerfully abandon all claim to the treasure for the pleasure of taking vengeance on you for all your country has made them suffer in these long years, hunted, degraded, outcast?

"Do you realise that I have but to raise my hand and you're a doomed man, and not the whole might of the British Empire could save you? But we shall take our time. You will not die too soon, my friend. First you shall speak! And if you remain obstinate, there is always the charming English girl..."

He clapped his hands. On a sudden the cave seemed filled with angry, shouting men. My head swam for I was worn out with want of sleep and faint with hunger. Something struck me on the back of the neck a violent blow. I felt myself falling, falling...

* * *

How long I remained unconscious I don't know. When I regained my senses it was to find myself in semi-darkness in a long, low-roofed shed. It was dimly lit by a ruddy light which fell through some kind of grating in the roof. I could see no windows. The atmosphere was stifling and the floor and walls fairly swarmed with enormous cockroaches.

They had laid me down on a pile of sail-cloth in a corner. My head was splitting and I had a raging thirst. My pockets had been rifled and my brandy-flask was gone. I leaned back on my hard couch, my head against the rough wall of planks, and idly watched the flickering reddish light that filtered through the grating. I was vaguely aware of some unpleasant news that lurked, like a robber in ambush, in some unfrequented corner of my brain ready to pounce out upon my first conscious thought...

Somewhere outside a guitar was thrumming random passages of Spanish dances, punctuated, now and then, by a little burst of castanets. The soft murmur of voices became audible every time the guitar stopped, with here a laugh and there an exclamation. Presently a voice called "Pablo!": the lilting rhythm of a dance theme stopped—suddenly in the middle of a bar—and the click of the castanets was stilled.

Then, to soft, plaintive chords heavily stressed, an exquisite liquid tenor voice began to sing.

> "Se murio, y sobre su cara
> Un panuelito le heche...
> Por que no toque la tierra...
> Esa bocca que yo bese!..."

The chords broke off abruptly on a single string that sung reverberatingly. There was laughter, applause, the confusion of men speaking together. Then a voice said distinctly in German:

"He hadn't come round when I looked in ten minutes ago. Karl knows how to send them to sleep with that blow of his..."

"He'll come out of dreamland quick enough when *der Stelze* gives Black Pablo the word!" another voice replied.

"O Pablo," cried one in Spanish, "O Pablo! You shall try your little persuasions on the Señor!"

"*Si, si,*" came from many throats.

"*Madre de Dios,*" answered a voice in guttural Spanish. "He shall speak for me, *muchachos*! And if he will not speak, then, *caramba!* maybe he'll sing for us and for the lovely *Señorita* as well!"

Then followed a roar of acclamation. Then Black Pablo said:

"Patience a little while, *amigos*, until the chief comes. I go to make ready the fire!..."

I sprang to my feet. I heard no more of the talk outside, the cries, the laughter, the chaff. The time had come for action. I must decide at once between complete capitulation to Grundt or one last bid for liberty.

But what guarantees had I that Grundt, with the heliograph in his possession, would respect any promise he might give me as the price of surrender? None. I could not trust him and, as he had told me, he had an old score to pay off. And if anything should happen to me before the yacht returned what would become of Marjorie? Free I might help her; therefore any risk was justifiable to secure my escape.

Escape? But how?

The shed was solidly built of heavy logs, the door the only visible means of egress. The grating which admitted the air was a steel-bound frame too narrow, as I could see at a glance, to admit the passage of my body. I scrutinised the floor. It was of planking, well-made and seemingly in good condition. It struck hollow to the foot and I surmised that, as is generally the case with sheds of this kind, the structure was laid on a concrete foundation.

In the course of my examination of the boarding I moved the pile of sail-cloth. Beneath it was a plank in which an iron ring was sunk. The sheer unexpectedness of my discovery, the prospect of escape it opened to me, left me with brain numbed, irresolute. The talk and laughter had died down outside, but, from time to time, my ear caught a measured foot-tread as though a guard were walking up and down before the shed...

The plank came up easily enough. My heart sank within me. It revealed merely a shallow trough about three feet deep going down to the foundations of the shed which, as I had guessed, were set in concrete.

I got down into the hole and crawled in under the floor. It was pitch-dark and abominably hot down there under the boards, with a strong smell of rats. Face downwards, my head frequently scraping the planks above me, I crawled along the concrete bed, hoping against hope that I might find some hole, where the outer wall of the shed rested on the concrete base, which would enable me to scramble through to freedom.

But I was doomed to disappointment. Here and there I found a cranny wide enough for the flat of my hand to pass. But nowhere was there an opening large enough to take anything bigger than a cat. I could only conclude that the trap

I had found was made for the purpose of allowing repairs to be effected to the lower woodwork of the shed.

Half-suffocated with the heat and almost blinded with dust, I was painfully crawling back to my trap when my head hit a plank along the wall with more than usual violence. The beam, seemingly rotten underneath, eaten perhaps by ants, splintered like touch-wood and my head came up through the floor. I found myself looking into the shed.

Then germinated in my mind the seed of a great idea. The next best thing to escaping is to give the appearance of having escaped, a theory which many of our war prisoners in Germany turned to good account. If my captors were not acquainted with the construction of the shed, if, as I calculated, they would, from the discovery of a large hole in the floor, jump to the conclusion, without further investigation, that I had burrowed my way out under the floor, the guard over the shed would be relaxed and I should, at any rate, have a little breathing-space in which to think out the next move. There were a lot of "ifs" about my plan. But it was the only one I could think of for the moment and I set about putting it into operation at once.

Where the rotten plank had given way I enlarged the hole as much as possible. Then I climbed back through it into the shed, replaced the plank with the ring and covered it up again with the pile of sail-cloth, and without further delay dived down again through the hole I had made under the floor. I crawled away among the beams and joists as far as I could go in the direction of the other side of the shed and then lay still.

38

THE ESCAPE

Good fortune, I have always contended, comes to those who make ready to receive it. I can well imagine the Foolish Virgins of the parable spending the rest of their lives lamenting their hard fate and attributing their wise sisters' preparedness not to prevision but to good luck. Throughout my life I have always tried to leave nothing to chance but the *dénouement*. It is in the *dénouement* that Fate lies in ambush, waiting to slay or to spare...

I had done what I could, I reflected as I lay up in my stuffy hole. Now Fate must take a hand. I had no settled plan. In course of time they would come to look for me and if they did not drag me forth by the heels from my hiding-place, I should watch for the best opportunity that presented itself for my dash into liberty...

I think I may have dozed off; for I did not hear the shed door above me open. What brought me to my senses with a shock and set my nerves a-tingling was the stump of a heavy footstep, a well-remembered halting step, that made my heart stand still.

Then came the hubbub of excited voices, the glare of torch-light filtering through the interstices of the floor and the roar of Clubfoot's voice shouting orders. A long beam of white light clove the darkness of my lair. Someone had climbed down into the hole. I held my breath and wondered whether against the white concrete on which I lay my drill suit might escape notice.

Heavy feet trampled above my head; a door slammed violently and a whistle shrilled thrice. Again there came that clumping tread, shaking the very fabric of the hut. Then silence fell and I breathed again.

Suddenly a voice spoke, almost in my ear, as it seemed, from outside the shed.

"He may have tunnelled," the speaker said in German.

"If he has," replied a voice in the same language, "he can't have gone far. He hadn't time!"

The voices moved away.

The speakers were obviously going to make the round of the shed on the outside to see where I had escaped.

They would find no opening and I should be caught like a rat in a trap. If I were to make a bolt for it, it must be now or never. I began to shuffle my way backwards towards the hole in the floor...

The shed was empty and, oh! thank God! the door stood wide. Beyond it I had a glimpse of an open space surrounded by half a dozen wooden huts, a fire burning low in the centre. I tiptoed to the door. The night was very dark. I could hear men crashing about on the outskirts of the camp. One of them carried a torch and its red and smoky glare flickered over the trees and bushes. But the little clear space between the huts was deserted. Once I could get away from the light thrown by the fire...

Now I was through the door. I could hear them on the far side of the shed. In three silent bounds I was past the fire and across the open. Then I was brought up short by a low building lying directly in my path. As I halted, nonplussed for the instant, a door facing me opened and a mulatto poked his head out. He recognised me for a stranger at once. He rolled his eyes at me in surprise and would have cried out.

But I leapt at him, my fingers at his throat, and as he toppled over backwards across the threshold of the door, I tightened my grip until I felt the breath choking out of him. However, having got him down, I released my hold and ran my hands over his filthy clothes.

In the hip-pocket of his striped cotton trousers I found a Browning and a large key. I thrilled at the touch of the pistol in my hand. After successfully travelling the first stage on the road to freedom I had now a weapon to help me over the next! Surely things were coming my way!

The mulatto, upon whose chest my knee pressed hard, was grey with fear. He was a picturesque-looking ruffian with rings in his ears and a gaudy bandana handkerchief bound about his brows. I tore off his head-dress and unceremoniously crammed it into his mouth. There seemed to be about three yards of it and it was far from clean. But the yellow-boy gobbled it down and by the time I had pushed the end of it past his thick lips he appeared to be very effectively gagged. Then I strapped his hands together behind his back with his own belt and tethered his legs with an end of rope which I found in a corner. He made no attempt at resistance.

This job satisfactorily accomplished, I rose to my feet and looked about me. Where was Marjorie? Had any harm befallen her? In my mind's eye there arose the picture of her as I had left her standing on the fringe of the forest, a slim, girlish figure, a little thrilled but making such a brave show of calm. What had they done with her? In which of these squalid huts was she confined?

The room in which I found myself, dimly lit by a single candle stuck in a bottle, was obviously the cook's galley. There was a stove in one corner and remnants of food on the table. The mulatto, of course, would be the cook. Then there crept into my memory something Marjorie had said about a hideous man in whose custody she had been left before I met her with

Custrin in the forest. And I turned over in my hand the key which I had taken from the mulatto's pocket.

At the back of the kitchen was a door. It was locked but that key fitted it. As I softly turned the lock and swung the door back, there was a little cry, a flutter of something white, and Marjorie stood in the pool of yellow light thrown by the guttering candle across the threshold. I beckoned to her and put my finger to my lips.

She was very pale and her face looked as though she had been crying. But her splendid courage never failed her. She seemed to take it at a glance the disordered room and the yellow-skinned mulatto trussed up on the floor.

"My dear!" she whispered softly as she came out and stood by my side as though awaiting orders.

The galley door gaped wide as I had left it. The open space about the fire was still deserted; but I yet heard the sound of voices and the crash of feet in the undergrowth beyond the circle of light flung by the dying embers. And I noticed with growing anxiety that the eastern sky was growing light.

"We can't afford to wait!" I whispered to the girl. "We shall have to run for it. If only we can make our way in the dark to the grave! I can find myself to rights after that..."

"There's a path through the forest to the grave," rejoined Marjorie. "I followed it this morning. I can show you where it is."

I made her drink a cup of rum from a wicker-bound jar that stood on the floor and took a dram myself. It was wicked stuff, raw and almost proof, but I felt a great deal the better for it. I also pocketed some cold meat and bread. Famished as I was, I would not stop to eat; but I meant us to make a meal at the first opportunity.

Suddenly, from somewhere quite close at hand, voices reached my ear. Swiftly I drew the galley door towards me and peeped through the crack. Silhouetted against the firelight two

THE RETURN OF CLUBFOOT

figures were striding rapidly towards the hut. One of them, a great black shape, went with a limp.

In a flash, without a noise, I pulled the door to and flattening my palm on the candle, extinguished it, plunging the galley into darkness.

"We must get out by the back," I whispered to Marjorie at my side.

"There is no way!" she replied. "There is not even a window in the back room!"

"Then stay here behind the door!" I told her. "And, whatever happens... whatever happens, do you understand?... don't make a sound but leave things to me. And when I say 'Run,' run!..."

In a bound I was at the mulatto's side and had dragged him by the feet into the inner room. It was a fetid, black hole. I felt the outline of a truckle bed against the farther wall. I flung the cook down on it and spread a blanket over him. I was back in the galley at Marjorie's side just as a heavy footstep rang on the hard earth without.

Then the hut door was violently flung open.

"Pizarro!" called a thick voice in Spanish. "Pizarro! *Nombre de Dios!* Is the man deaf?"

We pressed ourselves flat against the wall as the door swung inwards. A white gleam of light pierced the darkness of the room and showed up clearly the rough panels of the door at the other end.

"Well!" said the thick voice, in German this time, "the door's shut anyway!"

The hut shook to his heavy tread as he stumped in, the fair young German, the brother of the Unknown, at his heels. Noiselessly I slipped out behind them.

They stopped suddenly. Clubfoot was at the door. If they turned round now, I should have to fight for it...

"*Na nu!*" ejaculated Grundt, without looking back. "The key's in the door. Show a light, Ferdinand!"

I heard the door creak on its hinges, saw the flashlight pick out the vague shape beneath the coverlet on the bed. And then the full force of my error broke upon me. I had left the mulatto's head exposed and, instead of Marjorie's soft golden-brown hair, Ferdinand's lamp showed us a coal-black woolly thatch.

Clubfoot, half across the threshold, swung round to the young German who was close behind him. But, before he could speak, I pitched myself with every ounce of weight I could command at Ferdinand's back and propelled him and Clubfoot violently into the inner room. I heard the loud crash as they fell in a heap on the floor and a smothered screech from the bed as I slammed the door and locked it.

"Now," I cried to Marjorie, "run!..."

39

A FACE AMONG THE FERNS

In my ears rang angry shouting, the sound of heavy blows rained upon that inner door, as I dashed out of the hut. Marjorie flashed by the front of the sheds and took a rocky path which led off steeply to the left. As I tore after her a man stepped out quickly from the angle of the hut to bar my passage. But without faltering in my stride I drove my elbow into his face and he slipped backwards, striking his head against the split log facing of the shed with a horrid crack. I did not stop to see what became of him but ran on, congratulating myself that I had laid him out without using the pistol for which my right hand clutched in my pocket. For I knew that the sound of a shot would bring the whole horde buzzing about our ears.

Daylight was coming now with great strides. The morning mists clung sluggishly about the lower part of the steep incline leading up from the hollow where the camp was situated. As we topped the path we came into view of the shores of a little cove and glimpsed a long, grey motor-launch that lay at anchor. This, as Marjorie told me afterwards, was Sturt Bay which, I remembered, the "Sailing Directions" had mentioned as the only practicable landing-place other than Horseshoe Bay on the island. In that deep hollow the sheds must have been invisible both from the land and the sea side. When, later on,

Marjorie told me that Clubfoot's men, in their talk among themselves, always referred to the huts as "The Petrol Store," I thought I understood why such care had been taken to conceal the camp from prying eyes.

Now we were in the forest following a winding track. Though, on looking back, it seems to have been the height of foolhardiness, I do not think we could have acted otherwise. For it was essential that we should reach the high ground undiscovered before it was fully light and we might have wasted hours trying to find the way through these dense woods where, though day was at hand, the shadows of the night yet lingered.

The noises I had heard on the outskirts of the camp had ceased. The silence made me uneasy. We relaxed our pace to a walk and went along swiftly and softly, our feet making no sound on the spongy ground. Suddenly, from a clump of rich green ferns, not a pace away from me, a man's head arose. I did not require to see the heavily bruised features to recognise Custrin. If ever the intent to kill peered out of a man's face, it did from the quick, black eyes of the doctor of the *Naomi*.

It happened far quicker than it takes to write it down. I could not see his hands; but there was a warning rustle of the ferns, a sudden change in the face, which told me he was going to shoot. The index finger of my right hand was crooked round the trigger of my pistol as it lay in the side pocket of my jacket...

We fired together. Something "whooshed" by my ear. In accents of shrill surprise Custrin cried out: "Oh!" stared at me stupidly for the fraction of a second through the blue haze that drifted on the air between us, then pitched toward on his face into the clump of ferns. There was a horrid gush—a convulsive movement of the hands—and the body lay still. The woods seemed to ring with the report, and there was a smell of singed cloth in the air. The pocket of my jacket was smouldering...

Now silence descended once more upon the forest, broken only by a faintly audible drip! drip! from the drooping head at my feet. Then suddenly a distant hallo went echoing through the woods; another shout, much nearer at hand, answered it and was answered by another until the whole forest rang again.

I turned to Marjorie. White to the lips, she stood with her face averted from that limp form sprawling in the ferns.

"We must make a dash for it, partner!" said I.

Docilely, like a little child, she thrust her hand in mine. "Don't go too fast!" she pleaded, "I'm—I'm—afraid of being left behind..."

Hand-in-hand, like the Babes in the Wood, we set off again through the forest, pelting headlong down the track. Unmolested we reached the lip of the clearing and dropped down into the hollow where the grave lay bathed in the lemon-coloured light of the new day. In front of us towered the rugged mass of rock for which we were making and my eye sought on the topmost terrace that pillar of dressed stone which held, as I firmly hoped, the secret of the treasure.

Panting we scrambled up the shelving slabs of stone which led to the foot of the crag. In order to reach the first shelf I had given Garth a back; but I guessed that the track I had seen winding aloft from the first terrace must, somehow, find its way to the ground.

We followed the base of the rock round till, presently, we came upon a tiny, zigzag footpath, crumbling and precipitate, leading upwards. By this we were out of sight of the clearing, but the sounds of pursuit drifted across to us more plainly every minute... the noisy passage of men through the undergrowth, raucous shouts. They seemed to be beating the jungle, keeping in touch with each other by calling.

The attack, when it came, would come from the rear. Therefore, I made Marjorie go first up the path. I looked at her anxiously. She was game all through, this girl; but her eyes were wistful and her mouth drooped pathetically.

The path, winding its way across the face of the rock, brought us on to the first shelf and thence, from the far end, pursued its course aloft. As we stepped out on the terrace a shot rang out from below and at the same moment a bullet hit the rock with a rebounding thwack right next to my ear while another whined shrilly over our heads.

"Go on, go on!" I cried to Marjorie. Together we dashed across the terrace and then the winding of the path brought us under cover again. We toiled on, the path growing steeper and steeper. I kept looking round to see if we were followed; but the grey path below us remained deserted.

As we mounted higher I noticed that the shelves cut out of the rock face grew narrower. The second terrace was scarcely more than twelve feet wide. Since we had left the first terrace we had looked out over a stern landscape of barren rock and lonely crag without a vestige of green. But, when we were within measurable distance of the third and topmost terrace, the path suddenly bent to the left and a magnificent panorama of land and sea burst upon our gaze.

Far below us the belt of green jungle was spread out at out feet; the waving green trees sloped down to the cliff-sheltered anchorage where the white wings of sea-birds flashed in the sun; a broad belt of deep blue sea ran out to the horizon all round. In the foreground our narrow path zigzagged to and fro, like a fluffy grey ribbon gummed to the rock. Just beyond we looked into the cup-shaped hollow with the grave. Tiny figures, every detail clear-cut and distinct in that limpid air, were dotted about the clearing. One leant heavily upon a stick which, as we stood and gazed upon the view, he raised and with it pointed aloft.

"Hurry, hurry!" I cried to Marjorie, but almost before I spoke a rifle again rang out in the hollow below and the dust spurted at my feet. It was some thirty yards to where the path, turning once more, would bring us out of sight and we scrambled forward with the bullets "zipping" angrily in the dust or noisily flattening themselves out on the rock. Several of the men in the clearing seemed to be firing, for the bullets came pretty fast.

It was a harrowing experience to be shot at at that height, perched on a precipitate path like flies on a ceiling. I plunged forward, my heart in my mouth. Now Marjorie had reached the bend and having rounded it into cover, had halted, waiting for me to draw level. A bullet struck the ground between us splashing the grey volcanic dust knee-high and the next moment I had scrambled into safety. Then I saw that the topmost terrace was only a few yards from us.

I turned to the girl. She had gone very white and she seemed to be leaning for support on the rocky wall at her side. Before I could speak she heaved a little sigh and pitched forward. I caught her in my arms.

40

WHICH PROVES THAT TWO HEADS ARE BETTER THAN ONE

I don't think she fainted. It was just that her forces had failed her. She lay quite motionless in my arms, her red-brown hair a splash of colour against the white sleeve of my coat. But a few yards, as I have said, separated us from the shelf, so I lifted her up. I felt a soft arm steal round my neck as she steadied herself. I glanced at her face. Her eyes were open.

"Hold tight," I bade her, "and whatever you do don't look down!"—for at that height the clear drop down the side of the cliff was enough to make an Alpine guide dizzy. Looking steadfastly ahead and fighting down a horrible feeling of giddiness I carried the girl up the path and at length stood upon the ledge.

It curved round the face of the rock, a mere shelf not more than two paces wide but slanting inwards, which improved one's foothold. From it the face of the cliff dropped sheerly to the nullah hundreds of feet below. I ventured a peep over the side and my brain fairly swam; for I am no hand at heights. From somewhere above us a great bird suddenly went up with a vast flutter and, with a few strokes of its powerful wings, propelled itself through the air until level with us it hovered motionless at an immense height above the stony valley.

"I'm going to set you down now," I said to the girl. "Lie quite still and don't move until I come back. I'm going along the ledge a bit to see if it broadens out at all or if there's a cave."

As gently as I could I put her down. The wind blew invigoratingly on the pinnacle of the crag and I hoped it would revive her. I stood and listened. No sound came from below. But I knew that until I found a spot from which we could survey the ascent we should not be safe.

I edged my way along the shelf as it curved round the rock. A few steps brought me in sight of its termination. It ended in nothing; but what caught my eyes was the tall pillar chiselled out of the rock upon which the flash from my mirror had rested. Beside it was a low opening in the back wall of the cliff.

The pillar was merely a high expanse of "dressed" stone, as the masons say, which had been carved out of the soft surface of the peak. From pictures I had seen of the images on Easter Island I knew it to be the first state of one of those uncouth effigies, relics of a departed era, which are found in more than one island of the Southern Seas. The pillar was not inscribed or carved in any way. It stood just as some native mason had left it waiting for the sculptor's hand.

A touch on my shoulder; Marjorie stood at my side.

"I'm a poor kind of soldier, partner," she said, "to fail you at the critical moment. I was at the last gasp when you picked me up. How ever did you manage to bring me up here?"

"Don't ask me," I laughed. "I was terrified for fear you'd look over and get scared..."

"I don't mind heights," the girl rejoined simply, "we live a great part of the year in our place in Wales, you know, and I've done quite a lot of climbing in my time. Oh! Look! Did you ever see anything so wonderful? "

We were side by side on the ledge with our backs to the pillar and as she spoke she stretched forth her hand and pointed across the valley. Above the jagged crests of various isolated peaks in the foreground a gigantic solitary image raised its tall black form against the deep azure of the ocean which was spread out to the horizon. Its back set to the sea, its features, stern and enigmatic in expression, turned towards us, and clearly visible in that transparent atmosphere, it dominated the little rocky plateau on which it stood, dwarfing the tremendous blocks of stone strewn about its base. Before it, as if from a sacrificial altar, a thin spiral of black smoke slowly mounted aloft against the blue sky. It seemed to rise from the ground at the foot of the effigy.

It was, in truth, a wonderful sight, a spectacle of sheer majesty. That lonely Colossus with its cruel face seemed to embody the suggestion of sinister mystery which, I had felt from the first, brooded over Cock Island...

Marjorie gave a little shudder.

"This island frightens me!" she said. "To think of that awful-looking image standing there gazing out across the valley for all these hundreds of years as if it were waiting for something. Somehow it reminds me of that clubfooted man, so hard, so ruthless, so... *patient!* Grundt makes my blood run cold!..."

He had not molested her, it appeared. When I had left her to enter our cave on the beach, men had suddenly surrounded her and carried her away to the sheds. There she had been handed to the custody of the mulatto who had locked her in the room behind the galley where I had found her.

"At meal-times," she added, "they brought me out to their open-air mess in the space between the huts. No one spoke to me. But they eyed me silently, especially Dr Grundt. He always seems to be thinking, that man, and I'm sure his thoughts are wicked. And the man they call Black Pablo! He kept edging towards me and leering with his one eye. Oh! It was horrible..."

She had seen nothing of Custrin since her encounter with him in the forest.

Clubfoot, she told me, had had some trouble with his men. They were grumbling at him for having let me go. The

Germans, especially the blond young officer, were particularly bitter. But Clubfoot had rounded on them and said that, as long as there were trees on the island to hang mutineers on, he would have no questioning of his authority.

Somewhere in the green tangle of woods far below us a single shot rang out sharply. The report went reverberating down the valley and from the tree-tops a cloud of birds swooped up affrighted. I did not hear the flight of the bullet so I could not see that the shot was meant for us. Yet there were only Clubfoot's men on the island now. Was Grundt asserting his authority?

The girl had dropped to her knees, and now seated herself cross-legged on the ground.

"If you and I are partners," said she, "don't you think the time has come to take me into your confidence?"

She invited me with a gesture to seat myself by her side. I glanced down at the valley. Below us and to the left the ascending path twice wound into view. From our coign of vantage one might infallibly pick off anyone who tried to push our position from the path. Though I was inclined to think that the gang had had their fill of fighting for the day, I was glad to be in a position from which their next move must be unerringly revealed to me.

I followed the girl's invitation; for I was very weary. To tell the truth, I welcomed the chance of resting quietly for a spell. I needed to think out the grave difficulties besetting us. It was clear that we could not stay were we were, for I had only five rounds of ammunition left. And Marjorie, who sat by my side, her rich brown hair blowing out in the wind, her eyes fixed dreamily on the hideous image staring sardonically across the valley at us; I had to think of her. Henceforth, any risk I took must inevitably imperil her safety... it was a horrid thought.

When would the *Naomi* come back? And could we risk holding out till the promised gun announced her return? She could not arrive at the earliest before the evening, I calculated.

I brought out the meat and bread I had taken from the galley and we ate it together, side by side. Although the sun had not long risen, there was already a heat in its rays which warned me of what its noon-day fierceness would be. And I was keenly alive to the fact that we had no water.

"I can see by your face," said Marjorie suddenly, "that you are worrying about me. And I want to be a help, not an impediment. I made you an offer of partnership once before!"

"I know," I rejoined, "but I didn't know you then..."

"I was so anxious to help," she said. "And you would tell me nothing!"

"I'm afraid I don't know much about women," I said.

"Major Okewood," exclaimed the girl, turning round and looking me full in the face, "you surprise me!"

"It's true..." I began.

But Marjorie laughed merrily.

"You're too delightful for words," she said. "Why, my dear man, if you understood women you'd have..."

She broke off hastily and added:

"There are only two kinds of men: those who say they do understand women and don't and those who admit they don't and don't. But all the same don't you think it's rather insulting to one's intelligence to find a man locking up his secrets in his heart simply because he's read or heard somewhere that a woman is not to be trusted?"

I looked at her with interest. This young girl, with her ridiculous clump of reddish brown hair, her slim straight limbs, her calm child-like eyes, made me feel like a naughty little boy being reprimanded by his mummy.

"Yes," I said limply. "I suppose it is!"

For a minute her eyes encountered mine, and in them I read her reproach. She dropped them almost at once and a sort of embarrassment silenced us. Then it suddenly occurred to me that she and I were alone; I wondered to find that neither the prospect of spending the night, maybe several nights, in the company of a man of whom she knew next to nothing, nor the danger to which she was exposed, had shaken her out of her serenity. This girl was full of character. My wish, that poor man's wish which I had hardly dared to admit to myself on board the *Naomi*, rose to my mind with such force that I felt the blood mount to my face.

But Marjorie took my hand and patted it as she might have patted a child's.

"Tell me about your mission!" she said.

I kept her hand and seated at her side in the shade of that ancient pillar, with the fresh breeze caressing our faces, I told her how Fate had put into my hands the message left by Ulrich von Hagel for Clubfoot and his gang. I described to her my efforts to unravel the cipher which I repeated to her.

"How does it go in German?" she asked, for I had given her the English version.

"You know German?" said I.

She nodded.

"I used to have a German Fräulein," she answered. "She was a dear old thing and as a small girl I often went over to Boppard to stay with her people. I knew German rather well."

"Well," said I, "here goes!"

And I repeated the rhyme which had hammered its jingling measure into my brain:

> "Flimmer', dimmer' viel
> Die Garnison von Kiel
> Mit Kompass dann am besten
> Denk' an den Ordensfesten
> Am Zuckerhut vorbei
> Siehst Du die Lorelei..."

I broke off suddenly.

"By Jove I" I exclaimed. "By—Jove!"

I have spoken of the peaks which stood up in the valley between us and the stone image. The words of von Hagel's doggerel sent my gaze roving interrogatively across the open space and presently it fell upon a tall slender rock with a smoothly rounded crest which raised itself erect in the foreground. And it dawned upon me that there was The Sugar-Loaf of which von Hagel spoke.

I glanced across the valley from right to left, past the image frowning through the wisp of smoke at its foot, to where other peaks raised their crests aloft to the blue sky.

Suddenly I turned to Marjorie.

"If you've been to Boppard," I said, "you must know the Lorelei. Look where I am pointing and tell me if you see any rock which resembles it!"

Leaning over until her hair brushed my cheek the girl followed my pointing finger.

"Why, yes!" she exclaimed, "that square grey rock leaning over is rather like the Lorelei..."

At last I felt that I was within measurable distance of the end of my quest. But between me and my goal was interposed that unsurmountable four-barred obstacle, those enigmatical notes of music.

I had identified the peaks, but what did they signify? What bearing had they on the hiding place of the treasure? I felt utterly nonplussed and, for the first time, discouraged.

"What does it mean?" asked Marjorie at my elbow. "What has the Lorelei to do with the treasure?"

I laughed rather bitterly.

"If I were a musician," I answered, "I should probably be able to tell you. As I am not..."

"Please don't be mysterious," the girl bade me. "Tell me what you mean."

THE RETURN OF CLUBFOOT

I told her of the four bars of music.

"They're part of some German tune or other," I told her. "It's vaguely familiar to me, but I'm blessed if I can put any words to it. And I take it that the words are the thing!"

"Can you hum the melody over to me?" asked Marjorie.

Singing is not my forte. A combination of bashfulness and a cigarette-smoker's throat produce from my larynx when I attempt to sing sounds which I have always felt must be acutely distressing to my hearers. But Marjorie listening gravely with her head on one side, made me repeat my performance.

Then she said:

"But do you know you're trying to sing a song that was all the rage in Germany when I was there just before the war. Listen! I'll sing it to you!"

And in a clear young voice she sang:

"Püppchen, Du bist mein Augenstern
Püppchen, hab' Dich zum Essen, gern."

Then she checked herself suddenly and clutched my arm. "'Püppchen!'" she said. "Oh, partner, don't you see?"

"No!" I replied dejectedly. "I confess I don't! I know that 'püppchen' means a 'doll' or a 'little doll' but I really don't see..."

Marjorie raised her hand and pointed a slender finger at the saturnine image on the opposite side of the valley, seen between the Lorelei on the left and the Sugar-Loaf on the right.

"There's your doll!" she said.

And I knew at last that the riddle was read.

41

THE BURIAL CHAMBER

Much good the discovery did us, I reflected bitterly. A thousand, two, three thousand yards—in that thin atmosphere it was impossible to gauge distances accurately—of pathless mountain lay between us and the idol. Indeed, I hardly gave the solving of the riddle more than a passing thought now; for my mind was engaged in the more urgent problem of how to extricate Marjorie in safety from the perilous pass to which I had brought her.

We could not remain on the rock indefinitely; that much was clear to me. Already, under the influence of the sun's rays beating down ever more fiercely on that exposed ledge, the pangs of thirst were making themselves felt. It was Marjorie who mentioned it first. She asked if we could find water anywhere. At our level I thought it was doubtful and told her so. Marjorie Garth, I discovered, was a girl who liked to be told the truth.

"What about that cave beyond the pillar?" she asked, leaning across me to point at the low opening I had remarked in the back wall of our ledge.

"While it's light," I answered, "one of us must remain and guard the path. I don't know what their inaction means... but we must be prepared for anything. Why don't you have a look at the cave? But go carefully; the roof seems very low."

I gave her my hand and helped her up. She stepped across me, turned round and gave me a little smile, then bending down disappeared into the cave opening. And I, with my automatic in my hand, while I keenly watched the two little ribands of path below me, racked my brains to find a way out of our impasse.

I would try and hold out till dark. If, by then, the *Naomi* had not come, we would endeavour, under cover of the night, to reach our cave on the shore and wait for her. If, in the meantime, we were overpowered, I would capitulate and tell Clubfoot all I knew. In the meantime, I should have to abandon my hunt for the treasure.

A faint sound behind me made me start. It was shrill but distant. I listened. I heard it again and this time I recognised the call.

"Coo... eee!"

It was Marjorie calling from the interior of the cave. With a quick glance at the path below, I scrambled to my feet. The entrance to the cave was not more than four feet high and I had to bend almost double to enter. Within, for a few feet from the opening there was enough light to see that the floor, brittle and crumbly, sloped down into a dark void. I felt my way cautiously along the side of the cave foot by foot, stooping low to avoid the roof and seeing nothing. Then from somewhere far below, as it seemed at my very feet, the girl's cry went forth again:

"Coo... eee!"

I stopped.

"Right!" I shouted. "Where are you?"

From far below the cry came up, faint and a little quavery.

"Down here in the dark and I don't like it! But I've found water! There are some steps cut in the rock!"

The lure of the water was irresistible. I glanced at the path, above which hung a trembling curtain of heat. It was still deserted. I judged that I might safely risk a quick dash into the cave to quench my burning thirst.

The cave narrowed as it receded into the rock, and presently my foot shot out into space. I groped a bit and struck a shallow step. Then I suddenly remembered that I had a stump of candle in my pocket. I had picked it up on the previous evening when we had been loading the launch. An old campaigner never leaves candle ends lying about. They are apt to come in useful—as witness this case.

So I struck a match and lit my bit of candle and peered down. The feeble ray only illuminated a black void, a dark narrow shaft; but I saw that the steps descended almost sheer down one side. I was now able to stand erect, so clutching the side of the rock with one hand and bearing my lighted candle in the other, I started the descent. And I counted as I went.

I had counted fourteen steps when suddenly the ground appeared to give way beneath my feet. I clutched wildly at the side of the rock, my hand slipped over the smooth surface, and with a soft rumble the whole of the steps seemed to slide away. My light was extinguished and in a shower of crumbling rock and a cloud of acrid dust, I slithered headlong into the black shaft.

Well, I was blown sky-high once by a shell in France and I remember struggling madly with mind and body, as it seemed when I looked back on the incident afterwards, against the invincible force which bore me upwards until I gave up the struggle... and never even remembered the subsequent bump. But in this case, though I fought all the way to check my headlong fall, I never lost consciousness, and I felt in every bone of my body the terrific jar I received on landing on my back on a hard, rocky floor.

Some lingering echo told me that the girl had screamed, though I don't think I really heard her voice. But the next thing

I was aware of was a little whimpering sound. Then from the darkness the girl's voice said:

"Oh, Desmond!"

And I heard a little sob.

I felt dazed and shaken, but I staggered to my feet.

"Marjorie!" I called, "Where are you? I'm all right. There's no damage done..."

I heard a footstep, then a hand was thrust into mine, a small warm hand that entwined its fingers in mine and wrung them hard. Then, scarcely realising what I was doing or why I did it, I drew her to me and put my arms about her, felt the caress of her soft hair against my cheek as her head rested on my shoulder. And so we remained a minute or more in that inky darkness because we were glad to have found one another again.

By some miracle I had kept the candle in my hand all through my fall. When presently Marjorie drew away from me, I fished out my matches and rekindled the stump.

We found ourselves standing in a long, narrow chamber with a roof which, low to start with, sloped down until it stood not more than four feet from the floor. The place smelt damp and musty and here and there the walls gleamed wet where the light of the candle struck them. Along one side of the cave was a kind of stone slab.

Just behind where we stood was the narrow shaft by which we had descended, at its foot a jumble of debris. I raised the candle aloft and strained my eyes to see up the shaft. I stared into blackness; but I noted that where the stairs had been cut there now remained nothing but the sheer overhanging wall of rock.

I took Marjorie's arm and pointed to the wet glistening on the walls.

"Let's drink first!" I said.

My voice sounded strangely hollow in the vaulted place. I turned and led her to the rock. The water was dead cold and delightfully fresh to the touch. The girl put her lips to the wall and drank. I followed her example. She finished before I was through; for it seemed to me that the sun on that ledge outside had drained every drop of moisture out of my system and I drank and drank again. But suddenly she plucked my sleeve and whispered in an awed voice:

"What... what is that?"

She pointed at the stone slab of which I have spoken. It resembled a rough altar built up of big stones laid together like an Irish wall. And on it lay three or four long and shrunken-looking packets. The rays of my candle picked out a round substance that gleamed brightly through the wrappings of the nearest of these objects.

Even before I stepped up to the stone table to get a closer inspection I knew what they were. Here lay the bones of that forgotten race which had once inhabited Cock Island, the sculptors of the idol which had frowned at us across the valley. We had blundered into one of the island burial-places scooped out of the heart of the rock. The high light which my candle had caught up came from a hip-bone which had worn its way through the bark envelope. The girl saw it, recognised it for what it was, and shrank away.

"Let's get away quickly from here!" said Marjorie, nervously. "These... these mummies frighten me dreadfully. Desmond, take me out into the sunshine again..."

Her voice pleaded piteously and it went to my heart. For I was wondering...

"Good Lord!" I said, "They're naught but a handful of dust. There's nothing to be frightened of! Come and sit at the bottom of the shaft while I see about finding a way up!"

I sat her down on a pile of debris and gave her the candle to hold while, mounting as high as I could on the heaped-up rubbish, I sought for a means of scaling the shaft. But the face of the rock, from which the stairs had broken away under my weight, was now overhanging and so high that I could not see the top. The rest of the shaft was smooth and hard, and try as I would I could not get hand or foot-hold anywhere.

My initial surmise had proved all too correct. To return by the way we had come was impossible. To reach the top we should require to be hauled up by a rope. But, in order not to frighten the girl, I kept on trying to find a way to clamber aloft. And all the time I was thinking that, failing any other egress, those blackened mummies were to be our companions until...

At last, with torn hands and slashed boots, I climbed down again to where she sat.

"No good," I said.

She stared at me in a dazed sort of way.

"Oh," she exclaimed wearily, "there must be a way up! We can't stay here!"

She sprang to her feet and clambered up on the debris, peering aloft. I reached up and took her hand.

"We'll explore the cave and see if there's another way out," I said soothingly.

Marjorie turned and looked down on me.

"And if there isn't..." she began. "Oh," she added hastily, "don't think me a coward, but I have such a horror of shut-in places. And you've altered so much since we came down here, your voice is so grave, it scares me. Oh, Desmond, we're not caught here for good...!"

I smiled up at her.

"How you run on!" I said as cheerfully as I could. "God bless my soul, we're not at the end of our tether yet. There's certain to be another exit at the far end of the cave..."

There was an opening of sorts; for one of the first things I had done on landing in the subterranean chamber was to see what means of escape it afforded other than that by which we had entered. But it was a slit, a mere air-hole in the living rock which, to judge by a cursory examination, would scarcely afford passage for a dog.

I have been in some tight corners in my time and it has always seemed to me that the most frightening thing about death is not the prospect of death itself, but rather the realisation—and it usually comes upon one suddenly and without warning—of the inexorability of fate, the utter impotence of man to escape his destiny. And very soon after crashing down into the cave I had understood that our chances of escape were reduced almost to the vanishing point.

We had no food, only water and air. Death by slow starvation awaited us unless we could attract attention and secure help. Clubfoot and his people might be willing enough, in their own interest, to rescue us. But what chance had we, immured in the bowels of the earth as we were, of letting him know where we were? And how was Garth to find us when the *Naomi* came back?

Marjorie had risen to her feet. Her face was a little flushed and there was a glitter of excitement in her eyes.

"That's it!" she cried, "there must, of course, be another way out!"

And picking up the candle-end she darted across the cave.

I hadn't the heart to follow her. Better, I thought, that she should realise for herself our true situation. Sooner or later she must understand. I saw the yellow glimmer of light at the end of the rock chamber and watched great shadows flicker across the roof as she moved the candle to and fro. Then she was beside me again, the candle between us, and I knew by the convulsive movement of her shoulders that she was weeping.

What could I do? What hope had I to offer? I stretched out my hand and she clasped it. Then, to spare our sole illuminant I put out the candle. I had thirty-four wax matches left.

Thus hand-in-hand we sat for some time in silence. The darkness was thick and clammy like a black velvet pall, the sort of darkness of which the city-dweller has no experience. Presently the girl grew calmer, and with one or two shuddering sighs her sobs ceased.

"My dear," said I, "I want you to have faith in me. I have been up against it so often; yet always in the end I have come out all right..."

I broke off; it was hard to speak with conviction.

"I am afraid," the girl moaned, "so terribly afraid. At the front I used to be proud of having less nerves than the other girls. But to sit still, in the dark, and wait for death... I never imagined anything so terrible. Do... do you know that I have to keep a tight hold on myself to keep myself from screaming?"

"Yes," I said, "and I want to tell you, Marjorie, that I think it's wonderful how well you take it. I've seen men get hysterical with much less reason!"

"And you?" asked Marjorie, "Aren't you afraid of death?"

"When it comes, yes," I answered. "But this job of ours, my dear, teaches us to live for the present and let the future take care of itself. At the front the worst part of a push was the waiting for it; when the whistles went and the barrage lifted one forgot all one's doubts and fears. And the only way to get through that bad afternoon before zero hour was to live for the moment, concentrate on the petty fatigues and annoyances of humdrum life and to decline to cross one's bridges until one came to them..."

"But aren't you fond of life?"

"It's no good being fond of anything on this earth," I told her, "because you're irredeemably compelled to lose it in the end..."

The girl was silent. Somewhere in the cave there echoed the melancholy drip of water.

"Have you ever been in love?" she asked suddenly.

"Of course I have, the same as everybody else." But she was not content with generalities. I had to tell her about a girl at Darjeeling, when I was a young sub., whose abrupt change of mind had once and for all put all idea of matrimonial bliss out of my head.

"Have you ever been in love?" I challenged by way of changing the conversation. But she evaded the question.

"You'd marry if you met the ideal woman?" she queried.

"Perhaps circumstances would prevent it again!" said I.

"What is your ideal woman like?"

Again I heard that sad splash of water from the darkness and it brought me back with a pang to our position. I smiled to think of us two, imprisoned in this death-chamber of the Southern Seas, calmly discussing the eternal question of life.

"She's tall and slim and clean in mind and body," said I; "she must trust me and be a companion as well as a lover!"

"Have you ever met her... since the girl at Darjeeling?"

"My dear," I said, "the girl at Darjeeling is now a stout *divorcée*, who, as the price of her husband's freedom from her shocking temper, retains the custody of the children whom she neglects disgracefully..."

The girl laughed a low little laugh.

"How severe you are!" she commented. Then she asked: "But have you met your ideal since?"

"Yes," said I, knowing full well whither the conversation was drifting.

"Then why don't you marry her?"

"I haven't asked her," I said.

"But why not, if she is your ideal?"

"Because," I replied, throwing caution to the winds—and, after all, what was convention to us in our circumstances?— "she is too rich!"

"You don't ask *me*," said the girl after a pause, "whether I have an ideal?"

"Naturally," I retorted, "since you evaded answering my question when I asked you if you had ever been in love..."

"The man I marry," she said in a low voice, "must make me feel such confidence in him that even in the hour of death I shall not be afraid..."

I dropped her hand and stood up. It's all very well to be philosophical about meeting death when you have no attachment on earth; but this slim, proud girl with the grey eyes and the clustering brown hair was stimulating in me the desire to live.

I struck a match and lit the candle.

"It's now a quarter to four in the afternoon," I said. "In order to spare our forces as much as possible, we will shout once in turn every quarter of an hour in case there should be anybody above on the shelf. I'll start now!"

And raising my head up the shaft I hallooed. My voice started the echoes ringing through the cave but no human voice responded.

"And now," I said, "I believe we'll have another look at that air-hole. Some of this volcanic rock is very brittle, and we might be able to enlarge the opening..."

We crossed the cave together, bending as the roof sloped down towards the farther end. The opening was a long narrow slit, not two feet deep, the top-side jagged with snags of rock. The candle guttered as I held it in the orifice, and I felt the cool air on my face.

It was undoubtedly an outlet into the fresh air; but how could one hope to worm one's way through that narrow vent? I thrust my hand with the candle into the opening and my arm went in up to the shoulder. It seemed to be a passage; for my hand encountered no resistance and the roof, if it did not get any higher, was not any lower. The rock was hard and solid.

I drew back and scanned the opening. It reminded me of the entrance of some caves where we used to scramble at school.

"Cox's Hole" had just such a narrow squeeze at the entrance which, however, opened up into quite a stately grotto beyond. I peeled off my jacket, then took off my collar and tie.

"Where I can go," I said to Marjorie, "you can! I'm going to have a shot to get through!"

The girl made no comment. She knelt on the hard floor of the cavern, her hands clasped in front of her. But she smiled as though to encourage me.

I didn't get far. My head went through all right; but a jutting edge of rock hanging down caught my shoulders and pinned me tight. Wriggle and thrust as I would I could make no progress at all and at length, in order not to stick inextricably, I had to give it up.

As I turned and looked at her an idea struck me. Marjorie Garth was slim and very supple, and but for her softly rounded throat and the gentle swell of her bosom one might have taken her for a boy.

"My dear," said I, "you must have a try. It's only my breadth of shoulders that prevents me from getting through. I believe you'll manage all right..."

The girl looked at me open-eyed.

"And leave you here?" was all she said.

I took her hand.

"Listen to me! The yacht must be back very soon. You can hide somewhere near the shore and when you hear the gun, make your way to our cave on the beach and wait for the *Naomi's* launch. You run the risk, I know, of falling into Clubfoot's hands again. But you have a sporting chance. Believe me, if you stay here, you haven't even that..."

With a quick gesture the girl sank her face in her hands.

"No!" she exclaimed. "No, no! I can't do it! I can't leave you like this!"

Gently I drew her hands away from her tear-stained face.

"Fate has sent us this chance," I reminded her, "and we must take it. I told you I always come out on top in the end and this is our opportunity. Isn't it better to have a run for your life than to stay here and die like a rat in a hole? If there should prove to be a way out you can always come back to the air-hole and report to me. If there isn't we can be together again..."

Marjorie nodded silently.

"If Grundt," she said presently, "should capture me again, he may cross-examine me about the cipher..."

"Tell him nothing!" I answered promptly.

"But if he makes it a condition for rescuing you..."

"Then I have told you nothing. That is my secret, Marjorie. If Clubfoot is to be told, I shall tell him myself. We are so near the end of our adventures that I'm willing to risk everything till the yacht appears.

"Clubfoot will never guess that you know unless you tell him. Remember he is a German and therefore has no opinion of women. He would never imagine that I have told you anything about the hiding-place of the treasure. Trust me, my dear! Our luck is in again! If you get out, I shall, too, somehow—depend on me!"

Then while she took off her shoes I divided the candle in two. I thrust her shoes, together with her half of the candle as far as I could reach into the opening. I gave her half of my store of matches. Then I turned and we faced one another in the darkness.

"Good luck, partner," I said, "we shall meet again soon!"

"I feel that I am abandoning you," she answered in a low voice. "Supposing I should fail!"

"You'll have made me very happy in the knowledge that you've escaped!"

With a little catch in her voice she demanded:

"Don't you think of yourself at all?"

"It's more pleasant to think of you!"

She made a little pause. Then she softly whispered:

"Money doesn't count down here!" And lifted her face to mine.

I took her in my arms and kissed her whilst she clung to me in the darkness. Then she dropped to her knees and crawled into the opening. For a few instants the yellow glimmer of the candle was obscured and I heard her breathing hard. Then the faint glimmer of light reappeared and I heard her voice from the other side.

"There's a winding passage and the air is quite fresh. The wind is blowing in my face. Goodbye, Desmond dear!"

"Au revoir, my dear!" I cried out of the darkness and silence fell again.

I stood there listening for a spell, then, following the advice of the French sage who said that he who sleeps dines, I stretched myself out on the rocky floor and soon fell into a heavy slumber.

* * *

When I awoke I relit my stump of candle. My watch had stopped. In that clammy darkness it was impossible to tell whether it was night or day. I sat up and stretched myself with no other sensation save that I was ravenously hungry. The silence was oppressive. I lay back against the rocky wall and waited...

42

A LIGHT IN THE DARKNESS AND WHAT CAME OF IT

As I learned from Marjorie later, the slit extended for only a few feet. Then the roof sloped up again. Marjorie found herself in a narrow passage with the fresh breeze blowing on her face. In fact, the draught was so great that the candle went out directly and she had to put on her shoes and grope her way forward in pitch darkness.

Her great fear was the the passage might lead to others and that before she knew it, she would be involved in a maze of subterranean galleries and, if the worst came to the worst, not even be able to rejoin me. She tried to maintain her direction by keeping always close to the right-hand wall and by counting her steps. But the gallery was so dark and it twisted so frequently that she soon lost count. At last she went blindly along, stopping at intervals to satisfy herself that she still felt the wind on her cheek.

She had halted irresolute and was thinking about turning back when, out of the darkness in front of her, a little glow appeared. At first a mere suggestion of light, it grew to a steady yellow radiance that lit up, though but dimly, the rocky roof of the corridor. The light itself appeared to be concealed by a bend in the gallery.

Marjorie remained perfectly still, her heart beating fast. Footsteps were approaching; then the murmur of voices reached her ear. Her first instinct was to turn tail and flee; but then the footsteps stopped and the light stood still.

"Four and twenty hours already are they away," said a deep rumbling voice in German, "and not back yet! *De Stelze* is too confident, Herr Leutnant..."

"Yet the doctor described exactly where he tied up the launch," answered another voice, hard and metallic, with a more refined enunciation. "Do you know what I think, Schröder? This English nobleman and his orderly have seized the launch..."

"*Aber nein*, Herr Leutnant?"

"And gone off to fetch their yacht back. She only went to Alcedo, at least so the doctor told us..."

"Then the yacht may be back quite soon, Herr Leutnant?"

"Certainly! That's my conviction. And to think that Grundt had this cursed *Engländer* in his power and let him go!"

"Bah!" said Schröder, "he grows old, *der Stelze!* Here three days are gone and not a trace of the treasure. In a little while, who knows? These damned *Engländer* will be here and our chance of making our fortunes will be gone for ever..."

"You speak true, Schröder! If only I had any support I would depose Grundt and take charge myself. But with these filthy Spanish monkeys..."

"Speak softly, Herr Leutnant..."

Intent as she was upon this conversation, Marjorie did not notice the light advancing until it was too late. Round the bend in the passage came a big, yellow, bearded German sailor swinging a ship's lantern, the blond young German officer, Ferdinand von Hagel, at his heels. In an instant they were on her and gripping her by the wrists dragged her down the gallery in the direction from which they had come. In silence they hustled her along for some hundred paces, then stopped at a bend.

"Wait here!" whispered the officer to Schröder, an evil smile on his face, "I go to reconnoitre. This will be a pleasant surprise for our comrades..."

He tip-toed away. Suddenly, from without, a harsh voice cried loudly:

"You idle rascals, the launch *must* be there!"

There was a confused murmur and the voice spoke again:

"Then the English yacht may be back any time now..."

Von Hagel appeared in the gallery. "Bring her along!" he ordered softly, beckoning with his hand.

The harsh voice shouted:

"Well, we shall have to fight for it yet!"

"No, Herr Doktor!" said von Hagel at the mouth of the gallery, "No! There need be no fight!"

They had emerged into a rocky hollow, flooded with brilliant sunshine which almost blinded Marjorie coming from the dank, dark recesses of the cliff. An arm of vivid green tree hung across the opening of the passage and beyond it there was a glimpse of gorgeous-hued bushes, over which the painted butterflies hovered, of bright blue sky and, in the distance, sparkling green sea. And across the scene the keen sea-breeze romped, blowing the hair about the girl's eyes, a breath of life after the clammy atmosphere of the cave.

His back to a tree, a ragged blanket cast across his knees, the Man with the Clubfoot lay. His face was pallid and his huge body shook with ague. Before him stood two uncouth figures, each with a rifle and blanket slung, poncho-fashion, across him, the centre of an excited, gesticulating group.

"Sir Garth," the German lieutenant added, bringing Marjorie forward, "will surely listen to reason when he hears that his charming daughter is the guest of Herr Dr Grundt! And, maybe, even the spy, Okewood, will come to terms..."

"*So, so!*"

Clubfoot's thick lips bared his yellow teeth in a grim smile.

"Das ist ja hoechst interessant! Jawohl!"

He raised his eyes to the girl, dark eyes that burnt with fever beetling from under the enormously bushy eyebrows, eyes that gleamed hard and menacing.

But now the crowd, which had fallen back at von Hagel's dramatic interruption, surged about him and Marjorie, shouting and gesticulating. The hollow rang with German and Spanish.

"Where is the Englishman?" they yelled. "Grundt, what of the treasure you promised us? The girl knows! Make the girl tell!..."

Grundt raised a great hand and, for the moment, the hubbub was stilled.

"Old Clubfoot is not at the end of his resources. *Kinder*, we have a hostage, a hostage we mean to keep. Let the yacht return; as long as the gnädiges Fräulein is our guest, we shall have no trouble from the stupid Englishmen. And as for our clever young friend, Okewood... Herr Leutnant!"

"Herr Doktor?"

"The *Engländer* was last seen in company with the girl. Take two men and search the gallery!"

Von Hagel coloured up at the brusqueness of Grundt's tone.

"Schröder here," he said without a shred of respect in his manner, "has explored the gallery. It leads to a small air-hole through which he believes the girl crawled. No man he says, could possibly get through..."

"Then," said Clubfoot, "the *Engländer* will be in one of the caves on the topmost terrace. Unless he has escaped?..."

And he shot a quick glance at the officer.

"Impossible," replied the other. "There is only the one practicable descent and it is guarded..."

Clubfoot nodded. Then he raised his hand.

"Go now," he said, "and leave me with the girl!"

On that von Hagel bent down and spoke softly in his ear. He seemed to be urging something with great insistence. Suddenly one of the Spaniards—a short man with a fat grey face covered with blue stubble and little pig eyes—danced to the front of the group. He burst into a torrent of voluble Spanish, shaking his fist repeatedly at Clubfoot. The latter did not move a muscle but looked at the speaker with contempt in every line of his face.

It was not until some of the Germans broke in, that Marjorie could understand what the scene was about.

"We're sick of being fooled," cried the big seaman they called Schröder. "The Kaiser's deposed, d'ye hear, and we're all equal! You've bungled things long enough, Grundt. You let the cursed English spy slip through your fingers with the hiding-place of the treasure in his head! You're past your work, Grundt! You've botched our business long enough!"

"*Ganz recht!*" ejaculated another German. "And poor Neque got a bullet in the guts for saying as much to you in the woods yesterday!"

This explained the single shot we had heard in the forest when we were on the rock.

"And the doctor murdered by this *verdammt Engländer!*" shouted a voice from the rear.

"Three days we've waited here and not a sign of the treasure," said von Hagel, looking round the group. "What have you to say to that, Grundt?"

Clubfoot, who had remained impassive under all this abuse, now staggered to his feet. No man lent a hand to help him. He stood and faced them, towering above them all. Ill though he was, his personality dominated every man in that place. A flame of colour mounted in his haggard face; two veins stood out like knots in his temples and his eyes blazed. His two hands, crossed on the crutch of his stick shook.

"Are you a candidate for my succession, Herr Leutnant?"

He addressed himself to von Hagel alone and his voice was calm and steady. But then his feelings seemed to overcome him and with a roar he shouted:

"You insubordinate rascal! I can afford to let these curs yelp but when the whipper-in joins them, it's time for the master to use the lash!"

With that he raised his heavy stick and struck the other full across the face. With a scarlet weal barring his pink-and-white cheek von Hagel sprang at his aggressor, but a big automatic which Grundt had plucked from his pocket brought him up short.

"I used only one bullet on Neque," Clubfoot warned him in a quiet, grim voice. "There's one left for you, Herr Leutnant, aye, and more to spare for other mutinous blackguards like you..."

Von Hagel stepped back, broken, cowed. And Clubfoot cried:

"While this puppy wastes our time, the man we want, the man who can lead us to the five hundred thousand dollars in gold, is skulking trapped in a cave not a thousand yards away. Fools that you are, don't you understand that you have but to let him know that the English girl is in our hands and he will throw up the sponge? Otherwise..."

He paused deliberately and looked at Marjorie from under his heavy brows. The crowd shouted back at him in German the word on which he had rested.

"*Sonst?*"

"Otherwise be must know that I shall hand this delicate English lady to the tender mercies of any of our brave companions who has fallen a victim to her beauty—Black Pablo, for instance, or our handsome steward, Pizarro..."

At that the crowd roared approval. Black Pablo, his guitar slung across his back, a squat, toad-like creature, obese and disgusting, slouched over to the girl. He contrived to summon up from the depths of his single dull and fish-like eye an expression which made her shrink back in horror. Then, amid a burst of laughter, "handsome" Pizarro, the stunted mulatto cook, was pushed out of the grass. He shambled towards Marjorie, his eyeballs flashing white in his yellow pock-marked face.

"Go, children!" cried Clubfoot. "Drag this spy from his hole and bring him to me. This time he shall speak, by God!—or we shall finish with it once and for all!"

Again he looked at Marjorie. The gold in his teeth flashed as he smiled with cruel malice. Then, as though overcome by the demand he had made on his strength, he dropped back on his blankets once more.

The hollow was all astir as the men set out. They had camped at the foot of the terraced rock on the high ground overlooking the clearing with the grave, beyond it the broad sweep of Horseshoe Bay between the curved arms of land enclosing the lagoon.

"Take ropes!" counselled Clubfoot from his bed beneath the tree. "You may have to descend into the caves..."

The seaman, Schröder, brought out some lengths of rope and hurried after the string of men, who, in Indian file, streamed out of the hollow, talking and laughing like a pack of schoolboys. Not a man remained behind. Even Pizarro, the coloured cook, went along. Black Pablo, the leader of the party, who was the last to go, wanted to leave a guard over Marjorie. But Clubfoot would not hear of it.

"*Amigo mio*," he said. "El Cojo is not so old as that young jackanapes would make out. I cannot climb while this cursed fever is on me. But I can look after myself—and anybody else who does me the honour of spending this pleasant afternoon in my company..."

Black Pablo laughed stridently. They heard his feet ring sharply on the rocky ground. The next moment he was gone, and the peace of a summer afternoon descended upon the hollow, the soothing quiet of droning insects, of a little breeze stirring gently in the thick foliage, the distant drumming of the sea.

Clubfoot began to speak to Marjorie.

43

I INTERRUPT A TÊTE-À-TÊTE

"An unpleasant scene of violence, *mein liebes Fräulein*," he remarked, dabbing his forehead with a red handkerchief, "which might so easily have been avoided. But, when men take passion instead of reason for guide—*was wollen Sie?* The war destroyed logical thinking. Today it is rare to find anyone capable of taking a perfectly dispassionate view of life. *Jawohl!...*"

Marjorie wondered vaguely what he meant. His manner was ingratiating; but she was conscious that he was watching her closely to mark the effect of his words.

"We Germans lost the war. Therefore, a man like your friend Okewood believes that everywhere and in all circumstances, the German must be in a state of inferiority. How short-sighted, *meine Gnädige!* And what a blemish this want of logic signifies in an otherwise remarkable character! To go no farther a-field in search of an illustration than this delightful island-war or no war, the fact remains that the strength of my little party puts the Herr Major in an inferiority of thirteen to one. How much wiser on his part it would have been to have recognised this fact yesterday! Let us hope that you will not be so ill-advised as to ignore it! You take my meaning? How quick you are!..."

For a minute his thick fingers drummed on the blanket thrown across him.

"Your Herr father has gone to fetch the yacht, *nicht wahr?*"

"It is no use asking me," replied Marjorie. "I have not seen my father since I landed on the island"

"So, so!" placidly observed Grundt, "another question for friend Okewood presently. But perhaps you can tell me what has become of Herr Okewood? Where exactly did you leave him?"

Marjorie was thinking desperately. It was merely a matter of time, probably of minutes now, she reflected, before I should be captured and dragged out of the cave. But some instinct prompted her, as she told me afterwards, to give no information about me until she had actually seen me once more in Grundt's power. So she simply shrugged her shoulders.

"I trust that this gesture does not imply," said Clubfoot, "that you do not know where you left Major Okewood, for that would be acting a lie. And lying, *meine Gnädige*, would do you no good in your present predicament. You must not take advantage of our good nature, o, *nein!* Do not forget that on a desert island man is apt to sink back into his primitive state..."

His voice was gentle and caressing; but the implication in his words was horrible.

"You come to us unbidden. You throw yourself upon our chivalry. *Ja!* that is all very well. But have you made sure that the conventions of civilised life obtain in this little island republic of which I am president? *Hein, hein*, had you thought of that? But won't you please sit down?"

"I prefer to stand," replied the girl shortly.

"You make me do discredit to our old German courtesy, *liebes Fräulein*. I cannot sit while you remain standing, and in this hot sun... *bitte!*"

With his spade-like hand he smoothed out a place on the grass under the shade of his tree. Dully, almost against her will, Marjorie sank down.

A gleam awoke in the cripple's eyes as he pawed the girl's bare arm.

"Listen!" he said, lowering his voice confidentially and leaning towards her. "The Spaniards of my party come without exception from the lowest scum of the Central American seaboard. The table-talk is enlivened with anecdotes of their—shall we say conquests?—which fill even me with disgust and dismay. And my Germans, yes—I, a good German, must admit it—they, too, have forgotten something of the conventions of civilised life. For five years or more they have been outlaws, dirty Boches, the rejected of mankind—they who are of that race"—his voice rang out triumphant but then trembled and broke—"*Gott!* that is the salt of the earth!"

For an instant he seemed to be genuinely moved. Bitter memories kindled a spark of anger in his fierce, dark eyes. But the mood passed swiftly and his voice was gentle, his manner sleek as before when he resumed.

"You make it difficult, very difficult for me. You come here, a delicate, fair young maid and you expect to live unscathed in a camp of rough men; for I do not conceal from you the fact, Miss Garth, that unless your father is reasonable you may be with us for many days..."

He broke off suggestively. The girl dared not look at him for fear of the thought unspoken she might read in his leering eyes.

"Would you be surprised to learn?—it is always best to be frank, *nicht wahr?*—that it will require an armed guard to keep these men away from you at night?..."

At that Marjorie revolted. She sprang to her feet and walked away, sickened at the picture he had suggested to her by every word. Grundt made no attempt to follow her.

"I am sure you will be reasonable," he murmured.

A man burst turbulently into the hollow. It was von Hagel. He was smeared all over with grey dust and his heavy boots showed white gashes where the rocks had cut them. He was pale and the livid weal across his right cheek seemed to distort his features.

"Well?" said Grundt sternly.

The young man made a helpless gesture of the hands. Slowly Clubfoot sat up erect and a heavy scowl drew his eyebrows together. One could almost see the young German quake as he stood before his leader, dumb, confused, aimlessly moving his hands. At last he faltered out:

"He is not there!"

A convulsion of anger seemed to shake the huge cripple. The close-shaven hair of his scalp moved, his heavy nostrils twitched as solidly, viciously, his great jowl set.

"Not there!" he ejaculated hoarsely, his voice strangling with anger. "What do you mean 'not there'? Black Pablo's orders were to bring him down to me. Why has he not done so? *Himmelkreuz-donnerwetter!*"—his hairy hands beat on his knee with rage—"why don't you answer me?"

"We... we... gained the top shelf unobserved," stammered out von Hagel. "It was deserted. There is only one cave... with a clear drop down. The steps appear to have quite recently broken away. Pablo, Schröder and I went with torches—they let us down with ropes. We came to a lower chamber where some native dead are buried. At the end was the narrow air-slit through which the girl escaped..."

"And the *Engländer* was not there, you say?"

"No!"

"*Schafskopf!* He was never there!"

"We saw him enter it. Besides, we found burnt matches on the ground and the ashes of his pipe..."

"Then he went out by the air-hole..."

"It is too narrow. Ramon, who is slightly built, could not get through..."

"And there is no other cave?"

"No!"

"Evidently he left by the way he entered, and escaped under the noses of your sentries..."

"Impossible, Herr Doktor! By the way he went in, without ropes, both ascent and descent are out of the question! And since early morning the path, which is the only means of access to the cliff, has been guarded..."

Shaking with ague, Clubfoot was struggling to regain his self-control.

"*Erlauben Sie!*" he said in a voice half-suffocated with rage, "Let us get this right. I do not admit miracles. We know that the *Engländer* and the girl took refuge in this cave. *Gut!* The girl, we know, came out through the air-hole. Where is then the man?"

Von Hagel looked at Marjorie.

"Why not ask the girl?" he suggested.

"You've heard what he said," screamed Clubfoot, whipping round and shaking his finger at Marjorie. "Where did you leave this man?"

Then Marjorie told them she had left me in the cave.

"*Sehen Sie?*" roared Clubfoot. "He's escaped under your very snouts, *Schweinhunde* that you are! He's in that cave yet! Get out of my sight, you dog! And send Black Pablo here! Tell him he has to reckon with me now! And by God if I have to *go* to him myself..."

Von Hagel had turned and fled. The cripple had risen to his knees. The perspiration poured off his face as, with trembling limbs, he vainly strove to overcome the weakness that mastered him, while he mouthed and mumbled a stream of threats.

Then from the sea a gun spoke, a single report that broke the brooding silence of the island and went echoing and clanging among the tall, grave rocks. Clubfoot's babble ceased on the instant. He desisted from his attempt to rise to his feet and remained immobile save for the trembling of his great torso. Slowly he turned his head and looked at Marjorie who, transfixed with fear, was watching him.

Thus I found them as, a moment later, I stepped into the hollow.

"Sit down, Grundt!" I said.

44

CAPITULATION

Racked with fever though he was, his presence of mind did not forsake him. In a flash his whistle was at his lips and three shrill blasts rang piercingly among the rocks. With the other hand he snatched up his automatic.

It was done with such lightning speed that he had me at a disadvantage. Though I had my pistol in my hand when I challenged Grundt, I was completely thrown off my balance by the glimpse I had of Marjorie who, with the blood drained from her face, stood swaying against a boulder as if about to faint. For a fraction of a second I took my eyes off the cripple and in that instant he had me covered.

"Move and you're dead!" he snarled at me. "Drop that gun! Drop it, d'ye hear?"

"You're welcome to it," I said as I pitched it on a tussock between us. "I've come to capitulate, Grundt! You win!"

"Very clever! Oh, very clever, indeed!" he sneered. "You imagine, I suppose, that Clubfoot, the stupid old Boche, did not hear that gun from the sea just now? Your friends may have arrived back, Herr Major. But little good they'll do you. I am going to kill you!"

Even as he spoke, into the turquoise horseshoe of sea at his back the *Naomi* came steaming, the sun flaming here and there on her polished brass-work, a glittering white ship as snowy as the spume that creamed in her wake. So clear was the atmosphere that I could see the white-clad figures running about her decks. I strained my ears to catch if I might hear the clang of her engineroom telegraph ringing her down to "slow." But the wind was off the land and no sound came from the *Naomi*. She might have been a phantom ship, such a spectre as, they say, visits a man in the hour of death.

And, in truth, it seemed as though for me the hour of death were at hand. Grundt's evil eyes and grim mouth set above the gleaming blue barrel of the great automatic were ample evidence that his words were no idle threat. He shifted his grip to get a better aim and I looked away, away from that sinister face, away from the *Naomi* and her promise of home, away from the glistening sea and the swaying green palms, to Marjorie. She stood like a white marble statue. Only her eyes seemed yet to live and they were wide with terror.

Again Clubfoot's whistle rang out. I turned to see his forehead puckered in a questioning frown. I shrugged my shoulders.

"What chance has the *Naomi* against you and your men, Grundt?" I asked. "A pleasure yacht is not equipped to send off cutting-out expeditions, you know! You are fully armed and well-entrenched in the island! It seems to me that your fears are exaggerated!..."

"Fine words, fine words!" he muttered. "Nevertheless in a minute you are going to die!..."

He took out his watch and laid it on the blanket before him.

"When I told you I had come to capitulate," I rejoined. "I spoke the truth. I have found the treasure. And there is proof!"

I opened my left hand and flung at his feet a handful of gold. Twenty-mark pieces, they dropped softly on the blankets and lay there gleaming in the sunshine, the Kaiser's head and the Imperial Eagle plain for him to see.

I had shaken him. I knew it at a glance. He looked down at the gold, his eyes narrowing with suspicion.

"*Also doch!*" he murmured—that conveniently elastic German phrase which means "By Jove, he's done it!" or, "Well, I never!" or "I'd never have thought it!" or anything more or less along these lines, you care to fit to it.

"Let Miss Garth and me go free to rejoin the yacht," I said, "and I'll tell you where the treasure's hid!"

He stiffened up at once.

"It is not for you to dictate to me, you scum," he cried. "Unconditional surrender is the only kind of surrender I understand. Say what you have to say and I will then decide what I shall do with you..."

I glanced seaward. And my heart stood still. The *Naomi* had vanished. Had it been but a vision after all?

"Come on!" urged Grundt, scowling. "I have given you a respite. But I now grow impatient..."

I noticed that the ague had taken him again and that, do what he might, he was trembling violently all over.

"If you will allow me to put my left hand in my jacket pocket," I said, "I can show you something that will explain everything."

"*Bitte sehr!* But remember that I can stretch you dead before you will have time to shoot, even through your pocket..."

From my jacket I produced the little mirror. The sun caught its polished surface as I brought it out and it flashed and flashed again.

Between the curving arms of Horseshoe Bay the launch of the *Naomi* came flying. I could see the white spray thrown up in two curving sheets as her bows cut the green water. To my ears stole faintly the quick chug-chug of her propeller. I wondered if Grundt had heard it. But he was staring fixedly at the little mirror which I kept turning over in my hands so that it flashed and flashed...

"This was wired to the grave, Grundt," said I. "It was what failed you to read the cipher. You remember the line 'Flimmer', flimmer' viel'? That was the indication to throw a spot-light thus!"—I caught the sun's rays in the glass and flashed it seaward to the bay—"from the mirror set at an angle of 85 degrees; 'the garrison of Kiel,' 'die Fünf-und-Achtziger', you know, Herr Doktor! Incidentally it was you yourself who were good enough to recall the allusion to my mind!..."

And I reminded him of our talk in the ravine in the forest.

Savagely he bit his lip.

"So that was what made you willing to hand me the message," he commented. "I wondered what it was. But continue! We waste valuable time!..."

"The compass bearing indicated by 'the Feast of Orders' was, of course, 27, from January 27th, the date of the celebration, as you probably guessed for yourself. The spotlight thrown along this line fell upon a peculiar pillar in the topmost terrace which your men are now searching. From this pillar, between two crags, the Sugar-Loaf and the Lorelei, both quite easily identified. I saw the great image indicated by 'Püppchen' in the message. I don't know whether you know the song 'Püppchen, Du bist mein Augenstern?'

"*Augenstern*—star of my eyes—refers to the idol. It has one eye hollow. By mounting from the hill-side at the back you can look through the eye and see the little cairn of stones which Ulrich von Hagel, with the hand of death upon him, built to mark the hiding place of the gold. At the foot of the image the treasure lies buried. From a box at the surface I took this handful of gold. I could nor move the rest for I had neither pick nor spade and the ground is hard and rocky. And that, I think, is all!"

For the first time Grundt relaxed his forbidding expression.

"Your story sounds plausible, Herr Major," he said. "This time, I believe, you are telling the truth..."

I gazed out into the bay. The launch had disappeared. She must have gone in under the cliffs out of sight.

"In any case," Clubfoot was saying, "I propose to risk it. Being a practical man you will realise that I cannot afford to chance the valuable information you have acquired falling into the possession of your friends. Furthermore, I bear you a grudge, Okewood. It has been the rule of my life that no man shall beat me and live. Therefore, I am going to shoot you now..."

A little cry and even as I turned Marjorie pitched forward and fell prone on the grass between Grundt and me.

"Bah!" said Clubfoot, "let her lie! She will..."

He never finished the sentence. Quick as thought the girl half raised herself, two deafening reports rang out all but simultaneously, then, with a snarling cry, Grundt snatched at his wrist.

The next moment Garth and Lawless burst into the hollow. But I was staring at Marjorie who had fallen motionless on her face.

45

ULRICH VON HAGEL'S TREASURE

For me in that moment the world seemed to end. I had plucked this girl from a placid, unruffled existence and plunged her into a vortex of adventure. Was she to leave her life, laid down for mine, in this desolate island while I, the author of all the mischief, was to escape unharmed?

Lawless was at Clubfoot's throat, worrying him like a terrier with a rat. Then, of a sudden, Carstairs and Mackay were there, twisting together with a leathern thong those great hairy wrists, one of which dripped blood. I stood helpless, watching, as in a dream, Garth raise up his daughter and rock her still form in his arms. In her right hand she still clasped my automatic with which she had saved my life.

There was a shrill cry from the entrance of the hollow. With skirts flying Yvonne, Marjorie's French maid, darted in. "O, ma chérie! Ma chérie!" she moaned as with tears rolling down her face, she dropped to her knees by the girl's side. Now Garth was holding a flask to his daughter's lips. Presently to my unspeakable relief, she stirred slightly, then opened her eyes.

"I'm all right," she murmured, "quite all right really! Ah! Yvonne!"

And she closed her eyes again.

Garth stood up, a tall and commanding figure of a man in his spotless white drill, and looked at me, tatterdemalion that I was, with a four days' growth of beard and unkempt hair, my clothes torn and stained, my boots gashed almost to ribbons by those cruel rocks.

"Is she... is she... wounded?" I faltered.

The baronet shook his head and gulped.

"She's only fainted," he replied. "My poor, poor lass..."

Then, swallowing his feelings, he demanded fiercely:

"Where is this man, Custrin?"

"Dead," I answered. "I shot him..."

What had happened in the forest had seemed natural enough. But, with the *Naomi*, civilisation had returned to Cock Island and my admission sounded horribly cold-blooded in my ears. As briefly as might be, but without concealing any salient fact, I told Garth the story of what had supervened after his departure with Carstairs. With ill-concealed impatience and with reddening cheeks he listened to my tale; but he grew too angry to hear me to the end. When I told him how I had come upon Marjorie in the room behind the galley he burst out in fury.

"So this is the end of your wild-goose chase! My little girl, alone and unprotected, in the hands of these savages! By God, Major Okewood, if any harm has come to her through your doing..."

"When I asked your help to get to Cock Island, Sir Alexander," I answered, "I had no means of knowing where this adventure would lead us. Nor had I any suspicion that I would, that I could, be followed. Otherwise I should never..."

He cut me short with an angry gesture of the hand.

"I don't want to hear any more. It is no thanks to you that my poor girl has not lost her life through your reckless folly. I had my doubts all along as to how far I could trust myself to your judgment. If I had had any idea that you and that blackguardly doctor between you would have dragged my little girl into it..."

This was too much even from a distraught parent.

"It was none of my doing that Miss Garth came ashore," I retorted hotly. "And as for Custrin, it was you who unhesitatingly accepted him at face value. You even suggested that he should join our expedition..."

"But for you, Custrin would never have come on board. You'll not contest that, I suppose? I wish to Heaven the *Naomi* had never seen you..."

"I can only say how very deeply I regret the terrible experience Miss Garth had to undergo," I began,

But he only snorted.

"I don't want to hear any more from you!" he retorted and walked away.

I was keenly aware of the hostile atmosphere he radiated and it added to my utter sense of forlornness. But Lawless was speaking to me, as I stood dumbfounded, clapping me on the back, asking if I were all right.

"The gang's hooked it," he chuckled. "With the report of the *Naomi*'s gun they must have just bolted off to their launch in Sturt Bay, way across the island, leaving their skipper to his fate. A dangerous man, that, major! We saw the launch... it's a sea-going submarine chaser... crossing the bar and making for the open sea. Sir Alexander was all for my going after 'em. But I told him it was no good with their start..."

Then he told me of the immense surprise which the appearance of the *Naomi*'s launch had occasioned on board the yacht as she lay off Alcedo Rock.

"When the old man found that I had let Miss Garth ashore with the doctor," the captain continued, "I thought he was going out of his mind. He raged like a wild man. Whew! but it was hot work for a bit. He called me every name he could lay his tongue to and I'm damned if I know whether I'm in his service yet or no. I've been carpeted once or twice in my time and talked to rough but I never did see such a dido as Sir Alexander raised! And he's fighting mad with you, too..."

"I have the same impression myself!" I answered.

"We put about at once," Lawless resumed, "and ran for the island. Jock Mackay crammed on every ounce of steam he could raise. He had nightmare every night thinking of the coal-bill! We dropped anchor off the bar and took the launch ashore at once. As we came in through the lagoon, I caught through my glasses the flash of your heliograph from the cliffs in the centre of the island. So directly we landed we made for the high ground..."

"I hadn't a notion how to let you know where we were," said I, "until I thought of the mirror. It was rather a forlorn hope because, as you saw, things were getting a bit pressing when you arrived..."

Someone touched my elbow. Mackay stood there. "Yon great Gairman is asking to speak with you!" They had stretched Clubfoot out on his blankets beneath the tree. I hate to see a man trussed up anyway, and a queer sort of misguided pity stole into my heart as I looked down on Grundt, whom I had feared so greatly, strapped hand and foot.

At my approach he opened his eyes. They were still grim and fearless.

"If my men had come," he said truculently, "you would never have escaped. But they ran and left me—von Hagel, a German officer, with the rest. Truly, I begin to think the sun has set on my unfortunate country!"

He checked and seemed to think.

"Young man, young man, that you had known me in my prime! But the foundations of my life have been knocked away. Okewood, I am getting old!"

The perspiration was damp on his brow. I could see the sweat glisten on the bristles of his iron-grey hair.

"In my day, in the years of Germany's greatness, I was all-puissant! I had but one master—the Emperor himself! No one—*no one*, do you understand?—not the Imperial Chancellor nor even the head of the Civil Cabinet, who was a greater man than he—dare give me, *der Stelze*, orders! Yet I had no official position! My name was in no *Rang-Liste* and I held no decorations. *Der Stelze* was not to be bought by those glittering crosses and stars with which so many of my fellow-countrymen loved to hang themselves! No, I was the secret power of the throne, the instrument of His Majesty. And, with this one exception, the highest in the land trembled at my name..."

His voice sounded tired; and it seemed to me that, of a sudden, he had, in truth, become an old man. His figure had relaxed; he appeared to have grown grosser of body than of yore; the flesh of his face was sagging and his cheeks had fallen in.

"This was to have been the last adventure," he resumed and stared at me defiantly, "the last of how many? Friends of my master told me of this hoard and delegated me to proceed to Central America to track it down. What they would have given me for my pains would have sufficed to enable me to realise my dream of settling down on a little property I have in Baden, and of passing the evening of my days in peace..."

"And what did your friends want the money for?" I asked.

"That," retorted Grundt proudly, "is the business of my master!"

His words gave me my answer; for I knew of the existence of secret funds destined to bring the Hohenzollerns back to the throne which they had so shamefully abandoned.

"You matched yourself against me, Okewood," Grundt said suddenly, "at a time when already the axe was laid at the roots of the German oak. In the long seclusion which followed my wound—they found it necessary, as you know, to give out that I was dead—I used sometimes to think that our duel was a miniature reproduction of the struggle between Germany and England. And in neither case am I quite clear as to why the *Engländer* won!"

"Perhaps it was a case of conscience, Herr Doktor?" The German looked up at me in surprise.

"Conscience!" he exclaimed. "But that is not a means of warfare!"

Lawless at my side uttered a loud exclamation. He was bending down over the blankets.

"The treasure!" he exclaimed, "By gum, you've found it!"

And he held up a shining piece of gold.

Funny, I had forgotten all about it.

"On those blankets, captain," said I, "you'll find all the treasure we're ever likely to get out of Cock Island. I located the hiding-place all right. But the treasure's gone. There are fifteen gold-pieces there—I counted them. That's all that's left of it..."

Then Grundt spoke.

"So you were bluffing to the end!" he said and was silent.

"Then that was why the gang was in such a hurry to be off!" cried Lawless.

I shook my head.

"They didn't find the treasure either," I replied. "Somewhere scattered among the rocky ravines and valleys of this island, a hundred thousand pounds in American eagles and German twenty-mark pieces are lying. Old Man Destiny had it in for us, captain. He sent a volcanic eruption which blew the treasure sky-high!"

"Jimini!" exclaimed Lawless in a hushed voice.

"It's an awfu' pity!" ejaculated Mackay mournfully.

Yvonne came. Marjorie was asking for me, she said. I found her sitting up, Garth at her side. The light was slowly mellowing and the sinking sun cast long shadows across the hollow. The sky was all marbled with red and gold flecks.

Rather shyly Marjorie thrust a slim white hand into mine. It may have been my fancy; but I think I saw Garth wince.

"So you did come out on top after all?" she said. "Sit down there beside Daddy and tell me all about it from the beginning. You found the treasure then?"

"I found where it had been hid," I replied. "But it had vanished..."

"Vanished?" cried Marjorie, and I swear there was dismay in her voice.

"Vanished?" echoed Garth.

"But the gold pieces you threw to Grundt," queried the girl. "I don't understand..."

"That was part of one box which had survived the volcanic eruption which scattered Ulrich von Hagel's horde to the four winds. You remember that wisp of smoke we saw rising from the hillside in front of the great image? Well, I discovered that it came from a deep fissure in the mountainside at the foot of the idol. From the little cairn of stones, which still stands on the edge of the cliff, it was clear that the treasure had been stored in a cave which appears to have been hollowed out of the rock in front of the idol.

"Where that cave was is now a yawning hole belching forth smoke and streams of lava. In fact, as far as I can judge, the treasure was blown clean out of the mountainside. That this surmise is correct is shown, I think, by my discovery of the remains of a wooden box in which were still a few gold pieces. Other fragments of charred wood were scattered around. For the rest the treasure is gone and will never be recovered!"

Marjorie's eyes rested mournfully on my face; but I could not meet her gaze.

"But how did you discover all this?"

"The passage by which I escaped from the burial-chamber brought me out within a hundred yards of the image. The sulphur fumes from the fresh cone of the volcano caught me by the throat directly I emerged into the open. My one idea was to find you. So I crammed the gold pieces in my pocket and made for Horseshoe Bay to see if the yacht had returned. Finding no sign of her or you I started to reconnoitre. I guessed that Clubfoot and his party would be watching somewhere near the terraced rock and sure enough, as I was prowling in the undergrowth near here, I saw the whole gang file out towards the rock. I watched where they had come from and creeping up saw you and Grundt in conversation. The only thing that mattered then was to get you out of Grundt's clutches. I saw no signs of any guards but I made sure that Clubfoot would have help within easy reach. As I was turning things over in my mind I heard the *Naomi's* gun. So I decided to risk everything on a final bluff and I acted at once..."

"When they told me you were not in the cave," said Marjorie, "I couldn't believe my ears. How on earth did you manage to escape?"

"Well," I replied, "you remember that stone table on which the mummies lay? Under one of them I found, let in the table, a flat stone carved with a turtle. I don't know whether you realise the significance of that sign. The turtle was the mark of that celebrated buccaneer, Captain Roberts, who, in the old days, was a great man in these waters. The buccaneers are known to have used Cock Island for obtaining fresh meat and water—you can read about it in the 'Sailing Directions'—so the sign of the turtle set me thinking.

"I tried to get the stone up but it was firmly cemented in the table. However, in my pushing and thrusting I leant against the table edge and suddenly the whole top swung round outwards into the cave leaving a hole about five feet deep. The hole was the opening of a passage several hundred yards long which led into the open air..."

"But how did you manage to close the opening behind you?"

"Quite simply. I arranged the mummies as they were before, covering the turtle stone, then standing in the hole I drew the table-top back into place again. It is quite solid and does not ring hollow—the simplest and neatest device of its kind I ever saw. Roberts and his men must have used the burial-chamber for some sort of secret meetings, I imagine. Perhaps in their day Cock Island was inhabited..."

There was so much I had to ask, so much I would have said. But the presence of her father, dour and intractable, threw an invisible bar between us. I felt embarrassed and miserable—because I realised I suppose, that our island dream was at an end.

"It is getting dark," said Garth, standing up. "Come, Marjie, it's time we were back on board!"

He did not include me in the summons. Yet I should have to sail with him again. He could not maroon me there.

"You're coming with us?" said my dear Marjorie with her ready tact.

"Only as far as the beach," I replied. "We have to decide what's to be done with our friend yonder..."

In truth the problem of Grundt was beginning to obtrude itself in my mind.

"I'll come on board later," I said, "if Sir Alexander will allow me..."

"We must, of course, take Major Okewood back with us to Rodriguez," Garth observed stiffly.

At that Marjorie flared up.

"Daddy!" she cried indignantly.

We went down to the shore in silence. As we emerged from the woods, John Bard came striding up the beach.

46

THE END OF A DREAM

I don't think I was ever so glad in my life before to see anyone. There he was in the flesh, dear old John, tall and grave and courteous, like any Spanish don, in a clean tussore suit and the inevitable cigar stuck in a corner of his mouth.

"John!" I exclaimed. "How on earth did you ever get here?"

He stared at me in astonishment. It was obvious that, for the moment, he did not recognise me. Well might he wonder who this begrimed tramp might be who greeted him so familiarly. But then he cried out and clapped me on the back.

"Desmond, by all that's holy! Man, you've given us an anxious time! What have you been up to to get yourself in that condition?"

"It's a long story now ended," I answered soberly, "and it'll keep! At present I can't get over your turning up here!..."

"From inquiries I made about El Cojo and his gang after you left I got seriously alarmed about you," said this most faithful friend. "But when I heard that the Government coastal defence motorboat, the fastest craft in these waters, was missing, I decided it was time I came to look for you. One of my fruit-ships, the *Cristobal*, happened to be in harbour, so I came along in her. She's lying outside now. Before we do any more talking I suggest you come aboard with me and have a clean-up. And you look as though you could do with a drink as well!..."

I explained the difficulty I was in regarding the disposal of Grundt.

"El Cojo, eh?" commented Bard and whistled. "That's some capture you've got there, Desmond. We'll take him back with us to Rodriguez. He's hand in glove with the President, I believe, and I should like to give his Excellency a lesson."

So we settled it. Bard arranged to send a boat ashore to fetch Clubfoot to the *Cristobal*. He promised to see to it that my enemy was safely bestowed.

So I turned my back on Cock Island and left it brooding sadly beneath the stars with the terraced rock and the image and the little bowl-shaped clearing where Von Hagel slept. I went on board the *Cristobal* and for a good half-hour, with a long "peg" within easy reach of my hand, lay and soaked the stiffness out of my bones in a boiling hot bath. John had volunteered, in the meantime, to send a boat over to the *Naomi* to fetch my luggage; for I had told him how things stood between me and Garth, and he assumed that I would remain on the *Cristobal*. I had hesitated an instant before replying, for I desperately wanted to see Marjorie again. But, I reflected, a millionaire's daughter was not for me—and it was better we should part thus. So I scribbled a note for the coloured steward to take to her: just a line to say goodbye and to thank her for her action that had saved my life.

They brought me some food in my cabin and while, attired in a voluminous dressing-gown of my friend's, I ate, John Bard told me what he had learnt regarding the connection of El Cojo's gang with Cock Island.

"During the war," he said, "the island was the depot for certain important gun-running operations carried out by Black Pablo and his friends for the Mexican insurgents. The idea of the scheme, which was directed by the German espionage heads in the United States, was to keep things humming on the American border and to detain United States troops there.

"In those days Black Pablo had a ship of his own. He used to call periodically and collect arms and ammunition deposited on the island by some German commerce-raiders or other — there is talk of a mysterious vessel under the Swedish flag that used to stand off here — and take this contraband to Rodriguez. Here in port, under cover of night, it was transferred to a Mexican steamer which ultimately ran it ashore somewhere on the Mexican coast. On the outward trip to Cock Island, Black Pablo used to carry large stocks of gasoline for German craft operating in these waters..."

"There's a group of sheds on the other side of the island which Clubfoot's men called 'The Petrol Store,'" I put in.

"Precisely," said Bard. "There was a regular traffic here. The island is, after all, conveniently enough situated for the work they had in hand; not too far from the Central American coast yet well off the trade routes. It was naturally, as you might say, selected as the rendezvous in connection with what was intended to be German's biggest coup against the Americans in the war... the destruction of the Panama Canal!"

"By George!" I commented.

"If it hadn't been for the Armistice," Bard continued, "I believe they would have pulled it off. They spent months on the preparations; everything was worked out to the last detail. The most vulnerable points were to be dynamited; the Gatun Lock and the Culebra Cut, I know, were mentioned. The big bang was planned for November, '18..."

"I see! And the Armistice spoilt it?"

"Exactly. The H.E. had been passed by Black Pablo and Co. to the parties appointed to carry out the explosion, and it was agreed that, as soon as the coup had come oh, Black Pablo should make for the island rendezvous to receive his pay from a trusted German emissary who would await him there. The sum was one hundred thousand pounds in American gold dollars and German gold marks. But the Armistice, as you say, knocked the whole thing on the head. The entire German fabric collapsed, its plots and intrigues with it, including the canal coup. The Allies took a very firm hand with the Rodriguez Government and forced them to expel Black Pablo and confiscate his ship. Pablo went to San Salvador and did his best to charter a vessel there. But there was a heavy slump in German stock and everybody had the wind up. So nothing was done..."

"And Grundt—El Cojo?"

"I did not succeed in finding out a great deal about his movements; for the people from whom I inquired either did not or would not know anything about him. But apparently he turned up from Havana some months ago. The rest of the story—how they got on to Dutchey and his tale of the message taken by the Englishman from the grave—you know..."

There was a tap at the cabin-door. The dark-skinned steward of the *Cristobal* was there with my kit from the *Naomi*. "El Cojo," he told us, had just come on board. Bard threw a questioning glance at me.

"I leave him to you, John," I said. "I don't want to see him again..."

My friend grinned understandingly and left the cabin. In silence the steward laid out some clean clothes for me. He said nothing about my note to Marjorie. Had she had it? Surely she would have answered...

"You left my letter for the Senorita?" I asked at last.

"Si, si, Senor Commandante," the man replied. "The Señorita was on the deck with the rich Inglez, her father, and I gave the Senor Commandante's note into her own hands!"

"And she read it?"

"Si, Senor!"

"And there was... no reply?"

"No, Senor!"

Well, that settled it. I had my conge. Cock Island and those wonder days with Marjorie must go into the store-house of past memories... Yet there was a tug at my heart as for a moment I thought of her as I had held her in my arms in the burial-chamber and she had raised her face to mine. "Money doesn't count down here!" she had whispered; but now we were back in the work-a-day world where money could prove an insuperable barrier between true lovers...

In moody silence I dressed and went above. A crescent moon hung low down on the horizon and the deck was eerie with fantastic shadows. No one was about. On our starboard bow the rugged mass of Cock Island was a black blur against the stars.

It is one of the failings of the Celtic temperament that its moments of the highest elation are apt to be followed by phases of the deepest depression. Reaction had come upon me after our days of high adventure and floored me utterly. All the spice, so it seemed to me in that dark hour beneath the moon on the *Cristobal's* deserted deck, had gone out of the romance of my profession and left me with an ill taste in my mouth. As I paced up and down I revisualised the scenes through which I had passed in my quest; Adams gasping for breath in his hovel, Garth and I scrambling through the steaming jungle, that storm-tossed figure by the grave, Marjorie pillowing her gold-brown head on my chest in the darkness of the cave.

From every one of the pictures which passed across my mind her face seemed to look out, the narrow pencilled eyebrows above the clear grey eyes, the great tenderness of her mouth... Within a few hours, I pondered sadly, I had found my love and lost her just as I had found and lost the treasure...

A voice was hailing us out of the gloom that hung over the opalescent sea.

"*Cristobal* ahoy!"

The sound of oars came to me and presently a ship's boat emerged from the night, a white figure in the stern. A few minutes later Marjorie Garth, wrapped in a white blanket coat, stepped out of the boat that rocked in the swell at the foot of the *Cristobal*'s companion and mounted to the deck.

"You would have left me like this?" she said, and stood close by my side.

I shrugged my shoulders.

"It was not a friendly thing to do... partner," she added in a breathless sort of way.

"Your father..." I began.

"Oh!" she cried in a low voice, "I was ashamed of him. After what you risked to save me. But you must make allowances. I am all he has, you know. He'll be all right in a day or two. We're going back to Panama and home by way of America. And I've come to fetch you back to the *Naomi!* ..."

I shook my head.

"No!" I said.

"If I ask you to come. And I'll make Daddy apologise, if you like..."

She laid her hand on my arm.

"No!" I said again.

Hurt, she withdrew her hand.

"Your stupid pride..." she began.

"Don't let us quarrel," I pleaded. "Let me keep a wonderful dream unspoiled, Marjorie. But dreams can't last for ever, my dear. One has to wake up some time, you know!"

Questioningly her eyes sought mine.

"Even if Sir Alexander had not told me I was not wanted on the *Naomi*," I continued, "I think I should yet have parted from you here. My dear, my dear, don't you see it's hopeless? I care far too much for you to be able to know you merely as a friend. I must make an end of it. The barrier between us is insurmountable..."

"Barrier?" she repeated. "What barrier?"

"Money! You're too rich, Marjorie, for me to ask you the question which, almost from the moment I first saw you in the smoke-room of the *Naomi*, I have wanted to put to you. I make enough out of this odd trade of mine to keep a wife. But as long as I'm in the Secret Service I'd ask no woman to marry me. It wouldn't be playing the game by her—or by the service, either!..."

She listened to me in silence. Then she said quite simply:

"Desmond, if you'll ask me, I'll be your wife. I've never met a man I'd marry before; but I'd marry you. Why should you let money stand between us? I shall have enough for both..."

I loved her for her words. But I shook my head again.

"It won't do, my dear," said I. "And you know it won't do. If I'd found that cursed treasure, things might have been different. But now I've only to tell you I shall never forget that you paid me the greatest compliment a woman can pay a man... and to say goodbye..."

With a sob she turned from me and, ignoring my arm, ran down the ladder and stepped into the boat.

Before morning Clubfoot had escaped. Loud shouts from Cock Island where, by Garth's permission, some of the crew of the *Naomi* had spent the night ashore, discovered the news to us. The *Naomi's* launch, which they had drawn up on the beach, was missing, and at the companion of the *Cristobal* a severed length of rope showed that the painter of one of the ship's boats which had been tied up there had been cut.

Bard held an inquiry. But his crew came from Rodriguez, "and," he told me, "they have a holy fear of El Cojo. He simply blustered his way out of the lamp-room where I had him imprisoned! I'm not sure," he added with a grin, "that old Clubfoot has not himself presented us with the simplest solution of a very difficult problem!"

47

IN WHICH A BLACK BOX PLAYS A DECISIVE PART

A smear of smoke on the horizon was all that was left to denote the presence of the *Naomi* when John Bard came to me as I sat in the shade of the after-deck of the *Cristobal*, going through the mail he had brought me from Rodriguez. He dropped into a chair at my side.

"Captain Lawless and that Scots engineer of his," he said, "Spent the greater part of the night ashore grubbing for gold round the image. But they didn't find as much as a dollar. And then to discover they had lost their launch. Gee! They were as sick as mud!"

"Bah!" I answered. "I'm fed up with the whole place. The sooner we're at sea again the better I shall be pleased. I want to get back to work, John..."

"We're sailing at four o'clock," my friend replied. "But before we up anchor, Desmond, old man, I should like to have a look at that burial-chamber and the passage by which you escaped. What do you say to taking me ashore now and showing me round?"

"Anything to pass the time," I said wearily. "When do we start?"

"Right now. And I'll bring a pick and spade. If there's time we might have another grub for gold in the lava round the idol..."

"You bet the canny Scot hasn't left an inch of soil unturned," I laughed as old John went off.

Half an hour later we were pushing our way across the rocky valley at the end of which, against the mountainside, the great idol was set. We skirted the smoking volcano and at length stood before the narrow fissure, half-hidden by a gigantic boulder, through which I had emerged from the burial-chamber.

We had borrowed a couple of lanterns from the ship and Bard carried a pick-axe while I shouldered a spade. We left our tools at the entrance and lit our lamps. Then I led the way into the passage. At the end I found the solid masonry of the table hanging down into the passage. A steady heave swung it round and there, above our heads, was the black square opening of the death-chamber.

And now I struck. The place had too poignant memories for me. I hoisted Bard up into the hole, but I declined to accompany him. Swinging my lamp in my hand, I wandered back along the passage towards the cleft by which we had entered.

I had gone perhaps a hundred yards from the cave when the light of my lantern, striking low, revealed a square flag set in the floor of the passage. It sounded hollow to the foot. Setting down my lamp I stooped to examine it and then I saw that the stone was roughly carved. The carving was worn and filled in with dust. I scraped it clear as best I could with my hands and then saw that the stone was carved with the likeness of a turtle, the counterpart of the turtle carved on the table in the cave. I could see the head and tail and the four flippers roughly hewn.

"John!" I shouted. "Here, John!"

My voice reverberated weirdly in the low-roofed passage. I dropped to my kees and tried to heave the stone up. But it was firmly set and resisted all my efforts. Then I heard Bard's footsteps echoing along the passage.

"Will you look at that?" I said as he came up.

"By George!" he exclaimed. "Captain Roberts, his mark! Can you heave it up? Wait! I'll get the tools!"

And he darted off along the passage.

With the aid of the pick we prised the stone up. A slot had obviously been cut for it in the rock. A shallow opening was revealed and at the bottom stood a black box.

It was of black leather, discoloured but apparently in good condition, the corners bound with some dull metal which I took to be brass. It was about four foot long, with a rounded lid studded with nails. Bard lifted up one of the lanterns whilst I, lying on my face, dropped an arm into the hole. My fingers closed on a handle at the side of the box. I heaved. The box was immensely heavy and I found that I could barely lift it. I managed, however, to push it to one side, thus making room for my feet. Then I dropped into the hole, up-ended the casket and by dint of our combined exertions we landed it on the floor of the passage.

I looked at Bard and he looked at me.

"You — open it!" I said hoarsely.

The box seemed to be of Spanish manufacture for the leather was handsomely tooled in the Cordova fashion. It was fitted with an elaborately chased iron or steel lock with a hasp that rattled to Bard's touch. Without further ceremony he inserted the point of the pick under the hasp, wrenched, and the nails giving way in the rotten leather, the whole lock came off. Then he threw up the lid and we saw a layer of discoloured brown canvas. This I pulled aside and we fell back in amazement.

For the box was filled to the brim with magnificent gold and silver vessels, interspersed with them richly chased pistols and a couple of daggers with studded with gems. There were, amongst other things, a superbly wrought ewer and basin, both of which seemed to be of solid gold, a flat gold dish set with diamonds and rubies, a gem-laden crucifix, the Christ in pure gold, and an enormous variety of gold and silver forks and spoons. We laid all these treasures out on the floor of the passage and then, beneath some folded lengths of rich crimson brocade, came upon a long ebony box in which, wrapped loosely in a cambric scarf yellowed with age, was a superb collection of gems. There were no less than three magnificent *parures* of pearls, such as great ladies in the days of the Merry Monarch wore upon their neck and bosom, a number of diamond and pearl drops such as were worn on the forehead, diamond earrings, a huge emerald set as a brooch, several heavy gold chains, and some diamond buckles. Beside the ebony box, enveloped in a flowered silk wrap, was a curiously fashioned silver globe richly set with different precious stones to represent the various capitals of the world.

Bard heaved a deep sigh and looked at me.

"My word, old boy!" he exclaimed, "you've done it at last!"

"What—what do you suppose it's worth?" I asked rather unsteadily.

"A hundred thousand, two hundred thousand pounds," answered Bard. "Who can say? The antiquarian value, altogether apart from the intrinsic, of some of these things—that crucifix and that globe, for example, must be very considerable.

"That emerald and those brilliants, for instance... but you aren't listening."

I wasn't. A sudden vision had come to me of clear grey eyes trustfully raised to mine, of a tangle of copper-coloured hair that rested against my coat, of a slim warm body that clung confidingly to me. The discoloured leather trunk which lay at our feet was destined to change the whole course of my life. Hope, to which, with Marjorie, I had said goodbye, came surging back into my heart. Our island dream was not at an end... unless good fortune had come to me too late.

"When will the *Naomi* reach Panama!" I suddenly asked.

"In about a week or ten days," John replied. "Why?"

"Because," I said, "I *must* reach her by cable!..."

It was ultimately from Rodriguez that my message was sent. Akawa, Bard's Japanese butler, took it down the hill to the cable office. I was prostrate with a bad bout of malaria, which I must have contracted in the steamy woods of Cock Island. My cable was to Marjorie, and this is what it said :

"The barriers are down. When will you marry me? DESMOND."

But no reply came. All through the feverish days of my illness, a shadowy cable addressed to me flitted through my tortured mind. Sometimes, when I was light-headed, as Bard told me afterwards, I would fancy that Marjorie had replied, that Akawa was handing me the message... But when consciousness returned, I awoke to a dark world which even the leather trunk locked away in Bard's strong-room could not illumine...

It was weeks before I could travel to New York, where I placed the treasure in the hands of a firm of antiquaries. They advised that it should only come on the market gradually, piece by piece, in order not to depreciate its value. I do not, therefore, know even now exactly how much it will realise; but from what they tell me I am quite justified in regarding myself as a comparatively wealthy man. Bard will not touch a cent of the treasure. He does not need it, he says, and it belongs to me...

A cable from the Chief, to whom I had communicated my New York address, awaited me on my arrival from Panama. It directed me to go to Washington for instructions. The treasure disposed of, I accordingly boarded the train and proceeded to the capital.

From my hotel at Washington I telephoned to my old friend, Vincent Pargett, at the Embassy, and invited myself to dinner.

THE RETURN OF CLUBFOOT

Vincent made me welcome in his very comfortable bachelor apartment, and over the cocktails produced a batch of cables.

"You'd better read this one first, Desmond," he said. "It came only this morning. The rest have been here a week," and he tossed over the envelope.

It was from Marjorie. My heart seemed to stop beating as my eyes fell on her name printed at the foot of the message. It was from London, and I realised that my cable must have missed her at Panama and followed her home.

This was her reply:

"Whenever you like.—YOUR MARJORIE."

There are moments which justify even the Secret Service agent in abandoning his wonted habit of reticence. With Marjorie's dear message in my hand I told old Vincent, whom I had known all my life, the news which it contained.

"Three cheers!" exclaimed my friend, then raised his glass.

"I drink," said he with mock solemnity, "to the passing of England's premier sleuth!"

* * *

I wonder! Shall I, in the stay-at-home Government billet which the Chief procured for me and happy in the possession of Marjorie as my wife, always be able to resist the beckoning finger of romance luring towards high adventure and spirited endeavour? Shall I, to the end of the chapter, remain deaf to the call of the blood, aloof from the thrill of the man-hunt? *Quien sabe?* Who knows?

Of Clubfoot I never heard again, and to this day I do not know whether, weak as he was and single-handed in that little launch, he ever made the land. Garth, inclined to be difficult at first, resigned himself at the last with a good grace to our matrimonial projects. I think the argument that my share of Captain Roberts' treasure would remain in the family made a distinct appeal to his Lancashire horse-sense. Carstairs is with us still and is developing into an excellent butler.

For the Vice-Consul at Rodriguez, whose friendly services I had not forgotten, the Chief procured the C.B.E. I am told that he wears it very impressively, dangling from its purple ribbon on his shirt front, when, in evening dress, according to the protocol, he attends the President of Rodriguez at the opening of the Legislature...

A fan of Sherlock Holmes?
Then meet Solar Pons

The original fan fiction from the great August Derleth—the Sherlock Holmes of Praed Street.

"the best substitutes for Sherlock Holmes known."
– Vincent Starrett

"an excellent series of adventures in detection in their own right." – *The Chicago Tribune*

For more details and a full list of titles:
visit https://www.hachetteindia.com/home/yellowbacks

Love Golden Age crime fiction? Have you checked out the full yellowback range?

From Locked door mysteries to blind detectives through first women detectives, the yellowback reissues is one of the largest selections of classic crime fictions, in the original format with a modern clean easy read page layout. A sampling below.

For more details and a full list of titles:
visit https://www.hachetteindia.com/home/yellowbacks

H. Rider Haggard
MR. MEESON'S WILL

Melville Davisson Post
MASTER OF MYSTERIES
THE COMPLETE UNCLE ABNER COLLECTION

Jack London
THE ASSASSINATION BUREAU LTD.

Baroness Orczy
THE SKIN O' MY TOOTH
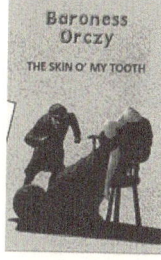

Earl Derr Biggers
SEVEN KEYS TO BALDPATE

Horace Walpole
THE CASTLE OF OTRANTO

Sexton Blake
THE SEXTON BLAKE COLLECTION VOLUME 1

Francis Beeding
THE HOUSE OF DR. EDWARDES

A. E. W. Mason
AT THE VILLA ROSE

Fergus Hume
THE MILLIONAIRE MYSTERY

Donald Henderson
A VOICE LIKE VELVET

Richard Hallas
YOU PLAY THE BLACK AND THE RED COMES UP